Siren's Snare : A Blood Re
By Crystal-Rain
Copyright 2013 Cryst

SIREN'S SNARE
A BLOOD REVELATION NOVEL
CRYSTAL-RAIN LOVE

PROLOGUE

The blood would never come out. Disgusted, Marilee shut off the faucet and threw her stained cutoffs across the bathroom. They hit the wall with a soppy wet thud and fell to the floor. She joined them there, her knees pulled up to her chin as the tears she'd fought back all day finally broke free.

I killed.

And it felt good.

Marilee's stomach turned over with her silent admission and she quickly lurched forward, hanging her head over the toilet bowl not a second too soon. She purged the contents of her stomach, flushed the toilet, and grabbed hold of the sink. It took effort, but she pulled herself to a stand, bracing her wobbly legs to support her slender weight.

She had to leave. She had to get away from the stain of other people's blood on her favorite pair of jean cutoffs. The soiled material taunted her from where it lay on the floor, reminding her of what she'd done. And why she'd done it.

How much I liked doing it.

Marilee traveled the narrow length of the hallway until she reached her small, cramped room. The voices of those she killed seemed to follow her, crying out in rage. She shoved the tortured sounds into the back of her mind and grabbed a duffel bag from her closet. Quickly, she grabbed clothes and stuffed them into the black bag along with the five hundred bucks she'd stashed under her mattress for an emergency. Becoming a murderer was an emergency, she assured herself as she struggled to see through her tears.

The cross her grandmother had given her when she was just a little girl still hung on her bedpost. She scooped it up, running a finger over the black and clear beads Gram had lovingly threaded together. A tear plopped onto the gold cross before Marilee raised it over her head and allowed it to hang from her neck. The cross was all she had left of the woman she'd loved more than anyone on earth.

Choking back a sob, she grabbed the duffel and left her room without a backward glance. She didn't leave a note for her mother before stepping out the front door of the little white shotgun house for the last time. If Becky had survived the attack, she wouldn't even miss her. If she hadn't survived… Well, there was no use worrying about that when the woman had never really been much of a mother. Gram had been everything to Marilee, and she knew she hadn't survived the attack because the vampires had taken over Gram & Grampa's house after killing them.

She'd done nothing to protect them.

Marilee tossed her duffel into the old pick-up truck and slammed the door closed. She didn't want to think of the dreams she'd had, the gnawing sensations in her gut telling her danger was coming. She didn't want to think of her grandparents' kind smiles or generous hearts. More than anything, she didn't want to hear her grandmother's voice, but the sound wouldn't leave her.

You have a destiny to follow, my sweet girl. You know things nobody else knows, and see things others are blind to. You will be called to do great things one day, and your gifts will bless many.

Marilee swallowed down bile. Her gifts didn't save Gram or Grampa. She'd foreseen their death, but like so many dreams before, she'd ignored the warning, never thinking the monsters from her nightmares would become real.

Now the feeling in her gut that had led her to the sheriff's department two nights ago, just in time to help a slayer destroy a group of vampires, told her it was time to leave town. Somewhere out there, her destiny called.

She prayed her true destiny was something more than being a killer.

CHAPTER ONE

"Move it, Blondie. Table nine's gettin' pissy."

Marilee glared at the chunky redhead in the two-sizes-too-small outfit and bit back a scathing retort. She usually didn't let Brenda get to her, but her gut was twisted out of shape tonight. Something was going to happen, something big and most likely dangerous.

She grabbed the basket loaded with mini corn dogs and fries, and the two plates of burgers and onion rings, and balanced them on her tray. Wedging herself between the bar and Brenda's fat ass, she managed to get past the skank-bag and onto the floor. A gyrating couple nearly backed into her, but thanks to her quick reflexes she managed to get the order out to the trio at the table.

A heavy man in a baseball cap sat with his arm wrapped around the shoulders of an overly made-up brunette. Opposite him in the booth, a tall lanky man ogled her unabashedly. *Bet those perky tits would taste real good.*

Marilee clenched her jaw and turned on her heel. It was better to leave than to cause a scene.

"Uh, excuse me, honey," the woman called out. "I need a refill!" *Stupid bitch didn't even ask when she saw my empty glass. Her tip just got smaller.*

"Another Coke coming up," Marilee called back over her shoulder with a tight smile. She barely restrained the urge to flip the skinny woman off. People couldn't control their thoughts like they could control their tongues, and if she'd been on her game, she wouldn't have read the woman's mind anyway. Her nerves had her off and she had to deal with the consequences.

As she grabbed a frosty glass out of the cooler and filled it with Coke she let her gaze rove over the room. Hank's Hoe-Down was just like the thirty or so other hole in the wall bars she'd worked in over the years since leaving

Hicksville without a backward glance. The music was loud, the food greasy, and the drunks plentiful.

This particular bar was decorated in a country western motif, not unusual for small towns in Texas, and cowboy wannabes filled the room. So did the cowboy wannabe groupies, in their short skirts and smaller tank tops. Couples danced in the middle of the floor, people sat wedged into the booths, chewing on greasy burgers or sloppy ribs, and in the far corner a group of men bet on the outcome of a pool game between two guys in T-shirts and tight well-worn jeans.

It was a normal Friday night at Hank's, except for the unease slithering around in Marilee's belly.

She delivered the Coke and two icy longnecks to table nine, careful to lockdown her mind so she wouldn't hear what other parts of her body Pervo-man wanted to taste, and took orders from two more booths.

"Order up, Charlie," she called to the heavyset man whipping up food in the kitchen before glancing at the clock. Two more hours until closing time.

A cold chill skirted up her spine and an unnamable force drew her gaze to the door as a tall, dark silhouette filled the entry. Her breath caught as he stepped forward into the light.

He stood about six feet two inches tall, with wavy black hair that fell just below his shoulders, and dark, piercing blue eyes that met hers across the room and refused to let go.

"Where did that big hunk of sex in the flesh come from?"

Marilee broke free of the man's gaze and turned her head to see Brenda pulling down her tank top and pushing up her breasts until they nearly toppled over the edge of her neckline. "I don't know what he's having for dinner, but I'm gonna be that man's dessert."

We might all be. Marilee swallowed hard as she watched Brenda sashay over to the man, who now sat leisurely at the corner table closest to the door. He wore black combat boots, black pants, a black T-shirt and a black leather jacket. Back to the wall, he tapped his long fingers on the table as he kept her in his sights, his perfectly carved face giving away nothing.

"Hey! You deaf or something?"

SIREN'S SNARE

Marilee jumped and turned her head to notice the grizzly looking man who'd parked himself right in front of her at the bar. "I asked for a Rattlesnake."

Blinking out of her stupor, she swallowed hard and nodded. "Sorry."

"Marilee! Get these orders out, dammit!"

She quickly made the drink for the man at the bar and turned to grab the food Charlie had set out several minutes ago. The looks she received from the cook and Hank himself, who leaned against the back wall, competed with those of her customers in the glare of death contest.

About damn time.

I bet that hair came from a bottle. Probably thinks she's hotter than me, and if John doesn't quit looking at her ass in those little shorts...

This food better be worth the wait.

Maybe if I leave a big tip, she'll let me in those shorts.

Hot little thing, but she sucks as a waitress.

Marilee ground her teeth together and fought to push the thoughts out of her head as she made her way back over to the bar. All the while, she felt the weight of the man in black leather's stare on her.

"Move!" Brenda barked as she cut her off to slide behind the bar. "Table five requested you," she said bitterly, grabbing two frosty mugs out of the cooler to fill up at the tap.

Marilee glanced over to the corner table where the man stared her down. "I have to get beers over to tables eight and ten."

"I'll take them," Brenda offered, grabbing two more mugs, "and I'll take your tips for those tables."

"Bitch," Marilee grumbled as she watched the she-devil carry the tray of beers over to one of the tables.

"Table five hasn't been served," Hank reminded her, a deep scowl etched into his face, as he stepped past her to get to the kitchen.

Biting back the impulse to tell him to go to hell, Marilee squared her shoulders and walked over to the corner table, where the trouble she'd sensed awaited.

She'd killed men like him before, but there was something about this one, some secret hidden in the depths of those inky blue eyes that told her this one wasn't like any man she'd come across before.

"What can I get you?" she asked in a low voice as she reached the table. "A Bloody Mary? Maybe a Bloody Nancy? Or Susan?"

The side of his mouth turned up into the slightest hint of a smile. "I like your accent, and your humor. Am I that obvious?"

"The leather jacket in the middle of a Texas summer was a dead giveaway," she answered, ignoring the little sparks of electricity shooting through her system at the sound of his rich, melodic voice. "A human wouldn't have lasted a minute without keeling over from heatstroke."

He glanced down at his attire, grinned, and then let his gaze slowly wander up her body. "You're certainly dressed for the heat."

Marilee folded her arms in front of her chest, desperate to stop the tingling sensation in her breasts caused by the man's perusal. He was a bloodsucker for crying out loud, the last thing he should be doing was turning her on. "What do you want?" she asked, wishing she hadn't worn such a snug T-shirt.

He cocked his head to the side and chuckled, low and throaty. "Isn't it customary for waitresses to be pleasant to their customers?"

"When those customers are drinking beer or Coke, not blood." She glanced around to make sure no one overheard her and found Hank watching her with narrowed eyes. He jerked his head toward table nine where the trio she'd served earlier were glaring at her, empty beers in hand.

"I've got other tables, so if you would just do us both a favor and I—" She turned around to see the vampire looking back at her with an air of impatience, a menu open in front of him on the table.

"I'll take the T-bone, very rare."

"I'll just bet you will." Marilee angrily scribbled the order onto her pad. "If you so much as look at anyone here the wrong way, I'll kill you whether there are witnesses or not."

"I was warned that you would, Marilee."

Her hand froze over the pad and she clenched her fingers tight around the pen to hide any visible shaking. "How the hell do you know my name? We don't wear nametags here and I sure didn't introduce myself."

"You have other tables, Marilee." He looked past her. "And your boss looks very irritated. I'd suggest you turn in that order and see to your other customers."

"Blood-sucking son of a bitch," she muttered under her breath as she turned to head for the bar, worry producing a ball of nausea in her stomach.

The vampire's deep chuckle let her know he'd heard her.

"I don't know what it is about you that fine hunk of sexiness finds so appealing," Brenda muttered as she continued putting freshly washed mugs into the cooler. "Barely a curve on you."

Marilee bit her tongue and continued wiping down the bar. She could always kick the more-fat-lumps-than-actual-curves-bitch's ass in the parking lot. After she got paid for the night. And what a night it had been, with table after table of customers. Friday and Saturday nights usually were busy, but in the three weeks she'd been in the little Texas town, she'd never seen it so packed. Her feet ached from the constant walking and standing, and a headache was starting to form from the concentrated effort it took to block out the thoughts of the people surrounding her. She was normally much better at blocking, but everything about this night was off. Especially the man still sitting in the corner watching her intently, the steak he'd ordered untouched. "Trust me, he's not my type."

"You can go on home, Brenda," Hank said, strolling behind the bar. "Tell that man over there we're closing up, would ya?"

"Love to." Brenda pushed up her boobs, sucked in her gut, and sauntered over to the table, her hips whipping back and forth so fast, it was a wonder she managed to move forward.

"You know that gangster?" Hank asked, his tone indicating his disapproval.

Marilee glanced up from the bar to see Mr. Tall, Dark, and Bloodthirsty following Brenda out the door. He looked back at her and that near-grin he was good at doing showed itself. Marilee's heart slammed into her throat. Brenda was a bitch, but if he so much as touched one hair on her head he would meet his maker before the night was through.

So dramatic. Which maker do you refer to? I already killed my sire.

Marilee gasped as the vampire's voice registered clearly in her head. She'd picked up on people's thoughts before, but never had anyone spoken directly to her through her mind, let alone read it.

Relax, little vampire killer. The redhead will not be harmed.

"Marilee!"

She jerked, and turned to see Hank's irritated scowl. "Where is your head, tonight, girl?" He slammed the cash drawer closed and started counting out bills. "Here."

Marilee took the small wad of bills he handed her and frowned. She didn't need to count it to know she was about to get really upset. "This isn't what we agreed to, Hank."

"That's the thing about working under the table," he said with a smug grin. "Who you gonna complain to?"

"You son of a—"

"Watch it, girl." He fanned the bills in his hand. "That tone might guarantee you don't see another dime."

Marilee's hands tightened into fists. "I'm leaving town tomorrow, Hank. I don't give a damn whether you employ me another night or not."

"Oh, just skipping out, are we?" He chuckled. "Wasn't even going to tell me, and you wonder why I don't give you the amount we agreed to? Face it, you're not the best waitress. You know the drinks, but your customer service skills are seriously lacking."

"I had an off night." *And yours is about to get even worse if you don't pay me right.*

"Whatever. I got several complaints about you. In fact, I could have lost business tonight thanks to you."

Marilee rolled her eyes. "You don't have any competition in this town, Hank. Your drunks aren't going anywhere else. Just pay me what we agreed on and you'll never see me again."

"You haven't earned the amount we agreed on." He leaned against the bar, his arms folded as his beady eyes roamed down her body. "But there's still time for you to earn the difference."

Marilee's stomach rolled as his intent dawned. "Hank, there's not enough money in the world for what you're wanting from me."

His eyes darkened. "I know your type. You come around looking for under the table work because you're running from something. You either knocked off a convenience store, ran a scam, or poisoned your cheating boyfriend. I don't know what you did and I don't care." He stepped closer. "You need money to leave with, and there's only one way you're going to get it."

"Prying it out of your cold, dead hands?"

He stepped back, swallowed hard at the implication, but the moment of fear was fleeting. Understandably. His six foot one bulky frame dwarfed her five foot seven slender form. "A little scrap of a girl like you can't do much damage."

He stepped forward again and trailed a finger over her shoulder, down the length of her arm. "Now are you going to earn the money or not?"

Marilee pulled away from the man's vile touch, and cursed her rotten luck. She was getting out of town, with or without the money he still owed her. She had bigger problems than being strapped for cash, and those problems had fangs and killer blue eyes. "Fry in hell, Hank. I'm out of here."

She rounded the bar and headed for the door, but didn't make it far before Hank's beefy hand clamped onto her upper arm and jerked her around.

"Maybe you didn't understand." He shoved her until her back hit the bar. "You're earning the difference."

Marilee ignored the pain in her lower back and quickly assessed the situation. She could smell whiskey on Hank's breath, his eyes were a tinge glassy. The man was drunk. Drunk men could be dangerous. She knew from experience gained long before she'd ever set foot in a bar to work.

"Hank, let me go." She'd stay calm. Calm would keep the situation from escalating.

"You'll like it, girlie." He accentuated his statement by unbuckling his belt.

How he could find it beneath his rotund belly, Marilee didn't know, and she intended to stop him before he found the snap to his jeans, too.

"I don't know about that, Hank. I'm not big on pork." She kneed him in the groin and made a run for the door while he was bent over sucking in wind. Calm had flown out the window the moment his belt buckle came undone.

Something grabbed the back of her waistband and she found herself back against the bar, a red-faced, thoroughly pissed off Hank bent, but not broken, before her. "You fucking whore. You'll pay for that."

Marilee struggled against his hold on her arm, but couldn't break free unless she snapped the bone. Though she'd broken bones before, she hesitated now. The jerk certainly deserved a maimed body part or two, but she couldn't do it so coldly. Not to a human. "Hank, you're drunk. Just let me go and we'll forget about this."

"Wrong, blondie." He used his free hand to tug at the snap to her cutoffs. "You'll never forget this."

Marilee looked around the bar for a weapon, seeing no knives or sharp instruments. The sound of her zipper sliding down sent her heart racing into her throat, her mind reeling back to her childhood. Not again!

She kicked out, knocking Hank off balance enough for her to climb over the bar. He grabbed her by the waist and tugged her back down, but not before she snatched a bottle of whiskey from behind the bar.

"Come here, bitch." Hank spun her around and his head met the bottom of the whiskey bottle. He groaned in pain, bending over as shards exploded against his skull, but he was quickly up again.

His arm whipped out and the back of his hand slapped hard against Marilee's jaw. Stars flew out before her eyes as her head whipped to the side.

"Bitch!" He grabbed Marilee and slammed her onto the top of the bar. "Hit me again and I'll break you into pieces."

He climbed over the stools and onto the bar, straddling her legs tight to keep her from kneeing him again. She kept a knife in her ankle boot. If only she could get to it. Hank slapped her again, the hit leaving a burning path along her other cheek and she reflexively covered her face with her hands to ward off more blows.

Whiskey dripped off his head onto her hands and she choked back a scream as the sound of his zipper rustled. All of the sudden she was fifteen years old and trapped under a man again. Then, suddenly, she was free.

She blinked as the weight of the large man disappeared, and lowered her hands to seek out the source of commotion she heard. Sitting up, slowly so she didn't throw up from the nausea the movement caused, she gasped at the scene she witnessed.

The mysterious vampire growled in rage, his eyes glowing with power as he bashed Hank's body repeatedly into the bar. The bar owner screamed in between sounds of agony.

"Stop! You'll kill him!"

The vampire paused mid-body slam and stared at her in disbelief. "You would have a problem with that after what he was about to do to you?"

Marilee looked down to find her shorts around her knees. Heat flooding her face, she jerked them up to cover her teal and black striped bikini panties and slid off the bar. The vampire reached out with one hand to help her, Hank dangling like a limp ragdoll from the other.

"Don't touch me." Marilee sidestepped his hand, earning a look of contempt, and quickly zipped up her cutoffs. Her head spun and her lunch threatened to rise. She vaguely recalled her head slamming into the bar and figured she probably had a concussion. Great. Like she needed another problem added to the already too long list.

Hank made a gurgling sound and the vampire focused his attention back on him. "Shut up, you filthy swine."

Marilee took advantage of the vampire's shift in attention and raised her foot so she could quickly extract the blade from the sheath hidden inside her boot. She'd paid a pretty penny for the custom dagger she'd designed herself, but it was worth it. The silver blade was sharp enough to slice through anything—she'd chopped off fingers, bones and all, with it—and had a handle made of hawthorn, a type of wood vampires couldn't tolerate.

The vampire raised Hank in the air, his hand clamped tight around the creep's throat, and directed his gaze back to Marilee. It quickly shifted to the dagger she held poised for attack. "You'd pull that on me, but not a man about to rape you?"

He made a sound of disgust in his throat, and Marilee felt a pang of... guilt? She shook her head, shaking the odd feeling away. The vampire protected her, but it didn't change what he was.

"I believe there's an issue of money."

She blinked, wondered how the vampire knew so much. "He didn't pay me the amount we agreed on for me working here."

"Get what you're owed, and let's go."

Marilee opened her mouth to tell the vampire she wasn't going anywhere with him, but he turned his gaze on her again. His eyes glowed with a terrifying degree of power. "Get what you are owed. Now," he added between clenched teeth and bared fangs.

Marilee looked at Hank's mottled, blue-tinged face, and swallowed hard. A human man was about to die and the blood would be on her hands. Fighting back another wave of nausea, she bent down to retrieve the bills Hank had dropped during their altercation. Careful to avoid shards of glass littering the floor, she collected the money—some of it wet from spilled whiskey—and shoved it into her front pocket.

"Is that it, or does he owe you more?"

"That's it." It was probably a little bit more than the agreed upon amount, but hey, being sexually assaulted gave her the right to charge interest.

The vampire nodded, turned his head toward Hank and lowered the bar owner so they were face to face. "Thank God for second chances and pray for forgiveness," he growled and effortlessly threw the man over the bar, sending his body crashing into the mirrored wall which shattered on impact.

She'd seen vampires in action before, but this one was different. He was far more powerful than those she'd fought, so powerful his energy sucked the air out of the room. And what was with the glowing eyes? She'd never seen that before.

When he returned his attention to her she looked into those dark blue eyes, full of simmering rage, saw herself being thrown across a room, and took off at a run right out the door. She was scared, beyond that, she was piss-in-her-pants terrified. It didn't matter that she'd killed vampires before. Instinct told her this one wouldn't go down easy.

She pushed away the nausea clawing at her belly and struggled to keep the world around her in focus as she ran down the street. It was late and all the bar's patrons were long gone from the area. She had to run. She had to find a place to hide.

She had to throw up.

Diving into a narrow alley, she braced a hand against a brick wall and bent over. Her lunch threatened to rise again, but all she could produce was a strong set of dry heaves. It reminded her she needed to eat more.

SIREN'S SNARE

"You really shouldn't overexert yourself if you're concussed."

Marilee spun around and came face to face with the vampire. He'd snuck up on her without a sound.

"Stay away from me." She held the dagger out, reminding him she was armed.

He frowned at the weapon. "It's disturbing how ready you are to use that on me, but not the man who attacked you."

Marilee recalled him saying something similar back at the bar and felt the twinge of guilt again. Why, she didn't know. "What do you want from me?" *To kill me, obviously. Duh.*

He grinned, but his eyes didn't show humor. "I'm not here to kill you, Marilee. If I were, why would I have bothered protecting you from that animal?"

Good point, unless he just enjoyed the thrill of the chase. And how did he know her name? "You never answered my earlier question."

He cocked his head to the side, raised an eyebrow.

"How do you know my name?"

"I was sent here to retrieve you."

Alarm bells rang out in Marilee's mind. A vampire sent to retrieve her? No way was that good. Her hand reflexively wrapped around the cross she never removed from her neck. She knew it wouldn't harm the vampire, but what it represented gave her courage. However, being courageous didn't mean being stupid. The best thing she could do was escape or at the very least go somewhere with people. The vampire might not act with witnesses around.

She turned to run and saw a tall chain link fence blocking her exit. "Oh, that's just classic stereotype. Dumb blonde goes down a dark alley while being pursued by the big, bad monster and meets a dead end." She stomped her foot and turned around to face her enemy, no other option left. It appeared she'd been cast in a B movie without her knowledge. The mask of anger on the vampire's face stole her breath.

"The big, bad monster is the man who beat you, tried to rape you. Why do you insist on giving me that title instead of him?" He turned and took a step as if he were about to storm off, but quickly turned back around, closing the distance between them. "Maybe I had it wrong. Maybe you enjoyed it, craved his touch."

She slapped the vampire's face, heedless of repercussion. "You bastard! How dare you think I'd like such a thing!" Years of repressed rage rose inside her and she raised the dagger to strike.

One hand rubbing his jaw, the vampire raised his free arm and the dagger flew into his open palm. He winced as the hawthorn handle touched his skin and dropped the weapon.

Blinking, her mind unable to believe what she'd just seen, Marilee backed away, but the vampire snaked an arm around her waist and pulled her closer. "I'm sorry, Marilee. That was a cruel thing to say." He raised his hand and she flinched, but after a brief pause, he merely wiped away tears she hadn't been aware of shedding. "I do not like being looked upon as a monster when compared to that type of man."

"Who the hell are you?" She reached out with her mind, trying to pull information but as was the case with most vampires, she couldn't get anything. She no longer felt the panic-fueled need to run from him, though.

"Have you paused to think that maybe the danger you've felt all day was due to the man who tried to rape you?"

Irritated with his intrusion into her thoughts, Marilee released a frustrated sigh. "No. The hint of danger still lingers, and it's lingering around you. Who are you? Why can you hear my thoughts?"

"I have the same psychic abilities you have," he explained, stepping away and turning. "Come now."

"I don't come on command." She stood with feet firmly planted, arms crossed before her chest.

The vampire turned his head toward her and grinned impishly. Her face heated. "You know what I mean."

"It's late, Marilee, and we have much to discuss. I'd rather not have that discussion in an alley in the dead of night." He glanced around. "I may have been followed."

Fear clawed at her insides, but still Marilee did not move. "You'll have to give me more than that to make me follow you off to who knows where, vampire. What happened to Brenda?"

"She made me a very generous offer of her body, to which I politely declined." He stuffed his hands into his pockets. "After implying I was homosexual she left with two men in an old, rusted pick-up truck. I imagine she's sandwiched between them as we speak."

Marilee's lip curled up at that image she so didn't want in her head and reached out with her senses. She couldn't read the vampire's mind but she could feel the truth in his words. Still... "Why won't you tell me who you are?"

"My name is Khiderian," he answered, his tone implying his frustration. "I'm a very old vampire with very little patience. Now, move."

Marilee just looked at him, bristling at his tone.

"I can make you come." His gaze held a hint of mischief, lending to the double entendre.

"Not in this lifetime, buddy." Bending down, Marilee scooped up the dagger and slid it into her ankle boot. The sense of danger swirled around the vampire, but the little voice inside her that forewarned her of things to come told her he wouldn't directly harm her. "I've killed vampires before," she warned, just in case. "Don't mess with me."

"I understand how little you value my race." He turned to lead the way to the mouth of the alley. "However, I was ordered to retrieve you and so I am. You should thank me for my help tonight, but I imagine it'll be a cold day in Hades before you admit a vampire was more honorable than a human."

"I could have taken care of that jerk by myself."

"Not if you weren't willing to kill or maim him because he was human." He glared at her as they walked. "Some human life isn't worth preserving. It amazes me that you would even consider sparing his but would kill a vampire simply because of his or her existence."

"Vampires killed my grandparents."

He stepped in front of her, halting her, as they faced each other. "And another vampire saved your life in that little town."

Marilee gasped, remembering the vampire-witch who'd healed the damage to her throat after she'd been attacked by another vampire while helping Jake Porter fight a trio of the bloodsuckers who'd taken over her hometown. "How do you know that?"

"I was given your bio before I was sent to retrieve you."

"My bio? What the hell are you talking about? Who sent you, and for what?"

"The Dream Teller," he answered. "The witch who watches over all vampires. Jacob Porter has been captured, and you are the person who's going to save him."

CHAPTER TWO

Dizziness engulfed Marilee. She nearly toppled backwards, but two strong leather-clad arms caught her.

"Don't touch me!" Batting away the vampire's hands, she straightened. "What do you mean Jacob Porter was captured? Jake couldn't have been captured. He's..." She struggled to find a word to properly describe the man who'd rescued little Bobby Perkins from a vampire lair. A vampire lair that had once been her grandparents' home.

She'd first met him at the jail when she'd gone to demand Sheriff Peewee Porter investigate her grandparents' disappearance. While there, she'd heard Jake screaming from his cell that something was coming and Peewee needed to let him out. Images of beast-like people feasting on blood flashed into her mind as chills overtook her body. She knew then that her nightmares hadn't been harmless dreams, but were premonitions.

Peewee ran to Jake's cell and she left his office, her feet moving on their own volition. Something, that feeling she got from time to time that fate was controlling her body, not her, led her to the front and there she saw them. Three people she'd known most of her life. Two men and a woman. Neighbors.

Newly turned vampires.

Something snapped inside her and she went into battle alongside Jacob Porter, killing a man she'd seen almost daily for the past several years. She'd watched as Jake mercilessly destroyed Peggy Sue Freebush without batting an eye. Granted, the vamp-bitch had damn near killed her, but still... She'd been mesmerized by his ferocity.

She hadn't hesitated to go with him to her grandparents' house and enter a lair full of vampires. He'd made her feel safe. She felt right fighting beside him.

"He's happily married to his soul mate, you know?"

Khiderian's crude comment snapped her out of the memory. The image of Jake and Nyla—his soul mate whom she'd accidentally shot—leaving in Jake's black Malibu after dropping her, Maybelline and Bobby Perkins off at the motel faded away as she glared at the tall vampire. "It wasn't like that, and stay out of my head."

"Then quit mooning over the man and start walking." Khiderian emphasized his command by turning around and again leading the way out of the alley. He was silent, brooding even, as they reached the street and turned back toward the direction of the bar.

"How was Jake captured? Who has him?"

"He was caught in a siren snare." He glanced around again, as if looking for eavesdroppers. "My car is in the parking lot of the bar. Do you have someplace we can stay for the day? We'll leave out at dusk."

"What?" Marilee stopped. "Who said you could stay anywhere with me?"

Khiderian reached back and grabbed her elbow, propelling her forward. "I did. Look, I'm the one at a disadvantage. I'm going to be with a vampire killer in the daylight hours, when I'm at my weakest." He leered down at her. "But The Dream Teller says you are the only hope for saving Jacob Porter and keeping the dark side from stopping the Blood Revelation so I'm trusting you. You could show me the same respect."

"Blood Revelation? Siren snare? Who is the Dream Teller, and what are you talking about?"

They'd reached the parking lot to Hank's Hoe-down and Khiderian led her to a shiny black sports car. Holding open the passenger door for her, he looked down into her eyes. "You were supposed to meet Jacob Porter. It's always been your destiny to save him if he ever fell into trouble."

Marilee fell into the car more than sat in it, her knees suddenly weak. Between the jelly-like feeling of her limbs, the pain in her back and head, and the nausea still rolling around in her stomach, it was hard to think. It was her fate to rescue Jacob Porter? *Jacob Porter?* No way. She wasn't worthy.

"He's not a god," Khiderian grumbled, sliding into the driver's seat and closing the door. He took up a lot of space in the small car, reminding Marilee of his powerful stature.

"You just can't seem to stay out of my mind, can you?" She huffed out a breath, now understanding what it felt like to have private thoughts invaded. No wonder the few kids she'd let in on her secret hadn't wanted to play with her after finding out.

Khiderian produced a key from his jacket pocket and inserted it into the ignition, bringing the sleek machine to life. "Where to?"

"I've been staying at a crappy little motel off the interstate. You can go to hell," she replied sweetly, adding a tight little smile for effect as she fluttered her eyelashes.

"I think I saw that motel on the way here." Khiderian grinned, pulling out of the parking lot. "I'm not a bad guy, you know." He sighed when she chose to sit in silence, looking out the window instead of answering. "I noticed you had a case of dry heaves back there. Can I get you something to eat?"

"No thanks. I don't eat people meat, preferring to stick with beef and poultry," Marilee muttered as heat filled her face. She reminded herself the man occupying the car with her was a vampire, and she shouldn't care that he saw her trying to blow chunks.

"I was thinking of something more along the line of McDonald's. We should be able to find a twenty-four hour fast food restaurant somewhere." He stopped at a red light and looked over at her. "You're probably concussed and I know your stomach is empty. Eating would be good for you."

"Keep talking about food and I'm going to redecorate the interior of your nice, flashy car," Marilee warned, her stomach doing a somersault. For being empty, it sure did churn.

"It's a rental."

She glared at the grin on the vampire's face and fought back her own. A sexy vampire with a sense of humor. Just what she needed. "I'm not hungry. Tell me about Jake. What exactly is a siren snare?" She blinked. "Wait. Are you talking about sirens from mythology?"

Khiderian nodded as the light turned green, and moved the car forward. "Creatures of the sea with the ability to cast themselves in the image of their intended victim's ultimate dream woman."

Marilee took a moment to digest the brief information, and what it implied. Apparently, Jake's love for Nyla wasn't enough to save him from being captured.

"I doubt any man on this earth could resist the pull of a siren. Well, except for a gay man, seeing as how they can only cast themselves as women." Khiderian turned right on the street which would take them to the interstate. "Jacob evaded a siren snare once before by dying and resurrecting. You knew he could do that, right?"

Marilee nodded. "I overheard him and Nyla discussing it. This crazy mad scientist guy injected him with some kind of serum that kept him from dying. Well, permanently, that is. I take it then that it's still working?"

"Yes, but we're unsure if it'll work indefinitely, which is why we need to rescue him."

A chill crept up Marilee's spine. She didn't want this task. It was too much responsibility. "You said he evaded a snare once. What happened this time? And what the heck is a snare?"

Khiderian's mouth curved upward as he glanced her way quickly before returning his attention to the road. "A snare is when a siren projects herself as a man's fantasy woman and lures him with her song. She mesmerizes him, and then kills him by sucking out his soul."

"Holy shit."

"Nothing holy about it." Khiderian's jaw clenched tight. "A slayer's soul can't be taken by dark forces, but a slayer can still be entranced. The first time Jacob met up with a siren, she ordered him to kill himself and he did. She was so surprised when he resurrected that she ran away in fear while he killed off the were-hyenas she was working with."

"But she came back."

Khiderian nodded again, and maneuvered the car onto the interstate. "With friends. They can't take his soul but they can keep killing him. The question is, how many times will he die before he no longer comes back?"

"Poor Jake." Marilee rubbed her temples, the pain behind her eyes growing worse. "So basically, I'm supposed to save him from a group of hussies from hell?"

Khiderian barked out a laugh. "That's one way of putting it."

"Why me? Why not Seta? She healed me when my neck was nearly broken, and she's female. A siren can't entrance a female, can they?"

"Not a heterosexual female."

"Seta's a lesbian?"

"No." His brow furrowed. "I don't think so, but that doesn't matter. The group that has Porter knew he associated with vampires and witches. They took precautions."

Marilee's stomach rolled again. "You're telling me that a group powerful enough to capture Jake Porter and protect themselves against a vampire-witch as strong as Seta is supposed to be stopped by me?"

"You're not alone, Marilee. Your job is rescuing Jacob from the sirens. I'll handle the rest."

Her head spun. "What does the rest include?"

"The usual. Vampires, shifters, demons, whatev—"

Marilee hit the button to lower the window at the same time she unfastened her seatbelt, and stuck her head out of the car just in time to throw up, for real this time. What little she'd had in her belly hit the moving road and her head throbbed harder in response to her body's upset.

"You all right?"

"Perfect." Marilee slid back into her seat, discreetly wiping her mouth with the back of her hand. "There's the motel."

Khiderian pulled off the exit ramp and drove to the motel, parking the car outside the room farthest from the manager's office. "Which room?"

"The one we're parked in front of." Marilee groaned as a sharp jab of pain ricocheted through her head. Her stomach didn't feel much better, all twisted in knots.

Her door opened and Khiderian reached in, slid one arm under her legs, the other behind her back. Realizing his intent, Marilee slammed her palm into his chest. "Back up, bloodsucker."

He halted, but didn't move out of the way. "You're in no condition to walk."

"I've been taking care of myself since I was in pigtails. I don't need help from you." She shoved him away and stepped out of the car on shaking legs. "I don't need help from anybody." *And I can't help anyone but me. I can't save Jake.* "Move!"

The vampire stepped away from her, nostrils flaring at her tone, and closed the car door. Marilee walked toward the motel room door, but her vision blurred and she lurched forward.

"Dammit." Khiderian grabbed her around the waist and slung her over his shoulder.

"Put me down!" She pounded her fists into his back.

"So you can pass out and I'll have to carry you into the room anyway? Be sensible." He stopped in front of the door. "Where's the room key?"

"In my back pocket, and don't get any bright ideas about feeling on my ass." Marilee quit beating his back and retrieved the plastic card key out of her back pocket. "Here, jackass."

"Your manners could use some tweaking," he commented drily as he opened the door. Once in, he quickly covered the distance to the single bed and gently set her on top of the comforter. "How's your head?" he asked as he crossed the room and closed the door, sliding the bolt into place.

"It's screaming at me." Marilee leaned back against the pillows to watch Khiderian adjust the curtains, trapping out the daylight that would fall within the next few hours. "I thought only direct rays of the sun could harm you."

"That's true." He turned, inspected the room. "But it's best to always stay hidden from your enemies."

"You really think someone could have followed you?"

"It's possible." His gaze caught on the tiny refrigerator unit and he walked over to inspect its contents, pulling out everything it contained: a bottle of water and half of a Subway club sandwich. "Eat and drink."

"I just blew chunks all over the interstate," Marilee grumbled. "What makes you think I want to eat?"

"It will help you." He shook his head in exasperation. "Take this, please."

"Fine." Marilee sat forward enough to eat and took the sandwich.

Khiderian placed the bottled water on the nightstand next to her. "Do you have anything to help with your pain?"

"I keep Tylenol in my bag."

He glanced around the small dark room again, zeroing in on the duffel bag resting on one of the cheap chairs encircling a cheaper looking card table.

A moment later, he sat at her side with two Tylenol in hand, the bottled water open and ready.

Marilee set down the sandwich she'd forced herself to take a bite out of and took the capsules from his large palm. The irony that she was being cared for by a vampire, the same type of being she'd been killing in the years since leaving Hicksville, didn't escape her. "Well, this is something I never expected."

"I'm sorry I'm not the bloodthirsty animal you decided I would be."

Marilee returned the vampire's dark glare as she downed the Tylenol and replaced the bottled water on the nightstand. "Who's judging who now?"

"I don't need to judge you," he replied emotionlessly. "I can hear your thoughts, remember?" He turned away, but not before Marilee caught the look on his face. From the tight set of his jaw, the stiffness of his shoulders, he actually seemed affronted.

Marilee pushed aside the guilt that reaction in him caused her and ate a bite of the sandwich. It landed in her empty stomach with a thud and she rolled her eyes. Why was she letting a vampire order her to eat when she didn't feel like it? More importantly, who was he supposed to be? Who was the *we* he'd mentioned earlier and why was he sent to *retrieve* her in the first place? "What exactly are you?"

"Psychic vampire."

"Not that." She took another bite of the sub. "Who is this Dream Teller you mentioned before, and why were you sent for me? Do you work for this Dream Teller or something?"

"You could say that." He swiveled his head to meet her gaze and she quickly focused her sights on her sub. She had the distinct feeling she could get pulled into those pretty dark blue orbs, even in the dark. Especially in the dark. "I'm kind of vampire special ops."

She nearly choked on the sandwich. "GI Vamp-Joe?"

"Yeah, kind of." He grinned. "You amuse me. Not many people can do that."

"Sorry to hear that." Marilee forced the last piece of sandwich down and wadded up the plastic bag, tossed it into the wastebasket sitting across the room. "You must be a real stick in the mud."

"I suppose so." He reached out and probed the back of her head. "How are you feeling?"

"Better." Marilee pulled away so he'd drop his hand away from her. She didn't like the warm sensation his touch gave her. Actually, she did like it. What she didn't like was the fact that it didn't repulse her as it should. "That was extra strength Tylenol. It works really good."

"What about the other?" His gaze softened. "If you want to talk about what happened?"

"What would I have to talk to you about? Other than your reason for *retrieving* me." She crooked her fingers into quotation marks.

"Marilee, you were almost raped."

"Almost being the key word," she snapped. Geez, what kind of devil worshiper wanted to make a girl rehash that? "And if you're looking for a thank you, forget it. I would have gotten him off me before he…" A shiver tap danced along her spine as the image of a red-faced Hank hovering over her entered her head.

Marilee shoved at the irritating man looking down at her with pity-coated eyes. She hated pity. It was right up there with ridicule, and she'd had plenty of both growing up in the sticks with Becky Mills as a mother. Some people would think being the town whore was the worst thing possible, but there were worse things. Namely, being the town whore's daughter.

Khiderian grabbed her wrists in his hands. "You've been attacked before."

"That's it!" Marilee kicked the vampire in the chest with all the strength she could muster, efficiently knocking him off the bed. "I didn't ask for a grief counselor! Stay out of my head or I swear, I'll kill you while you sleep!"

Khiderian looked up at her from where he sat sprawled on the dirty motel room floor, blue eyes open wide in surprise, and raised his hands. "Fine. Sorry I allowed myself to show a little concern." He pulled himself up and dusted his hands on the sides of his pants. "You obviously don't care for the emotion."

Another jolt of guilt hit Marilee in the center of her chest and she growled. Of all the times to go soft. "Look, I'm not trying to be a bitch."

"Apparently, you don't have to try." He turned and removed his jacket, exposing a long sword sheathed to his back, and a skinny blade strapped onto each muscular arm. "It seems to take very little effort on your part." He hung the jacket on the back of a chair. The sword and its sheath came off next. The smaller blades stayed on.

"So I see the nice guy routine was an act after all," Marilee responded, squeezing her hands into fists.

"I'm not an actor, I'm a soldier." Khiderian stretched his long body out on the plaid couch that smelled so musky Marilee hadn't dared sit on it, scrunched his nose at the offending odor, and shifted, trying to find a comfortable position. Marilee wished him luck. "If you can learn to be civil, we'll get along just fine."

He sent her a pointed look and eased the back of his head down onto the arm of the couch, raising his arm to cover his forehead. The move showed a bulging bicep that captured Marilee's attention. She let her gaze rove over the length of him stretched out on the couch, admiring the view. He might be a vampire, but he was Grade A, all the way.

She noticed his mouth curve up at the corners and realized he'd heard her thought.

"Bastard!" She threw a pillow at him.

He chuckled and caught the soft projectile effortlessly and positioned it under his head. "Thanks, babe." He winked at her and closed his eyes. "Now get some rest. We rise at dusk and head out."

"I thought you couldn't sleep if you had a concussion."

"Old wive's tale, and you don't have a concussion anymore anyway."

"I don't have a concussion any—" Marilee recalled the tingle she'd felt as Khiderian probed her head with his hand. "What did you do?"

"Nothing I'll be thanked for, I'm sure." He shifted, eyes still closed. "As charming as your southern accent is, I'd prefer your silence."

Grumbling to herself, Marilee punched her remaining pillow into some semblance of shape and turned on her side to settle in. "Kiss my ass."

He chuckled again, the low throaty sound managing to tickle her nerve endings as she summoned sleep. Before she could achieve the feat, she heard his whisper in her mind. *Don't tempt me, honey. Remember, I bite.*

CHAPTER THREE

Damn, it's cold. Marilee opened her eyes and instantly realized something was wrong. She no longer lay in a shabby bed in an equally shabby motel room off the interstate. Instead, she stood in the middle of what appeared to be the woods. Blue rays of moonlight shone through the trees, adding a little light in the darkness. There were no animal sounds in these woods, though, not even insects. Everything was dead. Still.

But something was here.

She felt it up ahead, watching. Waiting. The only thing she saw were trees stretching out into the distance before being swallowed by misty fog. Her heart pumped faster, her pulse revved. A prickle of awareness tingled up the length of her spine. She normally fed on danger, reveled in the adrenaline rush, but the emotion steamrolling over her now was the same one she'd felt since waking up the day before. It didn't give her strength. It made her want to cower like a little girl, something she hadn't done in ages.

She felt fear. Cold, ruthless fear.

"Interesting."

Marilee let out a squeak as she spun around to see Khiderian leaning back against a tree, arms crossed in a nonchalant pose. He raised his hands and said, "Sorry." The smirk on his undeniably handsome face showed her how truly sorry he wasn't.

Marilee's face heated, whether from anger at his amusement, or embarrassment over her near-scream, she wasn't sure. "What are you doing here?"

"Are you not happy to have a friend in this place which obviously frightens you?" He pushed away from the tree and walked toward her, his movements slow and stealthy. Like a predator ready to strike.

"I don't have friends. If I did, you wouldn't be one of them." Marilee stepped back as he stopped before her. "Where is this place?"

"Do I appear as if I know?" The smug expression on his face clearly said he did.

"How did we get here?"

His grin broadened. "How do you think?"

"Do you always answer questions with questions?"

"Only when it entertains me this much." He reached out to tap his fingers lightly against her cheek. "You develop twin spots of color here when you get mad."

She knocked his hand away, ignoring the tingle of his touch she had no business feeling. "Quit playing, dammit. Where are we? Is this a dream?"

"If it were a dream I imagine we'd be naked."

Marilee gasped, more from the effect of his heated gaze than the bold comment. "You're not my type, vampire," she advised, hoping he didn't pick up on the sudden breathlessness in her tone. "And the two of us being naked together in one of my dreams would be a nightmare."

He chuckled, the low grumbling sound again tickling Marilee in places she'd rather not acknowledge.

"Are you finished antagonizing the poor girl, Khiderian?"

Icy cold claws of fear gripped Marilee tight as the presence she'd felt watching her suddenly closed in at her back. She stood stock-still as Khiderian's gaze swept past her shoulder to settle on the owner of the rusty, aged voice. "I'm sorry, Dream Teller. I have retrieved the girl as asked."

"Good. Turn around, Marilee."

She couldn't. The fear she'd been sensing engulfed her now, threatening to drag her under and hold her there until she drowned. She stared into Khiderian's midnight blue eyes and willed him to help her.

Those eyes filled with compassion as he reached out to tip her chin with his fingers. "You're safe."

"The dream realm amplifies emotion, especially strong ones like fear or anger," the Dream Teller explained. "What you are feeling right now, Marilee, is your own fear you've been keeping locked away. You know it's time to face it, and that thought alone terrifies you."

"I'm right here with you." Khiderian braced his hands on her shoulders and turned her around.

Marilee faced a frail old woman with long, white hair spilling out of a dark gray hooded cloak. Her nose was long and hook-like, her face marred with a map of deep grooves, and her eyes were blinding white. The witch perfectly fit the description of a hag. She looked as if a strong wind could knock her right over, but Marilee sensed more power in her than in Seta, Jake, Nyla, and Khiderian combined. One being holding that much power terrified her, and she backed away, right into Khiderian's chest.

The vampire's arms enclosed her, offering warmth to chase away the chill creeping through her body. Too stunned by the powerful witch before her, she didn't fight him. "You're what I've been sensing."

The hag nodded. "I am a seer, a prophet of sorts for the good vampire race."

"The good vampire race?"

"Yes." The witch inclined her head in the direction of Khiderian, but didn't raise her gaze to him. It was then Marilee realized the white-eyed witch was blind. "Khiderian is a soldier for the side of good, as are Seta, Jake, Nyla—"

"Jake and Nyla aren't vampires."

"Jake isn't, but he has been gifted with immortality and is a true slayer, which makes him a supernatural being. Nyla is part vampire, and though her sire was evil, she didn't allow his darkness to claim her."

Marilee recalled the horrific-looking vampire who'd organized the attack on Hicksville, and had killed her grandparents, turning their home into his lair before abducting Nyla, and put two and two together. Jake hadn't just killed any vampire, he'd killed Nyla's sire. "Why am I here if you're a prophet for the vampire race?"

"The Blood Revelation protects the human race."

Unease churned in Marilee's belly. "What is the Blood Revelation, and what does it have to do with me, other than the fact I'm a member of the human race?"

"The Blood Revelation states that three sets of immortals who are predestined to mate will produce strong immortal warriors, one of which will be powerful enough to save the world from Satan's wrath." The witch smiled.

"Yet, the Blood Revelation involves more than just those specially chosen immortals. Even they need help, and help can come from me, their friends, and sometimes even a young human woman will be needed to make sure the Revelation unfolds as it should."

"No. I can't." Marilee shook her head from side to side, her knees weakening. Khiderian held her up when she grew dizzy from the enormity of what she was being told. "I can't possibly save Jake. He's the one who taught me how to kill vampires."

"You'd already impaled a vampire by the time Jacob Porter discovered you," the Dream Teller reminded her. "There was very little advice he needed to give you, and you have done well on your own since parting ways."

Marilee cringed at the reminder. She'd left Hicksville three years ago, right after raiding the vampire lair with Jake, and since that day she'd killed at least twenty vampires. And she'd enjoyed the thrill of it every time. It wasn't until later while washing the blood out of her clothes that she thought about what she'd done and the remorse set in. After that came the guilt, then the shame.

Khiderian's arms tightened around her and she knew the vampire had been fishing through her mind again. Growing tired of his constant intrusion, she shoved his arms away and stepped out of his hold. The move brought her closer to the old witch, but the fear she felt had simmered down, and now the feeling was closer to one of dread. "So I'm supposed to go in and kill sirens now. Is this really all I'm meant to be? A killer?"

The Dream Teller frowned, raised an old, gnarled hand to cusp her cheek. Marilee shivered at the cold, yet oddly comforting touch. "You are so much more than that, child." The Dream Teller dropped her hand away. "You have wonderful gifts at your disposal, some you haven't even discovered yet. Khiderian will help you to find these hidden talents and train you how to use them."

Marilee bristled at the thought of being the arrogant vampire's student, and the old witch laughed. "He is not a bad man, young one, even if he does like to tease you. Khiderian is a good warrior to have in your corner, a strong and just soldier. You are safe in his hands."

Marilee turned her head to look at the vampire who'd gone silent. He stood behind her with arms folded, showing off the corded muscles. He was handsome, dangerously so, with those deep blue eyes, straight nose, and chiseled features. His skin was a deep tan, and power rolled off him in waves. He wasn't an average vampire, and Marilee knew in her gut he would be more than the average soldier. And more than the average man. She seriously doubted safe was what she'd be in his hands.

"Why can't Khiderian save Jake if he's such a powerful warrior?" Marilee asked, turning back toward the blind witch.

"Because he is a male. He would get snared by the sirens and his soul would be at jeopardy."

"Of course." Marilee snorted in disgust. "All that power and he can still be felled by his own dick."

Khiderian growled behind her. "I assure you if you ever came across an incubus you'd be felled by your own—"

"Khiderian!" The Dream Teller's harsh tone stopped the vampire from finishing his statement. "The two of you must work together in order to succeed."

"I understand." Khiderian stepped up to stand by Marilee's side. "I apologize for my temper." The narrow eyed look he directed at Marilee held no apology for her.

She glared right back at him as she asked the witch, "What happened to Seta and Nyla to keep them from saving Jake?"

"Jake is not the only warrior in danger." The witch raised a wrinkled hand and twirled it in a circular motion. White mist grew from her palm and formed a cloud when she held her hand out to the side. In the misty cloud, two cherubic faces appeared. One, a tawny headed little boy with violet eyes, and the other a precious little girl with dark, wavy hair and green eyes. Her ethnicity was hard to tell. Both of them appeared only a few years old. "These special children must be protected at all costs."

Marilee's palms broke out into a sweat. "Those hell-hussies who captured Jake have those babies too?"

"No, thank God." The Dream Teller waved her hand and the image disappeared. "But they are who the dark side is searching for. They are the reason Jacob Porter was captured."

"And the reason why the vampires closest to Porter can't rush in to save him," Khiderian interjected.

"Who are they? What do the sirens want them for?"

"Not just the sirens," The Dream Teller corrected, "but the entire dark side. They are the first two warriors born to the side of light."

"The boy is Jacob and Nyla's," Khiderian added.

Marilee's mouth fell open as she searched his face for a hint he was joking, but the look she received back was deadly serious. "But if Nyla is a vampire..."

"Part vampire," the witch reminded her, "and a very special immortal chosen to mate with an equally important immortal to produce a powerful warrior. Rialto and Aria are also specially chosen vampires who were given the honor of bringing forth a warrior for our side. The little girl is theirs."

"And these dark supernatural creatures want the children. What will they do to them?" Marilee had a good guess and it made her stomach roll again.

"They want to sacrifice the warriors to Lucifer. If their blood is spilled over an altar for him, his power over the mortal world..." The witch shuddered. "Only God himself could save us then."

"Us?" Marilee frowned. "You said this Blood Revelation was designed to protect the human race. Why would you be harmed?"

"Because the only thing that keeps an immortal from crossing over to the dark forces is our humanity. Being among good mortals helps us retain it and if we lose that, we lose ourselves."

"Great, so the fate of the whole world is in my hands." Marilee thought of the little immortal warriors' sweet faces and forced herself to stand tall. "So where is Jake being held? What's the plan to get him out?" *How the heck am I going to pull it off?*

"You and Khiderian will figure out the plan once you locate him."

Marilee blinked. "Once we locate him? You don't even know where he's at?"

"My visions don't always tell me everything." The old witch smiled. "It's not my fate to find him, it's yours."

"How am I supposed to do that?" Marilee threw her hands up in the air. "I may be a pretty good killer, but I'm no tracker."

"Khiderian will help you."

Marilee looked at the vampire, noting he didn't seem thrilled at the idea either. "Great. Shouldn't we be doing something now to find Jake? Why are we here with you if you don't know where to find him?"

The witch continued to smile, seemingly unperturbed by Marilee's tone. "The two of you did not hit it off well so I needed to speak with you directly and make it clear that you are to work together at all times. Though I must say I'm pleasantly surprised you haven't tried to stake poor Khiderian yet. I had my concerns." She waved her hand in a circle again and another image appeared. "Remember him?"

Marilee peered closer at the image of a man dressed in a white T-shirt and drawstring pants. He sat on a cot in an all-white tiled room. Her lip curled the moment she recognized him. "That's the wacko who made Jake immortal."

"Curtis Dunn, or A.C. as he sometimes likes to be called." The witch nodded her approval. "You must retrieve him before you save Jake."

Marilee sighed. "Do you at least know where this one is?"

The witch laughed. "Yes, this one I do. Jacob took him directly to a mental institution after leaving Hicksville. It will be in or near the desert."

"Well, that narrows it down." Marilee folded her arms. "If that's all you got, can we go now? The sooner I can get through this, the better." *Maybe once I finish this mission or whatever it is I can finally be some kind of normal.*

"If you need me, I'll be here." She raised her arms toward the cerulean sky. "Play nice, children."

Marilee sat up and glanced around. She was back in her motel room, resting atop the bed, but goosebumps from the frigid temperature of the dream world provided evidence of her recent visit. She rubbed her hands over her arms to chase the chill away and observed Khiderian.

He lay on his back on the shabby plaid couch, one hand resting on his abdomen—she bet he had a six-pack—and the back of the other hand resting over his brow. The room wasn't dark enough to still be the wee hours of the morning so she knew the sun had already risen despite the curtains being drawn to block it out.

SIREN'S SNARE

A glance at the alarm clock sitting on the nightstand showed she had been asleep for about four hours. Another glance at Khiderian showed him still as a statue. Stepping softly across the carpeted floor, she crept over to the couch and studied him. His chest didn't rise and fall for several minutes. This was it. The deep sleep.

Jake had taught her a few things about vampires, the rest she'd learned from trial and error, and a little bit of psychic probing. When she came across newly turned vampires, although she couldn't clearly hear their thoughts through the raging hunger clouding their mind, she could extract vital information in bits and flashes from their memory. She knew there was a period during their sleep when their bodies slowed down and they mended whatever damage they'd sustained that night. They were vulnerable during this period of time, and she wondered if a vampire as old—and she instinctively knew he was centuries old—as Khiderian was vulnerable enough during this stage for a little mind intrusion. "Only one way to find out."

Marilee took a deep breath to steady herself and planted her feet firmly into the carpet. She closed her eyes, focused, and inhaled deeply, reaching out to Khiderian's mind with her own. She stumbled, nearly losing her footing altogether as she hit a wall of power like nothing she'd ever come across before.

She braced herself again, licked her lips, and psychically traveled the length of that wall, keeping her feelers out for a weak spot. A dull throb started between her eyes, but she pressed on, and eventually hit pay dirt.

It felt as if part of the wall broke away and she fell through. She physically moved closer to his body as she psychically pushed further into his mind. She travelled through a tunnel of bright white energy, and soon found herself standing in a darkened room, a shadow four feet before her.

She recognized the form immediately. That tall shadow, the thickness of the shoulders. Khiderian. His back to her, she couldn't see his face, but felt his sudden anger and knew he sensed her presence.

"Khiderian."

The anger in him whipped out and she felt a wash of heat pour over her. Gasping, she stepped back, bumped into a dresser. It became clear to her she was in a bedroom and Khiderian loomed over someone's bed. She craned her neck to see around him and was surprised to find Hank sitting in the bed, his knees raised to his chest and his eyes full of... nothing.

Shimmering particles of power spilled from his mouth, floating toward Khiderian, and she knew the vampire fed off of him. How it was possible to feed off someone without leaving the motel room, she didn't know, but that was exactly what he was doing. She could feel him actually strengthening as Hank weakened. Steadily. She looked back into Hank's eyes and realized why they were merely a void. Khiderian was sucking out the man's life force. Khiderian didn't feed off blood. He fed off something far stronger and from the looks of it, he didn't intend to quit until he drained the man dry.

"Stop it!"

I don't know how you breached my barriers, but I suggest you leave.

Marilee swallowed hard, unable to miss the threatening tone of Khiderian's mind-voice, but refused to follow his direct order. He was going to kill Hank. He was going to kill a human being and she had to stop it. Moving forward, she reached out to grab Khiderian's shoulder, but froze as she saw the particles of energy coming out of Hank's mouth going into Khiderian's nostrils. He stood with his eyes closed, breathing in heavily, as though he were literally inhaling Hank.

"What the hell are you?"

The feed stopped and Marilee felt it snap like the cracking of a whip as it shut down. Khiderian turned his head in her direction and opened his eyes. Eyes which had been the most beautiful blue she'd ever seen were now a bright white.

"Leave now before I lose control." The words were his, but the voice belonged to something far stronger than a mere vampire. It boomed, reverberating so powerfully, Marilee felt it deep in her chest, a sensation similar to feeling the deep bass of a drum during a rock concert. His form wavered and she realized he was shaking. His jaw clenched, indicating his struggle to hold in whatever power played with his voice.

"What's happening to you?"

He closed his eyes, and his face filled with lines of strain as he balled his hands into fists. *Go away, Marilee. Back out of my mind now before I release the power. I could hurt you.*

She shook her head despite him not looking at her to see the action. She wasn't leaving him with Hank. The barkeeper sat in the bed, rocking back and forth, his arms wrapped tightly around his knees. His eyes were void of life, but she could still sense him inside the shell of his body. He was scared. Beyond scared, he was absolutely petrified, and she had an inkling why.

Don't.

She ignored Khiderian's command and inched closer to Hank. Two steps closer to him and suddenly she felt the pull. His mind was wide open to her.

Marilee, please...

She glanced at Khiderian, noted the increased trembling as he struggled with the power inside him, and mentally told him to go to hell. She was going to find out what he was and what he was doing to Hank. And why he'd come back for the jerk. Closing her eyes, she breathed in deep, willing Hank's mind to meld with hers, and was suddenly sucked down a dark tunnel.

Marilee, noooooooo!

She couldn't breathe. She couldn't focus. She could only fall deeper into Hank's mind, images from his memory bank flashing before her at warp speed. He'd been beaten as a child, abused by his mother's boyfriends for... She gagged as she saw him peeping into his mother's bedroom as she had sex with different men. Inside his mind, she felt his emotions, experienced his arousal watching his own mother fornicate with a variety of men. Then he was caught and beaten severely. His mother ridiculed him along with one of her many suitors, called him a little pervert and taunted him. Hank hated her, hated her for choosing those men over him and not even letting him watch.

Suddenly the images changed and she saw Hank watching other couples having sex. Peering through their bedroom windows, watching through binoculars from the kitchen window of his very first apartment. He was a peeping tom, one who couldn't get it up she discovered as the memory of being laughed at by a prostitute flashed by.

Marilee gasped for air as the sensation of having her own soul sucked out of her body hit. She heard Khiderian growling, but couldn't look at him. She couldn't pull out of Hank's sick, twisted mind. She was forced to watch his memories of beating women and raping them after getting them drunk. She was forced to watch as his memories turned into daydreams. She saw his fantasies of her, the images he'd been thinking as she worked in the bar. If Khiderian hadn't saved her from the monster, being raped would have been the least of her problems.

The images changed again and she saw Hank being skinned alive, felt the excruciating sting as flesh was pulled from muscle. Tears sprang from her eyes as the pain ripped through her body. She tried to block out the images as they became more violent, but couldn't escape.

Pull out, Marilee. Get the hell out of here!

I can't! She screamed inside her mind, unable to get her voice to work without any air left in her lungs. *Khiderian, stop!*

Marilee!

There was a loud pop followed by a thunderous growl and a flash of light so bright it obliterated everything in the room, and suddenly Marilee was yanked out of the room, falling backward out of the tunnel she'd stumbled through to enter Khiderian's mind.

She fell to the ground hard but her rump had barely hit before she twisted, coming to a complete landing atop a rock-hard mass of muscle. Khiderian grunted as his back took the total impact and held her close to his body, one hand wrapped around the back of her skull to protect her head. No longer inside his mind, Marilee lay sprawled over him on the dirty carpet of the motel room.

His angry, smoldering eyes were blue again, but his body still thrummed with the power she'd witnessed him sucking out of Hank. Without even having to be near the man in the flesh. With a cry, she scrambled off of him, crab walking until her back hit the wall. "What the hell was that? What did you do to Hank?" More importantly, what the hell did he do to her?

Grunting, he raised his upper body off the floor and bore his gaze into hers. "You should have never entered my mind. I could have killed you."

Marilee swallowed hard, having no doubt about that. She'd felt him sucking something out of her. "What are you? And don't say vampire. You're way more than that."

His dark gaze never softened as he rose from the floor and stretched. Power practically snapped, crackled, and popped around his tall frame. "I'm... complex."

Understatement. Marilee jerked to a stand and moved sideways when he stepped toward her. "Stay the hell away from me."

He arched a dark brow. "I'm your teacher, and your partner. I can't quite stay away from you."

"You'll keep your distance if you value your life." Marilee inched closer to the bed and used it as a very poor wall of defense to separate herself from the imposing vampire-slash-whatever the hell he was. "You fed off a man and tortured him without even being physically close. How?"

"I told you I'm a psychic vampire." He crossed his arms over his chest, his feet separated so he stood in an intimidating stance.

"I thought that meant you could read minds, and move things," she added, recalling how he'd yanked the dagger out of her hand earlier without touching it.

"It does." He nodded, expression passive. "There are other things I can do with my... *abilities*." He took a deep breath. "My mind is a very dangerous thing, Marilee. You should not have trespassed."

She couldn't argue with that. She feared she'd never get over what she'd witnessed. "What were you doing? It was like you were sucking out that man's soul and literally ripping him apart."

"I'm a psychic, otherwise known as *pranic*, vampire, Marilee. I feed on more than blood."

Her mouth went bone dry. "What else do you do? Besides kill."

His eyes grew darker as they narrowed on her. "You entered that psycho's mind. Do you still believe he deserved to live?"

"Maybe he didn't." Marilee raised her chin. "And you can play God, judge and jury all you want, but it doesn't change the fact you're a monster. You... you..." She struggled to find the right word. "You mind-raped that man to serve your own purpose. You nearly did it to me! You're nothing but a predator."

"Takes one to know one." His stony face strained with barely held contempt. "You forget that I know more about you than you know about me."

Marilee ignored the alarms going off in her head and forced herself to hold Khiderian's ruthless glare. "What are you talking about?"

His mouth, set in a hard line, curved into a leer. "I know about Louisiana. I also know about the kids in the cemetery and what went through your mind as you slaughtered those vampires in Hicksville. I know about your dreams."

Marilee's heart froze in her chest. Unwanted memories flooded her brain and she felt him filtering through them, realized he was the one producing them inside her head.

"Call me whatever you want to, Marilee, but I killed Hank for you. I did what you know you wanted to do, would have done if not for the fear you'd be a murderer all over again."

CHAPTER FOUR

"You son of a bitch!" Marilee shook with anger as she raised her leg and snatched the dagger out of her boot. With the lightning fast reflexes of a vampire, she threw the weapon with alarmingly accurate precision.

Khiderian barely had time to telepathically alter the dagger's course, narrowly avoiding having his head sliced open, when Marilee was on him, beating him with her fists. Somehow she managed to see through the sheen of tears coating her cornflower blue eyes and land each blow with amazing force for such a willowy female.

Khiderian took the blows, the strength from his recent feed working as a shield against pain he would have otherwise felt acutely. As she hurled profanities at him, he inhaled deeply, willing her pain into him. It was the least he could do, considering he was the one who'd slapped her in the face with her dark secrets so callously. Even if he had been provoked, he'd went too far.

Marilee jerked away, subconsciously throwing up a mental wall so quickly his own power snapped back on him, and he staggered back a few steps. "What the hell? You were doing it again!"

Marilee ran her hands over her body, patting herself as if checking for anything missing. "What is that? What do you do to people?"

"Marilee." He reached out for her, but she slapped his hand away.

"Don't touch me! Don't ever touch me!" Her shriek bounced off the walls, hurting his sensitive ears. "I don't know how you know the things you know about me, but stay the hell out of my life!"

"I can't." He sighed, releasing his own frustration before being overwhelmed with hers. "We are in this battle together until we safely remove Jacob Porter from the siren's snare."

"No!" She shoved at his chest, knocking him back a step, so much strength in her slender frame when her anger engulfed her. He made a few mental notes how to best harness it for when they began training. "I'll find Curtis Dunn myself and figure this out. You stay the hell away from me!"

She gave him another good shove and stormed toward the door, grunting as she tried to open it only to find the knob wouldn't turn. Spinning around, she planted her fists on her hips and leveled him with a glare that would reduce a lesser man to tears. "What are you doing?"

Khiderian shook his head slowly from side to side, careful to keep his telepathic hold on the door knob from slipping. "I can't do that. You insulted me, Marilee, and I lashed out at you in response. I was..." He closed his eyes and ground his teeth together. Was he really going to apologize? Yes, he was. He had to. "I went too far and I apologize."

"How do you know about Louisiana?" Her voice quavered and it drew an ache from Khiderian's chest. "And the others you mentioned?"

Damn. He'd just had to go there. "That's not important right now."

"Not important right now?" Her voice elevated with each word, her eyes blazing fire. "You're in my head and you know my deepest, darkest secrets. How you're managing to do that is very important to me."

"You could do it, too. In fact, you have." Khiderian paused, waiting for the memory to pop into her head. "You knew when that man was cheating on your mother. You even saw a clear image of the other woman he was seeing."

"Stop." She closed her eyes as if doing so would stop her from seeing the image in her mind.

"It's a gift, Marilee."

"No. It's a curse." Her bottom lip quivered.

"It's kept you safe more than once. I can teach you how to control it better."

"No!" Her eyes opened, the normally light irises darkened to cobalt. "Is this the training that old hag mentioned? If it is, I don't want it."

"You need to control your powers."

"No, I need to get rid of them." She turned for the door and yanked on it again, a tear escaping her eye when the knob didn't budge. "Let me go before I blow this room apart."

"Like you blew apart that building in Louisiana?"

"I didn't mean to hurt those people." Her voice was so soft he barely heard it, even with his hypersensitive hearing.

"I know you didn't, but you'll do it again unless you learn to control your powers. Once you control them, you'll learn that they are gifts, not curses."

Marilee looked at him over her shoulder, a dull glimmer of hope in her eyes. "You can really train me so I won't accidently do that again?"

"Yes." *And I can show you how to tap into the powers you've yet found.*

"Can you show me how to turn them off for good?"

"No. They're a part of you." His heart constricted as the dull flicker of hope burned out completely. "The only way to turn them off is to stop breathing. Permanently. I'd really rather you not do that."

She smiled a little, just a slight tipping up of the corner of her mouth, and tried the doorknob again. It twisted freely and she slipped out into the daylight, pulling the door closed behind her.

Was that wise?

Khiderian bristled as The Dream Teller's haggard voice questioned him. He was one of very few she could come to during the waking hours. He was one of even fewer who knew her real name. "She'll come back, Krystaline. She knows I can help her gain control of her powers, which makes me the beholder of what she craves more than anything in this world."

You think you know her so well.

He didn't miss the laughter in the witch's voice, nor did he appreciate it. "You don't believe I do? I've watched over her since the day her power sparked." She was just two years old, having a normal tantrum children of that age tended to throw. Yet, for a child with so much power, a tantrum could be a dangerous thing.

He'd watched over her each time her power sparked, making sure she didn't accidentally hurt anyone, until she'd reached the age she wouldn't simply forget his presence. Those times he'd had to stay invisible to her and watch as she exploded, keeping his interference at a minimum when her powers escaped her. It was because of those times he felt the need to help her so strongly now.

Is that really why?

"Hey!" Khiderian threw up his wall of defense, shutting the witch out of his mind. "Stay out of my personal thoughts. Why are you here anyway? Just busting my chops?"

As fun as that is... Be careful with her, Khiderian. She's fragile, and we need her.

"I won't break her." Khiderian started to settle back onto the couch, then thought better of it as the musty smell rose to chase him away. He stretched out on the bed, deciding to nap and strengthen himself for when Marilee returned. "I'll have her fully trained as agreed and ready to help rescue the great Jacob Porter."

Why so bitter? She does not love him in that way. And you know—

"I'm not bitter. I'm tired. I need to rest but an old hag keeps talking to me."

Krystaline chuckled. *Be careful with her, Khiderian. You don't know her as well as you think. She's...*

"Human," Khiderian finished. "With all the hang-ups that entails. Believe me, I've noticed."

Just don't forget your kid gloves.

"Sure. Are we done yet?"

Sweet dreams, Khiderian. Behave yourself.

The slight pressure in the front of his head eased and he knew she was gone, back to the dream realm where she watched over the vampire race. Of course now she'd left him with enough on his mind that he'd never get back to sleep.

Sitting up, he ran a hand down his face. Marilee had breached his wall of defense and entered his mind while he was astral-feeding. That should have never happened. But it had. She'd waltzed right in as he was about to release his power and suck the life right out of the swine who'd put his filthy hands on her. She'd been hit in the crossfire and if he hadn't snatched her out... He shuddered at the thought.

She was just a human. A human with extraordinary power, but still just as fragile as the rest of them. And he was the one assigned to turn her into a weapon without sucking her soul out in the process.

Shit.

SIREN'S SNARE

"Why am I crying?" Marilee swiped her hands over her cheeks, vaporizing the traitorous tears. She didn't cry when her mother dropped her off at Grampa and Gram's and didn't return or even call for three years, nor did she cry when she swooped back in just to drag her off to Louisiana with her and her pig of a boyfriend. She didn't cry when she had to fill out papers at school and couldn't enter her father's name and contact number because she didn't even know who the guy was. Why should she cry now?

Sure, she'd almost been raped the night before. Wasn't the first time. Both times she'd been saved. Both times the bastard forcing himself on her had died for his actions. She shuddered and kept walking down the sidewalk, no destination in mind, just... away.

How did Khiderian know so much about her? She'd never told anyone about what happened in Louisiana. She damn sure never spoke a word about the cemetery, not even to her mother or grandmother who already knew she was a freak. A cold chill fell over her as she thought back to that night.

"Marilee is a big hill-bill-y," the kids sang out as they danced in a circle around her, taunting her with their words and sneers.

Why had she come? She could be home now curled up with a book, listening to the silence as she waited for her mom to return home from her date. If she returned home from her date. Becky had been staying out longer than usual the last few weeks. Marilee knew it was because of her. Becky could see something was wrong with her and it scared her.

Still, she should have waited in the trailer to see if she came home. Instead, she'd answered the knock on the door when Billie Jo came over to ask her to come hang out. Foolishly, she'd followed the girl to the cemetery where a group of kids waited. How could she have been so gullible to believe Billie Jo had wanted to be her friend? Nobody wanted to be her friend. She was a freak and they all knew it.

She twisted her hands, trying to break free of the rope binding her wrists together, but it wouldn't budge. The temperature had cooled considerably as the sun fell and now her legs were covered in goose bumps from her ankles to the hem of her shorts. She didn't actually feel the cold, though, not in her mind. She burned inside, where her anger raged. They'd tricked her. Made a fool out of her.

Billy Morgan made kissing faces at her as he circled her with the others. Miranda Lee grinned impishly, loving every minute of her torture. They'd tied her up, gagged her, and forced her into an open grave what seemed like an eternity ago.

"You'd be better off dead, hillbilly," Miranda had said, "so we're going to do the world a favor and help you die."

"One less hillbilly," April Hayes had added. "Next we'll have to find a way to get rid of your white trash mama."

"Nah, that one will just screw herself to death eventually," Billy chimed in with a laugh before dropping to a knee to peer over the edge of the grave. "What about you, Marilee? You take after your mama?" He turned toward the others. "Should I find out before we start to bury her?"

"She's nasty. You'd probably catch a disease," Chad Davis answered, kneeling next to the other boy. "Then again, she's kinda hot for a hillbilly."

Marilee pulled her knees up to her chest and pushed herself as far against the dirt wall as she could get. She wouldn't have family life class until seventh grade, but she knew enough to know what they were talking about, and she knew enough to know she didn't want them touching her in that way.

"Chad Davis, if you so much as think about doing that with her, I will never kiss you again," Miranda scolded him.

With a round of chuckles, the boys stood up and joined the others in circling the grave, following Billie Jo as she chanted some strange sounding stuff she read off a paper. "That should do it." She finally stopped and leaned over the grave to peer in. "The incantation has been read. Now we just bury her and the demons will come to take her soul."

"Yeah, right," Billy said. "Let's just start tossing in the dirt. I gotta get home before my dad's shift ends."

She heard their footsteps trailing off and relaxed a little. They weren't going to bury her like they'd said. They were just going to leave her in the grave overnight. She'd be fine. All she had to do was wait until morning. There would be a funeral and they'd see her in the grave and get her out. She'd tell on them. To the police. Surely the police would be called when she was found in the grave.

Something crunched above her, then again, and again. Her heart started racing. They were coming back. She looked up in time to see a cloud of dirt rain down upon her. She tried to scream, but the gag muffled the sound. More showers of dirt fell upon her, but she couldn't look up to see what the kids were doing without dirt getting in her eyes.

What to do? She tried to scream, to beg, to cry. Only gargled sounds escaped her mouth, and tears were useless. The kids didn't care. They didn't care at all how scared she was. She was the town whore's daughter, and an outcast. They just wanted her gone. She would be found in the morning, she realized as more dirt hit her, but she would be found dead.

We can help you.

Marilee jerked her head around, sure she'd heard someone next to her, but she remained alone in the grave.

Release us. Set us free to save you.

Who are you? Marilee asked in her mind, sure she'd heard someone.

You know. You know what to do. Release us.

Her chest tightened, then something inside swirled and she grew dizzy. Warmth flooded her body and her mind instantly filled with strange words she didn't recognize. More of a song, she realized as the cadence grew stronger. A chant.

Release us. Release us.

She closed her eyes tighter and concentrated on the strange chant, allowing it to grow stronger, louder. The sound of drums entered her mind, a tribal sound that vibrated through her body, then suddenly all was silent.

A wave of icy cold washed over her body then a burst of lava exploded through her system, and she opened her eyes to assure herself she wasn't being ripped in half as it felt her body was being torn from the inside. Something dark and sinister was coming out of her.

She registered the fact that no more dirt was falling and looked around the grave to find herself buried to her waist. With a shake of her head to get the dirt off her eyelids, she glanced up, only saw the dark night sky, full of tiny white stars. The kids were no longer circling the grave or tossing in mounds of dirt.

They were screaming as if the hounds of hell were after them, and she couldn't shake the feeling that was somewhat accurate. She'd released something, felt it claw its way out of her. Just as she had done when her mom was attacked in that alley. She'd felt the stirring inside her, the growing of pressure, and she'd released it. The building the man had run into exploded into a huge ball of fire and a dozen or more people had died. Innocent people. All because a man had stolen her mom's purse and she'd wished him dead.

She couldn't do that again. Her mom had told her she was crazy to think the explosion was her fault, but she knew it was. Just like she knew those kids were screaming because of something she'd done. Something she'd released. She had to get it back, draw it back inside her.

No! They were never inside you. You just gave them the power to take form. Do not draw them into you.

The voice! Marilee watched the top of the grave, waiting to see whoever belonged to that voice, but he didn't appear. He never did. He came to her when she was in trouble, never taking form. Sometimes he spoke, but normally she just felt him near, watching over her soundlessly as she struggled to hold in the power inside her. He was her guardian angel, if such a thing existed.

Who are you? She kept her gaze on the top of the grave, willing him to come to her and show himself. *Please don't hide. You understand me. You're the only one who could. Please help me.*

A deafening shriek filled the air, an inhuman sound that chilled her to the bone. She gasped as the earth shook, a low rumble that didn't last long, but she instinctively knew had been caused by a major flux of power. Whatever she'd released had been contained.

A dark shadow emerged at the top of the grave. A male silhouette, tall, with broad shoulders. She couldn't see any features, but knew this was the man she'd been feeling all her life. Her guardian angel.

The gag in her mouth loosened, falling free as if carried away by the wind, and the rope at her wrists and ankles unwound. He was going to save her!

You will be found in the morning. I will make sure nothing comes to hurt you. And in a blink, he was gone, and she was alone in the grave where she cried herself to sleep.

SIREN'S SNARE

A cemetery employee found her in the morning and the police were called. She told them the others had lured her there. She told them what they had done, but didn't utter a word about what she'd done or how her guardian angel had protected her.

The children were dead, except for two. Miranda swore demons had chased them that night. Billy didn't swear anything. He didn't speak at all. The only sound he made was a deafening scream when his gaze locked onto Marilee's.

Marilee froze, the voice of her guardian angel replaying clearly in her mind. He hadn't visited her since that night and eventually she'd convinced herself it was all in her head. He didn't exist, not in any physical form anyhow. He was a manifestation, something she created in her mind to help herself deal with the crap she went through as a child. But now she remembered. She heard his voice clearly and recognized the owner.

"Son of a bitch." Turning on her heel, she raced back to the motel, hot angry tears flowing freely down her face. He was real. He'd always been real, and he knew what she was going through. He could have helped her, at least talked to her and made her feel less of a freak, but he'd left her that night. He'd abandoned an eleven-year old girl in a grave.

Marilee flung open the motel room door and kicked it closed with her boot. "You bastard! You were there."

Khiderian cracked open an eyelid and sighed. He rose to a sitting position on the bed she'd vacated not long before, facing her with his legs hanging over the side. "You remembered. That means I didn't perform my job as well as I was supposed to."

"Your job?" Marilee blinked, her eyes burning. "What job?"

Khiderian sighed again, weaving a hand through his thick mass of dark hair. "I was drawn to you, to your power. I watched over you from the time you were just a toddler, barely able to speak, but I was supposed to stay in shadow. You shouldn't have ever seen me."

"Why?" Marilee shouted the question. "If you were so drawn to me and knew what I had inside me, that you could help, why didn't you?"

"Because I couldn't. The elders knew about you and how I..." He looked away. "They knew I was protective of you so they declared me your keeper. I was to observe you in shadow, report to them your abilities, and make sure you were not harmed."

"Not harmed? Not *harmed*?" Marilee laughed as a fresh tear dripped from her eye, and grabbed her dagger out of her boot. She flung herself at Khiderian, knocking the vampire backward on the bed. With the dagger gripped firmly in her hand, she straddled him. "What were you doing when I killed the people in that building? Why didn't you save those kids in the cemetery?"

"I couldn't step in and risk being seen," he answered, his gaze locked to hers. "I did as much as I could to contain your flares."

"My *flares*?" She lowered the dagger so the tip rested against his throat. "I *killed* people and you just let me."

"I tried to stop you when I could. Sometimes your power flared so fast that by the time I reached you there was nothing I could do. My mission wasn't to save your victims. It was to keep you safe."

"Well, you suck at your job. You just left me there in a grave."

"I stayed with you until dawn." Khiderian's eyes darkened. "I shielded myself so you couldn't sense me, but I did not leave you until the first rays of sunlight broke through the trees. I stayed with you until I had no choice but to leave."

Khiderian's hand wrapped around the hand holding the dagger and he flipped her over, pinning her to the bed. Marilee gasped as heat flooded her body. It was an intimate position, one she was surprised to find herself enjoying.

"Drop the dagger, Marilee. I won't hurt you."

"You already have." She released her grip on the dagger and let it hit the floor. "Every time I was alone and you could have let me know you were there. Every time I was scared and you could have let me know I wasn't the only freak with abilities. You hurt me a thousand times."

"I'm sorry." His eyes softened and in them she saw sincere guilt. "I wasn't allowed."

"Your job was just to keep me from being harmed?"

He nodded. "Yes. Without announcing my presence."

"You announced your presence at the cemetery."

"And I was severely reprimanded. I couldn't reveal myself to you again after that night."

"So would you have let my mother's boyfriend rape me if she hadn't stopped him?"

Khiderian stiffened, his eyes full of rage. "When did this happen?"

"When I was fifteen." She frowned, realizing by the deep growl in his voice and the slight shaking of his body, Khiderian was furious. This furious was a degree that came with just learning of a horrible thing. "You didn't know."

"Of course I didn't know. I would never allow a man to do that to you." He sucked in a deep breath and let it out slowly. "What happened? If you'd used your powers to protect yourself, I would have felt it."

"I fought him off. I screamed."

"But you didn't use your powers."

Marilee felt small under the condemning look in Khiderian's eyes. "My mom stabbed him in the back, killed him. I got away."

"What if she hadn't been there?" His voice held a hint of anger. "Would you have used your powers or just let him rape you?"

"If you were there, it wouldn't have mattered. Where were you?"

"If you had used your damn powers, I would have been there!" Khiderian turned his head to the side, looking at the wall, anywhere but at her. "I had other assignments, too. I couldn't always be hovering over you, but if your power spiked I would have felt it and tapped into your mind. If I'd seen…" He met her gaze once more. "I would have destroyed him if you couldn't. Why didn't you use your powers? Then and last night?"

Marilee closed her eyes, wondering how to make a vampire understand. "I can't just kill someone and be fine with it."

"You have no problem killing vampires."

She didn't miss the condemnation in his tone, and didn't blame him for it. Especially now that she knew he was the one she'd felt watching over her all those years ago, the one she'd called her guardian angel. "I do after it sets in and I realize they were once human, that they're really not immortal after all."

He rolled off of her and sat up. Marilee instantly missed his warmth. The thought made her chuckle.

"What is it?" He glanced at her as she rose to sit next to him.

"You're warm."

He frowned. "Yeah, so?"

"I didn't think vampires could be warm." She shrugged when he just looked at her. "All the books and movies talk about how cold you are. It's kind of funny realizing that we actually believe some really stupid things like that. I mean, you have blood flowing through you and you're a... or you were a human. Why would you be cold?"

He didn't laugh with her. He didn't even smile. "You'll never see me as a person, will you?"

The smile died on Marilee's lips, but she couldn't answer him when she didn't know for herself if she could look past what he was. What he'd done to Hank. Even if Hank was a bad man, he'd stopped him in the bar. He didn't have to kill him, and not the way he'd killed him.

"It's just as well, I suppose." Khiderian rose from the bed and walked over to the table to retrieve his sword. He turned with it in his hands, his face void of emotion. "You're going to hate me by the time I'm done training you."

CHAPTER FIVE

"Again."

Marilee glared at the vampire masquerading as a drill sergeant and balled her hands into fists. "It's not working."

"Of course it's not. How do you expect to focus your energies on locating Porter through all that anger?" Khiderian cocked his head to the side and looked at her pointedly. "Focus, Marilee."

"Here's an idea. Focus on kissing my ass." She stood up and left the table to stomp across the room. "It doesn't work."

Khiderian sighed and set down the pendulum he'd been holding over a map on the table. He leaned back in the chair and stretched his long legs out before him. "I've done it thousands of times. It works. You are the problem."

"If you're so damned good at it, why don't you do it then?" Marilee planted her hands on her hips and tapped her foot. "Time's wasting."

"You're the one with the connection to him. You're the one who can locate him this way."

Marilee rolled her eyes. "I barely met the guy. It's not what I'd call a connection."

"It's a connection. You have to find him."

"You're telling me you've located thousands of people using that pendulum thingy and a map, but you can't find Curtis Dunn?" Marilee narrowed her eyes. "Sounds pretty unlikely to me."

"I said I've used this method thousands of times. I never said I'd used it to locate thousands of people."

Marilee threw her arms up in the air and growled in frustration. "It's too hard. I can't do it. I don't have these frigging powers you think I have."

"You have them, you just haven't been trained to find and hone them. Now sit back down at this table and try it again."

"Bite—" She stopped herself when she saw the impish grin spread across his mouth and figured what his response would be to such a suggestion. "Go take a long walk on a nice, bright sunny day."

Chuckling, he laced his fingers behind his head and made a show of relaxing. "We don't leave until we have a direction, and if you waste too much of the night we won't leave for close to another twenty-four hours." His expression grew serious. "I wonder what all those sirens could do to Porter while we're sitting here playing games. Tell me, how painful do you think it is to feel your organs shut down as you die? Do you gasp for air?"

"All right!" Marilee stomped back over to the small table and sat in the chair she'd just vacated. "I'll try it again."

"That's my little warrior angel." He grinned at Marilee's death glare and scooped up the pendulum in his large hand. "Clear your mind of everything except the image of Curtis Dunn and focus on the pendulum."

He raised the instrument by the end of the thin cord attached to it and held it over the center of the map of the United States. Marilee stared at the diamond shaped crystal hanging at the end and did as she'd been instructed. Nothing happened.

"Relax, Marilee. Let go." His voice was a soft whisper, probably meant to be calming, but it was far too attractive to be calming. Her hormones were jumping all over the place.

"Clear your mind, Marilee. You should only be seeing the image of Curtis in there."

Damn. He'd read her mind again. She was sure of it. Ire sparked and she felt her body temperature increase. She quickly tamped it down and closed her eyes as she took a deep breath. Releasing it slowly, she recalled the face of Curtis Dunn, the man who'd injected Jake with the immortality serum, and focused on it.

"That's good, Marilee. Focus on Curtis Dunn. Now find him. Find him so we can help Porter."

She held on to the image as she opened her eyes and focused on the crystal. It didn't move. Panic rose in her chest. Jake had to be saved.

"Don't panic, Marilee. Focus."

Focus. She took another deep breath, released it, and pictured Curtis Dunn. Nothing happened. If only she had a phone number for the guy. She could call... A light bulb went off in her head. When she was a little girl and had a bad dream she would think of her grandmother, call out to her in her mind so the boogeyman she feared was in her room wouldn't hear her. Gram came to her every time. Focusing harder, she gave it a try.

Curtis. Curtis Dunn. Where are you? Help us, Curtis. Help us find Jake.

The pendulum moved. It rocked back and forth, then moved in a circle, spinning faster as its arc grew wider.

"That's it, Marilee. Keep on."

Curtis Dunn. We need you, Curtis. Where are you? Show us where you are. Please, Curtis, please help.

The cord of the pendulum stiffened into a straight line and the crystal fell on the map with a thump. Khiderian looked across the table and smiled. "He's in Nevada. Great job, Marilee. I told you the power was in you."

"Holy shit." Marilee stared at the pendulum in wonder.

Khiderian laughed as he rose from his seat, the pendulum in hand. "The pendulum will help us pinpoint his exact location once we draw closer, if we even need it at that close of a range, but for now we have enough direction to move on."

Marilee nodded and grabbed her duffel bag from the floor as Khiderian strapped on his sword and pulled the leather jacket on to cover up his weapons. "Do you have a vehicle?" he asked as they stepped out of the motel room.

"I had a truck, but it got stolen a month ago," Marilee answered as she followed him to the trunk of his car to deposit her bag.

"I'm sorry to hear that." Khiderian lowered the trunk.

"Yeah, well, it was just an old clunker." She turned away and headed for the passenger side of the car. Khiderian was before her, opening her door before she'd reached it. "So much for chivalry being dead."

"You forget I come from another time."

"Trust me, vampy. I haven't forgotten what you are." She slid into the seat and waited for him to close the door and join her. She didn't stop herself from enjoying the view as he rounded the hood to get to the driver's side and slide in. Vampire or not, he was still pretty good eye candy. Just her luck. "So, are we taking a plane? If so, you'd better be prepared to finance this trip because I'm a little low on funds."

"I never travel by plane."

She looked at him head-on. "From here to Nevada has got to be at least a full day's drive. I realize you have really dark tint on these windows but we're talking about driving through some of the hottest areas in America in daylight."

"We're not driving non-stop to Nevada." He glanced at her as he started the car. "Seatbelt."

Rolling her eyes, Marilee fastened her seatbelt. "So we'll be stopping somewhere before daylight."

"Yes."

She sighed. "If we took a plane, we'd get there a lot quicker."

"I do not travel by plane." He spoke each word firmly.

She smiled. "Don't tell me the big bad vampire is afraid to fly."

"No, the big bad vampire is not afraid to fly in a plane. He is afraid of crashing in a plane."

Marilee laughed. "Are you serious? A plane crash couldn't kill you, you big wuss."

"You have no idea how serious a plane crash could be for a vampire and everyone else on the plane." He looked at her with dark eyes so scolding her laugh died in her throat. "Vampires can be injured just as humans. A crash from that high of an elevation would tear us to shreds and the pain would be horrific, especially for a pranic vampire because we feel pain ten times more acutely than any other life form. Add in the fact that I'm an empath and can feel pain of all those around me and you can see why I would avoid it."

Marilee swallowed, thinking of how excruciating pain must be for him. "I'm sorry. I didn't know. But... couldn't a car wreck be just as bad for you?"

"No. For one, I'm in control of the car. For two, I'd be surrounded by more people in pain if I were in a plane crash. Regardless, injuries sustained from a plane crash are generally far worse than injuries from automobile accidents. I would be out of my mind with pain and the only way to heal would be to take in mass quantities of blood. If there were survivors, I'd kill them all saving myself."

A cold shiver danced along Marilee's spine as she looked out the window into the dark night. "So you drain people of blood and their souls?"

"Blood gives me life. Energy gives me power."

"Energy as in... souls?"

Khiderian's hands tightened around the steering wheel, his jaw clenched, and his nostrils flared as he took a deep breath and let it out slow. "There are some maps in the glove compartment," he said as he turned onto the expressway. "Find one that'll show us how to get to Nevada, or New Mexico at least. That'll probably be our first stop."

Realizing the tactic for what it was, Marilee stopped her line of questioning and did as asked. It took her a moment to find a map among the assortment in the glove compartment that would guide them to New Mexico. "We'll have to get another map in New Mexico, or just print out a map to Nevada from Mapquest if we can get to a computer."

"I have a laptop in the trunk." Khiderian glanced at the map as she opened it. "Do you know how to read a map?"

"Yes. I'm also skilled with tying my shoes and writing my name."

Khiderian grinned, and a small noise that sounded close to a chuckle came from his throat, but he didn't say anything. Marilee watched him as he drove, taking in the tense set of his shoulders, the wariness in his eyes. He was on guard. From her? From himself? It was so hard to believe he'd been the man she'd felt watching over her all those years before. Was it because he was ordered to or could he actually have some sense of decency? Would he kill her on command if the Dream Teller ordered him to?

He glanced at her with a look so dark, so haunted, she knew he'd heard every word she'd thought, but he didn't call her out on it. He punched the power button on the radio with his finger and turned up the volume. They drove the rest of the way in silence except for the occasional direction, and the sound of classic rock blaring from the speakers.

A feminine chuckle filtered through the haze of his mind, rousing Jake from his pain-induced stupor. He opened dry eyes and focused on what stood beyond the bars to his cell. It was one of the things that had captured him. A nasty creature that thrived on water and souls. It couldn't get his soul, but it sure as hell could make him wish he was dead. It taunted him by projecting itself in the physical form of his wife, but he could see beyond the visage to the scaly, amphibious thing underneath.

"Get my wife's image off of you, you fugly bitch." His voice came out harsh and cracked, the result of no liquids for far longer than he wanted to know. They'd shot him, stabbed him, sliced him, suffocated him, hanged him, strangled him, electrocuted him... Now it appeared they were going to make him die of thirst.

The siren laughed, running scaly fingers through the illusionary long black tresses so like Nyla's. "You amuse me, slayer. In all my centuries of capturing men in my snare, I've never come across one who actually envisions his own wife as his ultimate fantasy. I don't know if that means you're a truly honorable man, or just that damn lucky to have actually met and married your fantasy woman. Would you like to see her again?" She rubbed her body along the bars of his cell, dancing seductively. She wore a black tank top and jeans with boots, something Nyla would wear. She looked at him through Nyla's violet eyes, but a deeper look showed beady black eyes behind the illusion.

"You know I can see that monstrosity you call your real face." Jake sat up from where he'd fallen asleep on the hard floor of the cell and leaned his back against the wall. "Trust me, sweetheart, it's not doing a thing for Mr. Happy."

The creature growled. "You may be able to see through the illusion, and you may not find my true form desirable, but you can't deny my beautiful voice, can you?"

Jake grit his teeth together. Being a true slayer, he had some natural protection from supernatural creatures, hence his ability to see through the sirens' façade. However, their voices mesmerized him as well as they did normal men. He'd discovered this fact after his first run-in with the species. A siren had been working with a pranic vampire and a group of were-hyenas, snaring men with psychic abilities in order to build an army of psychic vampires, or prannies, as Jake liked to call them. The bitch ensnared him with her voice though he could see through the fake image she projected, and lured him into an alley. There, she ordered him to kill himself. He did, but when he resurrected it frightened her. She ran off while he busied himself killing the were-hyenas who'd intended on having him for dinner.

SIREN'S SNARE

He never told Nyla he'd been caught by the bitch's voice. It had seemed like a betrayal to the woman he loved so he'd told her the bare minimum of what had happened. He hadn't even shared the whole truth with Christian or Seta, the vampires he'd come to think of as allies rather than targets. He hadn't even told his own brother. He should have. He shouldn't have let them think he could handle the task of taking out a group of sirens. They could have found someone else, a heterosexual female vampire or a homosexual male. Surely, Seta or Rialto would have known of someone capable of the mission.

But no. When Seta had the vision of the siren returning to Baltimore, he'd let everyone believe it was safe for him to go after it. He'd walked right into a trap because he didn't have the balls to tell his wife he'd been lured by another female's voice.

"Go to hell, bitch. Fuck a cactus on your way."

She threw her head back and roared with laughter. "Insult me all you want, but it won't stop you from dying yet again. I know it hurts. I see the pain in your eyes. I've heard your moans and screams as the agony overtakes you."

Jake balled his hands into fists on his knees, wishing the freaky looking bitch would stick her neck through the bars so he could strangle her. Not that he had the energy left in him to reach the bars quickly enough to do it, but it was a nice thought regardless. "Do you have a point to your visit?"

"You know why I'm here, Porter. We go through this every day." Her ugly face grew serious. "Do you want to see her again? You know how easy it could be."

Jake let his upper lip curl into some semblance of a grin. "Kill me a thousand times, bitch. I'll never tell you how to find her."

"You were made immortal by science, an injection of a drug. You started drinking blood as a side effect. Do you know why?"

"It's healthier than Kool-Aid?" Jake quipped as hunger roared to life. Just the mentioning of it and he thirsted for a taste, though he'd never consumed more than what he could get off of a raw steak.

"Very cute. You need blood, Porter. It acts as a booster to the serum that traitor injected in you. It prolongs the serum's life. How long has it been since you've had blood, slayer?"

Panic rose in Jake's chest, but he quickly tamped it down. Freaking out like a scared little girl wouldn't help him get out of this mess. "The whole point of the serum was to create the immortality of a vampire without having to feed like one."

"Yet, you drink blood."

"I've had a little bit. One might think it could be the result of marrying a vampire."

"Really?" Beneath the illusion of Nyla's face, she raised a hairless eyebrow. "She drinks blood to live so you follow along to be closer to her? Why do I not find that believable?"

"Maybe she likes to bite during sex and it turned me on so I gave it a try and got a little blood in my mouth. Maybe I liked the taste."

"Maybe you're full of shit." The siren crouched down outside the cell so she was at eye level with him. "Carter Dunn failed at creating the immortality serum because he hated vampires too much. He refused to include the drinking of blood into his formula. His brother knew what he would not accept, and that is why Curtis Dunn could create the serum and make it work."

"Now who's full of shit?"

"Not me." The siren grinned before standing back up. "You're growing weaker with each death and resurrection. You'll realize soon enough that you won't live indefinitely without a little blood to help you out. And the weaker you get, the worse the torture will feel. You'll tell us where she is or she'll feel your pain and come to us once you lose enough strength that you can't possibly block her from your mind. Don't think we don't know it's what you're doing."

Jake swallowed, his dry throat burning with the effort it took. Nyla was probably already half out of her mind worrying about him. He could try and not allow the full extent of his pain to broadcast through his mind but as his soul mate, she would still know. If it continued, he feared the other vampires would not be able to restrain her. Especially if he reached the point of weakness that indicated permanent death approaching.

"We'll get her whether it be sooner or later," the siren advised. "The amount of pain you have to endure in the meantime is solely up to you." She shook her head in what looked a cross between pity and amusement, and turned, slinking her way up the stairs leading to the upper floor.

Jake let out a breath as the heavy door closed behind her. Dammit, the bitch was probably telling the truth. He felt horrible and the pain grew worse with each resurrection. He had to get out of this dark, musky basement prison and figure out where he was and how he could get back to his family without leading the monsters right to them. So far, they didn't know about Slade.

They knew Jake and Nyla were one set of the destined mates prophesized to create special warriors for the pending supernatural war, but they had no idea Slade had already been born. They'd already tried to kill him in order to prevent the baby from being born, but the immortality serum kept him from truly dying. Of course, if they beheaded him he probably wouldn't resurrect from that. So why hadn't they? Killing him permanently would stop the Blood Revelation from happening if he and Nyla hadn't yet had a child together, and since they didn't know about Slade...

He frowned, tried to think of a reason why the sirens and the were-animals they were working with hadn't killed him in a way that couldn't be undone but thinking made his head hurt worse. He was in too much pain, and suffering from thirst and hunger far too much to figure out what they were up to.

He fell back asleep with a prayer for Nyla and Slade in his heart.

Khiderian gently withdrew from the motel clerk's mind as he took the key from his pale hand and turned away. Wind whipped across his face as he stepped out of the lobby into the parking lot and he inhaled deep, testing the texture of nature's work. The wind was strong enough. He could use it in Marilee's training.

Moonlight streamed down on his car, showing each speck of dust coating the once shiny black luster as he approached. He knew Marilee still slept without having to see her. He could feel her utter calmness. He couldn't remember the last time he'd actually felt that sense of calmness from sleeping. For him, sleeping was often more work than wakefulness.

He opened the passenger side door carefully to reveal her still fastened into her seatbelt, head back against the headrest, lips slightly parted. She looked so innocent in sleep, his stomach twisted with guilt. But he had orders to follow and he knew better than to disobey.

He scanned the area, reaching out with his extra senses for signs of trouble. When the scan came back clear, he bent forward and unfastened her seatbelt. Carefully, his body tensed for attack, he wrapped his hand around her slender shoulder and shook it until her soft blue eyes opened. A small smile emerged as she woke, but once she realized it was his face she smiled up to, her eyes hardened. "You're in my personal space."

On a sigh he backed away, allowing her the personal space she requested as she emerged from the car. "I've checked out a room for us already, but I'd like to do some training before sunrise."

"What kind of training?" She cocked her hip out and planted a fisted hand on it, reminding Khiderian of the pose a petulant child would take if advised they had to do something not quite fun in order to get a new toy or dessert. The action reminded him how very young Marilee was and the smile forming on his face died.

"You're already aware of your pyrokinetic abilities thanks to the incident in Louisiana, but you can control far more than fire."

He'd caught her in the middle of a yawn, but at the mention of Louisiana she became fully alert. "I don't ever want to do something like that again."

"You didn't have control over your ability then so it escaped you and people suffered." He stepped forward, invading the personal space she prized. Tipping her chin with his fingertip, he made her look him in the eyes. "I can train you to harness that power and others so something like that never happens again. However, you may find a time when you need it."

She jerked her head away, freeing herself from his touch, and tried to back away but one step connected her with the car. "When would I need such a horrible thing?"

"When you find a lair full of hideous monsters hell bent on killing you, for one." He allowed her to mull over that thought as he turned away and started walking. "Come along."

"Where are we going?" She fell into step alongside him, scanning the parking lot.

"I saw a good area for practice from the expressway. It's just up behind this hill." He nodded toward the large hill stretching out just beyond the edge of the parking lot.

"You saw behind that from the expressway?" Her tone indicated her disbelief as she turned her head side to side, searching. "I can't even see the expressway from here. How could you have possibly seen what's behind that hill?"

Khiderian grinned. "One of the perks of joining the very exclusive vampire club is the excellent vision plan."

The hill was large but the size was due to width more than height so Marilee would have no trouble making it over. He would carry her without complaint if needed, but in his gut he knew she'd never allow it, not even if she walked on sprained ankles. The knowledge of that shouldn't hurt him, but he couldn't deny the twinge of pain in his chest knowing she thought him a cruel and unjust monster.

They covered the distance quickly and came upon the large flat area he'd seen from the expressway. The area didn't contain much foliage, just a few patches of dry grass here and there, and a large cactus to the right. It was mostly rolling earth, beautiful in its purity. No buildings flawed the scene.

"Geez. I thought I came from the sticks," Marilee said softly from his side. "You really know how to find a place in the boonies, don't you?"

"It's a good area for practice." He stepped away and took enough strides to place them six feet apart before turning toward her. "Feel the wind?"

She frowned. "Um, yeah. Why?"

"You're going to control it." Khiderian held his arms out at his sides. "Really feel it, Marilee. More than feel, experience it. Taste it. Know it until it becomes an extension of yourself."

"What the heck are you talking about?"

Khiderian laughed at the puzzled expression on Marilee's face. "We are created by God, as is nature. We are one with the wind, but most people don't have the ability to understand that. You do, and you can use it to your advantage."

"How?"

"You can use the wind as a weapon."

She stiffened. "I don't like weapons."

"Says the woman with a dagger in her boot."

"A dagger is far more containable than fire, or wind for that matter."

"With the proper training, nature can be a safe weapon as well." Khiderian let his hands drop back down to his sides. "You need to trust me to train you."

She shook her head. "There's no such thing as a safe weapon, but all right. Train me to control the wind, and I mean *control* it. Don't teach me to mess around with something that'll get away from me."

"Trust me." Khiderian knelt down and scooped up a handful of the dry earth. "Clear your mind and focus on the air around you. Take in the feel, the smell, everything."

Marilee closed her eyes and breathed in deeply. Khiderian found his own breath stalling as she tilted her head back and stretched out her arms at her sides, truly feeling the night air. A beam of pale blue moonlight shone down on her, casting an ethereal glow around her. She wasn't the most physically perfect woman he'd ever seen. She could use a little more meat on her bones. Her hair was pale and unremarkable, her features pretty, but not the makings of a Hollywood starlet. Her breasts would barely fill his hands.

Yet, at the same time she was the most beautiful creature he'd ever seen.

"What now?"

Now I throw you over my shoulder and... Khiderian shook his head, reminded himself he had a job to do and it wasn't a job designed to bring him pleasure. "Open your eyes and observe the wind's movement."

She did as told, looking around. The wind had momentarily stilled so Khiderian reached inside himself and used his own power to spur it along. A gust blew by, sending dirt flying. "See how it picks the dirt up, how the tiny particles dance in the breeze?"

"Yes." She nodded.

"Do it with this." He held out the handful of dirt. "Call upon the wind to pick this up and carry it out to your waiting hand."

"No, seriously."

He chuckled at her bewildered expression. "You can do it, Marilee. I believe in you."

Her expression drew serious, a trace of sadness filled her eyes. "I don't think anyone's ever said that to me."

Khiderian smiled despite the ping of pain in his chest around the vicinity of his heart, glad to be the one to give her a little confidence. "I don't think anyone's ever really known you."

Her eyes hardened as they narrowed on him. "Including you."

He grinned self-deprecatingly. "Maybe so, but I do know you have it in you to do this. I still believe in you as you should believe in yourself."

She blinked, the hardness in her eyes fading as she squared her shoulders and stood straight as a rod. "Whatever. What do I do?"

"Be one with the wind. Feel it flow through you, taste it on your tongue, let it wrap you in its embrace." He swallowed hard as the words he spoke brought other images to his mind. "Once you do that you can control it to move as you like. Direct it to take the dirt from my hand and carry it to you."

Marilee nodded, her body tensed as she stared at the mound of earth in his hand. Her brow furrowed from heavy concentration.

"I said become one with the wind, Marilee, not dominate it. You've got to relax," he added, allowing his smile to filter through to his voice.

The corner of Marilee's mouth turned upward in response as she visibly relaxed, her shoulders lowering into a more natural position. She breathed deep with closed eyes, opening them on the slow exhale. She continued to do so as the wind whipped around them. Khiderian could feel the shift in nature's design, could sense the manipulation in her dance as the air swirled between him and Marilee in a steady arc.

She extended her arm in front of her, uncurling her hand until it lay flat in the air, palm up, and focused her attention on his outstretched hand. The reddish brown earth in his palm swirled and lifted. The wind she controlled danced the dirt away and carried it out of his grasp.

"Shit!" Marilee cursed as the dirt hit the ground with the slightest whisper of sound.

Khiderian chuckled. "You didn't expect to get it right the first time, did you? Again." He bent down to scoop up more dirt and rose to meet a gaze full of murderous intent. Chuckling softly, he held out his hand. "Again."

A little over an hour later Marilee let out a whoop of celebration as the dirt in Khiderian's hand reached hers effortlessly. He smiled at her child-like excitement and dusted his hands together, removing the slight film of earth from them. "Not to say I told you so, but I told you so." He winked at her smile and stepped toward her. "Good work."

"Thanks." She turned her hand sideways and allowed the dirt to pour back down to the ground before dusting her hands together. "You're sure I can control it?"

He reached out and slid his fingers under her chin, tilted her head so their gazes collided. He could suck the doubt right out of her without much effort, but knew she didn't like him inside her head so he settled for soothing her with words. "I'm sure you can control it. We'll continue to train as long as it takes for you to feel totally comfortable with your abilities, but I have faith in you. You can control it. You're far more powerful than you know."

She smiled softly before stepping back, her arms wrapped around her middle, hands rubbing the pebbled flesh of her arms. The little T-shirt and shorts she wore provided little coverage. Khiderian hadn't paid much attention to it, weather never being a big deal for him, but the temperature had dropped during their training. "Are you cold?"

"A little." She shrugged. "It's not really that cool, but I guess all the wind whipping around us made it seem cooler."

"I suppose so." Khiderian slipped off his jacket and wrapped it around her slender shoulders. "The sun will rise soon. This will keep you warm until we reach the motel room."

"Thank you." She fitted her arms through the too long sleeves of the jacket and followed along at his side as he guided her back toward the motel. "I don't understand. Temperature obviously doesn't affect you or you couldn't make it through the desert in hot leather, but you're warm blooded. Don't you sweat?"

Khiderian thought about it. "I feel temperature when I think about it. I guess I don't sweat because as long as I don't think about it, it doesn't bother me."

Marilee frowned. "That doesn't make sense scientifically."

"It does if you quit thinking like a human." Khiderian chuckled. "Humans waste so much time trying to make sense of things that just are. It truly is a waste of time."

"Oh. I guess it is." She ran a hand down the length of the jacket. "Thanks again for letting me wear the jacket, and for training me."

"I don't need the jacket. It simply serves as a cover for my weapons," Khiderian explained. "Training you is my job."

"Is believing in me?"

He stumbled just outside the motel, something he never did. Turning, he saw her standing a few steps behind him, hands fisted on hips. She looked ridiculous standing there trying to look mighty with her slender body engulfed in his big jacket. Ridiculous and delicious. He could tell her that he'd lied about believing in her, simply said what he thought would get her through the training session, but he knew she could tell truth from lie and this was one lie he didn't have a chance of selling. Because he simply couldn't do it. He felt guilty enough for what he was already doing to her. "The sun is about to rise. Let's get to the motel room."

"I think I'll stay out here a little bit longer." She glanced back toward the direction they'd come from. "I bet a New Mexico sunrise is gorgeous, especially over that hill."

Khiderian glanced over to the hill they'd trained behind and imagined the beautiful colors that would streak the sky as the sun rose over it. "I imagine it would make a stunning portrait." He turned toward the motel, already sensing the sun's ascension.

"You don't want to watch it?"

He looked over his shoulder, his gaze colliding with hers and felt a sense of loss. "I can't."

Her brow furrowed. "From the window?"

"It's not the same." He turned away before she could see the sheen he felt coating his eyes and closed the distance to the motel.

He grabbed their things from the trunk of his rental and entered the room, setting everything on or next to the small dining table. He'd just removed the sheath from his back when the door opened and she stepped inside, closing and locking the door behind her. He inhaled, tasting the air. "The sun will rise in a few seconds. You're going to miss it."

"No I'm not, and neither are you." She parted the drab brown curtains and opened the blinds. "Come here."

Frowning, he took the few steps needed to join her before the window. Silently, they watched as the warm orange ball rose beyond the hill, bringing with it vibrant strokes of pink, yellow, and orange.

"Have you ever seen something so beautiful?' Marilee whispered, her head dangerously close to resting on his shoulder, an unconscious move that showed her growing trust.

Khiderian gazed down at her, his chest tight, and knew he was beyond screwed. "Unfortunately, I have."

CHAPTER SIX

"Jacob!" Seta sat straight up on the chaise, her back protesting the sudden movement.

On the sofa across from her, Christian arched an eyebrow. "Either you just had a vision or you've got some explaining to do to Nyla. I'm sure she wouldn't appreciate you dreaming about her husband."

"Funny." Seta stretched, wincing as her back made a popping noise. "You've spent too much time with Jacob and have adopted his need to make jokes at the most inappropriate times."

"It lightens the mood. The man knows how to keep his cool during the worst of times."

"You know what would lighten my mood? Not waking up feeling like I slept on a cinder block." She stood and further stretched out the kinks in her back and neck. "Seriously. Get new furniture."

"Seta." He held her gaze determinedly. "Spill."

"Fine." She took a deep breath, using her senses to determine how alone they were beneath the church Christian owned. The vampire lived in the underground home he'd dug out of the earth in case anyone got suspicious of his nature and came hunting for him. It was very secure. She knew because she'd been the one to create the wards that notified him of the presence of outsiders. "How is Nyla?"

"As good as can be expected. Malaika and Jonah are watching over her two rooms down, keeping a careful eye on her to make sure she doesn't try to seek out Jake on her own."

It was now Seta's turn to arch an eyebrow. "What's the danger level?"

"She's steadily growing more antsy. If not for the fear she's the best protector for Slade, I don't think we'd be able to stop her from leaving. She said she can feel him. He's in great pain."

"She's right." Seta shuddered, recalling the images from her vision. "They're killing him over and over again in cruel ways. I don't know how much more of it he can stand."

"We have to save him." Christian stood, his eyes expressing his fear. "He'd go in for us."

"We don't know where in is," Seta reminded him. "No matter how hard I focus I can only get snatches of what's happening and all I see is a dark, rank holding cell. I don't even know if he's still in Baltimore. They've obviously prepared themselves for an attack and set up barriers against my magic."

"All that tells us is they know Jake works with witches. Let's not track them like witches, but as humans."

"Track them as humans?" Seta scoffed. "Like a human would even know of their existence."

Christian rolled his eyes. "I mean we use our common sense, Seta. If we can't rely on you or Malaika's magic, we rely on the hard facts. You saw a siren tempting him. What do we know about sirens?"

"They're pure evil and deserve a slow and cruel death." Seta's blood boiled in her veins as she thought of the way the sirens tempted poor Jacob with his wife's image. There was once a time she'd thought nothing of killing the slayer herself, but he'd proven his heart was full of love, not hate. He was on the side of good and an important member of their small army. Seeing the sirens put him through hell and him still not break sparked a fury inside her the sirens would surely regret.

"I mean factually, Seta."

"That is a fact but I know what you mean." Taking a calming breath, she thought hard. "They're water creatures. They would never travel far from a sizable body of water."

"Right." Christian stood, tapping his chin with a finger as he started to pace. "They've always been along the Inner Harbor when Jake has confronted them before. That's also where he was headed when we last saw him."

"So they were in the area due to its closeness to the water and that's where they snatched him."

"Right." Christian nodded. "Even if they've traveled, they would travel along the water."

"You're right." She shook her head. "Something's off about all this, though. From what I can glean from the snatches I'm receiving, they don't know the children have been born. Why haven't they just killed him to stop the Blood Revelation before it has a chance to happen?"

"Seta!" Christian stopped pacing, his eyes full of anger which was unusual for the kindhearted vampire who insisted on searching for the good in everyone. "How can you be so callous about Jake's life after he's fought at your side?"

"I'm not, you fool." Seta glared at the young-looking vampire but before she could unleash her anger on him she reminded herself that Christian and Jacob had formed a bond somewhere along the line of their long history. After Nyla, Slade, and Jacob's brother, Jonah, Christian was next in line in his level of concern for the missing slayer. Seta would miss him if he left them permanently, even shred to pieces whomever was responsible for his death, but the emotional damage would be far greater for those four. She cut the vampire minister some slack. "I'm thinking about the big picture here. They're torturing him, not killing him, and surely they know he can die permanently if his head is removed from his body. What do they want?"

"They expect his mate to come for him."

"Exactly." Seta twisted her hands together. "They don't want to just stop the Blood Revelation. They want to do something far worse than that."

"What could be worse than that? They stop the Blood Revelation and they win. Are you sure they don't know two of the children have been born?"

"I'm sure." Seta threw her hands up in the air. "I hate this. I know there's so much more going on but I can't see it and wherever they are, they have me blocked. Dammit, they're planning something huge, and I'm afraid we won't know until it's too late."

"Relax, Seta. You've had your abilities blocked before and you got around it." Christian stepped closer. "The last time we were up against demons."

"So we could be up against demons this time."

"Possibly. The sirens don't have the ability to block you, nor do the were-hyenas we know they were working with last time."

Seta thought back to the past year and a half when they'd last faced off with the sirens. "There was only one siren that time and she was working with a pranic vampire and the were-hyenas. This time I think it's more than one siren. All I see when I see them in the visions are women in Nyla's image but there's a different feel about some of them. Jake seems to tell differences between them too."

"So...?" Christian inclined his head. "What are you saying?"

"I'm saying we don't know what the hell we're going up against and sadly, we can't do a damn thing until we do."

"We can't just stand by and do nothing while they keep torturing Jake."

"It's the only option for now." She shrugged, hating having to make the statement. It wasn't in her nature to just sit and wait.

"No, Seta, it's not. We really can't let them keep abusing Jake." Christian stepped before her, his eyes grave. "Jacob has been drinking blood."

Seta's heart slammed against her ribcage, his implication sinking in quickly. "What? How long? How much?"

"He's been doing it for a while now. He can get by on the blood from rare meat but he's taken a little blood from a bag before. Fortunately, he doesn't need large quantities like we do, but if he goes without long enough..."

"Are you telling me he won't be able to regenerate if they keep killing him?"

"I fear that he won't." Christian looked away. "He trusted me not to tell. I don't even think Nyla knows about anything other than his sudden preference for his meat to be prepared rare. Curtis Dunn created the serum his brother could never perfect because he knew blood was a requirement and that small doses would be needed as a booster."

"Dammit." Seta knew her voice had risen and quickly brought herself back under control. She didn't want to upset Nyla. If the woman thought for one moment that her husband could die permanently there'd be no restraining her. She could turn into mist and escape within the blink of an eye. Seta feared even her and Malaika's combined power couldn't hold her if she were in full panic mode.

"Seta, we have to get him back."

"How do you propose we do that?" She knew her tone was bitchy but her nerves were rattled. She hated feeling helpless. "We can't send any of the men because the sirens will ensnare every one of you, and Nyla is out of the question because they are laying out this trap for her. Malaika isn't wise enough. She's only recently discovered that she's a witch. I haven't had enough time to train her for a battle of this proportion."

"Which leaves you."

"It would leave me if I had any idea where the hell they're holding Jacob." She growled, dragging a hand through her hair. "We have no choice. I might not be getting visions as quickly as I'd like but at least I'm getting something. My visions are our best defense. If I go out of here half-cocked we could all suffer because of it." She closed her eyes and felt the sag of her shoulders. "I care for Jacob Porter, too, but my first responsibility is guaranteeing that these children live to grow up and save humanity."

"I understand." Christian turned away and walked the length of the room. He tried to hide it, but she could hear the disappointment in his voice and it cut her deep inside.

She stepped forward, ready to go to him when a vision assaulted her with such force she rocked back and had to grab the edge of the table to keep from falling back. A warrior with great strength was training a young woman with abilities that rivaled her own. And they had the same goal in mind that she had, to find Jacob Porter. But the warrior was the same kind of creature that had tried to kill Jacob Porter once already.

"Seta!"

She snapped out of the vision to find her shoulders caught in Christian's iron grasp. "I know what to do now."

He blinked before stepping back, letting go of her shoulders. "You had a vision."

"Yes, and we are not the only ones seeking Jacob Porter."

He frowned. "These others... are they good or evil?"

"One I know is good." Seta remembered the girl clearly, remembered mending her throat after an enraged and newly turned vampire had come close to ripping it completely out. "The other I'm not sure about. He's very powerful, and seems to be training the good one, but his aura is full of darkness. He has shed much blood and darkness pulls heavily at his soul."

"Who are they?"

"The young woman who helped us in Hicksville, and..." Seta swallowed. "A pranic vampire."

Christian's eyes darkened. "Pranic vampires were working with the siren who escaped Jake, the same one we're sure came back with friends."

"I know. And once I find this one, I'll determine how he knows of Jacob."

"And if he's working against us?"

"His head will make a lovely trophy."

Khiderian sat up so quickly, Marilee jumped a foot. "Shit, Khiderian. Scare the hell out of me, why don't ya?" She paused in her folding of her pajamas, noting the alarm in his wide eyes. "Khiderian?"

"We're leaving right now." He rose quickly from the couch and grabbed his sword, sliding it into its sheath. "Someone's on our trail."

She stilled. "Who? What?"

He glanced at her sideways as he hoisted her bag onto the top of the table and unzipped it, snatching her pajamas from her hands to shove inside. "An old ally of yours."

"Huh?" Marilee cocked her head to the side, frowning. "What ally?"

"Seta." He zipped up the bag. "Do you have everything? We need to go now."

"Why?" Marilee recalled the vampire-witch who'd saved her life after the attack in Hicksville. The woman hadn't done anything to justify the alarm in Khiderian's eyes. "Why are we running from Seta? She helped me before."

"The fact that she was once your ally doesn't mean she will be now." He pulled on his coat and grabbed her elbow, prodding her toward the door despite the fact the sun hadn't gone down yet. "And even if she sides with you, it doesn't mean she'll side with me."

"Why wouldn't she?" A sinking feeling hit Marilee in the gut. Something wasn't right. If Khiderian was what the Dream Teller called a good vampire, and Seta was a good vampire, they should be on the same side. Marilee yanked her arm free of Khiderian's grasp a foot away from the car. "What's going on? If both of you are really supposed to be fighting for this Blood Revelation thing you should be working together."

"You would think so." Khiderian unlocked the car doors and tossed her bag into the backseat. "Come on, Marilee. I can't stand the sun for long. Pranic vampires are more susceptible to its damage than the regular blood-sucking variety."

Marilee folded her arms and planted her feet firmly in the ground. "I know. The fact that you're willing to start traveling before sundown didn't get by me. You're supposed to be this big, bad psychic warrior but the thought of Seta on your trail sends you running for the hills."

"And?" His eyes darkened beneath his furrowed brow. "Get in the damn car."

"No." she shook her head. "Not until I get the truth. All of it."

She blinked her eyes and found Khiderian standing directly in front of her upon opening them. His hand clamped around her upper arm as her mouth opened and she was shoved into the passenger side of the car before she could form a word.

Mouth hanging open, eyes blinking, anger rose inside her as the door closed with a loud slam and a very agitated Khiderian rounded the front of the car. She reached for the door, pausing as the lock engaged. "I hate pranic vampires."

"So does Seta," Khiderian said as he slid into his seat and started the car. "Put your seatbelt on."

"Make me."

Khiderian directed a wry look her way as her seatbelt fastened around her. "The more psychic power I use, the more energy I'm going to need to feed on to stay in fighting form. Seeing as how you are all alone with me on this trip you might want to do as much as you possibly can to keep me from needing to feed until we get somewhere more populated."

Huffing out a breath, Marilee crossed her arms and sat back in her seat. She knew the pose was reminiscent of a cranky child but didn't care. The vampire didn't play fair. "Fine, but you could answer my questions."

"I told you. A former ally isn't a guaranteed future ally, and an ally of yours isn't necessarily an ally of mine." He put the car in reverse and backed out of the parking space before turning out onto the street which would take them to the expressway. "What more do you need to know?'

"Everything. Are you really one of the good guys?"

"The Dream Teller explained to you what our mission is." His hands tightened around the steering wheel as he maneuvered the car onto the expressway. "You can believe her, even if you don't have any faith in me."

Ouch. Marilee flinched, surprised by the ferocity behind the simple statement. Unable to look at the vampire next to her, she focused her gaze out her window while guilt twisted low in her belly. She shouldn't feel anything for the vampire, she argued with herself, especially not guilt. He'd known of her abilities since she was a young girl and could have helped her at any point. But no, he'd waited until he received a direct order to announce himself. He was using her to help complete a mission, plain and simple. Who cared if he seemed upset by her inability to completely trust him. What had he really done to earn that trust?

"Don't act as if we've been lifelong friends and I should have some sort of blind faith in you. We've just met."

"Is that really the way you see it?"

Marilee risked a glance at the warrior next to her and saw that his jaw was clenched as tight as his hands. His eyes stayed forward, focused on the road, but even from her angle of sight, she could tell a slew of thoughts and emotions swam through them. His mind was definitely on more than where they were going.

"Part of my mission is to protect those directly involved with the Blood Revelation," he said softly. "Rescuing Jacob Porter is our mission, not Seta's. If she finds us and comes along she won't be where she's most needed. It's best for all involved if she doesn't catch up to us."

Marilee frowned. "Why didn't you just say that?"

"Why did you just assume I was hiding some dark secret?" He glanced at her for a brief moment, but in that small sliver of time Marilee saw a world of hurt. "You angered me by jumping to the worst conclusion so I reacted. It's childish to behave that way, though, and regardless what you think of me, we're in this mission together. We both need to remember that."

Marilee looked down at her hands lying in her lap, shame creeping over her. "I don't trust easily. Maybe it's offensive but it's protected me all my life."

"Maybe in the past, but you have to trust me now. I'm your partner and your teacher. If I don't have your trust, I'm not going to be able to keep you alive."

Marilee swallowed hard. "This mission of ours is part of our destiny, right?"

"Right."

"So it's already been determined what's going to happen?"

He frowned, seemed to mull over his answer. "To an extent. Why?"

Marilee took a deep breath. "I need to know something. If I trust you, do everything you say, will we really survive this mission?"

"Trust me completely, Marilee, and I guarantee you will survive." He glanced at her briefly before returning his gaze to the road. "I swear it on my own life."

Seta crept through the utility room of the worn down building, stepping lightly as only a vampire could to avoid the creaking of boards beneath her feet. The room she entered through gave only the light that slipped through the gap in the dark curtains drawn over the windows. A human would stumble through the dark, but Seta had the gift of perfect night vision. She trained her eyes to the darkness, an action that took a mere second, and walked deeper into the small house, bypassing the kitchen to step into the living room.

Samuel, the gray-haired psychic fisherman, sat in a recliner, drinking from a mug. Seta inhaled and took in the scent of coffee touched lightly with cream. He looked up as she entered, no surprise registering on his face, which was highlighted by the vanilla candle burning on the table next to him.

"Good morning, Seta."

"You were expecting me?"

"I wouldn't be a good psychic if I didn't sense you coming." He grinned before setting his mug on the small table and swept his hand out in a gesture for her to take the seat at the opposite side of the table. "I would offer you coffee but I don't think you'd drink it."

Seta nodded her head in appreciation—Vampires could drink or eat anything they wanted, but the digestive problems that came with most common foods made the act unappealing—and crossed over to the chair, settling in. She glanced about the room, noting the minimal décor. A couch lined the opposite wall, a fireplace and a large screen TV each took up a side wall. Other than a braided throw rug and a painting which looked like nothing more than haphazardly splotched colors, the room was plain, beige, and boring. "Do you know why I came?"

"I think so." Samuel sat back in his chair, folding his hands over his sizable belly. He wore a dark short-sleeved T-shirt and brown trousers, the clothes as haggard as his face and unkempt hair which hung to his shoulders in gnarly waves. His white-streaked beard was a little neater, but not by much. "Something's happened and you need my help."

"Yes." The word was harder to get out than Seta had thought it would be. She rarely asked for help, and never from a human. Despite his psychic abilities, Samuel was human all the way. "You tried to warn away humans who came to the siren two years ago. You could tell what she was without being ensnared yourself."

"Funny. I recall being captured."

"But not by the siren." Seta tilted her head and studied the man. "You're gay."

"Is that a crime?" Samuel delivered a hard glare daring her to say something against his sexual nature.

Seta enjoyed the man's courage. She might be petite but a psychic would feel her power acutely and it took a brave one to not cower from it. "Not at all. I'm only trying to understand what happened then. The creature you saw was a siren."

"I know. I overheard the people who rescued me talking about it. It sounded like one of the fabled sirens who lure fishermen to their deaths. Is that right?"

"Yes, though you would never have to worry about that happening to you." Seta grinned. "You have immunity."

"Because I'm psychic or because I'm gay?"

"Because you're gay. The men the siren hunted were all psychic to some degree. The sea-bitch was snaring them so the pranic vampire she worked for could turn them into what he was. She projected herself as their ultimate fantasy and lured them in. A siren can only take on female form though."

"Which explains why she had no effect on me. It was just one, right?"

"Yes, though she took on different forms."

SIREN'S SNARE

Samuel nodded. "I thought it was just one woman, judging by the strange aura. I couldn't figure out how she always looked so different though." He shifted in the seat. "So, Seta, what do you need from me? I doubt you've come to me two years later just to rehash the circumstances surrounding my abduction. This is about the babies born the night I was rescued, isn't it?"

Seta instantly tensed. Samuel had been brought back to Christian's church after being rescued along with Jake's brother, Jonah, and Malaika, the witch she'd been training. Jonah and Samuel stayed upstairs in the church while Malaika helped her to deliver the babies in Christian's underground dwelling. The fisherman shouldn't have known of their births. "What do you know of the babies?"

"I know they are very special." He frowned as he glanced away. "I know their existence goes against all logic. One was born to the man who brought me to the church and his wife... a woman who can take the form of a panther and drinks blood like a vampire. The other, a beautiful little girl, was born to a pair of vampires, one of them your son."

"You know a lot." Seta swallowed hard. "Have you told anyone?"

"No." His eyes hardened. "The vampire who abducted me that night searched my mind and though he found the image of your granddaughter being born I carefully managed to keep the parents' names secret. My gut told me to. Only he and one other pranic vampire in his army knew of that vision anyway. They both died that night."

"None have come to visit you since?"

"His army was wiped out by the slayer. I sensed the births of the children and saw them in my mind's eye at the time of their birth. I have had no other contact with vampires or any supernatural being for that matter since that night. I even quit working, terrified I'd run into one of those things again." He held Seta's gaze steadily. "Even if I had been approached by one, I would not tell what I witnessed that night. I know those children are special. I know vampires can't have children but those babies were still born and they were born for a great cause."

"You are a very wise man." Some of the tension drained out of Seta's body, but she still couldn't fully relax. There were too many unanswered questions. "The vampire who captured you, Xander, was working with a siren. She got away and came back with friends, others just like her."

Samuel sat forward. "What happened?"

"There were signs that sirens were in the area so Jacob, the slayer, went to kill them. He'd told us he was immune to them and we believed him, but he hasn't been heard from since he went after them. It's been weeks." Seta took a deep breath. Though she didn't physically need the oxygen, it did help to keep her calm. "Are you sure Xander didn't share any information about the children with the siren?"

Samuel closed his eyes, shook his head. "Damn," he muttered before opening his eyes again. They were bleak enough to make Seta's stomach take a dip. "I don't know. I barely remember the vampire taunting the woman there, the witch."

"Malaika?"

"Yes. He said something about seeing her help bring one of the babies into the world while raiding her ex-boyfriend's mind before changing him over into a pranic vampire. Obviously, he knew of at least one child before he captured me."

"So he could have shared that vision with the siren. That's why she's back and why she brought her own army." Hot fury engulfed Seta's body. Malaika had delivered Njeri, her granddaughter, so the sirens knew about her. They had to know she was alive and would be hunting her relentlessly. However, if they'd only seen the one birth... "Would the sirens have any reason to believe Jacob was one of the immortals chosen to create a special child?"

"Not from any vision I had." Samuel shrugged. "My vision was about your granddaughter. Malaika's vision was about your granddaughter. I've told no one of the slayer's child."

"Then why do the sirens have Jacob?" Seta ran her hands through her hair, more confused than she was before she visited the fisherman. "They haven't killed him. Nyla would know. They seem to be keeping him to lure her out. They have to know the baby has been born or they would just kill him to prevent the conception. They're trying to lure her and the child to them. How do they know? Jake would never tell."

"They may not know. They've obviously received some information from someone indicating the slayer is or will be the father of this special child. However, if he's not telling them anything, or even if he's swearing that the child hasn't been conceived they'll keep him as insurance just in case."

"They'll keep him until they can draw out Nyla and kill them both." Seta's eyes burned with rage. "And they'll still look out for signs of the baby."

"Makes sense to me." Samuel sipped from his mug before setting it back on the small table. "I've had visions of the births and I know what you are. What I don't know is what the children are. What is their purpose?"

Seta narrowed her eyes on the man, protective instincts flaring. "Why do you need to know?"

He laughed. "Before that incident I thought I was the most abnormal person in the world. Then I met Malaika, a witch, and you, a greater witch. Throw in the vampires, shape-shifting beasts, and even the slayer with his own special powers, and it was a full circus of utter craziness. I was caught up in all of it." His mouth thinned into a hard line. "I was beaten and abused by those creatures from hell and through it all I managed to hold back information that could have endangered all of you. I didn't know you at all. Hell, I knew you were vampires and witches, but I did what I could to throw Xander off and help you out. Now you're coming to me and I know you're going to ask me to do something, aren't you?"

Seta looked away. Rarely did she feel guilt, but it tried to work itself into her conscience now. "I've been blocked by someone I need to track. I need the help of a non-witch with psychic abilities."

"Then I need to know more than I do." He sniffed, leaned forward in the chair. "I need to know exactly who I'm protecting and why. I deserve that much considering if whoever captured your slayer is working with a psychic of their own like they were the last time, there's a good chance my help might be discovered. That means there's a good chance I might take another ass-kicking for you people. I don't bounce back as well as your kind."

"You're right. Your help is greatly appreciated." Seta sat straighter and looked the man in the eye. "There is a prophecy called the Blood Revelation which states three sets of immortals will be chosen to mate, creating special warriors. One of those warriors will be the Child of Light. The Child of Light will save the world from Satan's wrath."

Samuel's dull gray eyes widened with interest. "One of these children is the special child?"

"We don't know yet." Seta frowned. The grandmother in her wanted her son's child to be the special one who would save them and fulfill the prophecy, taking the great honor, and had hoped for some sign, but there were none. The children were normal toddlers, except for the fact they both drank blood. "Whether one of them is the Child of Light or not, they are one of the three special warriors born to fulfill the prophecy. All three have important roles. All three must be protected at all costs."

"Even the cost of a life?"

Seta nodded. "I would die for them, yes."

"But you want to save the slayer?"

"Of course I want to save him if his death can be prevented and the children protected. His son is part slayer, and who better to train the boy than the slayer who sired him?" Seta didn't mention her fondness of the slayer. To do so would be a sign of weakness she wasn't comfortable with. Being psychic, the ex-fisherman probably knew anyway. "And the children need protection at all times. As a slayer, Jacob Porter can sense supernatural beings before anyone else. We need him fighting with us to make sure these children survive to fulfill their destiny."

"And you need me to locate him?"

Seta studied the man. He was psychic which gave him some protection. He could sense impending danger. Of course, he had been captured once before and she knew better than anyone that psychic powers could be unpredictable. He was human, though, and too old of a human to be much use in combat. Despite his immunity to the sirens, he couldn't go in to their lair to save Jacob. "Even if you located him it wouldn't do us any good until we could find someone who could take out the sirens and whoever is currently helping them."

"You couldn't?"

"There's a chance I couldn't." Seta fisted her hands until her nails threatened to break the skin of her palms. Feeling useless was a cruel punishment, one she wasn't used to. "The fact that I'm only seeing very little in the visions I have of Jacob tells me the sirens are working with someone who knows how to block a witch's powers. I could go in and be caught in a witch's net."

Samuel tilted his head, his eyes showing understanding. "Malaika, the young witch Xander caught, was kept from using her powers when they threw silver dust on her."

"It's called a witch's net. We can't move in it and we can't call upon our power. Whoever the sirens are working with have already taken precautions against the power of witches. I'm sure they'd be ready to capture me or Malaika if we went in to rescue Jacob."

"What about the others? Your son?"

"He would be caught in the siren's snare. All the men in our small army are heterosexual and no use in this fight."

Samuel shook his head. "Then send in your son's wife."

"She hasn't been a vampire long and still has much room for improvement in her combat skills." Seta sighed in defeat. "We aren't ready to infiltrate the sirens. We need to know more about who is involved and what their plans are before we rush in blindly."

"What can I do to help you?"

Seta captured Samuel's gaze and held it steady. "I've had a recent vision of a couple who are hunting down Jacob Porter's location. I believe the young woman is trustworthy, but I'm unsure of the man she is with. He's a very strong pranic vampire and he felt my intrusion. He blocked me so I can no longer see him."

Samuel frowned. "And you think I can?"

"Yes. I need to know where to find him so I can find out what he is up to, and how pure his intentions are."

Samuel licked his lips and glanced away. "I can try but if I don't have anything he has touched or even an image of what he looks like—"

"I have his image and I'm going to put it directly into your head." Seta stood and stepped around to stand behind Samuel's chair. She placed her fingertips on his temple. "Tell me where I can find the vampire."

CHAPTER SEVEN

Marilee felt the chill the moment Khiderian jerked the steering wheel to the right and sent the car careening down the off ramp. Something was coming. "What is it? What's happening?"

"Do you feel it?" His eyes were wide and alert though they focused on the road before him.

"The danger? Yes, I feel it. What is it?"

"I told you I thought I might have been followed. Whoever's following me must have made the decision to show themselves because they're almost on us." He swerved around a crate in the road and continued to speed down the dark street, trees whipping by so fast looking at them would make Marilee nauseous. She concentrated on the sense of danger instead, trying to determine which direction their followers would come from. It seemed Khiderian was racing in the opposite direction to buy them some time to set up for battle unless they got lucky and were able to outrun their foes. "I need to know exactly what you feel right now, Marilee."

She blinked. "Danger, I told you. The same thing you feel."

"We don't feel things the same way. I need to know what you sense."

"What?" Marilee gripped the dashboard as they took a turn at break-neck speed. "How do you know how I feel things or—"

"You have a gift I don't have," Khiderian snapped, whipping around another corner, taking them farther from the interstate and deeper into what looked like the boonies from what Marilee could tell in the dark. "What do you feel?"

"What gift—"

"I don't have time to explain right this very minute!" He was yelling now, his nostrils flared. "Just answer the fucking question before you get us both killed, dammit. What. Do. You. Feel? Exactly," he added, glancing at her for a brief second before swerving to avoid a small, furry animal in the road. They flew by so quickly Marilee couldn't make out what it was.

Bristling at Khiderian's tone, and cold with fear over the implication of his words, Marilee focused on what she felt and tried to put it into words. "Fear. Danger. I don't know."

"Do you feel anyone calling you?"

She cut a glance at the vampire, confused. "Calling me? No. Why would I?"

"If you do feel someone calling you, asking you for help, or anything like that, ignore it. Understand?" He pulled the car to a screeching stop in the middle of a field that appeared to have been recently plowed and turned toward her, his eyes stern. "Do. Not. Answer. The. Call."

"Alright," she said softly, baffled by the adamancy in his tone over something that made no sense to her.

"I mean it, Marilee. Don't answer to anyone but me."

"Okay, I got it."

He held her gaze a moment longer then pushed the button to pop the trunk and stepped out of the car. "Come on."

The sound of their doors slamming shut after them was the only sound in the still night as they quickly made their way to the trunk of the car. Khiderian passed her bag to her and yanked off his jacket to make his own weapons easier to access.

"Are you sure we couldn't have outrun the enemy?" Marilee asked as she withdrew her Browning 9mm Hi-Power pistol from the bag and loaded it.

"I wouldn't take a chance on fighting now unless it were unavoidable." He frowned at the gun in her hand. "I smell hawthorn."

"What else am I going to shoot into vampires?"

His eyes registered surprise. "Where did you get hawthorn bullets?"

"I made them." She smirked at the expression on his face and grabbed the bottle of oil she applied whenever she went on a hunt. "Make sure you don't touch me."

Khiderian shook his head as she rubbed the hawthorn oil on all exposed areas of her skin, which was a lot considering she wore a tank top and cut-off jeans short enough to give her grandmother a fit if the woman were still alive. "Noted."

She tossed the oil bottle back into the bag, grabbed the pistol, and stepped back so Khiderian could close the trunk. No sooner had the latch clicked, a rustle sounded behind them.

They turned in unison. Nothing stood before them but they knew it was there. Marilee narrowed her eyes and looked around. The field left them exposed, and the dense thatch of trees bordering it hid their enemies. "We're kind of sitting ducks out here, Khiderian." She kept her voice to a whisper, knowing it was futile. To a focused vampire a whisper was no different than shouting through a bullhorn.

"I'll sense any type of projectile and change its course. Focus on the pattern of the wind and you'll be able to as well. Our enemy will draw close to attack and being in the open will help us. There's nothing for them to hide behind here except the car so be careful of it." Khiderian moved so they were positioned back to back, preventing an option for their enemy to sneak up from behind.

Marilee...

Marilee jerked her head to the left where the voice came from but only saw the bare field stretching out for yards before the dark outline of trees appeared. The trees were too far away for anyone to call her name out loud and be heard. "Did you hear that?"

She sensed Khiderian tense. "I heard nothing. Is something calling you?"

"Yes."

"Ignore it or we're dead where we stand."

Swallowing hard, she nodded. "What is it? How can I hear it and not you?"

"Focus!"

Marilee blinked once and within that second an army appeared before her. She rose her hands and took aim as what looked like dozens of vampires emerged from the trees, coming toward her in a blur of speed. The Browning held thirteen bullets and she made quick use of them, wincing against the ear-splitting howls of the vampires she injured with the wooden bullets.

She didn't dare turn to look at him but she could hear Khiderian's sword slicing through air and blood spatter rained around her as he hit his marks. With a quick lift of her knee, she reached into her boot and withdrew the hawthorn dagger, slicing as quickly as she could to injure her attackers before they could latch on to her. The ones who did manage to make contact hissed in pain as their fingers connected with the hawthorn oil she'd drenched her skin with and drew away.

A loud shriek rent the air and a new batch of predators arrived. Marilee watched with growing dread as the sky filled with dark birds. "Now's a good time to use the wind to our advantage," Khiderian called out to her and she felt the shift in the air as he collected the wind and forced the dark birds back as they lunged for them.

While parrying with the vampires still among them, she noted the birds falling to the ground were ravens, but unusually large. She discovered why they were so big as they transformed into humans before their feet hit the ground. "Oh shit!"

"Hawthorn won't stop them," Khiderian advised. "You should have brought some silver bullets."

"How do I kill them without silver bullets?" she asked, sidestepping a vampire claw.

"Taking their heads off or their hearts out will work. Take my sword." The sword appeared to her right and Marilee quickly snatched it. The second her hand connected to the hilt, she swung and cleanly beheaded a trio of enemies. "Watch your back!"

She felt Khiderian step away and knew he had to do it because they were being surrounded. She kept her back to the car and swung the sword at her attackers, simultaneously kicking a few in the stomach when they got too close. Her heart threatened to explode, her breath wedged itself inside her throat, but she somehow managed to keep swinging. She was used to vampires, had actually grown somewhat comfortable fighting them, but seeing birds change shape into men and women seriously messed with her head.

She swung the sword, leaving deep gashes in the chests of three men, but before she could pull back her arm for another swing, a fist connected to the side of her head and she fell back against the car. As she slid down the side, stars shooting out before her eyes, she caught a blurry glimpse of canine teeth coming at her.

Marilee... We will help you. Marilee.....

A roar sounded and air whipped around her as her attackers flew backward. She knew Khiderian had blasted them back to buy her time. She rose to her feet and willed the dizziness in her head to subside as she took her position, sword raised, ready to behead whoever stepped before her. In her other hand she held the dagger for the ones who got too close.

Marilee... Release us...

She stilled, her entire body frozen as she recalled the night at the cemetery. Whatever she'd released that night had spoken to her in the same way, begged her to release them, and children had died. They were back. Whatever it was that destroyed those children were back, ready to cause more carnage.

Pain ripped into Marilee's thigh and she screamed, glanced down to see a man biting into her leg. She brought the sword down, splitting his back in half. He fell to the ground, head still attached, and opened his mouth in a silent scream as blood spilled from his lips. Marilee turned away to throw up but had to swallow down the bile and duck out of the way as a woman lunged at her.

The woman shifted into a raven before hitting the car and rose into the air before diving toward Marilee. She barely stepped out of the way before a man was on her, his hands wrapped around her neck as his mouth opened wide. Not a vampire, she deduced from the zero-effect of the hawthorn on his skin. Two curved fangs grew from his gums and he lowered his head toward her neck just as she raised the sword, planting the silver blade into his gut. She twisted it as he screamed and pulled up, shoving at his chest to push him away as she tugged the weapon out, spilling his intestines.

The raven-shifter landed on her head before she could react to the fact she'd just ripped out a man's innards and started clawing at her scalp. Screaming, Marilee swatted at the creature, but couldn't dislodge it.

"Stand still!" She heard Khiderian's command and a moment later the bird lay on the ground, split into two equal halves.

She turned around and gasped as she took in the cuts marring Khiderian's face and arms. Though his clothing was dark she could tell it was covered in blood and he didn't seem to possess as much power as he had the night they'd met. "Your power is dwindling."

"Don't let them know that," he growled, turning to cut an approaching shifter with one of the blades he kept strapped to his forearms. "No time for breaks, Marilee."

She felt a rush of wind at her back and turned just in time to duck as a claw came at her face. Unfortunately, it sliced into Khiderian's back, eliciting a sharp grunt of pain. Knowing she'd failed to protect him while he'd watched her back fueled her anger and she ignored the pain in the leg that had been chomped on. Quickly rising, she head-butted the man with the bear-like claws and brought up the sword. The sturdy piece of silver entered his body at the groin and made a deep cut before she drew back and swung again, this time cutting a deep wedge between his neck and collar bone. Two more hacks and his head rolled off his body.

Twisting around with both blades before her, she managed to slice a man's neck with the sword and stab her dagger into a woman's gut. The woman hissed and wrapped her hands around the hilt of the dagger but cried out when she touched the hawthorn handle. Vampire. Marilee kicked the dagger, shoving it deeper into the woman's stomach.

The man she'd sliced with the sword came at her despite the blood gurgling out of his mouth and Marilee punched him in the face, sending his head back. He made sounds of pain and fell to his knees, perfectly positioned for the death blow Marilee delivered with the sword.

Release us. Release us now before it's too late. Marilee.... Release us!

"Shut up!" she screamed as the voices echoed inside her head and earned a wary look from Khiderian.

"Fight them, Marilee." He kicked a man in the stomach, propelling him backward before grabbing a woman by the head, breaking her neck with one swift motion. "Try to push them out of your mind. Whatever you do, do not invite them in or repeat anything they put in your head."

Marilee gritted her teeth and followed Khiderian's command. She tried to push the voices out of her mind as she and Khiderian battled back to back, slowly but surely taking out the dwindling army. They took blows and cuts of their own, even a bite or two, but managed to stay upright. As the battle went on, she noticed Khiderian used less mental power and drew upon his physical abilities to fight off the creatures attacking them. His movements, though still fast in comparison to humans like herself, grew slower as well.

She let out a cry of relief as the last body hit the ground, its head tumbling a foot away from the rest of it. "We did it."

"Not yet we didn't."

She swung around at the grave note in Khiderian's voice and looked toward the trees where a hooded figure emerged. "Vampire or shifter?"

"Witch." Khiderian's body tensed as he took a step forward. "Get behind me."

He's not strong enough. We can save you. Release us.

"Go away." Marilee clutched her head as the sound of drums beat through it. "Get out of my head."

"Ignore them, Marilee. Build a wall in your mind and fight them. Don't let them in."

Nodding, she tried to do what he said but didn't really understand and she couldn't focus on understanding while watching the hooded figure and wondering if whoever spoke to her in her mind was telling the truth. "The voices say you can't protect us."

"They're lying." His voice came out a low growl. "They'll tell you anything. Get behind me and focus on keeping them out."

"You've weakened."

"Marilee."

"Khiderian."

The witch rose her hands and bolts of lightning shot out. Marilee screamed as the lightning came toward her but it bounced back on the witch, catching her robe on fire. The witch screamed, spun quickly in circles and vanished, leaving behind no trace she had ever been there.

Khiderian fell to his knees, slumped over. Rivulets of sweat snaked down his face, his breathing labored. Marilee fell to her knees beside him. "Are you all right?" She touched his arm and quickly pulled her hand away as he winced from the traces of hawthorn oil still on her skin. "I'm sorry."

"Can you drive?" The words were ground out from his mouth, barely audible.

"Yes."

"Good." He fell face first to the ground, his body completely drained of the power she'd once felt roll off him in waves.

"Khiderian?" No answer. She reached for him but stopped short of touching his arm. She'd covered herself in hawthorn oil and as weak as he was, she didn't want to touch him with it.

She glanced around at all the dead bodies and shuddered before rising to a stand, doing her best to block out her own pain while walking around the car. She reached inside the driver side and popped the trunk. She already knew she didn't have any gloves in her bag and she would have seen some in the glove compartment had they been there. She rooted through the trunk, debating that given the circumstances Khiderian wouldn't mind her going through his things.

She opened a large suitcase and sorted through clothes—everything the man owned was black and looked like mugger wear—until she came upon black leather gloves. "Thank goodness."

She slipped the gloves on and lowered the trunk before squatting next to Khiderian. She gave him a nudge and said his name again. The only response she received was a garbled groan. The man was finished.

"Okay, big guy. Here we go." She wedged her hands beneath his arm pits and tugged. It felt like her arms were going to rip out of their sockets as Khiderian's body stayed right where it lay. "Oh come on." She pulled again, grunting with the effort. A sharp, stinging pain ripped through her leg and she collapsed, crying as the wound in her thigh burned. "Son of a bitch!" she screamed, bringing her fists down on the ground in a temper tantrum. "I can't do this, Khiderian. Get your six-foot-whatever-ass up and help me out here." He didn't move. He couldn't. He'd completely drained himself fighting to help her complete her mission. He didn't even seem to like Jake but he'd put his life on the line to keep her safe so she could rescue the slayer.

Wiping at her tears, Marilee took a deep breath and stood up. Glancing at the sky, she noticed the subtle lightening. Smoke already rolled off some of the bodies on the ground. Khiderian was old and had undoubtedly built up some immunity to the sun which he'd demonstrated earlier but in his weakened state he wouldn't last long. She had to get him to safety before sunset. "How?"

Fortunately no voices answered her in her head, or begged to be released so they could help, but she heard her grandmother clear as day as if the woman were standing right next to her. *Marilee, you are a strong young woman. Once you buck up and set your mind to something, you can move mountains, girl. But when you cry and throw fits you're just wasting precious energy.*

That was it. She was wasting energy, and if she'd quit panicking and focus her mind on it, she could move Khiderian. "Thanks, Gram," she whispered as she stepped over to the car and opened the back door. "You always knew the right thing to say."

She braced her body, took a deep breath, and then relaxed. Just as Khiderian had showed her outside the motel in New Mexico, she focused on the wind, felt its subtle pattern. Though it barely moved now, she could feel it and gave it a nudge. Slowly, it started to sway back and forth, picking up momentum. She wrapped it around Khiderian's body and lifted him off the ground.

Sweat broke out along her brow and upper lip, pain exploded in her head, and her limbs shook with the effort it took to lift such a heavy object with something as light as the wind, but she kept her mind trained on the task, drawing in more wind until it completely enveloped Khiderian.

She stepped aside and slowly, carefully, directed the wind as it carried his body and placed him gently along the backseat. Once his body rested on the seat, she released her mental hold on the wind and collapsed against the side of the car, pain shooting through her skull. "Shit, I think I sprained my brain."

Gripping her head with both hands, she waited until the pain in it subsided and slammed the car door shut. The field looked like a war zone with bodies littered all over. She had to get out of there before the owner showed up. There were a lot of farmers in Hicksville so she knew they started their days out severely early. First, she had to make sure she couldn't be traced.

Some of her and Khiderian's blood would be on the field, but it would be mixed in with the blood of the dozens who'd attacked them. There was far too much of it for her to worry about the narrow chance it would be tested and linked back to them. Wisps of smoke rose from the vampire bodies scattered on the ground, whatever immunity they'd built up completely gone in death. They wouldn't last long in an open field in the middle of an Arizona summer.

Grimacing, Marilee extracted her dagger from the stomach of the vampire she'd stabbed earlier. Her stomach rolled as it made a plopping sound upon exit but she pressed on, walking on her injured leg to retrieve Khiderian's sword and the other blades he'd used in the fight.

After securing all the blades and her gun in the trunk of Khiderian's rental she took a final look at the bloody mess. The shapeshifters looked like any other humans now and their deaths would be investigated. There was no way to hide the bodies, not by herself, and not with the little window of time she had before whoever owned the land came by to check on it.

She sank into the car, adjusting the seat Khiderian had sat in earlier to her smaller size, and turned the key in the ignition. They'd left tracks entering the field and would probably leave tracks while leaving, but there was nothing she could do about that. She couldn't carry Khiderian to safety and she damn well wasn't leaving him behind. As she navigated the car onto the road, she glanced at Khiderian's still body where it lay on the backseat and hoped she made it to safety in time.

CHAPTER EIGHT

Marilee breathed a sigh of relief as she moved the car so that it sat outside the door to the room she'd just rented at the Lazy Day Motel. All she had to do now was get Khiderian—who still hadn't moved a muscle—out of the car and into the room without being seen. Fate smiled upon them by providing a room in the back. She hoped it would smile a little more and help her lift Khiderian without bursting a blood vessel.

She stepped out of the car and rushed over to open the motel room door. Leaving it ajar, she walked over to the car as quickly as her sore leg would allow. She'd washed up with disinfectant wipes she kept in her duffel and thrown one of Khiderian's dark T-shirts over her tank top to hide the blood on it but hadn't dressed her wound. Luckily, the guy at the check-in counter was too engrossed with the Playboy magazine he was drooling over to pay her any attention when she'd signed in. Now she had to get Khiderian inside before her luck ran out and someone came out of one of the neighboring rooms. As seedy as the motel looked, someone carrying an unconscious body inside probably wasn't all that odd. Of course she'd be levitating an unconscious body. You didn't tend to come across that very often, regardless where you stayed.

She opened the back door and poked Khiderian in the chest, confident she'd wiped all the hawthorn oil off her hands. He didn't budge. "Come on, Khiderian. If you can move at all, please do it."

Nothing.

After growling in frustration, she took a deep fortifying breath and relaxed her mind, not the easiest thing to do with pain burning through her leg and ricocheting across both temples. As she concentrated on the wind around her the pain in her head increased until tears streamed from her eyes and her skull felt it would nearly split. Gripping it with her hands she choked back a whimper and breathed in deep to compose herself. This wasn't going to work this time and the sun had set fifteen minutes ago. She had to get Khiderian into the room the old-fashioned way.

"Son of a bitch." She bent at the knees, gritted her teeth, and slid her hands under Khiderian's armpits. "One...two...three!" She pulled as hard as she could and Khiderian's body slid out of the car onto the gravel parking lot. Once he was on the ground the task became more complicated. Bent over to haul him, more weight was put on Marilee's leg and it ripped through her with every tug she gave.

"You're going to give the man gravel burn if you keep dragging him like that."

Marilee gasped, nearly dropped Khiderian's upper body to the ground as she turned her head to see a petite but curvy Hispanic woman with dark eyes and long brunette hair. In black jeans, a tight black top, and black leather knee high boots, the woman looked like any other fashionable nineteen-year old, only she was far older than that. "Seta."

"You remember me." Ruby red lips turned up at the corner. "I remember you, too. You helped a friend of mine out of a jam which is why I'm giving you the benefit of the doubt right now instead of ripping out your organs."

Marilee swallowed hard. She hadn't actually seen Seta in action as far as fighting, but she's heard enough conversation between Seta, Nyla and Jake to know she wasn't someone to mess with. "Benefit of the doubt about what?"

The vampire-witch lowered her gaze to Khiderian and then looked up toward the sky. "Pranic vampires don't have a great deal of immunity to sunlight, regardless of their age, and especially not drained as this one is. Let's get him inside and then we'll talk."

Seta walked forward and placed an elegantly fingered hand on Khiderian's shoulder. Marilee gasped again as they both disappeared. Her heart seized in her chest but then the two reappeared inside the room. Seta laid Khiderian on the bed as if he weighed nothing and rose to her full height, which wasn't considerable, before arching a black crescent eyebrow. "Waiting for an invitation?"

Marilee closed the car door, making sure to lock it first, and entered the room, securing the door behind her. She quickly closed the shades, blocking out the light. When she turned toward Seta it was to see her scowling at

Khiderian. Suspicion settled in her chest and she wished Khiderian would wake up to help her. "Khiderian said you were tracking us. Did you decide to just sit back and watch while we were attacked?"

The witch's eyes widened at this news, and from what Marilee could tell, she appeared genuinely alarmed. Of course she was centuries old. She'd had plenty of time to hone her acting skills. "I would never sit back and watch a fight. Trust me when I say I would choose one side and help destroy the other." She glanced at Khiderian again. "Your vampire appears to be psychically drained and physically weakened to an alarming degree. He's in the deep sleep now."

Marilee nibbled on her bottom lip as she studied Khiderian lying supine on the bed, dried blood smeared on his skin though the scratches were already starting to heal. "Will he be okay?"

"He will heal with the deep sleep and some blood," Seta answered as she turned narrowed eyes on her. "But whether he makes it out of here living or dead depends on the answers I get from the two of you. I saw you trying to locate Curtis Dunn and discussing Jacob Porter. Why?"

"Move away from Khiderian and I'll answer your questions." Marilee tightened her hands into fists, more to stop the trembling in them than to appear threatening. She knew she could breathe fire and shoot lasers out of her eyes and still not threaten the powerful being in front of her. However, she could bargain with Seta. "I'll tell you nothing if you harm him."

Seta grinned, clearly amused, and stepped away from the bed to cross the room. "You realize I could kill him just as easily from over here," she said as she leaned against the opposite wall and folded her arms beneath her ample breasts. "Especially in his state."

"Why would you want to kill him when you're part of the same team?"

The twinkle of humor in Seta's deep brown eyes faded out. "What team would that be?"

"The team that rescues Jake from the hell-hoochies," Marilee answered carefully, not sure how much information Khiderian wanted the vampire-witch to have. She wished again he would wake up but he needed the deep sleep to heal him.

"How do you know about the sirens?"

SIREN'S SNARE

"How do *you* know about the sirens?" Marilee turned the question back around on her, delighting in the flicker of annoyance she caught in the woman's eye. "Don't look at me all suspicious and demand answers. Were you not with Jake more recently than I was?"

Marilee felt pressure in her head, a strange sense of filtering going on inside and realized Seta was trying to read her mind. Just as quickly, she felt a snap as if Seta's attempt to intrude snapped back on her. The pressure quickly subsided. Seta's hands tightened, giving away her temper. "Is there a point to that question?"

"I wouldn't do anything to harm Jake Porter. I don't believe you would either so why are we playing this game?"

"Game?" Seta scoffed. "Do you really think I'm here to play a game with you, mortal?"

Sweat trickled down the center of Marilee's back as she held Seta's glare of death. "No. I think you're here because Jake has been captured and you want to free him, but can't. Khiderian and I are going to free him. We are on the same side."

Seta cast a glance at Khiderian. "This is a pranic vampire. The same type of vampire brought Jacob Porter to the sirens' attention in the first place. The same type of vampire worked with were-hyenas to try and kill him." She redirected her gaze to Marilee. "How long have you known this man you claim to be your ally?"

Marilee licked her lips, discovering them suddenly dry. "All my life."

Seta raised an eyebrow to that. "You didn't seem to know a great deal about vampires when we came upon you in Hicksville, but you did learn quickly and proved to be helpful in combat. Now it makes sense."

Marilee shook her head at Seta's accusatory expression. "You don't understand. I knew him all my life yet I've only just met him. There's no big trick here."

"Really?" Seta cocked her head to the side, studying her. "You meet Jake in Hicksville, walk out of that dreadful little town without a scratch after the majority of it was killed off, and now I happen upon a vision of you aiding a pranic vampire in the supposed rescue of Jacob Porter by searching for a demon? I don't believe in coincidence."

"You believe in prophecy."

Seta's eyes widened briefly before becoming slits. "What do you know of prophecy?"

Marilee glanced over at Khiderian, who still lay still as death on the bed, and chewed the corner of her bottom lip. "Khiderian can answer any further questions you have when he comes out of the deep sleep." She met Seta's gaze. "We really are on the same side. I wouldn't go against you and Jake after you saved my life."

Seta nodded, seeming to be mollified by that response, then wrinkled her nose. "You are a filthy mess. Go shower and change. We'll discuss this attack you two fell under after you're clean."

"And leave you alone with Khiderian while he's vulnerable? Hell no."

Seta blinked. "You are very brave for a human."

"Or very stupid," Marilee muttered. "Doesn't matter. I'm not leaving him alone with you."

Seta chuckled. "Fine, then, but he's taken a lot of damage and the deep sleep will hold him longer than I have patience for. I can heal him and you, then we can all have a nice little chat."

Marilee stepped before the foot of the bed as Seta made to approach Khiderian. "How do I know you won't do something to hurt him?"

"Could you really stop me if I chose to hurt him?" Seta angled her head to the side before shaking it. "Know which battles to fight, young one. Trust me to take care of him as I took care of you in Hicksville."

"You've already threatened to kill him."

"I want the truth, Marilee. If the truth reveals he has malicious intent toward Jacob Porter I will kill him. Would you not?"

Marilee swallowed hard. Khiderian had defended her in battle, but so had Jake. If one was against the other, she would have to pick a side, even if it meant going against the one person who knew what she really was. Hoping she was making the right choice, she stepped away from the bed and let Seta approach.

The vampire-witch grabbed Khiderian's shirt by the collar and effortlessly ripped the material in half, revealing a muscular torso marred with cuts and blood. A spark of jealousy flared as the vampire-witch lay her hands on Khiderian's perfectly sculpted chest and closed her eyes. Marilee turned away, angered by the thought of another woman touching the vampire, and confused as to why. Despite being exceedingly attractive, Khiderian was still a vampire. Nothing would change that.

Her emotions somewhat in check, she turned back to watch Seta work her magic. Literally. Nothing seemed to be going on. There was no glow of light from her hands, no hum of power in the room though she did feel a slight shift in the air, a gathering of energy. As she watched, Khiderian's wounds healed within seconds, the blood on his skin the only indication they'd ran into trouble.

"Now for you." Seta took a deep breath and pointed to a chair next to the small wooden table by the window. "Sit and let me close up that wound on your thigh."

Marilee did as told, watching Khiderian as Seta rested her hands over her injured leg and focused with eyes closed on repairing the damage. A slight heated sensation traveled the length of her thigh and then all the ache and discomfort disappeared. She glanced down to see her skin smooth and unmarred, just a little blood remaining where the wound used to be. "Thanks."

"No problem at all." Seta straightened. "As I said, you helped Jake once. However, if I find out you are not loyal to him you will have far worse wounds to worry about."

"Keep threatening her and you'll be too dead to do a damn thing." Khiderian sat up on the bed and Seta instantly flew backward, smacking into the wall where he held her immobile with his power. "Thanks for helping me out with the flesh wounds, witch, but I haven't been in the deep sleep for at least the past five minutes. I was astral feeding. Marilee, go shower and change into clean clothing."

Marilee glanced between the two powerful vampires, noting the contempt they both held in their eyes as they stared one another down, and shook her head. "No. What are you going to do?"

"Do as you're told, Marilee." His eyes never left the vampire-witch pinned to the wall.

"I'm not your child to command." She stood and planted her hands on her hips. "We're all working on the same team here. I don't want anyone hurt."

"No one will be hurt if you do as I say and go clean yourself off now." His voice came out as a growl and the vein in his right temple bulged.

"Do as he says, young one." Seta spoke softly. "He needs blood and he can smell yours. He's listening to your heart pumping right now."

"She's right, Marilee. Please go wash up before I lose control."

Marilee glanced down at the blood still coating her exposed skin and quickly ran out to the car to retrieve her bag from the trunk. Seta remained pinned to the wall when she returned, locking the door behind her, and Khiderian still hadn't taken his eyes off her. He didn't even blink as she crossed between the two of them to get to the bathroom. "I want both of you alive when I get out of here," she said, pausing at the door.

"We should be." Khiderian's tone held a hint of warning. Marilee swallowed hard and prayed for the best outcome as she closed the bathroom door behind her and turned on the shower.

"Make any sudden moves and you will not live to regret it." Khiderian released his psychic hold over the vampire-witch before he gave in to the desire to wince from the pressure in his head. Astral feeding off the nearby motel clerk and some of the people currently occupying other rooms in the building had helped him to regain the mental power lost in the attack, but the witch was right. He needed blood and he needed it badly. Until he got it, he was no physical match for her. He had to make her believe his psychic abilities more than compensated in case she did anything stupid. He knew enough about the petite beauty to know she had a volatile nature.

Seta pulled away from the wall and straightened her top, shooting daggers with her dark eyes. "Man-handle me again and see what happens, parasite."

Khiderian grinned as he made a show of taking off his damaged shirt and relaxing against the pillows mounted before the headboard of the bed. "Well, if that isn't the blood-sucking pot calling the kettle black."

"I feed off blood, yes, but what else do you feed off?" She folded her arms, the action pushing up her breasts. "You know why I'm here. You somehow knew I had a vision of you and blocked me."

"Just a little witch's net worked into my mind shield to keep you away. Nothing to get upset over."

"Let's cut to the chase, soul-sucker. What do you know about Jacob Porter and why are you looking for the demon who nearly got us all killed?"

"If not for Alfred or Curtis Dunn, whatever he's calling himself these days, Jacob Porter wouldn't be alive now." He looked Seta straight in the eye. "The immortality serum he injected into Porter has saved the man's life quite a few times already. We need to locate him to make sure Porter survives even longer."

"You know what's happening to Jacob?"

"Do I know that he's being killed repeatedly? Yes. Do I know there's a chance the serum will quit doing its job without blood to act as a booster? Yes."

Seta stepped forward. "Why waste time looking for Dunn instead of going in to save Jacob?"

Khiderian shrugged. "I have my orders and my orders state Marilee and I locate Dunn first."

Seta frowned at this news. "Orders? Orders from who?"

"The Dream Teller."

The vampire-witch's eyes darkened. "You work for that old hag?"

"That old hag has helped save your loved ones more than once." Khiderian leaned forward, his ire sparked. "You should show her more respect. It's not her fault you didn't listen when she tried to warn you that your son would be taken from you if you continued to think with your foolish young heart and not your head."

"How dare you speak to me like that."

"You don't scare me, Seta. I respect your power and believe me, I know what you're capable of." He grinned at her shocked expression. The fiery witch wasn't used to being cut off by those who knew the extent of her power. "Kill me if you like but you'll be screwing yourself in the process. I'm a pranic vampire and older than you. You can't rip off my head and work a spell to get answers from my ashes like you've done with others in the past. When I die, all I know goes with me. You can't break into my mind because when it comes to mental abilities, I'm a heavyweight contender and you're barely able to step in the ring."

The vampire-witch fumed, and Khiderian could imagine steam building up inside her head just waiting to escape through her ears. The image brought a grin to his face. "Face it, Seta. If you want to know something from me, you're going to have to ask nicely and hope I'm in a generous mood."

"Just who the hell are you?"

"Khiderian, one of the oldest pranic vampires still standing and one of the Dream Teller's most trusted soldiers. Ask her. She'll vouch for me."

Seta looked him over, studying him with contempt. "So you know Jacob Porter is more than just a slayer?"

"Yes. I know about the children. Slade and Njeri," he added, earning a startled look. "My job, Seta, is to protect those children and all involved in their upbringing. My current mission is to save the slayer so he can train and protect his son."

"Why are you with the human?"

Relief flooded his body as he concluded the witch didn't realize Marilee had special abilities. He'd feared it despite knowing the slayer himself hadn't picked up on her skills. Being human, albeit a human with a very rare ability, shielded her from their radars. Then there was the added protection she had from witches. "Sometimes humans can be useful. Jacob Porter's capture was prophesied, as was his rescue by a human. Marilee is that human."

Seta gawked. "That little sprig of a girl?"

"She's a full grown woman." Khiderian grinned. "You should talk about size, Seta. You're not exactly an Amazon."

The vampire-witch rolled her eyes. "I'm not exactly human either and I've been battling immortals far longer than she has. How is she supposed to rescue Jacob?"

"I'll be with her. Her job is to take out the sirens. I'll get the rest."

Seta arched an eyebrow and stared pointedly at the places on his body she'd healed. "For both her and Jacob's sake, I hope you do better than you did this time. What happened?"

"We were attacked by vampires, shape-shifters, and even a witch," he snapped. "Trust me, I didn't go down easily and if I'd had enough blood I wouldn't have. I'll be sure to properly feed from now on."

"You should have before this last battle." Seta's mouth curved into a half-grin, half-sneer. "I'm guessing the human frowns on feeding. You've neglected to take care of yourself in fear of repulsing her."

Khiderian glanced away as the heat of embarrassment crept up his neck. "I blocked you for a reason. There's suspicion the other side is working with powerful psychics, otherwise they wouldn't know about the children, which we suspect they do."

The mention of the children worked, grabbing Seta's attention and forcing her off the topic of his feelings for Marilee quick and efficiently. "They know the children have been born then."

"We believe so. The Dream Teller has been trying to locate Jake and get a full picture of his surroundings including his captors."

"So have I." She turned up her lip in a sneer. "He's surrounded by sirens who taunt him relentlessly, but they can't be alone. They worked with pranic vampires last time, and were-hyenas."

"There were multiple shape-shifters in the attack tonight," Khiderian informed her. "Ravens for sure. I believe there were werebears and weresnakes too. The vampires who attacked weren't pranic, just the regular blood-sucking variety. They weren't very old."

"You mentioned a witch." Seta frowned. "Witches have psychic abilities. Depending on how powerful the one you went up against is… Did you get a feel for the witch's age?"

"Old enough that I was completely drained of psychic power after reversing her magic on her," he admitted. "It would have injured her badly but I seriously doubt it killed her. She's still out there, still working her dark magic and you know what she's looking for."

"The children." Seta's eyes widened, a flicker of fear—an emotion the witch wasn't known for showing—flashed behind them.

"Exactly, which is why I blocked you. You're the most powerful witch on our side. Saving Porter is a mission for Marilee and me. Your mission is to guard those children. You shouldn't be here." He frowned, wondering how she'd found them. He'd witch-proofed his mind, ensuring she couldn't locate them through him, and being what she was, Marilee had natural protection against witches. "How did you find us?"

Seta grinned impishly. "You're not the only vampire who uses humans when they prove valuable." She turned her head toward the bathroom as the water stopped and the shower curtain swished aside. Her dark eyes held warning as she swung her head back to look at him. "I'll trust you for now. I know the Dream Teller wouldn't reveal herself to someone unless they were a part of the prophecy, but if it's just the two of you on this mission you have to take care of yourself, regardless what the human thinks, or how you fear her revulsion."

Khiderian opened his mouth to deny the accusation, but Seta disappeared just as Marilee stepped out of the bathroom in a clean pair of cutoffs and a little blue Hicksville Roosters T-shirt, the fragrant smell of soap wafting around her. The hand she used to towel dry her long hair stilled as she looked around the room and her heartbeat increased. "What happened to Seta?"

"I didn't kill her." Khiderian quickly stood, desperate to get away from her beating heart and find sustenance but he fell back onto the bed before he could manage a step. The room spun and his stomach cramped. Damn, he needed blood.

"Khiderian? Are you okay?" Marilee sat on the bed next to him. "You look pale."

He couldn't help laughing at that. "According to lore, I'm supposed to be."

"Yeah, well, obviously the books and movies got that part wrong. What's the matter with you?"

He ground his teeth together as her heartbeat boomed through his head, teasing him. "I have to get out of here."

"You're too weak."

"Simple fix for that." He rose again, slower this time, and headed to the door, straining to keep it in focus through the dizziness while pushing his legs to carry him farther.

"Khiderian, you're in no shape to go out in daylight." She cut him off at the door. "You said you'd fed while Seta was here. Shouldn't you be okay until nightfall?"

"I need blood, Marilee." Sweat broke out along his brow as he struggled to stand upright. "Astral feeds give me psychic power but they don't give me strength. I hadn't fed well before the attack and with the blood I lost, I have no choice. I need blood and I need it now."

He moved to step past her but she gripped his arms, halting him. "You're sweating. You never sweat. Geez. How much do you need to get by until nightfall?"

Realizing her intent, he backed away. "No. I won't take it from you." Black spots floated before his eyes and he backed up until the back of his legs hit the bed and fell on it to stop the waves of dizziness. "I'll be fine as long as I lay down. I'll survive, but I'm hungry. You can't be in here."

"Khiderian."

"Your heartbeat is driving me crazy!" He breathed in deep, closed his eyes, and tried to push out the steady staccato as blood pulsated through the organ but his hunger was far greater than his focus. "Please leave. I can reach into the motel clerk's mind from here and secure you another room." The mattress dipped and her sweet scent—flowers and vanilla—surrounded him. Her heartbeat blared as her light weight settled over him. He opened his eyes to find her straddling his lap, her wrist held out in offering. "Take enough to get you by until nightfall."

Blinking, he rose to his elbows while trying to think through the hunger consuming him. "You're really offering your blood to me?"

She nodded, swallowed so heavily he could see it. "I know it's kind of late but I do need to thank you for saving me from Hank. I might not like what you did with him later but you protected me. I owe you for that."

He licked his lips and glanced at the offered wrist. The thin blue vein pulsing with life called to him. Scrounging up the willpower, he shook his head. "No, Marilee. I went too long without feeding and then lost blood. As hungry as I am now I don't trust myself to stop after just a little. It'll take a lot of psychic energy but I can lure someone to the room and feed off their blood. Then I'll just astral feed again to regain—"

"I can't sit by and allow you to feed off someone unwilling." Marilee rose and crossed over to her duffel bag sitting on the table. He tightened his fists against the urge to psychically force her into sleep so he could feed. If he used mind power on her, she'd never trust him again and there'd be no use trying to train her. Their mission would fail.

She turned around and held up her hands, showing the shine of hawthorn oil on her palms. "I'll stop you if you don't stop yourself," she said, coming back to the bed. Instead of straddling him, she sat closer to the headboard and held out a wrist. "Drink, Khiderian. I'm not leaving this room so you can feed off someone against their will and I'm not going to watch you suffer through the day."

He mustered the strength to sit up and she stretched out her arm. Leaning forward, he stopped short. "The hawthorn oil will touch my face. I can't drink from your wrist."

"Oh." Marilee's eyes widened. "Not my throat, Khiderian. That's too much like an attack."

Guilt punched Khiderian in the gut. He should have fed adequately and avoided this predicament, being forced to feed off someone repulsed and genuinely frightened of the act. "I won't do anything that makes you feel threatened, Marilee." He lowered his gaze to the little scrap of denim she wore. "There's another place I can feed from."

She followed his gaze and gulped. "Khiderian."

"Trust me, Marilee. The femoral artery is right here." He reached out and touched the inside of her thigh, thankful for the little shorts she liked to wear. "Right in plain view. I would never violate you."

He watched as emotions ranging from curiosity to fear and even a dash of excitement swirled in her eyes, and finally she nodded. "Okay, but don't get greedy."

He grinned. "I'm bare from the waist up, remember? Plenty of places to burn me with the hawthorn oil and make me stop if I do."

"Don't you forget it." The tone she used hinted at bravado but the tremble in her voice gave away her anxiety. Her body stiffened as she stretched her legs out on the bed and took a deep breath. "Go on."

He massaged her inner thigh, frowning as she jumped. "Relax, Marilee. It won't hurt if you don't tense up."

She took another deep breath and eased the tension in her body though her heartbeat steadily increased. The sound of it whet Khiderian's appetite and made it hard to pace himself, but he was determined to hold true to his word. He wouldn't hurt her, and if he had any power over it, he wouldn't scare her. Hand trembling, he massaged her thigh until the stiffness completely left her leg. "Lie back, Marilee, and bend your knee."

"No. I want to see you."

Anger burned behind his eyes. "I'm not going to rip your leg open. You can trust me that much."

"I do, but it's like getting a shot. If I see the needle go in, it's not so bad because I'm ready for it."

He'd never had a shot, his natural immunity making such things unnecessary even before he'd been changed into a vampire, which of course was long before such things were invented anyway, but he could see her logic. "Are you ready?"

"Yes."

He rose to his knees, fighting off dizziness and the animalistic hunger that urged him to do exactly what he said he wouldn't and tear into her, and stacked the pillows behind her, easing her down on them. "There, you're still elevated enough to see what I'm doing."

She nodded in agreement and looked at him with eyes begging him not to hurt her. His gut clenched, Khiderian slipped a hand beneath her thigh and raised her leg so it bent at the knee. He leaned over her and ran his tongue over the flesh covering the thick vein he would puncture. Marilee jerked away, scooting as far back against the headboard as she could. "What are you doing?"

Khiderian closed his eyes and breathed in deep, fighting back irritation. "My saliva has properties that heal the flesh after it's been broken and also serve as anesthetic to prevent pain. If I just bite into you, it will hurt and I know you don't want me using my power to mask the pain psychically."

"Oh. Okay." She eased back down and positioned herself for him to feed. "Sorry."

He offered her a little smile, letting her know he wasn't angry, and leaned forward again. The leash on his hunger barely there, he forced himself to take his time and lave the area he'd be biting into. She let out a little sigh that fueled his hunger even more but he managed to remain calm as his fangs extended and he carefully slid them into her thigh.

Marilee gasped, but didn't pull away which Khiderian was thankful for. The last thing he wanted to do was rip her flesh because she yanked away while his fangs were in her. Pulling back, he allowed blood to well above the marks and lapped up the life preserving nectar. The coppery liquid poured at a steady pace from the wound, ebbing his thirst and fueling his body with much needed strength.

Marilee squirmed and let out a soft gasp, and suddenly Khiderian was starving again, but what he wanted from her involved more than just her blood. He'd intended to only take a few sips to get by until nightfall, but the sound of her pleasure egged him on. He grew hard as he suckled at her thigh, wishing he could taste other places, and he was thankful she couldn't see how turned on he was from her vantage point. Feeding off her had been a bad idea, a very, very bad idea.

He had to stop. It was easy. Just quit drinking and seal the wound.

But he couldn't do it. Her blood tasted sweeter than any he'd ever sampled and he'd been around long enough to have sampled his fair share so he continued to drink her life essence, one hand caressing her outer thigh as the other played with the hem of her T-shirt, slowly easing underneath.

"Khiderian."

His name as a whimper from her mouth sounded so good, he hoped with everything he had she wouldn't ask him to stop, but even in the haze of his hungry, aroused mind he knew he could only take so much blood. He forced himself to stop drinking and sealed the punctures with his tongue. They would have sealed themselves from the saliva already there, but he wanted the excuse to lick her once more.

He started to pull away but she squirmed again, let out a labored breath, and he was a goner. Before he could think better of it, he whispered a kiss across the spot he'd drank from, trailed a few over her hip until he reached the exposed skin at her belly. He'd already inched her shirt up to just below her breasts while feeding and she hadn't stopped him so he slid his hands all the way underneath, cupping the small mounds over the lace of her bra. When she arched her back, pushing them further into his hands he nearly burst through his zipper. Pushing up the fabric, he suckled her over the bra until she whimpered and dropped kisses up her chest, along her jaw... He wanted to kiss her lips but feared her reaction to the taste of blood in his mouth, so he bypassed that treasure to drop open mouthed kisses along her throat, easing into the crook of her neck.

"No!" She gripped his shoulders and shoved, the flesh where she touched him burning from the hawthorn oil. Khiderian quickly jerked away, escaping the pain, and she leapt off the bed, falling to her knees.

"Marilee."

"Stay away from me." She turned toward him and watched him cautiously as she scooted farther away, eyes wide with fear. She jerked her shirt back down over her breasts and raised a hand to the side of her neck.

Khiderian cursed his ignorance. "I didn't bite you there, Marilee. I wouldn't do that after you told me not to."

"You were supposed to take some blood from me, not manipulate me."

"Manipulate you?" Anger surged as he recalled the way she'd squirmed as he suckled her thigh, breathed heavy with the arousal she felt just as much as he had. She hadn't told him to stop until her shirt was almost over her damn head, hadn't thought about stopping until he'd settled his mouth over the vein in her neck, reminding her he could rip into it. Until that moment, she'd enjoyed every bit of his attention and he opened his mouth to tell her, but stopped as he took in the fear still in her eyes.

She was so young, just a baby compared to him. Despite being ravenous he should have been in control of the situation. Looking down at himself, disgust churned in his stomach. Maybe he had manipulated her in some way. Why would she have wanted him inside her while he still bore the blood of his enemies on his skin? "I'm sorry, Marilee. It won't happen again."

He rose from the bed, stretched, felt the strength of her precious blood zinging in his body. "Can you get up?" He wanted to hold his hand out and help her stand, but knew she'd just bat it away. That simple act would burn more than if she allowed him to touch her hawthorn covered hand.

She slowly managed to get to her feet and stand straight. "I'm fine. I just got a little lightheaded when I first got up."

"Are you better now?"

She nodded meekly and he felt even more like a heel. "I'm sorry. I should have made sure you ate first before I even thought of taking any blood. I forget sometimes the importance of being well nourished before donating."

"I'm fine. I just need to rest."

"The bed is yours," Khiderian offered as he noticed she'd rented a room that only had one bed. A small loveseat rested against the other wall. He'd cram his body into it or just take the floor if he couldn't manage to. Marilee's bag rested atop the small table in front of a plastic display stand that bore an ad for a 24-hour pizza delivery place. His things were nowhere in sight. "Did you get my sword?"

"It's in the trunk. So are your other knives. I didn't bring any of your things in but I can get whatever you need."

"Thank you." He swallowed hard, shame flushing heat into his face. He'd been so drained he'd collapsed after turning the witch's magic back on her and the deep sleep had claimed him at some point soon after, but even it couldn't fully heal his body until he fed. He'd woken to find Marilee confronted by Seta and had to astral feed before being able to step in. Anything could have happened. "If you can get me a change of clothes, I'd appreciate it, and..." He walked over to the table and picked up the ad for the pizza place. "There's cash in my bag. Order yourself a pizza."

Marilee took the ad from him and nodded, avoiding his gaze. "Thank you."

"Order as much food and drink as you like. You need to replenish the nutrients you just lost." Khiderian turned and headed for the bathroom. He paused inside the doorway and turned back to look at the woman who'd defended him against Seta, yet still looked at him as if he were vile. "Thank you again, Marilee, for sharing your blood. I know it was a hard thing for you to do. I'll make sure you'll never have to again."

She didn't respond, didn't even look at him, and though he half expected that reaction it still hurt deep in his chest as he stepped inside the bathroom, pulling the door closed behind him. He cared too much, wanted something that would never be, and he had to stop it for both their sakes. She was still dazed by everything that happened but she'd remember the voices and ask him what they were, how he knew about them. He would have to tell her the truth.

Then any shot of them ever being anything more than partners on this mission would be completely obliterated, he thought as he stripped and stepped under the shower spray.

CHAPTER NINE

Marilee's hands shook as she set Khiderian's bag on the table along with his sword, two knives, and her dagger. All of the weapons needed a good cleaning but she didn't have the stomach for it now. She scooted the bag so it hid the weapons from view and stepped over to the bed where she'd left the pizza ad.

Her stomach was queasy, but Khiderian was right. She needed to eat. She should have stopped him from drinking after a couple minutes had passed, but his warm mouth on her thigh had felt too good. Almost as good as it had felt on the rest of her body.

What was I thinking? She hadn't been. If her brain had been functioning at all she would have never let a vampire that close to her neck. It was bad enough letting one feed off her, but to allow one near such vulnerable spots? The neck? The femoral artery? She might as well have just asked to die. He could have killed her easily and she would have allowed it to happen because she craved the feel of his lips on her skin. "Stupid fool."

Marilee fumed silently as she punched in the number of the pizza place on the motel phone. Someone way too cheery for the early morning hour answered and recited their specials. "No, no, I want—"

She was cut off again as the bubbly woman listed the new breakfast pizzas. Marilee scrunched up her nose at the thought of eggs on a pizza and waited for the woman to end her spiel so she could place her order, a large cheese pizza, an orange juice, and six bottled waters. Surely that would be enough to get through the day.

The bathroom door creaked as she lowered the phone back into its base. Turning, she caught sight of Khiderian emerging in a white terry towel slung low over his hips. Rivulets of water ran from the ends of his hair down his muscular torso as he walked over to his bag and extracted clothing. As usual, he chose to wear all black.

Glancing her way, Khiderian arched an inky black eyebrow. "Are you all right?"

Marilee realized she'd stopped breathing, the air stolen from her lungs as she took in the perfect vision before her, and quickly amended that problem. "I'm fine. I just ordered something to eat. It'll be here soon."

"Good." He peered over his bag at where the weapons lay. "I'll get these blades cleaned off. I would clean your dagger, but the hawthorn makes it difficult for me to do so."

"It's okay. I don't mind cleaning it myself once you're done in the bathroom." As she spoke, her eyes strayed to his tight stomach, where ridges bisected his six-pack abs. Her hand reached out on its own volition, aching to trace those lines. Realizing what she was doing, she tightened her hand into a fist and closed her eyes, shutting out temptation. She stayed that way until she heard the bathroom door close.

By the time Khiderian emerged from the bathroom a few minutes later, she'd already switched through a variety of channels on the small television set sitting on the dresser across from the bed. "Nothing's on."

Khiderian directed a curious look at her before glancing toward the television set. "Oh. I don't watch T.V. anyway."

"Never?"

"No." He leaned his sword against the wall and attached two sheaths to his forearms before sliding his other two blades into them.

"Well, we both need to watch it today." Marilee sighed. "We left a lot of bloody mess back at that field. I'm sure it'll make the news."

Khiderian stiffened. "How bad did we leave it?"

"The vampires were smoking when we left so they probably went up in flames shortly after I started driving away, but the shifters were still scattered all over the field. It was a bloodbath, if you remember, and there wasn't anything I could do except grab our weapons and go. The sun was starting to come up and I had to get you to safety."

He winced as he sat next to her at the foot of the bed. "I'm sorry, Marilee. Had I properly fed—mentally and physically—I'd have been in much better shape and could have cleaned up our mess."

"It's not your fault." She clicked through a few more channels until she found an online guide. She read the listings, searching for a news program, and turned the T.V. to a station that would be airing news in twenty minutes. "Without your help, I wouldn't have made it out of that. I've never seen such things before."

"Shapeshifters generally don't work together, but I know I saw ravens, snakes, and bears in that mix. The fact they were united against us is alarming to say the least."

"How did they find us?" she asked, her body chilled. "And where did the voices in my head come from?"

Khiderian ran a hand down his face and leaned forward, resting his elbows on his knees. He seemed to study the grungy brown carpet for a moment before speaking. "I'll tell you about the voices after you've eaten. As for how we were found, I think the witch worked some kind of magic."

"Like Seta did?"

"Seta used a human, I would guess a psychic, to locate us. The witch working with the other side may have as well, or..."

"What?" Marilee prodded.

"I'll explain after you've eaten."

"Explain it now." Her tone came out sharp. The look in Khiderian's eyes did nothing to calm her frazzled nerves. "I just sliced and diced animal-people for crying out loud, while voices filled my head, the same voices that spoke to me in the cemetery when I was a kid. I want to know what all this was about and I want to know now."

"After you've eaten." Khiderian stood and walked across the room, turning back toward her with arms folded. "The answers won't change from now until you get a good meal."

"So why wait?" Marilee threw her arms up in exasperation.

"Because if I tell you now, you might not have the stomach to eat, and it's important that you do."

She stared at the tall, imposing vampire until her eyes burned and he didn't so much as blink the entire time. Giving up that particular line of questioning, she rubbed her fingers over the spot on her leg that Seta had healed. "Then at least answer me this. A man bit me in the leg really bad. I don't know if he was vampire or shifter because I sliced him open so quickly it was hard to tell if he fell away because of that or the hawthorn oil on my skin." She looked up to see the closest resemblance to fear she'd ever seen in Khiderian's eyes. "Am I in trouble?"

Sitting next to her on the bed, he touched her forehead with the back of his hand and ran it down the side of her face to the base of her neck. "There are different types of shape-shifters. Skin-walkers, therians, weres, and lycanthropes. Therians and skin-walkers are very rare so the likelihood of any of those being in the battle with us is miniscule. Weres don't tend to socialize outside their own sub-race and I know I saw ravens, snakes, and I think bears."

Marilee nodded, recalling the man with two fangs in his mouth, and the bear-like paw she'd barely dodged. "So we were dealing with lycanthropes? As in lycanthropy?"

"You're not running a fever." He glanced over at the clock on the nightstand. "You would be running a fever by now if you were infected."

She gulped, her heart racing so quickly it was difficult to breathe evenly. "So I could actually be turned into one of those things?"

"If you were badly bitten by one, yes." Khiderian placed an arm around her shoulders and pulled her close, tucking her into the side of his body. "I think a vampire bit your leg, sweetheart. You don't have to worry."

"Until the next time we go up against those things and one does take a bite out of me!" She broke out of his embrace and crossed the room, pacing the floor, her arms folded to keep the shakes under control. "I can't do this."

"Yes you can." Khiderian stepped in front of her and gripped her shoulders, halting her before she spun around to retrace the path she'd just taken. He held her tight until she looked up into his stern blue eyes. "You were chosen for this mission. You are the only one who can complete it."

"No." She shook her head. "I'm human. I may be able to get past the sirens without them sucking me into one of their snares, but I have no immunity against the others. I can be turned into a vampire or a lycanthrope or... I don't even know what else. Hasn't my life been bad enough? I just want to be normal."

"You're as normal as anyone else, Marilee. We all have our own quirks, even humans. You're not a freak."

"Yeah? Then why can't you tell me what the voices in my head belonged to?"

Khiderian opened his mouth to respond, but was interrupted by a knock on the door. Irritation flashed through his eyes and he turned his head toward the door, his brow knit in concentration. Figuring her pizza had arrived, Marilee stepped toward the door, but Khiderian's arm shot out to block her.

The bolt on the door slid to the right and it swung open. Khiderian stepped out of the path of sunlight that shone through and instructed Marilee to pay for her order as the deliveryman stood stock-still, his eyes glazed over as he stared straight ahead.

"What are you doing to him?" Marilee asked as she rooted through Khiderian's bag for the money he'd told her about.

"Depending on what we hear on the news, we may not want anyone to know of our presence here. Don't worry. I'm not hurting him, I'm only keeping him from remembering us after he leaves."

Marilee found a wad of cash and pulled it out of the bag. The deliveryman didn't move as she approached so Marilee unzipped the red heat absorbing nylon bag he carried and removed the pizza inside. Another bag, a cooler one, held the orange juice and waters she'd ordered. After depositing everything on the bed, she found the ticket with the amount she owed on it and slipped enough bills to cover the charge plus a hefty tip into the innocent man's hand. She had to clamp his fingers around it. "Okay. You can release him now," she advised as she backed away from him.

"Thank you for ordering from Night And Day Pizzeria. Have a great day," the man said, his tone robotic, as he turned sharply and walked toward the car he'd parked next to Khiderian's rental. The door slammed closed behind him and the lock slid back into place. Khiderian sat down hard on the bed and lowered his head into his hands.

"Are you okay?" Marilee crossed over to the bed and kneeled on the floor before him. He jerked back as she started to rest her hands on his knees.

"Don't touch me. You still have traces of the hawthorn oil on your hands."

She looked down at her hands and let out a soft curse. "Sorry. I forgot." She quickly rose and went into the bathroom to wash the oil off.

When she returned, Khiderian was in the same position. "You didn't feed well off the motel clerk, did you?"

"He wasn't guilty of anything except enjoying porn a little too much," Khiderian answered, "so I only fed from him. It was nothing like what you witnessed me doing with the man who attacked you. Despite what you believe, I don't go around randomly killing to strengthen my power."

His accusation stung as she put the bottled waters she'd ordered into the small refrigerator in the room and sat on the bed to sip the orange juice. "You'll need to feed both ways before we leave tonight then."

"Are you going to give me any trouble regarding that?"

The juice suddenly tasted bitter. Marilee twisted the cap back on and lowered the plastic bottle. "You weakened during the battle because you hadn't properly fed, didn't you?"

Khiderian sighed as he straightened, and ran a large hand down his face. "Yes, which is why regardless how you feel about it, I must feed properly from now on. My ability to protect you and see that we complete this mission depends on it."

He could have died on that field because of her. Guilt slammed into Marilee's chest and nearly drew a tear to her eye. He'd saved her when cruel children tried to bury her alive. He'd saved her yet again when she'd been attacked by Hank, and she'd been nothing but an ungrateful bitch to him just because he drank blood and could do things with his mind that scared her. She could also do things that scared people. Didn't it hurt when they labeled her a freak and a monster? Yet she'd went right ahead and did it to him. And she'd accused him of manipulating her when he'd done exactly what she'd wanted. His mouth and hands on her body had been what she'd craved since meeting him, if she were being honest with herself. She'd have been madder if he *hadn't* shared the desire she felt. But her fear of the unknown made her reject him, and in such a cold way too. Disgusted, she lowered the juice bottle to the floor and crawled over to him. She scooted up against his back and wrapped her arms around him, lowering her head onto his shoulder.

He stiffened instantly. "Marilee?"

"I'm sorry." She turned her head to meet his surprised gaze. "You've done nothing but protect me and teach me how to protect myself and I've been such an unappreciative brat." She chuckled as he raised his eyebrow, too stunned to speak. "You've never actually sucked out a person's soul, have you?"

He grinned. "No."

"Why didn't you tell me that when I accused you of doing it?"

He shrugged, as much as he could with her draped over him and lowered his head, breaking eye contact. "I figured you'd believe whatever you wanted to believe. As long as you allowed me to train you for the mission, I chose not to argue with you unless I absolutely had to."

Another pang of self-disgust flared in Marilee's chest as she stared at the corner of Khiderian's mouth. She'd wanted him to kiss her so bad, still did, even though she didn't deserve it from him. Biting her lip, she wondered what he'd do if she kissed him right now. It didn't matter. She'd never do it, too scared of screwing up and embarrassing herself. Despite her age and being the town whore's daughter, she'd never actually kissed a man. The closest she'd come to being intimate with a man—she wasn't going to count the attempted rapes—was what she'd done with Khiderian earlier. Seeing the way her mother was treated because of her promiscuity, and often being labeled a slut herself due to it, she'd vowed to not have sex, not even kiss a man unless she really cared about him and had his respect. The fact that she wanted her first kiss to be with a centuries old vampire frazzled her nerves. It figured she'd pick a man who would have to have more experience than every leading man in Hollywood combined.

"Marilee?"

"Yeah?"

"You're boring a hole into me."

"Oh." Feeling as though she'd been caught with her hand in the cookie jar, Marilee quickly scooted back and opened the pizza box. "Sorry."

"What were you thinking?" He turned his body toward her.

She frowned as she angled her head to study him. There was nothing on his face that suggested he knew her thoughts and was teasing her about her fear of the attraction she felt for him. Come to think of it, he hadn't seemed to really be that in tune with her thoughts for a while. "I thought you could read my mind like a book."

"I could before I pissed you off by bringing up the tragedies of your past. You subconsciously threw a defensive wall up, blocking me out."

"So you haven't been able to read my mind since then?"

Khiderian shook his head. "Surface thoughts and emotions, but nothing deep. You've sealed your mind up good and tight."

Marilee smiled, realizing he hadn't heard her begging him to touch her while he fed from her thigh, or all the other thoughts that made her blush as she recalled them passing through her mind. "Good. It wasn't fair having all my thoughts read while I couldn't read yours."

Khiderian smiled as he leaned back against the headboard. "It is kind of nice, the unpredictability."

Marilee was sure she blushed as she bit into a slice of cheese pizza. "Do you want some?" She gestured with her hand toward the pie. "I mean... Can you eat pizza?"

He grinned. "Are you asking because it's food or because it's food made with garlic?"

"I asked for it to be made without garlic," Marilee admitted, heat filling her face. "Was that stupid?"

"Yes." Khiderian chuckled. "To my knowledge no vampire has ever been killed or even injured by garlic. Or onions. Or carrots or—"

"Alright, alright." Marilee struck an indignant pose. "I get it. I fell for Hollywood ridiculousness. So can you eat food?"

Khiderian frowned and sat forward to inspect the pizza. "I don't know."

"You don't know? You haven't tried to eat food since you were changed into a vampire? In all that time?"

He shook his head, looking curiously at the pizza. "I see a lot of humans eating those. Are they really good?"

"You've *never* ate pizza?"

"No." He frowned at her. "What?"

Realizing she must be looking at him like he'd just grown a second head, Marilee quit staring. "I'm no history expert but I'm pretty sure pizza's been around since like the 1800's. When were you born?"

"I've been around far longer than that," he replied and Marilee realized he was avoiding a direct answer so she scrutinized him. He appeared white... but he was pretty tan so it was possible he could have a little Hispanic blood in him. He didn't look like those plain, sad-looking people in paintings she'd seen in art classes or like people she'd seen in black and white photos from history books. It seemed he would look like those people if he came from that time. And were men ever so muscular before fitness became so popular? Weren't men from long ago generally portly like Washington or reed thin like Lincoln? "You're staring at me again."

Rolling her eyes, Marilee took a bite out of the pizza. "Of course I'm staring at you. You won't give me an actual answer so I have to figure out your age myself."

"Breaking News. A recent mass killing in the area..."

Marilee nearly snapped her neck turning toward the television set as the news came on and a brunette woman in a rose blouse unfolded the story of multiple bodies being found butchered in a field along with smoking piles of ash. Car tracks indicated there had been at least one person to escape the mayhem and that person or persons were wanted for questioning. "Shit," she muttered as the local sheriff was shown being interviewed.

"I've never seen anything like it in all my years on the job," the graying man said into the camera. "It looks like some sort of sacrifice was done here."

"It's all right, Marilee. They found the bodies but no one actually saw anything."

She quickly shook her head, swallowing hard past the fear clogging her throat before she could speak. "In your condition, I wanted to get you to safety so I didn't drive far. The motel clerk barely looked at me but what if he did while I was walking away? I was worried about you and may not have noticed. I used one of your shirts to cover up but I still had that wound on my leg. If the police come around to local mo—"

Khiderian reached out and cupped her chin. "Relax, Marilee. While I astral fed I cleared the clerk's mind of what he actually noticed and implanted a cover."

She blinked. "A what?"

"I put information in his head suggesting only regulars have been here this week. I know you're smart enough to use a false name when you sign in to a motel. If the log is checked, the clerk will say whatever name you chose belongs to a married woman who comes here often with her lover and always uses an alias."

"Yes." Marilee nodded, her heart still clammering. "But what about when they see your rental with out-of-state plates?"

"It's a rental and can only be traced to the rental company which will be a dead end because I cleared any trace of me out of their mind. They don't have my photo or any other pertinent information because I dipped into the manager's mind and made him hand over the keys, no questions asked. I planted a cover that they gave the car to a charitable organization so it wouldn't be reported as stolen. If asked about it, the motel clerk will tell the police that the car has been sitting there for a couple of weeks and whomever the owner is, they never stayed at this motel."

"You're sure?"

"Positive." He offered a reassuring grin as he lowered his hand. "I'm a vampire, Marilee. I know how to cover my tracks. Now eat."

She looked at the pizza, her stomach now queasy, but she knew he wouldn't tell her about the voices she'd heard until she ate so she picked up another slice. "Do you want to give it a try?" she asked, remembering the curiosity in his eyes as he'd looked at it earlier.

He frowned as he glanced down at the pizza. "No. Now isn't the time to experiment with human food. Suffering ill effects from it would not be good while we're on a mission." He leaned back down against the pillows at the headboard of the bed, waving a hand toward the pizza before resting both hands behind his head and closing his eyes. "Finish your meal and then we'll discuss what happened last night and get some much needed rest."

"Don't get sucked into the deep sleep while I'm eating, thinking that'll buy you a way out of that conversation," Marilee warned. "I'll crawl back in your mind and yank your ass out."

Khiderian's jaw clenched. "If you ever do that again, Marilee, I'll..." He frowned, his eyes still closed. "Just don't do it again. I could accidentally hurt you if you pop in at the wrong time."

Marilee didn't taste the chunk of pizza she swallowed, knowing he told her the truth. "I won't, but don't go into the deep sleep without telling me what I—"

"Eat, woman. I'm not going anywhere."

Grinning, Marilee finished up the pizza, eating the entire pie before chugging down the orange juice. Fighting and forgoing decent meals for a while had made her hungry despite the nerves dancing in her stomach.

SIREN'S SNARE

"Okay, I'm ready to talk," she announced as she rose to set the pizza box next to the wastebasket and toss the empty bottle of juice inside.

Khiderian sat up straighter, leaning forward as she returned to the bed. Face to face, they stared each other down. "What I'm going to tell you isn't going to be an easy thing to hear."

"Wow. Starting off like that isn't helping to keep me calm."

"I'm sorry, but I want you to be braced for the truth. You have a very rare ability, Marilee, but you must remember that despite this gift you are still a human."

She took a deep breath, willing her heart to slow down. "Why would I need to know that before you tell me about the voices?"

"Because you'll think horrible things about yourself. You'll think of yourself as a monster, but you're not. You are very much human, just one who has an ability others don't."

Tears burned at the back of Marilee's eyes. She gritted her teeth and kept them at bay. "You're scaring me, Khiderian. Just spill it already. What is this ability I have?"

"You are a *drac chemare*."

She rolled the odd title through her mind. "What is that? I've never heard of it."

"*Drac chemare* is a Romanian title. It means 'devil caller', which is pretty fitting. You have the rare ability to call demons. Because of this ability, they sense when you are near and try to persuade you to release them."

Marilee's body grew cold as she registered what Khiderian was telling her. The incident at the cemetery came to mind and she remembered the voices she'd heard begging her to release them. "You're telling me that I released demons in the graveyard that night, and they killed those kids?"

Khiderian nodded, his eyes full of sorrow. "You didn't know what you were doing and had released them before I arrived. Thankfully I kept you from drawing them inside yourself. That is the worst thing you can ever do."

"The worst thing I could ever do? The *worst* thing? Are you out of your mind? I killed *children*!"

"The demons killed those children." Khiderian's eyes darkened. "You were just an innocent child yourself."

"No, apparently I wasn't." She stood and raked her hands through her hair. "I bring demons to life! How could I possibly be innocent? I'm a mons—"

"No you're not." Khiderian suddenly stood before her, his hands clamped onto her shoulders. "Look at me. Look at me, dammit." He shook her until she met his gaze. "You are not a monster, or a demon. You're still very much human, Marilee. You just have a very dangerous ability, but as long as you control it, no harm will come from it."

"I don't even know what *it* is. I just hear those things calling me in my head. How am I supposed to control something I don't understand?" The tears she'd been fighting back broke free, trickling down her face as she heaved in a breath. "How do I get it out of me?"

"You don't." Khiderian pulled her close, wrapping his arms around her as he rested his cheek on the top of her head. "I'll teach you how to control the demons just like I taught you how to manipulate the wind. I'm going to be right here with you, all right?"

Marilee sobbed against his chest, dampening the black cotton T-shirt he wore as she circled his waist with her arms and held on tight. "How can you teach me when you don't hear them?"

"I can't call them like you can, and they don't seek me out, but I can destroy them like I did in the cemetery. I have an ability opposite of yours. It's what makes us such a good team."

"How does it work? I remember that night when I wanted to draw back in what I'd done and you said they were never in me. Where did they come from?"

Khiderian sat on the edge of the bed and pulled her onto his lap, his arms still cocooning her in a net of security. "Demons are entities formed of pure evil. They can take on physical form when they possess the weak of faith or when they are called by a *drac chemare*. There are portals between this world and hell. They can't be seen by the naked eye, not even a vampire can see them, but when you are in the vicinity of one they'll sense you and call out to you. You'll feel compelled to respond, especially if you are in danger and frightened."

"Like I was at the cemetery, and during the attack last night."

"Yes. With my ability to kill demons, I also have the ability to sense hell portals. Within seconds of feeling the enemy upon us I felt a portal near. That's how I knew you might be called and how I knew to warn you in advance. I had to stop though and give us time to set up for attack. I think they planned it that way."

"The demons?" Marilee wiped away the wetness from her eyes. "They were working with the others?"

"The Blood Revelation foretells of immortals defeating Satan. Demons serve Satan. The first attack on a chosen immortal was by two demon-possessed men, one of which was the same man who injected Jacob Porter with the immortality serum. He has been very instrumental in the prophecy. Whoever is against us is working with Satan."

Marilee's body grew colder as she recalled the attack in Hicksville. "When vampires invaded Hicksville and killed off most of the town there was a fight inside this little boy's house. Jake made me stay in the car while he and Seta went in to help Nyla. I remember Nyla and Jake talking about how Seta had been burned inside. She'd been burned by hellfire while trying to read one of the vampires' minds."

"That's one of the ways Lucifer protects his minions. Didn't you feel the call in Hicksville? Curtis Dunn was there. You should have felt something."

Marilee nodded. "It wasn't like at the cemetery or what happened last night though. I sensed something off about him when we went in to rescue Nyla and Bobby from the vampire who'd been transforming everyone in town into his own vampire army, that or killing them straight out." She closed her eyes for a moment and choked down a sob recalling how her grandparents were two who'd been murdered for the vile creatures to feed off of.

"Curtis Dunn is a special case. Alfred Dunn died long ago and made a pact with the devil to reincarnate along with his son through his own family line. His son, Patrick, came back as the full-fledged demon, Carter Dunn. He was a demon with a human body. Alfred came back as a split soul. Alfred is his demon side, but Curtis is the new soul. The two are meshed together inside Curtis Dunn's body. It might explain why you didn't feel as compelled to call upon him, or why he didn't call upon you. Curtis has spent his life fighting against the demon portion of his soul."

Marilee shook her head. "What? How can he be two souls?"

"It's hard to explain. He's kind of the mental embodiment of a Siamese twin. Curtis is pretty much a normal, everyday man, but Alfred is inside him."

"So he's just possessed?" Marilee asked, trying to understand the bizarre story.

"Very similar. You could still call out his demon."

"Alfred?"

Khiderian nodded. "It's a good thing Curtis had control over the demon in Hicksville when your paths crossed. If I'd swept in unannounced to help you Jake would have fought me and I wouldn't have had a choice but to defend myself. He also may have turned on you if he realized your ability. You can never tell anyone you are a *drac chemare*."

"Why would I want to?" Marilee shuddered. "I wish I didn't know."

"Knowledge is power. In this case, knowledge is the difference between life and death. If you unknowingly let a demon inside you the outcome would be very bad."

"How could I draw one inside me?"

Khiderian glanced away. "I'm not sure on the specifics. It's such a rare ability I've only come across one other person with it in all my centuries."

Marilee threw her hands up in the air, agitated. "Well, if I don't know how to do it, how can I make sure I don't do it by accident?"

"That night in the cemetery you felt the desire to pull the demons back into you. Do you remember?"

"Yes." She shivered, thinking what could have happened if he hadn't warned her against the action. Khiderian rubbed her arm in response, warming her.

"I think that's how it works. It's a mind thing. You feel the urge or desire to draw them back into you the opposite of how you let them out."

"I let them out with a chant. I heard the voices begging for me to release them and then there were drums and a strange chant. It kept growing and I kind of joined in. The more I focused on it, the stronger it grew until everything went still. Then I heard the kids screaming."

"The words were in you but the demons brought them out so you could add your power to make them work." Khiderian closed his eyes and took a deep breath before shaking his head. "I can imagine how hard something like that is to ignore, but you must ignore it when you aren't willingly drawing out a demon."

Marilee jerked in alarm, something in the vampire's tone setting off warning bells. "Why would I ever willingly call out a demon?"

"You never know when something outrageous might be necessary to defeat the enemy."

"Oh, no." Marilee quickly rose and crossed the room before turning around, arms folded in front of her. "Not on your life. I might be a country girl from the sticks, but I'm not as stupid as you apparently think I am. Whatever crazy idea you have brewing in that psychic head of yours is going to stay right there."

"Marilee, I haven't suggested anything. You're getting yourself excited over nothing." He patted the mattress next to where he sat. "Come, sit back down and quit wasting energy. It's bad enough you're not sleeping right now while we have daylight on our side."

Marilee scoffed. "Is the daylight going to keep the shape-shifters away?"

"Sunlight has no effect on them," Khiderian admitted, rolling his head as if there were a kink in his neck, "but if those shifters were lycanthropes, and I'm pretty sure they were, they work under the command of someone else. As prone as they are to run off and do their own thing without any form of order, whoever is running the show will most likely want to supervise over any action they take. Vampires, witches, sirens, all are most powerful at night. They'll attack when they're in peak condition for battle."

"You're sure about that?"

"I follow my gut, Marilee, and so far it's kept me alive for several centuries. I seriously doubt it would just all of a sudden fail me now when it's needed most."

She stared at the handsome vampire, taking in his relaxed, confident demeanor, and nodded. She didn't feel any impending danger and she always had before any sort of attack, even if her own gut didn't give her much warning, it always managed to give just enough. "I guess with our psychic abilities together we would feel any danger before it reached us, like the other night."

"Yes, and speaking of which…" Khiderian worried the corner of his bottom lip, eliciting a little spark of yearning low in Marilee's belly. "We need to discuss this wall you've thrown up to keep me out of your mind. It's a hindrance that needs to be remedied quickly."

She narrowed her eyes on the sexy vampire. "Why am I not surprised you want the ability to shuffle through my thoughts without a problem again?"

"It's not like that." Khiderian shook his head adamantly. "Your ability to call demons is very dangerous and could cost us everything. Marilee… I think you led our attackers to us. They must have latched on to you through use of the demons as soon as you blocked me out and came right at us. That can't keep happening if we plan on staying on track with this mission."

Marilee's stomach rolled as Khiderian's implication registered. "Are you telling me I'm like some kind of demon homing device?"

He nodded. "That's a pretty good way of putting it."

"You said they only sense me when I'm close to a portal."

"When I'm tapped in to your mind, they only pick you up when you're in the vicinity of a portal. Sit and I'll explain." He pointed to the mattress as he scooted far enough to rest his back against the head board and waited until Marilee had taken a seat in the middle of the bed to continue. "I was drawn to you when you were just a toddler because you'd had a tantrum which sparked your temper and flared your power. In that flare of power, the part of me that repels demons recognized the part of you that calls them. I was alarmed at how young you were and already showing the ability so I did what was necessary and forged a very small mind-link with you while you slept. You had no idea what we were doing."

Marilee swallowed hard and folded her suddenly trembling hands together in her lap. "You manipulated me into forming some kind of psychic link to you when I was just a little girl?"

"I know it sounds deceitful." His eyes held an apology. "It had to be done. At that young of an age, you had no defense against any hell portal you might have possibly come across. It was better to be manipulated by me than a demon."

Marilee sighed, shrugged off the moment of betrayal she'd felt. "I guess I can understand. So this link was shared between us all this time?"

"Up until you blocked me out, yes. It's why it was always so easy hearing your deepest darkest thoughts and why no matter where you were I could feel you if I tapped into that link, and any time you used your power in any capacity I instantly felt it."

"So that's how you knew I was at the bar in Texas without me using my power. The Dream Teller didn't tell you where to find me. You tapped into the link."

"Yes." He nodded.

"And somehow this link between us can keep the demons away? It didn't work in the cemetery."

"That was an unbelievable trick of fate. When I'm linked to you, my ability to repel demons can keep them from finding you through dark magic. However, that night those kids read a chant while they taunted you. They'd actually found a very real latin chant for calling demons for a sacrifice but were too young and stupid to understand what they were doing that night wasn't a game."

Marilee remembered the chant the kids read off the paper. "That's right. The voices started a little after that, but the chant I heard in my head was a little different. It was—"

Khiderian surged forward and clamped his hand over her mouth, his eyes wide. "Don't speak it, and whatever you do, don't think it."

Marilee tried to verbalize her agreement but it came out muffled so she nodded her head. Khiderian removed his hand and she moved her jaw to get the feeling back in it. "Sorry. I didn't think about it."

Shaking his head, Khiderian let out a frustrated sigh. "What I was trying to explain is that the demons found you that night because they were called by a chant some stupid kids probably got off someone they knew who was into voodoo, not that surprising considering the proximity to New Orleans, the voodoo capitol of the world. The chant brought them to the cemetery where your power immediately caught their attention. They recognized you as a *drac chemare* and called out to you. Not knowing what you were doing, you called them and as a result, you gave them form so they could attack the children. However, at no other point in your life, with the exception of last night, has a demon been able to locate you away from a portal, because of our link. We have to establish that link again." He looked at her sternly. "Now, before they work some dark magic and trace us again."

Marilee bit her lip, taking everything in while carefully avoiding thought of that night and the words of the chant the kids had taunted her with. "Linking my mind with yours will keep me from calling them altogether?"

"No." Khiderian shook his head, and she could see the glint of disappointment in his eyes. "Unfortunately, there's no way to completely shut off the ability. If you come into the close vicinity of a portal, the demons will still sense you, and they will still try to get you to call them. The urge to do so will always be strong, especially in times of stress. So far, the times you've come across demons have been great opportunities for them, but you didn't call them into you in Louisiana, and you didn't release them last night. That shows your strength, but if we don't link up, they can find you anywhere, anytime, with just a little dark magic used. If they keep coming at us, bringing vampires and shape-shifters from the other side with them, heightening your stress levels, you could give in."

"So it was the witch in the field who worked a spell so the demons could find me."

"I believe so. I can always feel an intrusion and the only witch who broke through my mind shields was Seta. The witch from last night, or some other psychic working for the other side, discovered our existence and our mission. He or she recognized you as a *drac chemare* which isn't that hard for those who work directly with demons to do, and without our mind link protecting you, was able to use the demons to track us and since we were traveling along the path of a hell portal..."

"They planned the perfect point of attack."

"Yes."

Marilee frowned. "If you sensed the hell portal, why did you get off the expressway and go toward it?"

"I didn't." Khiderian scowled at the implication. "Hell portals can be very small or they can be large. This particular one covered a pretty good distance. The moment I felt that we were about to be ambushed I sensed the portal and I got off the expressway to travel *around* it. Had I kept going we would have driven *inside* the portal, and if I'd had the choice I would have gotten us farther from it before we took up fighting positions, but your weapons were in the trunk—that's going to be a big no-no from now on, by the way—and our attackers were gaining on us. We didn't have any time to lose preparing you to fight."

Marilee lowered her head into her hands. "I'm screwing up left and right. You'd be better off without me."

"Hey." Khiderian reached out and gently gripped her chin with his hand and turned her head to face him as he leaned forward. "Without you, I wouldn't have a chance at completing this mission, and Jacob Porter would be a dead man walking. He has hope at survival, because of you."

"As long as what I am doesn't get us killed before we reach him."

"You never know. What you are, your ability, could end up doing some good."

Marilee felt a ball of unease roll around in her stomach, but couldn't pinpoint why. As long as Khiderian was with her, everything should work out fine. "If I call demons, and you repel them, how can I call them if we're linked?"

"Your ability to call outweighs my ability to repel, but I can still destroy anything you bring forth. It's hard, and takes a great deal of my psychic power, but I can contain your accidents." He rubbed his thumb along her chin. "Just don't ever call one into you."

Her stomach took a dip as Khiderian's eyes suddenly filled with a mixture of fear and something akin to pure misery. "You're holding something back. If you can destroy anything I call forth..." She remembered what he'd said earlier. "You mentioned another *drac chemare*. If I need training to handle my ability, it should come from someone who has the ability too."

He lowered his gaze, focusing it on the floor. "If that were possible, but it's not. The other *drac chemare* called a demon into herself."

Marilee's hands shook, something in his tone sending a chill through her. "Did you destroy the demon?"

"Yes."

She tried to swallow and found her mouth too dry. "What happened to the other *drac chemare*?"

The eyes Khiderian turned toward her were haunted by the sins of his past. "I had no choice. Once a demon is drawn into a *drac chemare* it takes total control of the body and the power in it. It will draw hundreds, thousands of demons from the portals to kill everything in its path. Without the *drac chemare* able to expel the demon from her body, I had to destroy it inside her. She died horribly." He closed his eyes and lowered his head. "If you draw a demon into your body, I'll have no choice but to kill you along with it."

CHAPTER TEN

Marilee sat cross-legged before Khiderian on the bed, her hands shaking as she placed them in his and looked into the bluest eyes she'd ever seen, not just in color. "We're back to square one, aren't we?"

She blinked. "What?"

"You don't trust me." He spoke softly like a child who'd been hurt so much they grew afraid of speaking their concerns, afraid doing so would make them real.

"I trust you, Khiderian." She sighed, her heart heavy. "I trust you to train me and see this mission through, and I trust you to kill me if I screw up."

"That's a fate you don't have to worry about as long as you're careful."

She nodded and tried to offer a little smile, but her heart wasn't in it. He would kill her if she called a demon inside her. It was necessary, she knew, and completely unavoidable if she were foolish enough to do such a thing, but still the knowledge that he could kill her after what they'd almost shared… She shook her head. Khiderian was a grown man who'd lived for centuries. He could have bedded thousands of women in his time, and most likely had. With those good looks, finding a willing woman wouldn't have been a great difficulty. What they'd almost shared didn't mean anything to him. She didn't mean anything to him. "Let's get this over with before the other side works some magic and finds us, if they haven't already."

"Good idea." He rubbed his thumbs over the backs of her hands. "Have a little faith in yourself. You're strong enough to resist the urge to call."

She shook her head, exasperated. "Please hurry and do this. My nerves can't take much more right now."

"Okay. Relax."

Marilee did as told, and closed her eyes on a deep inhale, letting the air back out slowly. When she opened them, Khiderian stared back at her with an intensity that made her palms sweat. She hoped he didn't notice.

Smiling softly, encouragingly, he placed her left hand over his heart. A hiss of air escaped her mouth as her fingertips connected. Through the soft cotton of his dark T-shirt, she felt the hardness of his steel chest and the trace of life it protected. "Your heart beats so slow."

He nodded. "To conserve energy." He placed his right hand over her heart, lightly spreading his fingers over the swell of her breast. Marilee wondered if he noticed her heartbeat kick up a notch, and if he knew it was from his touch. "Now we touch temples and merge our minds."

Marilee watched as he reached out with his free hand and touched three of his fingers to her temple. Looking into his eyes, she repeated what he'd done and felt a thrum of power the moment her fingertips made contact with his temple.

"Close your eyes, and just let go."

Marilee closed her eyes and took a deep breath, relaxing on the exhale. She relaxed her mind as she'd done when they'd worked with the crystal and allowed calm to settle over her. The thrum of power grew and suddenly she found herself inside a white room facing a huge wall of bricks. Peering closer she noticed the white bricks were held together with silver in place of cement, and strands of hawthorn and sparkly dust were woven into the bricks themselves. "Where am I?"

"Behind the shield you've erected to protect your mind. I'm on the other side." Khiderian sounded miles away though she knew in reality he sat right before her. "I need to get beyond your shield to forge the mind link with you. Remove one of the bricks, or just take away the hawthorn."

Marilee stepped closer to the wall and ran her hands along it. It was as solid as any wall in the physical world. "The hawthorn is built in to the bricks. I can't remove it." She poked at the silver cementing the bricks together. "It's put together so well. How can I break it?"

"You made it with your mind, Marilee. You can destroy it just as easily as you built it, but I don't want you to demolish the whole thing. You need some level of protection."

She chewed her bottom lip as her gaze roamed over the sturdy wall. The task looked daunting. "You'll have to guide me. I don't know what to do."

"Study the wall like you studied the wind. Do you remember how?"

"Yes." She nodded though he couldn't see her, remembering their training session in New Mexico. "I focused on the wind's pattern of movement. What do I focus on about the wall?"

"It's power and construction. Take it all in. Study it until it becomes part of you."

Marilee frowned, then smiled thinking how close Khiderian came to sounding like a new age hippy type. Staring at the wall wasn't helping so she closed her eyes and felt along the structure with her hands. Her fingers dipped in the indentations of the stones, traced the silver encompassing them, and buzzed with power when she came across the special elements buried within. "What's the sparkly stuff?"

"It keeps witches from getting into your mind. As a *drac chemare*, you're born with that level of protection. You have solid protection against most psychics as well, only a very strong one with no non-human blood could get through, and me until you added the hawthorn to the mix."

Marilee felt a stab of guilt. "It's not easy having your deepest darkest memories brought up and used against you. Or having every single thought read."

"I'm sorry. I should have used more decorum, but you have to admit you didn't really give me much of a chance at first."

Marilee chuckled. "No, I didn't."

"And you've killed vampires before. I had to stay in your head to make sure you didn't try to attack me. I'd rather know in advance so I could fend you off without hurting you."

"If I let you back in, will it be the same?" Heat filled her face as she thought of all the things she'd thought about Khiderian since the battle. How attractive he was. He'd heard those things before and teased her, but if he knew just how sexy she thought he was now... The heat in her cheeks grew.

"I can be more restrained. I just need you to allow me enough space to put a little of my essence inside you. It will keep the demons from tracking us through you. From now on if I dip into your mind, it'll be out of absolute necessity."

Part of the wall shimmered then blurred. "Something's happening to the wall. One of the bricks is blurring."

"You're trusting me again. Focus on that trust, and visualize the hawthorn evaporating from that part of the wall."

Marilee walked over to the blurry brick and inhaled, absorbing its energy. She could smell the scent of hawthorn and imagined it as tiny particles. The particles formed before her and she blew them away, watched them dance in the air before fading out of existence.

The rest of the wall shimmered and Khiderian reached a hand through. "Come on."

Marilee took his hand, amazed by the fact she could now walk through the shimmering wall, and allowed him to lead her through. They stood together with her wall shimmering behind her, and another shimmering behind Khiderian. "What is that?"

"The shield I protect my mind with. We no longer have any solid barriers between our minds, but it is still important to never step into my mind uninvited, Marilee. You understand that great harm can come from it?"

Marilee nodded, recalling what had happened when she'd interrupted his astral feed. "So now we're linked?"

"Almost. Open your mind and take me in." He closed his eyes and breathed in deep. Marilee followed along, unsure what she should be doing, and the moment she breathed in a wave of power crashed over her. She felt Khiderian in it as if the power were a physical extension of him. She could feel it knocking on the door of her mind, seeking entrance. It didn't take long to make a decision. He'd protected her from Hank, and he'd protected her during the attack. He'd proven himself worthy of trust, and she needed him to help keep her safe from her own dark ability. Visualizing the door to her mind, she threw it open and the room filled with bursts of bright white and blue light before the power in the room cracked like a whip and her physical body jerked.

She opened her eyes to see Khiderian staring back at her, his limbs trembling as badly as hers. It took a few blinks to stop the room from moving around them. "Now we're linked," he said softly as he ran a hand down his face and stretched. "How do you feel?"

"Like I drank too much. I think," Marilee added as she rubbed her temples. She'd always stayed away from alcohol despite serving it up in various bars across the states. She'd seen what it could twist people into. "You did this to me when I was just two years old?"

Khiderian grinned. "It was much simpler then. I came to you as you slept and there was no wall keeping me out. Coincidentally, the link wasn't this strong."

Marilee nodded, feeling the difference. "I feel you in my head."

"It's just my power." Khiderian rubbed her temple. "Now that you're older and more powerful yourself, a whole new level of trust was required for the mind link to work. It allowed a stronger bond. Even if you slam the door to your mind closed to keep me out, my ability to repel will still be there."

"But I can't use it?" Marilee frowned, trying to understand.

"No. But it can still serve you well by keeping you from being tracked unless you're right on top of a portal."

"You said even if I close the door."

Khiderian chuckled. "Figures you'd latch on to that. We created a doorway this time. Either one of us can lock it against the other if we need privacy. Just visualize it like you did when you let me in and visualize locking it. I won't be able to read your mind."

"Will you be able to find me if I don't want you to?"

Khiderian's grin fled. Hurt filled his eyes before they burned with anger. "I'll always feel when you use your power but as long as you don't, if you really don't want to see me again—"

"It was just a question, Khiderian. I'm not planning on escaping you or anything." She sighed. "We have a mission to complete *together*."

Deep frown lines marred Khiderian's forehead as he rose from the bed. "The demons can't track you now. Let's get some sleep so we can leave at dusk. I don't think we'll have any problem with the local law but it's best to play it safe." He wobbled a little bit as he walked past but otherwise appeared fine.

Marilee laughed as he attempted to fit his body into the small loveseat along the opposite wall. "You know you can't possibly sleep there."

He directed a dark look at her. "Why didn't you get a room with two beds?"

"I was a little preoccupied with getting you to safety and not wanting the motel clerk to notice the big gaping wound on my thigh." She stood. "You take the bed so you can be comfortable. I'll fit on the loveseat."

"Absolutely not." Khiderian pointed to her, snapped his fingers, and pointed to the bed. "Lady takes the bed. It's a firm rule."

Marilee rolled her eyes, then chuckled as he slid to the floor and closed his eyes. "You are not sleeping on the floor, you old-fashioned lug. We can share if you're that adamant about it."

Khiderian popped open one eye, studying her warily. "Just what are you suggesting?"

Butterflies took flight in Marilee's belly as his question sunk in. "I, uh...I... Oh for Pete's sake, what do you think I mean?" She turned away and started fluffing a pillow, anything to hide her red face from the vampire awaiting an answer. "You've probably already read my mind anyway so I don't know why you bother to ask," she grumbled as she sank down onto the bed.

"No. I told you I would show more restraint if you trusted me enough to form the link. I won't go back on my word." He sat up and rested his elbows on his knees, watching her curiously.

"I appreciate that."

He nodded. "I can sleep on the floor, Marilee. I've done it before. I've slept in far worse places, actually."

"Don't be silly." A yawn escaped her and she quickly covered her mouth with her hand. "I'm sure the two of us can manage to share a bed without any problems. We can sleep at opposite ends if you like."

Something close to disappointment flickered through Khiderian's eyes as he hoisted himself up from the floor. "No, that won't be necessary." He lay down next to her in the Queen-sized bed and relaxed his body while he rested flat on his back. "Sweet dreams, Marilee."

"Sweet dreams," she said back as she lay on her side, watching him, yearning to trace his mouth with her fingertips.

"What are you doing, Khiderian? Have you learned nothing from previous experience?"

Khiderian looked straight ahead at the old woman in front of him, refusing to blink despite her blindness. It would show weakness to *himself*, and even that he would not allow in her presence. "Was it necessary to drag me here, Krystaline?" He looked around at the blue-tinged forest he and the witch stood in the middle of. To most it was freezing and scarier than their worst nightmare. It had never affected him at all. "You could have spoken to me telepathically instead of taking me away from the woman I'm supposed to protect."

"Now that you've allowed her a doorway into your mind?" Krystaline laughed, the sound menacing as her form flickered, revealing a momentary glimpse of a younger woman with flowing platinum hair and vivid blue eyes. He'd seen it happen before, but never commented on it, sure it was another secret he wasn't supposed to know. Upper management already thought he knew too much. "She managed to get in your mind before without you helping her along. Now you've just lain out a doormat for her to step over any time she wants to get herself killed... or learn things she isn't privileged to know."

"She knows better than to cross into my mind now. Our telepathic discussions will remain between only us."

"I wish I had that confidence." The old—or young, depending on which form was her true self—witch said on a sigh. "Your mission is to train her, keep her from doing anything foolish, and use her to save Jacob Porter."

"That's what I'm doing."

"Is it?" She grinned. "I understand you find her attractive, Khiderian, and I realize how much of an inconvenience it must be to spend so much time with someone who makes you feel—"

"I'm not stupid." Heat grew behind Khiderian's eyes. "I'm also not a schoolboy. I can separate my attraction for her from the job."

"Can you? Can you survive this time if you have to kill another *drac chemare* you've foolishly allowed yourself to grow attached to?" She cocked her head to the side. "You nearly lost everything you've worked for the last time. You won't be given another second chance to rectify your mistake."

This time, Khiderian laughed, the sound brittle and scathing at the same time. "As I am constantly reminded."

"You are lucky. Surely you realize this? Your brothers and sisters could have destroyed you for your past transgressions."

They could have tried. Khiderian ground his teeth together instead of speaking his mind. "If you only brought me here for a tongue lashing, Krystaline, I'm going to have to disappoint you. I'm working."

"Which is why I brought you here." The frail looking woman folded her arms across her chest. "You are nearing Dunn. It's time to train Marilee for what she must do."

Unease gnawed at Khiderian's stomach, scraping the sides savagely. "You never really told me what her task is supposed to be other than locating him." Which, miraculously, she'd done without calling the demon out. "I have a feeling I'm not going to like it."

Krystaline grinned, the expression bordering on malicious. "What else do you do with a *drac chemare*? She is going to draw the demon, Alfred, out of Curtis Dunn's body."

Had he needed oxygen to live, Khiderian would be in trouble, because he could no longer form a breath.

"Relax. You will be right there with her and if you do your job correctly, no harm will come to her."

Khiderian shook his head as the sound of his rapidly beating heart pounded in his ears. "Why? I can kill the demon inside Dunn. Why in the hell does she need to draw it out?"

"Because Curtis Dunn has done his part in this prophecy and as payment, he deserves peace."

"So let me kill them both. One soul will go to the heavens while the other is destroyed. There's no need to take risks."

"Train the girl and there will be no risk," Krystaline snapped. She rarely showed anger, especially at him. She liked to play games with his mind from time to time, and they exchanged banter regularly, but he knew he was one of her favorites. "You're far too attached, Khiderian. If you want to have your fun with the girl, be my guest, but having real feelings for her is just asking for pain. You know it is. The past has taught you that!"

She raised a hand and projected an image of Gwen, the last *drac chemare* he'd been assigned to partner with on a mission. Beautiful Gwen, with her long chestnut hair and curvy body that could make a man's teeth sweat. Gwen, who he'd lost when she drew a demon into herself. "Don't show me that," he pleaded as he viewed the projected image, seeing Gwen approach the demon-possessed man while he stood in the back of the room, watching them. The fact she'd drawn the demon into herself with him standing right there never ceased to torment him. He was so close, yet it still happened. "I lived it. There's no need for the replay. I'll never forget that moment." Or her blood he'd had to wash from his body after he'd obliterated her. Her screams had rang out in his head for decades afterward. Sometimes he wondered if they were really hers. Sometimes they'd sounded like they came from him.

"Then remember it better so history doesn't repeat itself. If she fails and draws a demon inside her, you must kill her and complete the mission alone. You know that can't be done, and if you fail to complete the mission, I can't say your siblings will be very gentle with you."

Khiderian nodded. For all his tough talk, he knew what his siblings were capable of. It didn't matter how strong, brave, or experienced he was in battle. He could never run, could never hide, could never recuperate. And he had only a fraction of the power they wielded.

"You must interrogate the demon before it is released. Find out all you can about the other side and what you can about Jacob. The demon will know something. They always know what their brethren are up to. Being kept from them or sharing a body with another soul won't change that."

Khiderian nodded, his jaw clenched tight, knowing how dangerous having Marilee interrogate a demon was. The whole time she dragged information out of it, it would be clawing its way into her psyche. "If it seems she is going to draw it in I will kill Dunn, regardless whether the demon is inside him or not," Khiderian declared. "I will not risk her life for Curtis Dunn's soul."

Krystaline frowned, the wrinkles bracketing her mouth deepening. "If she is in extreme danger, it is your job to protect her, but don't jump the gun. We need to know what information the demon can provide us."

"So why didn't you interrogate him sooner?" Khiderian fisted his hands, recalling the other vampire he'd seen with Seta after sensing her in his head. "I know it was another like me who destroyed Carter Dunn. He still walks, and he's with Seta and the others now. He's a part of this prophecy. Why aren't you making use of him?"

"Because Christian doesn't know why he can kill demons, and telling him why could ruin the test he's being given," she added in a warning tone.

"Stay away from him, and don't even think of asking for his help if Marilee does end up taking a demon inside herself. She is your responsibility, and your responsibility alone."

Khiderian growled, unable to stop the reaction. His brethren loved their damn tests. Everything was a test. From what he could sense from the vision he'd had, and what little information he'd received about the vampire from Krystaline—and now he knew why she'd told him so little about the vampire who'd destroyed Carter Dunn—Christian was old, and the poor slob had probably been tested for centuries. He deserved to know what he was.

"Don't even think about it." Krystaline's mouth was a pinched slash in her deeply grooved face. "You both made the same mistake, and you both must make amends in the ways that have been set out for you."

"Yeah, I know how it works." Khiderian sneered at the woman, sensing she could feel it even if she couldn't see it. The damned woman saw everything else. Too much.

"Be angry with me if you like, Khiderian, but you got yourself in this predicament. I am your friend, but I won't sugarcoat the unpleasantries of life for you." She sighed softly, her shoulders slumping. "You chose this pain."

"Do you really think I need the verbal reminder?" He tightened a fist, ached to send it crashing into the woman's face. She appeared old and frail, but he knew the body was just a shell hiding immense power. He would bring up the other form he saw breaking through the old hag façade, ask her what she'd done to find herself trapped in the dream realm, and how she liked it. He would ask her if it were all one big test, too, but he knew better. He didn't dare enrage the woman and unleash the power she possessed behind the phony appearance of a weakened old woman. "Will Dunn be able to lead us to Porter, or was I instructed to locate him only to use Marilee as a way of allowing Curtis Dunn his freedom?"

"The demon will know where Jacob is being held, and who is holding him. Question him well and you will find all the information you need."

"And possibly lose Marilee in the process."

"Have a little faith."

"My faith is in very short supply these days," he muttered before turning away. Unlike most, he could come and leave the Dream Teller's little world as he pleased.

"You're still angry with me?"

"Hell yes, I'm angry with you. All of you!" He whirled around to face her. "I can understand why I had to kill Gwen, but you're telling me that if Marilee draws a demon inside her, I have to be the one to kill her? There's another like me who can do the task just as well, without shredding his heart in the process, and I could just whisk in, grab him, and make him do it in my place, but I can't touch him? I can't get him to do this one thing for me because he's not supposed to know what he is?"

"He's being tested, and unlike you, he doesn't remember where he came from." She licked her dry, cracked lips. "Khiderian, he has a chance of righting his wrong well enough to be taken back."

And he didn't. He'd committed far too many wrongs, and he'd done it while knowing what he was... what he was supposed to be. Willful disobedience was more than just frowned upon. If not for the fact he was aiding in the Blood Revelation, he'd probably have been cut down centuries ago. "Good for him."

"For what it's worth, Khiderian, I think Marilee is a lot stronger than Gwen... and though you cared, Gwen didn't have your love like Marilee does. Your belief in her makes her even stronger."

"I pray so," he whispered before willing himself away from the dream realm.

"Krystaline."

The Dream Teller shivered as the voice, a voice more beautiful than the tinkling of piano keys, whispered her name across the wind. Strange how such a beautiful voice could send a chill of fear down her spine. Her old, withered spine.

"Coming," she responded, and closed her eyes, whispering the spell to teleport her into the cave where she met with upper management, as Khiderian liked to refer to his former family. Not that she would ever call them that directly.

She felt the loss of wind and knew she'd reappeared in the cave. The presence of her superior radiated strongly to her right, standing at the mouth of the cave. Despite her blindness, she knew the woman shone brighter than the most golden of sunrises. She could feel the warmth against her skin. "Yes, Kiara."

"My lost brother is behaving very defiantly."

"He is concerned about the *drac chemare*." Krystaline sighed, wishing she could say more to defend him. She'd been hard on Khiderian, but not out of spite. She knew what it was like to care for someone, in a way his brethren would never fully understand for they behaved, thought, and felt the way they were designed to. They loved all humans equally. To adore one in the way she and Khiderian had done, the way Khiderian did now, simply wasn't acceptable. Not for them.

"Women were always his downfall, no pun intended." Kiara bristled. Krystaline didn't need to see it to know. The woman's tone gave away the action.

"He's been with a very small amount of women considering his length of time roaming the earth." Krystaline braced herself for the reaction she feared, and immediately felt the heat of Kiara's disagreement wash over her.

"We could have thrown him into the pit, but we have allowed him to live this lifestyle he chose over us." The once delicate voice now sounded like the boom of thunder. "Even one woman taken in lust was bad enough. Comparing him against other human men does not make him appear better before us. He was not born a human man. He was created as something much higher, but chose to throw his blessing away. We will not overlook that, no matter how you pity him."

"Yes, Kiara. I understand." She did, in theory, but her once mortal heart would never follow. The thought of never giving one's heart to another, loving all equally... It was just too unimaginable. But then, she hadn't been created for that purpose. Khiderian had. He'd made his bed. Now he had to lie in it, tossing and turning for the rest of eternity.

"Good. And you understand how important this mission is?"

"Yes, of course." She was viewed by the vampires as a prophet for their kind, and in a way she was. Cursed to live in the dream realm, she acted as messenger between the vampires and elders... and Khiderian's former brothers and sisters.

"Then you know he mustn't fail. He must use the *drac chemare* to break the demon in Curtis Dunn's body and give us Jacob Porter's location."

"Yes, I told him." Krystaline frowned. Why couldn't Kiara and her siblings just do it? If they could kill the creatures, why couldn't they get information out of them? And why couldn't they swoop in to kill the *drac chemare* when a demon was taken in? Why did they force their lost brother, as they called him, to do it, knowing how it destroyed him inside? There was so much about them she just didn't get.

"And you yourself felt his resentment, his urge to refuse the order."

Krystaline nodded meekly. "But he'll do it. He knows the mission is more important than anything else." *And he knows what you'll do to him.* She bit the inside of her jaw to keep her own resentment in.

"He'd better. And if he drops any clues to our other lost brother, you will be held accountable."

"Me?" Krystaline's voice came out a shriek.

"Yes, you. It is your job to guide them."

Why? She wasn't even a vampire. Krystaline expelled a breath slowly, hoping the time it took to do so would cool her tongue before she forgot which one of them was the superior being. "I'll make sure he doesn't."

"Good. The interrogation will take place soon and Khiderian will take the woman to where Jacob is being held. I suggest you stick to him like glue, and make sure he stays focused on the mission."

Krystaline would have liked to give Kiara a suggestion, but bit her tongue lest she lose it. "I will, but I have a small favor to ask. You know I don't make many requests."

"No, you don't. I will hear your request."

"Thank you." She nodded, hoped she looked respectful. "Khiderian suffered greatly after killing the last *drac chemare*. He is much fonder of this one, and has done a wonderful job guarding over her as asked. If the worst happens and she draws a demon inside her body, wouldn't it be more merciful for one of Khiderian's brethren to destroy her?"

"Khiderian separated himself from us of his own free will." Kiara's tone parlayed her anger which still burned after so many centuries had passed. "He wanted to be with the humans so badly and experience life as they do. He can experience loss and mourning."

Hasn't he experienced enough of it already? Krystaline closed her eyes to stop a tear from spilling out.

"I will be watching to make sure everyone is carrying out their duties," Kiara warned. There was a gathering of wind and a flapping sound, then Krystaline stood alone in the cave fighting back the urge to scream out in anger for her friend.

Angels. She would never understand how beings supposedly so merciful and just could treat Khiderian the way they did.

CHAPTER ELEVEN

Marilee yawned, rolled her neck to get rid of the stiffness, and stretched before sitting up. She glanced around the room to confirm what she'd already felt before opening her eyes. Khiderian was gone. She could still feel him nearby though, and deduced he was feeding, most likely off others in the motel.

She shuddered at the thought, wondering if he was feeding off someone's blood or energy. Then the image of his mouth wrapped around a woman's neck or thigh flashed inside her mind and she growled low in her throat, her hands automatically forming fists. She was less than an inch away from the door before she caught herself. Khiderian was a vampire. It didn't matter that he was incredibly attractive or that he'd protected her. He was not human, therefore not someone she should care about in that way. They would never work out.

If only she could believe in the rational advice she gave herself.

Raking a hand through her disheveled hair, Marilee turned to see an assortment of food on the table. Donuts, beef jerky, bananas, barbecue chips, and a loaf of bread. Khiderian had brought her breakfast, or dinner, she supposed, judging by the hour. A very odd dinner, but it was food all the same.

She took care of business in the bathroom, where she found her dagger in the sink, blood-free—Khiderian must have used a rag to handle it—before grabbing a water out of the mini fridge and settling down at the table to eat her weird meal. The door swung open as she finished off the last of the chocolate donuts and Khiderian strode into the room. "Eat quickly. We need to leave as soon as we can."

The last piece of donut hit the bottom of Marilee's stomach with a thud. "What happened?"

Khiderian shook his head as he sat opposite her. "Nothing to worry about, but there were police officers here speaking with the motel clerk."

"Oh my gosh, and you let me sleep?"

"You needed the rest." Khiderian frowned. "I can evade human law, Marilee, and make sure you don't get into trouble. I'm not new to this."

"I guess not." She eyed the vampire while peeling the skin off a banana. He was gorgeous, radiating an air of authority stronger than he had when he'd first walked into the bar in Texas. She could *feel* the power coming from him. "You seem... healthy."

"I fed well." His eyes narrowed. "I told you I would have to in order to maintain my strength for this mission."

"I know." She took a bite from the banana, but didn't taste it. Her stomach dipped a little as she ate the fruit, but she knew she needed to eat what she could get when she could get it. "You didn't leave any... *evidence* behind, did you?"

"I didn't kill anybody!" His voice came out as a thunderous boom before he pushed up from the table and grabbed his bag, flinging it onto the unmade bed. "Hurry up. I want to get us a new car before we head into Nevada, and there's some other business to take care of." He stomped into the bathroom, returning with Marilee's toiletries, which he crammed into his bag.

"I guess you're mad at me."

He whipped his head around, flames in his eyes. "Irritated, Marilee. It's very frustrating when nothing seems to sink into your head. I don't go around randomly killing."

"Well, how am I supposed to know that?" Marilee tossed the banana peel onto the table and stood with her hands outstretched. "The only time I saw you feed, it was on Hank and look what you did to him!"

"Him, I intended to kill." Khiderian stepped closer. "He deserved it. I don't feed in that way with everyone. If you'd ask me how I feed instead of just assuming I go around slaughtering innocents, you would know that."

"Well, pardon the hell out of me if I don't know the basics of vampire dining," Marilee snapped, her anger fueled by the brooding man before her. "All you had to do was tell me. No need to get your panties in a twist."

"I don't wear panties."

SIREN'S SNARE

"Yeah, I know. You don't wear anything," she responded, recalling the lack of underclothing she'd found in his bag, and blushed as she realized what she'd just said. "I mean, not that I noticed, er, cared for that matter."

He arched an eyebrow, but said nothing, thankfully. Marilee quickly turned away and grabbed up the last of the food he'd provided for her, opting to take it along. "Thanks for getting me something to eat, but what did you do, knock off a quickie mart?"

"You didn't like it?"

"It was fine, just..." She glanced over at him and paused, registering the disappointment in his eyes. She suddenly felt like she'd put down a gift he'd bought for her, and felt horrible. "You don't usually eat chips and beef jerky with donuts." She didn't mention the loaf of bread. Had there been a toaster in the room, or some peanut butter or lunch meat it would have made sense. "How long has it been since you actually ate food?"

He shrugged, and tugged on his leather jacket as if straightening it. "I have more important things to focus on than when was the last time I ate. Have I left anything?"

Marilee shoved the food into a plastic bag and grabbed the remaining bottles of water from the refrigerator. "Looks like you packed up everything."

"Your dagger?"

"In my boot."

"Let's move." He nodded his head curtly and led the way outside. The early evening sky hovered over them as they got into the car and fastened their seatbelts.

"You're not putting the bag in the trunk?"

"I think we learned our lesson last time. It's best to be prepared." He offered a reassuring smile her way as he backed out of the parking space and exited the motel parking lot. "I don't think we'll have any more sneak attacks though now that we've formed the mind-link."

"Thank goodness." Marilee shivered at the reminder of the beasts she'd battled against the night before, and how much damage Khiderian had taken. She still couldn't shake off the guilt that he'd been injured so badly protecting her. "In case anything does happen, are you alright? If you need to feed more—"

"I'm good." He cast a sideways glance her way before taking a left turn.

"The expressway was back that way." Marilee pointed in the opposite direction they were going.

"I know. We're getting a new vehicle before leaving Arizona. Just in case."

"Oh." Marilee tried to keep the quiver out of her voice. Khiderian was a vampire. He was powerful enough to evade police, but she was just a person. Eventually she would need a job or to get a drivers license renewed. Something would happen to draw attention to her if she was on a most wanted list, and get her thrown behind bars where her ability to move the wind wouldn't come in that handy.

"Relax, Marilee. I've got us covered. The police have no idea who to look for."

She stiffened. "Already back in my head, I see."

"No, I'm not. I don't have to dip in your head to know what's going through it. I see it all over your face. You just love to assume," he muttered as his hand tightened on the steering wheel.

"Fine. I assume things, and it makes me an ass. So what? Bite—" She stopped herself from saying the most ignorant thing a person could say to a vampire, and earned a deep chuckle. "So, how do you feed enough to get up your strength without killing people in the process?"

"Wow. Did you just ask me a question instead of jumping to your own conclusions?"

"Yeah, smart-ass. Now answer it since I was so nice to ask and all."

Khiderian laughed, showing straight, gleaming white teeth. "Since you asked so sweetly, I can take so much blood from a person without doing any damage to them. Non-pranic vampires can feed off one person and the blood keeps them strong for a week or more depending on how much they physically exert themselves. Pranic vampires need to feed on blood at least once daily if we want to maintain our strength."

"Why? I thought you astral fed off energy or brain cells or whatever it is you feed off of to keep up your psychic abilities. That's the only difference between you and non-pranic vampires, isn't it?"

"Well..." His brow knit in concentration. "Seta most likely feeds more when she uses a lot of magic. The blood gives us physical strength but whenever magic or, in my case, mental abilities, are used, we draw on a little of our physical strength along with our mental power."

"How often do you have to astral feed to keep up your mental strength?"

"At least daily, but it really depends on how much power we use. We have to resupply whatever we use." A pensive look ghosted over his face. "The way I would have fed off Hank if you hadn't interrupted would have given me immense power. Anytime a life is taken, the power received is tremendous. That one feed would have gotten me through at least three days, even with the attack we fell under. But, if I don't kill, which I rarely do and only for good reason—" He directed a pointed look Marilee's way before returning his focus to the road "—I feed off energies multiple times a day, from multiple sources."

"You didn't kill Hank?" Marilee blinked, confused.

"No. If I had, you would have died, too. However, he'll spend the rest of his life in a coma."

Marilee frowned. "So it's just energy that you feed off of?"

He nodded. "I feed off energies, emotions. It's not always unpleasant, as it was with Hank. I can feed off people from a short distance and them never notice a thing, especially if they're... deeply engaged."

"Emotions? So you feed off of fear and anger?"

He nodded. "And love, lust, joy. Any emotion."

"Really?" Marilee shifted in her seat so she faced Khiderian better, intrigued by this new information. "So what gives you the most mental power?"

"Sex," he answered without batting an eye.

Marilee swallowed hard. "Sex? You *feed* off it?"

His jaw clenched. "Yes, Marilee. I feed off sex. Think about it. What goes through people during the act? Excitement, adrenaline, lust, curiosity, love, pleasure, disappointment, anger, shame... No matter what the circumstances leading to it, sex produces more emotions than anything so yes, I feed off it."

Marilee turned her body to face forward again. She'd already angered Khiderian with the question, judging by his tone, but she still had to know one thing. "So when you yourself have sex, you're feeding off your partner?"

"I can't not do it. It's automatic." He sighed heavily, frustration thick in the sound. "Let me guess. I disgust you."

"No." She shook her head, but couldn't look at him. Every time she did she imagined them together, him feeding off her while sharing something that was supposed to be special. It could never be special to him if he only saw his partners as food.

Khiderian slowed the car to a crawl as they drove through an affluent neighborhood, and eventually stopped outside a house with a long driveway which held a variety of cars. "This looks good enough," he murmured as he guided the car up the drive, pulling alongside the row of cars. "Let's go," he instructed as he exited the rental.

Marilee quickly stepped out and caught up to him as he walked toward the front door of the large white brick house. "What are you doing?"

"Getting us a new vehicle. The owner of this home can certainly spare one or from the looks of it, two or three."

Marilee looked back at the row of expensive cars, and her heart rate kicked up a notch. "We're stealing a car?"

"I wouldn't be walking up to the front door if I intended to just steal the homeowner's car like a common thief," Khiderian advised as he stopped before the door and rang the bell. He grinned at her as footsteps sounded from within the residence.

The door opened and a harried man with a hairline that started somewhere along the very top of his head, an expensive-looking suit and blue silk tie, and a Bluetooth attached to his ear frowned, then held up a finger as he said something to whomever was on the other end of the Bluetooth.

Marilee felt a slight tingle and the man suddenly went rigid. "I'll call you back, Wayne." He focused his full attention on Khiderian, and smiled, showing a shiny set of capped teeth. "It's so nice when old friends drop by. Please do come in." He stepped back and gestured for them to enter.

"Old friends?" Marilee asked as they stepped inside.

Khiderian winked down at her and followed his new 'old friend' deeper into the house. Marilee's jaw dropped as she noted the huge flat panel TV and pool table in one of the rooms. Through the glass wall, she could see a swimming pool the size of a small lake. "Geez."

The man took them deeper, guiding them into a massive kitchen. "Take whatever you need. I have plenty to spare."

Marilee glanced at Khiderian and received a nod in return. "Go ahead and grab something to eat while Ron and I... catch up on old times."

Marilee attempted to read the man—Ron's—mind and came up with static as though his mind were a television set and no one had bothered to turn it off after the last program ended. Khiderian had to be so deep in the man's head, he had no mind of his own, just functioned like a robot. Shrugging off the eerie feeling it gave her to know the man was basically walking around brain-dead, doing Khiderian's bidding, Marilee started looking around the kitchen as Khiderian and their host stepped through a side door she presumed led to the garage.

After the pizza, sandwiches, and other assorted junk she'd been dining on for longer than she could recall, Marilee's taste buds wept with joy when she came across a variety of leftovers in the refrigerator. Actual, home-cooked leftovers. Real food.

Licking her lips in anticipation, she removed plastic Tupperware filled with turkey and dressing, green beans, mashed potatoes, and macaroni and cheese, and found a plate to heap a portion of each onto.

She feasted on the food like a woman starved, so focused on the wonderful array of flavors rolling over her tongue, she didn't notice the sound of footsteps coming from the hall until she was face to face with a leggy brunette in a deep V-necked red blouse and black leather skirt that might have actually been a belt, and the fact that Marilee thought such a thing was really saying something. Gram had constantly nagged her about her own short shorts.

"Who the hell are you?" The heavily made-up woman crossed her arms beneath her bountiful chest, which defied gravity like nobody's business, and narrowed her green kohl-lined eyes while tapping a stilettoed foot on the floor. "I suppose the better question would be, where did Ron pick you up at?"

Marilee blanched as she realized what the woman was thinking. Glancing at her perfectly manicured hands, she saw the biggest diamond she'd ever seen in her life adorning a very important finger on the woman's left hand. She quickly dove into the woman's mind and after sorting through the cacophony of vile names the woman labeled her as, she learned the woman and Ron had been engaged for over a year, but Ron kept putting off the wedding. His fiancé worried there were other women, and was now convinced Marilee was one of them.

Marilee ignored the white trash barb the woman mentally threw her way and set down her fork. "I'm here with my... boyfriend. He's an old friend of Ron's."

The woman's perfectly shaped eyebrows rose into her hairline and Marilee could hear the doubts in her mind though she didn't choose to say anything.

"Lisa!"

Marilee and the woman turned as Ron and Khiderian entered the room. Ron smiled from ear to ear as he approached the woman and bussed her cheek, but the brunette's eyes never left Khiderian. Marilee didn't need to read her mind to know what she was thinking, but she made the mistake of doing it anyway, overhearing thoughts that had her gripping her fork so tight she nearly bent it.

"Ron, darling, who is your friend?" The brunette, who she now knew was named Lisa, stepped in front of Ron to get closer to Khiderian and held out her hand. "I don't believe we've had the pleasure of meeting."

What a hussy! Marilee fumed as she watched the woman—who'd had the nerve to call, er, well, *think* her skanky white trash—openly undress Khiderian with her eyes. Her ire grew as Khiderian smiled at the woman with a predatory gleam in his eye, the same type of gleam she'd seen in men's eyes as they scoured bars for easy targets.

"This is my old friend from college," Ron explained, his eyes unfocused, his tone odd. It sounded as if he were reading from a script. "We had some great times, and he really came through for me whenever I was in a pinch. I've done some thinking and decided I have too much wealth. I should share it."

Lisa's eyes widened in surprise, and Marilee thought the jig was up. Little Miss Uppity was about to throw a royal fit, but before a single word of disagreement could pass her lips, Khiderian focused intently on her, and her eyes glazed over before she gave off a drunken smile. "How nice of you to help out your friends, Ron. Is there anything I can do to be of assistance?"

"No, hon. I gave them my old Mustang. They're about to go on a trip and could use a better car."

"How nice." Lisa stepped closer to Khiderian, and both of them stared at him as if he glowed with pure radiance. Marilee could have been invisible for all the attention they showed her.

"Actually, while my friend eats, I could grab a... bite... myself." Khiderian's eyes narrowed as they caressed Lisa's form. The gleam in them was pure wickedness. Marilee's stomach churned with acid as he stepped back and Lisa followed him. "Relax for a little while, Marilee. I'm going to feed."

"You son of a bitch." The words slipped out before Marilee could make a conscious decision of whether or not to voice her opinion.

Khiderian's eyes registered surprise as he turned toward her, and Lisa speared her with a lethal look as she growled, unhappy Khiderian's gaze on her had been broken. Khiderian held up a hand and Lisa calmed. "Marilee, we've had this discussion. You know I have to do this."

Marilee forced out a bitter laugh. A man saying he *had* to have sex. How original. "You can stop pretending it's a chore. It's not like you don't want to do this. Go ahead. Don't let me stop you." She sat back with her arms crossed, hoping what she'd sensed from him was real. He'd wanted her, and would have had her if she hadn't freaked out when he got too close to her neck. But if he *fed* from this woman as if it were nothing, then it would mean she was nothing to him. It would mean everything she'd sensed had been all in her mind. She felt a slight pressure in her head and realized it was Khiderian trying to get in. She visualized the door they'd formed when linking their minds and slammed it shut. Pining over a man who openly desired another woman in front of her was bad enough without him knowing how his behavior hurt her.

Khiderian reached out and tilted her chin, his gaze softening as it collided with hers. "I won't hurt the woman."

Marilee's mouth dropped open as Khiderian withdrew his hand and started toward the doorway, Lisa on his heels. "Are you serious? You're just going to leave me here while you go *feed* on some woman?"

"Do you want to watch?" Khiderian whirled around and expelled a breath of frustration. "I need strength, Marilee. I'm trying to be considerate of how you feel, but—"

"Considerate?" Marilee rose from her seat, chest heaving with the deep breaths she had to take to keep from losing control and smacking the baffled look off Khiderian's face. Was it really that confusing trying to figure out why she was upset? Apparently it was. Shaking her head, she waved a hand dismissively and walked out of the kitchen.

She'd hoped he would run after her as she fled the room, but he didn't. Twenty minutes later, she sat huddled in a lounge chair, her gaze on the flat screen TV but for the life of her, she couldn't name the show she was watching. Her mind was too riddled with questions to focus on anything but her own stupidity. Watching TV was out of the question. Khiderian needed energy. Fine. He got the most from sex. Fine.

So why hadn't he come to her? "Because he doesn't really want you when there are other options around," she whispered to herself, then laughed. Why whisper? Ron was probably still standing stock-still in the kitchen waiting for permission from Khiderian to move. Lisa was under his trance and didn't give a damn if Marilee was torn up inside thinking about the two of them together, and Khiderian... He'd proven he didn't truly care about her feelings. Never had, apparently. She was a tool he could use to complete a mission, and nothing more. It didn't matter if he heard her. It wouldn't change the fact she'd allowed herself to feel something for a man—No, a vampire—who wasn't worth her emotion. How could she have been so stupid? She'd seen what men were like, had witnessed the way they'd treated her mother. She'd allowed herself to believe her mother brought her own abuse to her because of how loose she was, but maybe her mom knew better than her. She used men to get what she wanted and they used her right back. She might have been beaten a time or two, but she'd never had her heart broken. She was wiser than Marilee in that area. She never involved her heart.

"Marilee."

She closed her eyes and breathed in deep to fight back the anger that rose at the sound of his voice. As he neared, images of what she imagined him and Lisa had been doing flooded her mind and her stomach churned in response. "Done so soon?"

She felt him in front of her and opened her eyes to see him squatting in front of the chair, his head at an angle as he studied her. "You seem upset."

She laughed, a tear threatening to escape her eye as she pushed past him. "I'll get over it. Can we go now? There's a *good* man being held by a bunch of sirens that I think we need to rescue, in case you forgot that while you were playing."

"Playing?" He stood up and stepped toward her. "Marilee, I have to feed to keep my strength up. I don't do it just for pleasure."

"Oh, save it. I'm not as stupid as you think!" Marilee shoved Khiderian's chest and sent him back a few paces, his eyes wide with surprise. "I would leave your ass right now, but Jake's life depends on us working together. If you're done with our lovely and oh so generous hosts, let's move."

She turned on her heel and left Khiderian gaping after her as she stormed through the house, passing Ron in the kitchen. He smiled at her, his eyes still glazed over and empty, as she stepped into the garage. Lisa wasn't downstairs. Marilee growled as she imagined the woman lying in bed, recuperating from her recent exercise. What a skank, and to think the hussy had thought *her* a slut! "Bitch."

"Me?"

Marilee swung around to see Khiderian leaning against the door jamb, his brow creased as he watched her warily. She glared at him for a moment before turning to look for the car she'd overheard Ron talking about loaning to them. A Mustang. There were none in the garage so she stepped out a side door and looked among the ones lined in the drive. She spotted a cherry red Mustang facing the street and realized it had been moved because it was behind the car they'd arrived in. She didn't have to look behind her to know Khiderian was there. "So this is our new ride?"

"Yes."

"The tint isn't as dark as it is in the rental. Sure you won't fry?"

"We'll only travel during full dark." She heard him huff out a breath. "Why do I get the feeling you want me to fry?"

Marilee shrugged. "Maybe on some level you know you deserve it."

"For what? Feeding? We've discussed this to death. Why are you acting like this? It's not as if you didn't know I'd need to feed with all the psychic power I was using in there to secure us a new vehicle."

"Maybe I expected you to have a little more class about it!" Marilee snapped as she opened the passenger side door of the Mustang. She checked the backseat and saw her and Khiderian's bags had already been put in the new car. "Looks like we're ready and I'd rather get this mission over as quickly as possible so let's get a move on, unless you need to tell your new special friend goodbye one last time."

"Special friend? What do you mean by that?"

Marilee rolled her eyes and looked back at the vampire. Even in the dark she could see the confusion in his eyes. The man deserved an award for his acting ability. "I'm done with this conversation."

"I'm not." His eyes narrowed. "What exactly do you think I was doing?"

"Oh, what? Do I need to draw pictures?" Marilee expelled a breath to keep from raging as her body heated with anger. Did the jerk get a thrill out of messing with her head? She wanted to tell him what a pig she thought he was and point out that he'd just screwed an engaged woman. What kind of person was he to do something like that? But if she started yelling at him, she'd never stop and in the end she'd only feed his ego and that was not the way to deal with the situation. It was bad enough she'd fallen for the jerk, but despite sensing he already knew that on some level, she wasn't about to let him know just how deeply.

She bit the inside of her jaw to keep from spilling her guts and turned to get in the car when the pressure she'd felt before entered her head. Her anger flared as she realized the bastard had decided to raid her mind when she didn't answer his questions sufficiently. Well, screw that, and screw him too. She spun around and faced him as her body temperature rose.

"Stay the hell out of my mind!" A rush of heat poured out of her and Khiderian fell back against the rental. The back and side windows of the car exploded as flames shot out, and Khiderian quickly stepped away, looking between her and the rental with wide eyes.

"Calm down, Marilee." He stepped toward her slowly, hands held up in front of him as if to ward off an attack. "You remember what happened the last time you got this angry. Innocent people were harmed."

"You're not innocent." She didn't recognize her own voice. It was far too deep. Tears burned her eyes as they spilled down her cheeks and her breaths came too fast, making her lightheaded.

"Marilee, do you want to hurt me like this? Do you really want to kill me?"

"Yes," she answered as she shook her head no. He was a jerk, a bastard, a filthy rotten pig. He'd acted like he wanted her, flirted with her constantly, then moved on to Lisa with her big, fake boobs right in front of her. But she didn't want him dead. He'd saved her life more than once. Even if he was a jerk, he'd been there for her when she needed him, and would always be.

The windshield of the rental burst and flames grew higher. Marilee sobbed, knowing the flames would soon find a way to spread, consuming everything in their path. "I can't stop it. Tell me what to do."

"It's okay, sweetheart. I'm right here." Khiderian inched closer, watching her as if she were a snake, waiting to strike. Shame made her already overheated skin burn more. The fact that she felt ashamed when he should be made her anger grow, and as a direct result, the flames grew higher.

She tensed as Khiderian eased next to her and slid an arm around her waist. "Don't touch me."

"I'm not going to hurt you. Close your eyes."

"No."

"Do you want everything to burn? Do you want to burn Ron alive inside his home? You know that's what will happen if you let this get out of control." The windows of another car burst as its interior caught fire.

She closed her eyes, forcing more tears to spill. They fizzled as they dripped down her hot cheeks. "Help me."

"I am, sweetheart. I'm going to help you control it." He wrapped another arm around her, seemingly oblivious to the intense heat she could feel rolling off her. "You're very mad at me, and your anger is consuming you. When you get this mad, you tap into your pyrokinetic ability. You need to get your anger under control."

"I get angry all the time. I don't do this." She gasped on a sob.

"What's different this time? What happened this time that happened when your mother was mugged?"

Marilee thought back to that day, pictured in her mind the moment her mother's purse was stolen. She was scared. Her mother was crying. Then the building the mugger ran into burst into flames. "I don't know. I don't know why I lost control that day."

"You were a child then. Your emotions were probably harder to contain. But what set you off now? That I fed off the woman? I fed before we left the motel and you were fine knowing that."

"The woman?" Marilee's temperature rose even higher. "You can't even bother learning their names?" Had he fed off sex with another woman before leaving the motel? She'd thought he'd only fed off blood back there, but now that she knew what he was capable of... She shoved Khiderian away and gasped as flames burst between them.

Khiderian quickly held up his hands and the flames died out, leaving black smoke in their wake. "Dammit, Marilee. That was close. I can't shield fire for too long. I'm a vampire. Fire is very deadly to me. You don't want to do this!"

"You're making me want to do this!" A tree two feet behind Khiderian burst into flame. "Just stay away from me."

Khiderian nodded. "Okay. Let's contain this situation first though." He took a deep breath. "Close your eyes and think of something that makes you happy."

"Screw you. I'm not in the mood to think of kitties and rainbows right now. I'm not emotionless like you!"

"I hurt you somehow. I get that and I'm sorry. I'll make it up to you, I swear." He stepped closer to her, his hands held up in surrender, ready to block any fire she sent his way. "You know you don't want to hurt me though, or any innocent people. You never want to feel that guilt again."

"No." She shook her head, her body trembling. "I can't go through it again. Make it stop."

"I can't help you like this. If you can't calm down and draw it back, I have to link with you. You'll have to quit slamming the door in my face when I try to get in your mind."

"Fine." Marilee breathed in deep. "Just make it stop. Please." The pressure she'd felt before formed in the front of her head and spread. Marilee fought against her instinct to shut him out.

Khiderian crept behind her and wrapped his arms around her waist, pulling her closer as their minds melded together. "Focus on the flames just like you did with the wind. Watch them dance."

She did as instructed, and studied the way the flames bent and twisted, dancing without music in the night air. With Khiderian in her mind, it was easier to focus on the flames themselves, and not the emotions inside her fueling them. "Now call upon the wind to snuff them out."

Marilee breathed in deeply and called upon the wind, commanding it to encircle the flames. They died down, but didn't disappear completely. "I can't make it stop."

"Yes you can," Khiderian whispered, his breath tickling her ear. "It's yours. Command it."

She felt a tingle in her body and suddenly knew what to do. She braced her body and inhaled deep as if sucking the fire into her own body. The flames roared up in defiance, but only for a second before dying completely, leaving two charred vehicles and a crispy tree behind.

"You did it."

The prideful tone of Khiderian's voice after what he'd done flared Marilee's anger anew and she slammed the door in her mind closed, effectively kicking him out. "You did it. I felt you inside of me controlling it, guiding me how to make it stop. Now get away from me before I decide to burn your clothes this time."

Khiderian loosened his hold and stepped back, leaning against the hood of the Mustang. Marilee wiped the remaining tears from her eyes and studied him. Despite using his power to help her, he still seemed vibrant, but she couldn't help letting out a snide remark. "Do you need to go reenergize? I'm sure Lisa wouldn't mind another round."

His lips parted as his brow knit, and a smile slowly spread across his face. "You think I slept with her."

"No, I know you *fucked* her." Marilee ignored his raised eyebrows and stepped toward the passenger side of the Mustang, only to be yanked backward and whirled around to face the vampire she desperately wanted to get away from. "Let me go, Khiderian. I don't want to start the fire again."

"You won't. You've spent your anger, and now you're just sad." He spun her, changing positions so she was trapped between him and the car. "Why is that?"

"You were just in my mind. Didn't you get all the information you needed?" She swallowed hard, fighting back her embarrassment knowing he'd seen inside her head again and had to know the depth of her attraction.

"I was a little too busy helping you learn how to control your pyrokinesis to go looking around in there," he murmured, pulling her so close to him a sheet of paper wouldn't fit between them. "I did not have sex with that woman."

Marilee blinked, studied his face. If he was lying, he was damned good at it. "I saw the way you looked at her, practically drooling all over her big fat boobs."

Khiderian grinned. "I used a lot of psychic ability on Ron, then I had to add her into the mix when she showed up. I was hungry, and she was attracted to me which made her adrenaline spike, increasing her flow of blood. Of course I looked at her like that. I'm a vampire, Marilee. Blood is my cocaine and I was in need of a hit."

"So why didn't you take it from Ron?"

He frowned. "I admit it. If given a choice, I take blood from women only. Putting my mouth on men isn't something I enjoy and avoid doing unless it's in the heat of battle and I'm ripping them to pieces."

"So you admit it's a sexual thing." Marilee sniffed and tried to escape Khiderian's hold, but couldn't budge.

"No." He frowned, licked his lips. "Drinking blood is something I must do to survive. I prefer drinking from women since I am attracted to women, but that doesn't mean I want to have sex with every woman I drink blood from."

"You certainly let your mouth and hands wander when you drank from me. You're going to stand there and tell me you didn't do the same with anyone else you drank from since?"

"I drank from her wrist, and the only reason I did it in private was because I didn't think you wanted to see." He cocked his head to the side. "One would think you were jealous."

She glanced away. "Don't be stupid. I just don't think it's right having sex with someone when they're under your control."

Khiderian stiffened. "Do you really think me capable of such a thing?"

"No," she confessed, recalling his rage when she'd been attacked by Hank. "I'm just tired and cranky right now. I'm not making any sense. Let's just go before those people come to their senses and call the police."

"Not until we get something settled." Khiderian bent his head until his lips hovered over hers. "When you were fourteen years old you had a run-in with a bully at your school and your power flared, drawing my attention, so

I came to make sure you didn't do anything. You were wearing a white tank top, ripped jeans, and brown boots. I couldn't take my eyes off you, you were so beautiful. I knew I had to have you, but then I remembered how young you were. I knew what I was feeling toward you was wrong so I stayed away from you, helping you during your flares from as far away as possible until The Dream Teller had me fetch you for the mission. Despite the power it gives, I haven't had sex with a woman since that day. I haven't desired anyone but you since then."

Marilee stared at him, her mouth hanging open as she tried to form a response. He'd gone without sex that long because he wanted her? She shook her head, unable to believe the enormity of what he'd just claimed.

"I only get aroused when feeding from you," he murmured huskily before touching his lips to hers.

Marilee's heart seized and her first impulse was to push him away, but she ignored it and allowed Khiderian to slide his tongue past her lips and move his mouth against hers, giving her her first kiss. To her surprise, she couldn't taste blood, but she wouldn't have cared if she did. Gripping his shoulders, she followed his lead, hoped she was kissing him back the right way.

Khiderian stopped abruptly, and pressed his forehead against hers. "We can't do this. We have a mission to fulfill."

Marilee let out a little gasp as he stepped back, already missing his closeness, but she knew he was right. "We should go if we want to hit Nevada and get situated before sun-up."

"I guess we're good now if you no longer want me to fry." Khiderian grinned as he pressed his lips against her forehead. "Even if I can't have you, I'll never choose another over you," he said softly before backing away and walking toward the driver's side of the Mustang.

Marilee watched him, wondering what he meant by the statement, why he felt he couldn't have her, but feared his answer too much to ask. Instead, she glanced at the damage she'd caused one more time and joined him inside the car. "I guess we got some training in, at least."

"Yeah, we needed to work on your ability to draw and control fire." He studied the burnt remains of the two cars as he fit a key into the ignition and started it. A haunted look passed over his eyes. "Get some rest, Marilee. You're going to need it for the training we have to do once we hit Nevada."

Marilee frowned, wondering what type of training was ahead of her, and why Khiderian couldn't look her in the eye when telling her about it. And why his tone was full of apology.

CHAPTER TWELVE

"Seta! You'd better get in here!" Christian called, his tone urgent.

Seta cracked open her tired eyes and rose from the chaise in Christian's living quarters. She could sense the others' panic as she raced down the length of the hall which took her to where they held Nyla.

A few hours earlier, Seta had conjured a large plastic wall to hold her in her room after she'd shown signs of fleeing. For some reason, plastic was the only thing that could contain a therian. They could shift into their animal form and everything on them transformed with them, except for plastic. Their magic didn't work on or through it, so Seta had erected the thick plastic pane to cover the doorway.

"What's happening now?" Seta froze as she saw the spider web-shaped crack in the plastic barrier, and a large black panther crashing against the pane from the inside. "Shit."

"She's determined to break loose and go find Jake," Aria said as she stood in the hallway with the others, watching Nyla attack the pane in her animal form.

"Yes, I noticed." Seta raised her hands and spoke the words to strengthen the spell she'd cast over the doorway. The crack in the pane disappeared, but Seta's strength waned from the amount of magic needed to keep the plastic strong enough to sustain the constant pressure of Nyla ramming into it.

"Are you alright, Mother?" Rialto stepped away from his position behind his wife and approached her, his eyes showing his concern.

Seta smiled at her son. "I'm fine, darling, but I fear I'm going to have to keep reinforcing this wall and it'll zap every last ounce of my strength. Thank goodness there are no windows in the room for me to seal."

"You need a good feeding."

"Yes." She nodded her head in agreement. "Unfortunately I don't have time to go hunt for sustenance and you know it's too dangerous to bring food here into Christian's living quarters."

"If you can't maintain the barrier, she'll eventually break loose. With her ability to turn into mist, none of us will be able to stop her." Rialto turned his head toward the doorway and watched as Nyla rammed into it again. "We've all tried to talk her down, but she insists Jacob is going to die if we don't do something to save him immediately. She feels him fading."

"I'm sure she does." Seta sighed, her heart going out to the therian. She knew what it was like to feel a loved one fading. Her own sire had nearly died after being tortured by Carter Dunn, the first of many demons they'd had to kill since Rialto and Aria found each other, starting the Blood Revelation. Eron still remained buried in the earth, healing from the severe damage brought on from starvation and excessive torturing during his captivity. "We need help."

"You said a pair of warriors were searching for Jacob," Christian said. "Can you reach them and see how they're progressing?"

Seta scoffed. Warriors? Puh-leeze. Though she couldn't deny the vampire reeked of power, he thought and acted like a mortal human in love. And the girl? Marilee had proven a capability in the area of vampire slaying, but she was still just a small town hick with little meat on her bones, and plenty to learn. "No, but I know who can. Get Samuel," she instructed her son, "and bring him to me. Christian, call Malaika and get her here. I have to teach her this spell so she can sustain the barrier while I do something to stop this poor woman from losing her mind."

"And Jacob from losing his life," Christian said softly, stepping past her to do as told.

Nyla hit the plastic pane and fell back, shifting back into her human form as she fell to the ground. Tears stained her face and continued to run from her violet eyes as she heaved in a breath. "Let me out! I have to save Jake! He's dying!" She crawled forward and placed her hand against the pane. "Please, Seta. Please don't let him die."

Seta kneeled in front of the pane and placed her hand against the cool plastic, over Nyla's. "I will do everything in my power to save Jacob. We're going for help now, but Nyla, you have a child to protect. You must think of Slade."

"Where is he? Where did you take my son?"

"He's in the playroom with Njeri. He's safe, and he will remain safe as long as you stay here and let us get Jacob back for you."

Nyla's beautiful, uniquely hued eyes narrowed as a low growl erupted from her throat. "You say that but you're not doing anything to save him! You're locking me up here when I could be out there getting him back!" She shifted into panther form within the blink of an eye and rammed into the pane.

Seta sighed as she rose to a stand. "It's going to be a long night."

"I'll check on the children." Aria cast a sympathetic glance at Nyla and walked away, leaving Seta and Nyla to face off across the plastic pane, two powerful women not used to sitting idle while their loved ones were in danger suddenly forced to do just that.

Seta watched the large panther hit the barrier and clenched her teeth tight. The vampire Khiderian had better know what he was doing or he and Marilee would both feel her wrath.

Marilee yawned as she came awake and instantly realized she was no longer in the car. Opening her eyes, she found herself in a queen sized bed lying atop velvety soft red sheets. She sat up and looked around the room, noting how much nicer it looked than any motel rooms she'd ever rented. It was so clean, and the smell... She'd never been anywhere that smelled so nice, like fabric softener and lilacs.

Khiderian sat on a plush red sofa across the room, fiddling with items on the wooden coffee table. He glanced up as he felt Marilee's gaze. "Sleep good?"

"I must have. How long have we been here?"

"A few hours."

"Hours? Plural?" She found the alarm clock on the polished nightstand and blinked her eyes. "It's been at least four. Why did you let me sleep so long?"

"You needed it," Khiderian said sternly. "I strengthen my psychic abilities by astral feeding. You strengthen yours by sleeping. You're no good to this mission if you're worn out. Now eat something. You still have the food you brought along, or you can call room service."

"Room service?" Marilee swung her legs off the bed and spotted the binder next to the phone. She opened it to find a menu with different foods available for breakfast, lunch, and dinner. Her mouth watered as she found steak on the menu. "Why such a nice room?"

"Why not?" He shrugged as he sat back deeper in the couch. "The fact that I'm basically a mercenary doesn't mean I can't have nice accommodations. No offense but if I stayed at another cheap motel of your choice I'd lose it. There's only so much mildew a person can inhale, and I don't even want to know what I smelled coming off that last couch I slept on."

"Well, excuse me if I don't have the money to pamper you like a little princess," Marilee responded indignantly. "Waitressing only provides so much cash, especially when you have to sling beers in the trashiest dives on the planet because they're the only ones that'll hire you to work under the table. I guess if I had the power to mind-control people into giving me their money, I'd rent nicer places and drive flashier cars too."

Khiderian chuckled. "Don't worry about it. I don't intend on being too incapacitated to rent the rooms in the future, should we need them, and I actually hardly ever pay for rooms if you want to know the truth."

"So how do you…" Marilee rolled her eyes. "Mind control again. You just trick the clerk into handing over a key."

"Yes, and when I leave, there is no memory of me. While I use a room, they simply ignore it as though it doesn't exist."

Marilee frowned. "But how can I call room service then? Are you going to mind control the person on the other end of the phone, and everyone in the kitchen?"

"I paid cash for this room. The hotel staff still won't remember us after we leave, though."

"Thank you… for the room and considering room service."

"Not a problem." Khiderian shrugged. "You should eat now. I've spoken with the Dream Teller and also had a vision. We're going to have a guest soon."

She started to ask who but an image flashed through her mind along with a sense of intense anger. "Seta, and she's not going to be in a good mood."

"No she's not." Khiderian grinned. "Good psychic work."

"I have my moments." She stood and stretched before walking over to the small kitchenette where she rummaged through the bag of food she'd brought along. Knowing Seta would be arriving soon, she chose a long strip of beef jerky for breakfast and started on it as she sat at the bar separating the kitchenette from the rest of the room. "What do you have over there?"

Khiderian glanced at the items lying on the table—A bottle of clear liquid, some brown powdery stuff in a mesh bag, and a variety of flowers and twigs, some dried—and leaned forward, clasping his hands together. "The materials needed for a very powerful spell we're going to have to use in order to help Jacob."

Marilee's stomach rolled as she took in the worried look in Khiderian's eyes and she set down the remainder of the jerky, her stomach too nervous to continue eating. "Why do we need a spell? I thought we were going to get the location from Curtis Dunn and go in fighting."

"You're not ready for that." He glanced her way for the briefest of seconds before returning his attention to the items on the table. "Unfortunately, Jacob doesn't have time to wait for you to be ready so we have to make sure he gets some blood in him to boost the immortality serum he was injected with. We have to do it this way."

"What do you mean he doesn't have time?"

"His captors have been killing him over and over in order to draw out Nyla, and they've almost succeeded. He's going to die soon, and this time he won't resurrect."

"No!" Marilee's chest ached as tears burned her eyes. "We have to go in now. We can reach Curtis Dunn tonight."

"You're not ready for Dunn!" Khiderian's voice came out as an angry shout and he clenched his jaw, closing his eyes briefly. "I'm sorry. I don't mean to yell at you. Jacob will be fine. The spell will work."

"What kind of spell is— Aah!" Marilee bit back a scream, and automatically went for the dagger in her boot as a woman appeared in the room.

By the time she realized it was Seta, Khiderian was standing at her side, glaring at the furious vampire-witch. "I've been expecting you, and before you start on a rampage, we are aware of Jacob's situation and are prepared to save his life."

Seta opened her mouth to issue what would undoubtedly be a nasty barb, then closed it, frowning as if just registering what Khiderian had said. "You've located him and are going in to retrieve him now?"

"No. We haven't physically placed him yet, but we will very soon."

"Not soon enough!" The witch screeched, her eyes blazing. Marilee gulped, praying the fiery vampiress didn't choose to act on the rage she clearly felt, and tightened her hand around the hilt of her dagger. "He is dying. He probably won't make it through the night and we can barely keep Nyla contained."

"I know, which is why we're about to perform a spell. As I said, I've been expecting you. I have all you need, but you must cast it. Despite my many skills, I'm not a warlock."

"Jacob doesn't need a spell. He needs blood!" The rage in Seta's eyes simmered as she studied the materials on the table, her brow creasing as she looked back up at Khiderian. "Exactly what spell did you plan on using?"

"*Immortalis prosapia cruor*."

"I can't do that. Jonah is a heterosexual male. Even in spiritual form, if he catches sight of the sirens, he'll be entranced and won't do what we send him in to do."

"We're not sending Jonah in. We're sending in Marilee."

Marilee's heart skipped a few beats, but before she could say anything, Seta was already arguing. "But in order—"

"I know the requirements of the spell." Khiderian's body stiffened as he stared straight into Seta's eyes. "It will work."

The vampire-witch studied her so intently, Marilee felt naked on display. Seta's gaze suddenly whipped away and her eyes narrowed as she looked at Khiderian. Marilee tried to ease into his mind but the door between them remained bolted shut. She didn't miss what was obviously going on though.

"You're telling her something telepathically." She stepped back, looking between them, noting the briefest of guilty expressions before they quickly brought their features back in control, both of them wearing masks of nonchalance. She saw right through the crack in Khiderian's. "You're telling her something about me. Something about this spell you're going to do."

"Calm down Marilee." Khiderian turned toward her, his eyes soft and imploring. "I keep no secrets from you that will do you harm."

"Oh yeah, right." She scoffed. "What about—"

Don't say another word! If she finds out you're a drac chemare *she and countless others will hunt you down until your heart lies in their hands!*

Marilee looked up into Khiderian's stern eyes, glittering with authority, and swallowed. Casting a glance at Seta, she found the witch peering at her with a scary amount of curiosity. "What exactly is this spell and why am I the one going in? I thought we didn't know where Jake was."

"Physically, we don't, but through this spell you will project yourself to Jacob astrally, similar to what I can do when I feed from afar."

"Okay, and even if this works and I manage to do this, how am I going to get him blood?"

Khiderian took a deep breath, which she knew was more for calming his nerves than a necessity. He didn't actually need to breathe. "This is a very powerful spell. It will allow you to interact with Jacob in the spiritual form in a way I wouldn't even be able to."

Marilee frowned. "How? Why me?"

"We have to send you in. We..." He blinked and in that moment Marilee knew his next words would be a lie, or at the very least, an avoidance of truth. "We need to send in a human, and one who won't be ensnared by the sirens."

"So the sirens will be able to see me?"

"No."

"Then what does it matter if whoever you send in is attracted to the sirens?" Marilee threw her arms up in exasperation. "You're not making any sense. Why the hell am I doing something this dangerous? I'm going to be leaving my freaking body, aren't I?"

"Sirens are so powerful that a human man or woman attracted to them can be rendered useless by one glance," Seta interjected, her tone indicating her shortage of patience. "Sirens don't have to be able to see whoever we send in in order to screw up our plan. Right now, we don't have anyone else to send." She exchanged a quick look with Khiderian before continuing. "We will guard your body while you go to Jacob's side. You must wait for him to die and while his soul is separated from his body you must allow him to drink from you."

"What?" Marilee stepped back, her stomach churning. "That's gross."

Khiderian's eyes flared with hurt and Marilee instantly regretted her outburst. "It must be done, Marilee. If you want Jacob to live." He narrowed his eyes on her. "No matter how *gross*, you'll be saving his life. If you won't do it, we might as well write Jacob off now. It's a shame though considering he would do whatever necessary to save a life. I thought you admired that about him."

Marilee looked away, between the hurt in Khiderian's eyes and the condemnation in his tone, she felt lower than she'd ever felt in her life. "You're right. Jacob's a good man, and he has a child to raise, and a woman who loves and needs him." She squared her shoulders. "So... I appear by him and I'm pretty much invisible?"

"Yes," Seta answered as Khiderian just stared at her. Marilee half-wished she knew what he was thinking, but at the same time half-feared it. "Since you won't actually be dead you won't be seen by necromancers or witches, should there be any around. However, when Jacob dies and his spirit leaves his body it can be seen by either of those beings so if they're around..."

"They'll see him drinking from me."

"Not necessarily," Khiderian said. "They won't see you, but they'll see him. If there are any witches or necromancers around him you'll have to make sure he drinks your blood discreetly."

"Oh, is that all?" She ran a hand through her hair as a bead of sweat trickled down her spine. "How badly can I screw this up?"

"I wouldn't send you in if I thought you would screw it up." Khiderian folded his arms and looked at her sternly. "You can do this and you will succeed."

Marilee nodded, and tried to borrow some of Khiderian's confidence. "So you send me in through the spell. How do I get back out?" Her voice quivered on the tail end of the question as she thought of being trapped as a wandering spirit.

"The spell is kind of a round-trip ticket," Seta answered. "When Jacob drinks your blood the spell will bring you back. You won't be lost, and we'll be right here protecting your body."

"Protecting it from what?" New fear slammed into Marilee's chest.

"Nothing." Khiderian shot Seta an annoyed look. "Seta's just letting you know your body will be safe in case you're worried about being apart from it."

Oh, great. She hadn't even thought about that, but now that it was mentioned... "If I'm not actually in my body, won't it, like... start to rot?" She shuddered.

"No, it will not rot." Khiderian closed his eyes, his tongue pressed in his cheek, clearly impatient. "Just trust me, Marilee. I wouldn't allow anything to happen to you. You know that."

Seta looked between the two curiously, then jerked. "Oh, hell. We have to do this now. Nyla's going berserk. Jacob's on his last breaths."

Marilee didn't question how the witch knew this. She was, after all, a witch. Her psychic abilities had to outweigh her own. Bracing herself, she nodded firmly. "Alright. Let's do this."

Khiderian grabbed the bottle of clear liquid from the table as Seta quickly scooped up the other things he'd gathered. "Holy water," he explained as he doused her with it, smoothing the water over her clothes and body. He paused as he reached her arm. "You're going to need an open wound he can feed from. He's not a vampire and although you won't feel a thing in spirit form, gnawing on you will take too much time. He could waste away completely before he breaks through flesh."

Marilee cringed at the image that provoked. "So you're going to bite me first?"

He shook his head, eyes apologetic. "My saliva would seal the wound right after inflicting it. I'm sorry, but I'm going to have to cut you. I can take your pain away empathically so you don't feel the sting."

Marilee considered the offer as Seta sprinkled the powder for the spell in a circle on the floor. She didn't want Khiderian altering her mind. "No. I'll do it myself." She bit her lip. "Can I do it while in spirit form?"

"No. You can't take anything with you and you won't be able to touch solid objects."

"Well, that sucks ass." She sighed and closed her eyes as she quickly sliced her arm with her own dagger. She sucked in a hiss of air as the sting of her cut burn, and handed Khiderian the dagger.

He arched an eyebrow, reminding her the hilt was hawthorn. "Just toss it."

She wiped the bloody blade on her shorts and returned it to her boot before inspecting the gash in her arm. Blood welled above the surface and started to drizzle down her skin. "Am I going to bleed out while I'm doing this?"

"No. the spell will protect you," Seta answered. "Lie down in the circle. Hurry!"

Marilee looked into Khiderian's eyes and absorbed the reassurance she found there before carefully stepping inside the circle Seta had formed with the powder and herbs. She lay down in a straight line, her arms resting at her sides.

"The spell will work as soon as it's cast," Khiderian said from outside the circle. "Wherever Jacob is, you'll appear there. When he dies his soul will separate from his body and he will see you. You must quickly tell him why you're there and make him drink from you. When he drinks enough, the spell will bring you back to your body and return him to his."

"What if he doesn't drink from me?"

"Pour your blood down his fucking throat," Seta snapped.

Khiderian shot her a lethal glare. "It shouldn't be a problem. He'll be starving for it."

"It's time," Seta announced as she crushed flowers in her hand and tossed them over Marilee's body. At the outer edge of the circle she raised her hands and hummed.

Thick, heavy static crackled through the air. The room felt electric as Seta's humming grew stronger. As the humming turned into a bunch of Latin words, most of which Marilee didn't follow at all, she looked up at Khiderian. He nodded his head encouragingly before lethargy stole over her body. The room faded as her eyelids grew heavy and slowly closed. Seta's chanting slowly grew softer, sounding as though it came from miles away. The last word Marilee heard was one she did remember from her high school Latin course. *Prosapia*. Family. What did that have to do with... She couldn't remember what she was thinking as everything died away, leaving only silent darkness.

Seta's shoulders sagged as her arms lowered and she slowly opened her eyes, looking as if she'd woken from a week-long slumber. "It worked. She's gone."

"I know." Khiderian stared down at Marilee's lifeless body, his heart somewhere in the vicinity of his throat. He'd known what the spell would do and mentally, he'd been prepared for it, but his heart cried, seeing her lying there, no soul in her body.

"She's not dead. You don't have to look so devastated."

"I know how the spell works," Khiderian snapped, irritated by the witch's overly observant nature.

"So do I. The Immortal Family Blood spell. From your warning I know she's unaware, but does Jacob have any idea the girl is his sister?"

"Half-sister," Khiderian corrected. "I don't even think he suspects the man who raised him isn't his biological father. He doesn't know how slayers are created, does he?"

"Not to my knowledge." Seta sighed. "You know slayers have a natural protection against mind intrusion which explains why your little playmate here also has a natural defense against me. Other than the barest of surface thoughts, I can't get anything off her." She directed a narrow eyed leer Khiderian's way. "I don't know what he does or doesn't know about his paternity or how slayers are created, but I figured something was amiss when I met Jonah. Jonah is the oldest brother. By all means, he should have been the slayer had they shared the same father. Jonah has a natural defense against pranic vampires though." Seta folded her arms and angled her head to study Khiderian closer. "Why would he have that?"

Khiderian shrugged. "I've never met Jonah Porter. It's possible there's a little psychic background in the mother's family. They may be sensitives. It could explain why Jacob isn't the raging beast most slayers are."

"Very possible." Seta redirected her gaze to where Marilee's body lay. "So why don't you want her to know the truth?"

"Because it won't help our mission. Could even hinder it," Khiderian explained. "Marilee never knew her father, and has always wondered about him. She feels a closeness to Jacob but doesn't know why. She attributes it to him saving her life." He sighed. "She has enough on her plate with this mission. She doesn't need all of this piled on her right now, and if she knew Jacob was her half-brother it's possible she could do something rash. I need her thinking with her mind when we go in to save him, not her heart."

"I understand." Seta nodded her head. "So as the daughter of a slayer she must bear a gift. I'm curious why I can't detect it. Apparently Jacob couldn't, either."

"Maybe you're not as great a witch as you think you are." Khiderian lifted his gaze from Marilee only long enough to serve Seta a glare before returning it to Marilee's body. "There was nothing there for Jacob to detect. Marilee is a human, even if she does move quicker in battle due to her paternity."

"So that's it? The only gift she received from her father was speed?"

Khiderian closed his eyes and willed his temper to maintain stability. "You're not the only one who uses a little psychic human help."

The witch chuckled. "I knew there had to be something more to her. So why didn't you let on that she was a psychic?"

"Because she's *my* psychic human."

Seta giggled in delight, a sound that stabbed right through Khiderian's brain. "My, aren't we protective of our mortal?"

"Yes, and don't you forget it." Khiderian pinned Seta with his glare, allowing his eyes to glow as he offered her a small taste of his power. Her eyes widened briefly before she schooled her features to appear unmoved, but he knew she'd sensed his intent and understood in no uncertain terms that he would kill her if she touched one hair on Marilee's body, so he drew the cloud of power back into his body, saving his precious energy. "Enough distraction. You focus on Nyla while I focus on Marilee."

"Agreed." Seta quit staring at him, and turned her body away to look toward Marilee. "So you've fed from her?"

He growled low in his throat and Seta got the point. She didn't ask any more questions.

CHAPTER THIRTEEN

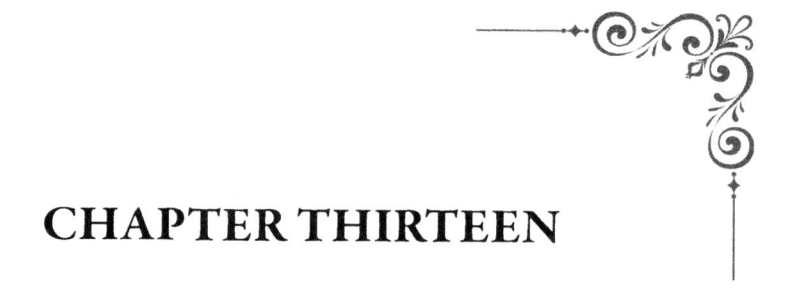

A scream ripped through the nothingness cloaking Marilee and she opened her eyes to a dark brick wall. Another scream, this one cutting off abruptly. Behind her. She turned and her blood froze in her veins—figuratively speaking—as she saw Jacob Porter, his eyes bulging out of his head as electrical currents ran through his body.

Three...Nylas? ... circled him as he hung from the ceiling, his wrists bound above his head with a metal chain. His feet dangled in a bathing pool full of water and every other second they each dipped some sort of taser-like things into it. The rough and bloody marks along his bare chest and arms were evidence they didn't always electrocute him through the water.

"One last time, slayer. Tell us where to find the child already born and we'll end your torment." One of the Nyla clones Marilee assumed were sirens stood face to face with Jake. "We'll let you go. Just say the words we need to hear."

Jake's eyes were closed now, his head lulled, but he managed to raise it and work his throat just enough to spit blood into the face of the bitch taunting him. She recoiled, lips pulled back in a snarl. "Bastard! Bring him down."

Marilee studied her surroundings as the women detached Jake from the ceiling hook he was chained to. She was inside a small, dank cell in what looked like a basement. Whether it belonged to a residence or an abandoned building, she couldn't tell, but she knew from experience the other side liked to kill families and establish headquarters in their homes. That's what the vampires had done back home in Hicksville. She returned her glare to the sirens and vowed her grandparents' death would not be in vain.

Jake was on the floor now, his body burnt and broken, his chest barely moving. As disabled and harmless as he was, the bitch he'd spit on still kicked him in the gut. Marilee surged forward, then remembered there was nothing she could do to them. She was nothing more than a ghost. All she could do was sit by and wait for them to finally torture the poor guy to death. But once she got back to her body and found out the address to this prison from Dunn, she was so kicking the bitches' asses. Marilee stilled. She was in the prison now. Even if she was just a spirit, she had vision. She could find the address and cut out the trip to Dunn altogether. It wasn't as if she were chomping at the bit to go anywhere near a man who shared his body with a demon after discovering what she was.

The sirens were circling Jake, taunting him further, but so far he still clung to life. She'd have to feed him her blood as soon as he died, and then she'd be sucked back into her own body. If she was going to get the address, she had to do it while he was still alive. That didn't leave much time.

She looked around. There were no windows in the basement, let alone the cell. She'd have to find her way into the upper level of the building and exit through the front door. She cast a quick glance at Jake. He was completely unrestrained, yet he didn't move a muscle. He couldn't. It wouldn't be long. She had to hurry.

Marilee took a deep breath, which was completely absurd, she knew, but she did it anyway out of habit, and took off at a run. She ghosted right through the bars of the cell but snapped back to where she'd started once she got three steps past. "What the hell?"

She quickly jerked her head around to see if the sirens heard her, and found them taunting Jake as if nothing had just happened. They still had no clue she was there. She looked out past the cell. There was nothing there. She hadn't even felt anything before she snapped back to her starting point, but she couldn't find the address to Jake's prison by going that way. If she could walk right through the cell bars... She turned the opposite way and walked through the wall... only to find herself in another empty, dark, musty room. "Come on." She walked farther, heading for the outer wall but just as she reached it she snapped back to her starting point again. "Dammit!" She stomped her foot, not surprised the action made no sound. She was catching on. As Khiderian had said, she'd appear by Jake. Apparently, she couldn't stray too far from him. She was going to have to face a demon before she found the address to his prison.

SIREN'S SNARE

The sirens huddled together, discussing whether or not to continue Jake's torture, and Marilee tried one more time to figure out where she was. Outside the cell was a table covered in metal instruments. She could only imagine the indescribable pain inflicted on Jake by those tools. There was no writing on anything that she could see. No markings, no brand names. There was no television, no radio, no newspaper, no magazines. Nothing with the name of the state they were in, and of course nothing like a household bill. That would just be too easy. Giving up, deflated by the failure, she returned her attention to the trio of hell-hussies chatting over Jake's broken body.

"He's dying," the one who still bore his blood on her face stated, studying him with her head tilted at an angle.

"That's the point, isn't it?" another one asked, studying her nails. "We've only been doing this for weeks now."

"This may be the last time," the first one answered. "He's had no blood to boost the serum that half-breed idiot injected him with. He can't take much more."

"What's the problem?" the one who'd been silent asked. "I'm growing tired of torturing him. I prefer men who come to me willingly, men whose souls I can suck out while they die. This waste of testosterone leaves us empty."

The first siren rolled her eyes. "We're doing this for the greater good, Lura. We haven't found the location of the child Xander told us about nor have we learned whether or not the slayer's child has been born."

"Are you sure there even is another child?" Lura asked, her voice a harsh whisper as if even while knowing Jake was knocking on death's door she feared him overhearing her secrets. "We got that information from a demon. Demons lie."

"So do we," the one Marilee decided was the ringleader snapped. "Who doesn't? But this is the fucking Blood Revelation we're talking about. This isn't something anyone bullshits about! How is he?" She directed the question to the siren who knelt by Jake's side, checking his pulse.

"Barely breathing."

"Let's just kill him and get it over with," Lura said, leering down at Jake. "I'm hungry for a soul."

Marilee froze, but remembered they fed off souls while they were in the process of a kill. They couldn't see her. She was safe. The wound on her arm was still open, blood that disappeared once it left her 'body' still seeping out. She wondered if it would dry up before Jake died.

"He couldn't answer us now even if he wanted to," the ringleader said on a sigh, squatting down to take a closer look at him before narrowing her eyes on the siren next to him. "I told you not to taser him in the throat. You fried his vocals."

The other siren shrugged, grinning impishly. "He still managed to spit in your face."

The ringleader's hand shot out and within the blink of an eye she'd drawn blood from the other siren's face. The siren's image flickered so that for a moment Marilee saw a blue-green scaled creature behind the Nyla costume.

"Bitch!" the siren snapped, her hand covering the fresh scratches along her cheek.

"Keep trying me and see what a bitch I can really be," the ringleader said, standing. "We have nothing to report back to Jaffron."

"Fuck Jaffron," Lura snapped. "If he's such a bad-ass vampire, why couldn't he capture and torture the slayer?"

"Because he can't make himself look like the love of the slayer's life," the ringleader answered. "We might not have gotten anything out of the slayer but we taunted the hell out of him better than anyone else could just by appearing in this image."

"He really would die for the bitch," Lura commented, a little awe in her tone.

"He really is... in a few more minutes, if that." The ringleader shrugged. "Come on. I'm tired of looking at him. Having a straight man deny me doesn't settle well in my stomach. Let's get through the ordeal of telling Jaffron we have no useful info and then grab a little something to make up for all this work."

"Please let there be some enticing choices tonight," Lura said to no one in particular as the three of them stepped away from Jake and walked over to the door of the cell. The ringleader inserted a key and led the other two out. Despite thinking Jake was truly on his deathbed this go-round, she locked the door behind her and the trio disappeared around a dark corner. Marilee could hear their footsteps traveling up a staircase and another lock being undone before a heavy door slammed shut.

She knelt down next to Jake and attempted to feel his pulse, but despite her fingers looking solid, she couldn't make them physically connect to him. He moaned, the sound coming from his raw throat so low, she barely heard it, but the degree of pain he felt came through clearly. "It'll be over soon, Jake, and I'll make you stronger." She thought so, anyway. She'd save his life at least.

Looking at the small pool of water he'd been hung over, the chain he'd been hung with, and the hook in the ceiling that had held him, fury raged in her gut. "You're going to get through this, Jake, and you will see your family again. I swear to you that I will get you out of here even if I have to reach into those bitches' chests with my bare hands to rip their hearts out. Just hang in there long enough to buy Khiderian and me the time we need to do it."

She reached out to brush the matted, bloody hair away from his brow, forgetting she couldn't touch him. Sighing, she closed her eyes and waited for him to die, helpless to do anything else. Poor Jake. She remembered the first time she'd seen him in the jail in Hicksville. She'd just impaled a vampire when he strolled into the lobby like a warrior angel, slaying the hell out of the remaining vampires. She'd been in awe.

She grinned to herself, recalling the way Khiderian acted when they'd first discussed him. He seemed to think she had a crush on the slayer, but she never had. Oh, he was gorgeous. There was no denying that, but she'd never felt an attraction to him like that. There was just something about him that didn't do it for her, but she respected him. He was loyal to his loved ones, and as evidenced by what remained of him in the cell, he would go through hell to protect his family.

Marilee had never known her father, not even as much as a name, and her mother might as well have died during childbirth. The only thing she'd ever done for her was kill her boyfriend when the drunken slob had assaulted her. That one incident was the only time Marilee felt the woman cared for her on some level, but in the back of her mind she couldn't help wondering if Becky Mills had just been jealous of the fact her boyfriend had shown her daughter attention she herself craved. Becky always seemed to care more about getting laid than about caring for her daughter. Maybe it wouldn't have been so bad if she'd had siblings to share the horrors of her childhood with, but Becky had only had one child. One birth control failure, as she referred to her. Marilee imagined if she did have a sibling, it would have been nice to have had a big brother like Jake, someone who would keep her safe. But she didn't and there was no sense dwelling on that now. She was grown. Gram and Grampa were killed by the vampires, and Becky most likely had been too. She was on her own. Just her and her very own vampire, if he wanted her. She grinned at the irony. Vampires had taken her family. Now one of them was the closest thing she had left to family. Crazy.

"What the hell?"

Marilee opened her eyes to see Jake. Twice. His spirit which looked as solid as a brick wall was sitting up inside his dead body. "Wow. That's disturbing."

His brow creased. "What? What are you doing here?" He narrowed his eyes, scrutinizing her. "You're not a siren."

"Do you recognize me, Jake?"

He nodded slowly, wariness thick in his eyes. "You're the teenager from Hicksville. You helped me raid the vampire nest in your grandparents' house."

"I'm not a teenager anymore, but looks like I'm going to have to help you out again. Drink." She held out her arm.

Jake looked at the arm and jerked back. "What kind of trick is this?" He glanced down, saw his dead body and let out a startled gasp as he backed away from it. "What the fuck?"

"The sirens successfully tortured you to death. I'm here to make you live again."

"What?" He looked around wildly. "What kind of scam is this? What are you?"

"I'm Marilee from Hicksville. You remember me." She cursed Khiderian in her mind. No problem, her ass. Jake wasn't lunging for the blood like he'd predicted. He didn't trust her and after what she imagined he'd been going through the past few weeks, she couldn't blame him.

"How the hell can I see you if I'm dead?"

"You're not fully dead, if what I gathered from what Seta and Khiderian told me is correct, but you don't have much time before you are."

"Seta!" Jake stood up, running his hands down his torso, feeling the solidity of his spirit form. "She knows where I am?"

"No." Marilee stood up to be closer to eye level with the tall slayer. "She worked some spell that brought me here in spirit form and told me I had to feed you blood. It'll act as a booster to the serum Curtis Dunn injected you with and allow you to resurrect again. We're going to save you, Jake. I promise, but we need a little bit more time to track down your location. However..." She held out her arm again. "If you don't drink my blood now you are going to be permanently dead and it won't matter whether we find this place or not."

He licked his lips as he studied her wound but the wariness didn't leave his eyes. "If this is a trick—"

"If it's a trick you'll figure it out soon enough and kill me. If it's not a trick then I'm telling you the truth which means you either drink this blood or you die and leave your son abandoned. It's your choice."

He shook his head, but stepped forward, grabbing her arm. "How can I touch you like a solid thing but I was just sitting *inside* my body?"

"I don't understand this magic stuff, I just do as I'm told. So far Khiderian hasn't led me wrong."

"Who's Khiderian?"

"The vampire who's going to kick everyone in here's ass while I take out the sirens... once we find out exactly where here is. He works for the Dream Teller," she added when Jake looked at her suspiciously.

Seeming mollified by that explanation, he bent his head and licked the blood oozing from her arm. Marilee felt nothing, odd since both of them looked solid and could touch each other, but as she'd told him, she was learning to just go with the flow where all the magic stuff was concerned. "What can you tell us about this place?" she asked as he drank from her. "Who else is here other than the sirens?"

"Vampires," he answered. "A witch, a shitload of shifters, and I think a psychic, but it's mostly the sirens who come down here. When is this supposed to cause me to resurrect again?"

"I don't know," Marilee answered as he continued drinking her blood, more greedily now that he trusted her a little. "I suppose whenever you get a certain am—ah!" Marilee was jerked back, cocooned in darkness again as she fell into a bottomless pit, Jake nowhere near her.

"Marilee."

Khiderian! Marilee opened her eyes, unaware they'd been closed, and gazed up at the hotel room ceiling. Lowering her gaze, she caught sight of Khiderian, what looked like relief in his beautiful blue eyes. "I think I did it."

"Can you get up?"

She rose to a sitting position, nodding as she came up, and looked at her arm. "I'm still bleeding."

"I'll fix it." Khiderian stepped into the circle, apparently it no longer mattered if it was disturbed, and knelt next to her. He took her arm in his hands and raised it to his mouth. "If you don't mind," he added, and Marilee was reminded of the way she'd reacted when told Jake would have to drink from her.

"I don't mind when you drink from me."

He grinned, the subtlest upturn of his mouth, before laving the marred area, quickly healing the flesh.

To avoid focusing on the intense sensation his tongue on her skin caused, Marilee took the opportunity to study Seta who was standing still with her head cocked to the side as if listening to something. Her fingers rested against her temple. As Khiderian finished healing her arm, Seta let out a sigh of relief. "Nyla has calmed down. We succeeded."

"Was there any doubt?" Khiderian delivered an unfriendly look at the witch before pulling Marilee to a stand. "How do you feel?"

"Fine." Marilee checked the smooth flesh of her arm, found it hard to believe what had just happened but there was no debating it had. "I tried to find out where Jake was being held but I couldn't move very far away from him."

"The spell keeps you close to him," Khiderian explained. "It would've been great if you could have gotten his location but things are never that easy."

"Did you get any information at all?" Seta asked.

"I know he's being kept in a cell in a windowless basement but I have no idea whether it's a private residence, public building, or abandoned warehouse. He was able to tell me that he's seen vampires, shifters, a witch and possibly a psychic."

"A witch who practices dark magic," Seta practically spat. "And working with a psychic? No wonder I can't get a lock on their location."

"Marilee and I will have the location soon enough." Khiderian glared at the witch. "Your job here is done and we appreciated the help, but now it's time for you to leave."

Seta straightened her shoulders, raised her chin. "You could try a nicer tone, soul-sucker."

"He doesn't suck out souls," Marilee said, surprising herself. Common sense would tell her to leave the volatile witch alone, but she continuously found herself trading barbs with the woman when Khiderian was the topic of discussion.

Seta raised an eyebrow as she angled her head to study Marilee more intensely. "I'm growing tired of your sassy attitude."

Khiderian stepped in front of Marilee before she could respond. "Leave now, Seta. Don't make me... make you."

The vampire-witch's nostrils flared as she split a venomous glare between the both of them. "I didn't help you buy Jacob more time just so he can be tortured in vain. You'd better save him and you'd better do it quickly."

Marilee folded her arms and stepped around Khiderian. "You're welcome."

Seta frowned. "What?"

"I said you're welcome, although you don't have the decency to thank a person after they've helped you." Marilee held the witch's glare as it grew colder. "You might have cast the spell, but it looks to me like Khiderian got all the stuff together and had everything in place for you just in the nick of time, and I'm the one who stepped into the danger zone. If I overheard correctly, you couldn't have done this spell without me. Jake would be dead right now without us so why don't you can the attitude and be a little respectful yourself?"

Seta's mouth dropped open, clearly not expecting someone to speak their mind to her. As she closed it, her eyes burned with anger. "Yes, you're correct. Khiderian did have everything I needed for the spell. Even ingredients I didn't know existed."

She leered at Khiderian as he tensed. "It's time to go, Seta. Now. Protect your grandchild and the other chosen."

The fire in her eyes simmering, lips pressed tight together, Seta gave a sharp nod. "Just remember that despite blocking me, I'll always find a way to find you should things not work out as planned. You'd better not fail or all your fears will come true."

Marilee jerked as the vampire-witch disappeared. "Even when I expect her little disappearing-reappearing trick it still manages to surprise me every time."

"It's teleportation. I can do it too but it takes a ton of energy. Now that Nyla's stable, Seta will most likely feast to replenish what she's used tonight." Khiderian turned toward the mess on the floor and focused on it. Within a minute, the powder and crushed flowers were resting in a wastebasket. A moment longer, and the blood that had pooled onto the carpet was no more.

"Cool. Can you teach me to clean house with my mind or is that out of my range?"

"You already know how," Khiderian answered. "It's the same thing we worked on in New Mexico."

"That was controlling the wind. There's no wind in this room."

"Controlling the wind is your first baby step into telekinesis. You just apply the same principle to objects. Focus and control. The more you use it, the easier it gets." He walked over to the sofa and plopped down, stretching out with his arm resting over his head. "You did good work tonight, Marilee. Now order up something good to eat and refuel."

"You sure can be bossy," she grumbled, earning a deep chuckle that made her shiver. "Speaking of which, what's with you and Seta?"

"What do you mean?"

"Please. You two are like cats and dogs." Marilee walked over to the nightstand and grabbed the room service menu. "Of course she does have a nasty attitude, but it seems like it really comes out around you."

"Seta is used to being feared and being in charge. When she doesn't get her way, she's a real…"

"Bitch?" Marilee supplied as she sat on the bed and perused the menu.

"Yeah. A supernatural bitch." Khiderian sat up and leaned forward, resting his elbows on his knees. "I should feed again before daylight."

Marilee glanced up from the menu. "Blood?"

He nodded. "I didn't find those spell ingredients down the block. I did a good amount of teleportation myself tonight. I didn't want to leave you alone long."

Marilee set the menu aside. "How much do you need?"

"I'm not bad off if you're worried about me getting in the condition I was in the other day." He scratched the back of his neck. "It's best to be safe though."

Marilee checked the time on the clock and walked over to where Khiderian sat on the couch. "It'll be daylight soon." She dropped to her knees between his legs and pulled her hair back, baring her neck. An extreme offer was needed to make amends for the pain she'd seen in his eyes earlier when she'd practically gagged at the thought of Jake drinking her blood. That look had haunted her since. "Here. You can feed better tomorrow night, but this should work for now."

Khiderian's jaw slackened as he focused on her neck. "You're offering me your neck?"

Marilee nodded, swallowed hard against a sudden onslaught of nerves. "Earlier I said that allowing Jake to drink my blood was gross. That's because it was Jake. I didn't mean that..." She lowered her eyes so she wasn't so fully aware of Khiderian's unnerving gaze on her. "I just didn't like the thought of some guy's mouth on me, but with you I..." Oh great. What was she going to say, that she liked Khiderian's mouth on her? Trashy much? Maybe she had taken after her mother a little. It just took the right kind of guy to bring it out in her.

Khiderian's finger slid under her chin and she allowed him to turn her face toward him. "You don't have to prove anything to me, Marilee. I know the thought of a vampire drinking from your neck scares you."

"True." She placed her hand over his wrist. "But you're not just a vampire. You're Khiderian, and you're kind of great."

His lips slowly spread into a closemouthed smile before he lowered his head to press them against hers. Marilee leaned into him, angling her head to allow him better access, and felt herself being pulled upward until she straddled his lap on the couch. Slowly, he made his way across her jaw and down the side of her neck, licking the point he would bite down into. Marilee braced herself for the bite, but was pushed away instead. Khiderian breathed heavily as he rested his head against the crook of her neck.

"Khiderian?"

"Room service. Order something. Lots of it." He pushed Marilee's thighs until she stood, and leaned his head against the back of the couch, looking up at her, eyes glazed over with hunger. "Go on. Jacob drank from you earlier. I'm not drinking from you until you've eaten something, and I want you to have something readily available in case you need it when I'm done."

"Oh. Okay." Marilee turned around, tripped a little as she rounded the coffee table, but quickly caught herself and walked over to the telephone. Sitting on the bed, she checked out the room service menu. Never having ordered before, she took a moment to read how it worked, and then dialed the extension listed. Khiderian's intense gaze warmed her skin as she placed her order, and her voice shook as she thanked the person on the other end of the line.

"About fifteen minutes," she said as she lowered the phone back into its cradle and wiped her clammy hands on her shorts. The same shorts she'd been wearing since they left Arizona. "Hey, can you get the food when it gets here? I want to take a shower and change."

"Sure." Khiderian tilted his head to his right. "Your things are in the bathroom already."

"Okay. Thanks." She stood up and paused, drinking in the vision of Khiderian sitting on the sofa, legs parted, head slightly back, raw hunger in his eyes as they stared back at her. Shivering, she hurried into the bathroom, quickly closed the door and leaned against it where she took a few deep breaths. If the man had taken off her clothes on that sofa she wouldn't have raised one finger to stop him. Hell, she probably would have urged him to move faster before her nerves caught up to her and scared her into stopping.

What are you doing, Marilee? He's a vampire. Hell-O. Big, brooding, fang-owning vampire... And who the hell cares? Shaking her head, she stepped forward to unzip the bag Khiderian had laid out for her on a white marble counter next to the sink. She spotted bottles of shampoo and conditioner, bars of scented soap, deodorant, wrapped toothbrushes and toothpaste, and even shaving supplies so she didn't bother rummaging for her own toiletries. She reached in to the bag and pulled out a white cotton tank top, a pair of pink boyshorts, and a pair of little gray cotton drawstring shorts to wear over them, and set the clothes aside before she stripped and stepped into the shower.

Her hands shook as she lathered a washrag with rose-scented soap and started to clean her skin. An image of her and Khiderian tangled in red sheets flashed through her mind and her legs wobbled so bad she had to sit down. Before the night was over she was going to have sex with Khiderian. She knew it with the same clarity she knew he and Seta had hid something from her. She started washing more vigorously, determined to be perfect for him, as determined as she was to find out what the secret was between the two vampires.

CHAPTER FOURTEEN

Khiderian dipped inside the hotel employee's mind while the young man set up Marilee's food on the bar, learning the man was a college student who relied a great deal on tips to get by and whose only concern at the moment was being quick and courteous so that Khiderian gave him a good amount of money. He barely paid attention to what Khiderian looked like as it was, but Khiderian was never one to take chances. He altered his image in the man's mind and made it appear he was alone.

"Will that be all, sir?"

"That will be fine," Khiderian answered and handed a wad of bills to the young man whose eyes lit up as he counted the money.

"Did you mean to give me this much, sir? The bill was only—"

"I appreciated the quick service," Khiderian cut off the man and led him out of the room. "Enjoy the rest of your shift."

He chuckled as he closed the door in the surprised man's face and walked over to the bar separating the kitchen area from the rest of the room. Marilee had ordered a thick steak and a baked potato, along with a slice of... cheesecake? Khiderian had befriended some humans, witches, and shapeshifters during his long time on earth, so he was familiar with quite a few foods even if he had no idea how they tasted, but some things still threw him. Food had never been a priority for him. Blood was.

His body ached at the reminder he needed to feed, and he ground his teeth together, fighting the impulse to go out in search of sustenance. After Marilee's reaction the last time he'd fed with her fully aware of what he was doing—granted, she'd thought he was feeding in another way entirely—he didn't want to risk another blow-up. She'd nearly burned him. Even as powerful a being as he was, fire was dangerous.

SIREN'S SNARE

He couldn't help grinning as he recalled the rage she'd shown over the thought of him with another woman. He'd longed for the willowy woman for a decade of his too-long life, never expecting her to return the feeling, especially after vampires had killed off her family. Then, throw in the fact she was a slayer's daughter, and the chances were almost impossible. Being female and not the first-born, she of course never had a chance of inheriting the full slayer gene but she still had traits. Quickness in battle, heightened awareness of danger, great instincts, and a natural instinct to distrust anyone not human. He'd sensed her attraction, but never expected it to go past an appreciation for his appearance. And now she offered him her blood because she didn't want him to feed from anyone else?

He should leave. Lowering himself to the foot of the bed, he rested his head in his hands, damning himself for his greed. He'd rented the nice room with the single bed in hopes of something he had no right hoping for. He was delighting in the fact she wanted him to drink from her willingly when he should be turning down her offer flat.

He wouldn't even tell the woman that the man they were assigned to rescue was her own flesh and blood because her emotions could hinder their mission, yet he was ready to go as far with her as she'd allow. What if something happened to him on the battlefield and she had the opportunity to escape unharmed, but didn't? What if he was trapped and instead of finding her own freedom she foolishly went back in for him? He had to push her away. He would still train her for the job they had to complete. There was no way he was allowing her to lose another family member, regardless of the Blood Revelation, but he couldn't allow her to grow feelings for him, even if for the first time in centuries, he felt true happiness. He'd cherish the moment she revealed her jealousy, giving away her feelings, until the day he drew his last breath, and maybe even thereafter, but he couldn't allow this disastrous train to keep rolling.

As the bathroom door clicked softly and creaked open he lifted his head to tell her as much, but the words died in his throat. Long golden legs glistened with moisture. A thin scrap of gray cotton barely covered her lower half, and an inch of smooth, taut skin peeked out between the top of the little shorts and the hem of her thin cotton tank top that fit snug against her body, showing the lack of a bra to hide her small, but perfect breasts. A small hint of her minimal cleavage erased any willpower he'd had. He was going to drink from her, and if she allowed him, he was going to taste more than her throat.

"Oh good. The food's here." She rubbed a towel through her damp hair before hanging it over the back of a stool and sliding onto one next to it. "I'll eat the steak and potato now so you can go ahead and feed."

His gaze fell to her thigh and he instantly hardened at the thought of feeding from the femoral artery again. Shit. "You know, there's still time left for me to find a donor and feed well without worrying about the sun coming up. We're in a hotel. There's plenty of people here."

"Is there something wrong with my blood?" Marilee's nostrils flared as she gripped a fork tightly in her hand. Khiderian had the instinctive feeling that fork could end up in him any moment.

"I don't want to hurt you."

"You've fed from me before and it didn't hurt." She tilted her head, studying him. "Are you hungrier than you let on? I can use the hawthorn oil if you're afraid of taking too much."

"No, that's not necessary." He shook his head and sighed as he ran a hand through his hair. There was no way out of feeding from her without pissing her off, and there was no way he could put his lips against her skin and not want more. His only hope of salvation now was that she'd come to her senses and refuse him. "If you're sure you're up to it. My concern is with your health."

"I'm healthier than a bull with a hard-on." Her cheeks infused with color as she closed her eyes and turned away. "Sorry. Hillbilly-ism from my time served in Hicksville."

"Time served?" Khiderian grinned. "Isn't that a prison term?"

"It felt like prison there." She started working on her steak. "I was trapped in that pathetic excuse for a town because my grandparents refused to leave, and I didn't want to leave them. Not that I had a lot of money. I was putting it away, trying to save up for when... I kind of had an instinct I'd have to leave one day."

"You knew the vampires would come."

"I had dreams about them. They became pretty regular the closer it got to that day. I guess that's why I was able to retain my sanity while everything was going nuts. Maybe if the others hadn't been so surprised by what they were seeing, they would have had a chance."

Maybe if the others had slayer blood. She couldn't do all the things Jacob could do, would never be able to sense a supernatural creature from as far a distance and pinpoint the make, model, and year like Jacob, but she had instinct and speed on her side. "Maybe if the others had your gifts."

"Are you referring to my psychic abilities or the demon bait thing?"

"Demon bait?"

"Isn't that what I am?" She speared a piece of meat onto her fork and slid it inside her mouth. Khiderian glanced away, enjoying the sight a little too much for comfort. "So my little curses kept me alive?"

"Gifts, not curses." Okay, so he fibbed a little. The ability to call demons, even if incredibly useful at times, was a curse. More than that. It was a death sentence if she was discovered. He recalled Seta's abundance of curiosity about Marilee and what she'd received from her father, and fear slivered along his spine. He didn't fear easily, but the thought of Seta discovering what Marilee could do had him damn near pissing himself. Seta was smart. She knew the right combination of slayer and faithless could produce a *drac chemare*. He had to be very careful with the vampire-witch. It would be a shame to kill the most powerful witch they had on their side, but if it came down to protecting Marilee's identity, he wouldn't hesitate. "You shouldn't feel guilty about surviving that massacre."

"I don't feel guilty about surviving it." She stabbed another piece of meat and popped it into her mouth, chewing angrily. "I feel guilty about having those dreams and allowing those beasts to kill my grandparents. I completely ignored my gut instincts and they paid the price."

"No, they didn't," Khiderian said quickly, unable to bear the pain in her voice. "They're in a better place now. No pain. No suffering. You're paying the price as long as you blame yourself for their deaths."

"Do you really believe that?" She twirled her fork in her baked potato. "You're saying they're in heaven, right?"

"Yes, and yes, I believe they are there now. They were good people who lived a full life and held no regrets that would prevent their souls from leaving this realm and becoming wandering spirits. They'd be unhappy to know you're taking the blame for their deaths."

Marilee looked at him curiously for a moment before turning her attention toward her food again. "Where do good little vampires go after they... if they lose their subscription to immortality?"

The image of flames licking at his body entered his mind. He lay back on the bed, shut his eyes, and forced the nightmare image out. "I'm not entirely sure there's such a thing as good little vampires."

"I could have sworn you said you were one of the good guys."

"Hmm." He rested an arm over his eyes and wished for a change in topic. "Less talk. More eat." Weight settled over his groin and he looked up to see Marilee straddling his lap.

"All done. Now it's your turn." Marilee pulled her hair back from the side of her neck and tilted her head, hoping her nervousness didn't show.

Khiderian's gaze roamed down the front of her body, warming every place it touched, before he raised himself onto his elbows. "You're trembling."

So much for hiding her nerves. "I'm a little nervous, but I'm okay."

"I told you already you don't have to prove anything to me. You don't have to do this."

"And I told you that I want to." Doubt crept inside her head as he didn't make a move toward her throat. "Look, I know that back there in Arizona I was a little... Well, I was a little crazy."

Khiderian chuckled. "You were jealous." He trailed a smooth fingertip down her throat, stopping just above her breastbone. "I like your jealousy. It shows you don't think of me as the big bad monster you once wanted so badly to believe I was."

"So if you don't think I'm a clingy psycho-stalker, why are you acting like you don't want to drink from me?"

He leaned in, pressed against her, and let his lips hover just under her ear. "I don't drink from your neck," he whispered, his breath tickling her skin, before flipping her over, changing positions so she now lay under him. "But thanks for the offer."

He slid down and Marilee gasped as his tongue rolled over the inside of her upper thigh, anesthetizing the area before he lowered his fangs and sank them into her flesh. Her heart raced as he suckled at her thigh, and she ran a hand through his dark, wavy hair, holding his head in place. The feel of his mouth against her body was so good, she could forget all about the fact he took what kept her alive.

Fortunately, Khiderian appeared to remember. He pulled back and licked the area he'd bit into, healing her flesh before kissing a path from her thigh to her midriff, dipping his tongue inside her navel, eliciting a squeal as the erotic tickle hit. "Why do you wear such little clothes? Are you trying to kill me?"

"If I was trying to kill you, I'd do it with my dagger," she quipped, earning a chuckle as he crawled up her body.

"Trust me. Showing all this skin works, too. It's just a slower, more agonizing death." He pressed his lips against her smile and slid his tongue inside. This time, she tasted the hint of blood but as his hand slid under the waistband of her shorts and inched them down her thighs, she couldn't conjure the ability to care. She just wanted more of him.

As her shorts were freed from her body, she tugged his T-shirt over his head, revealing the perfect torso underneath. "How is it you stay so golden when you hardly get any sun at all?"

"It's a vampire thing," he murmured against her lips, then stilled. "Marilee, you know I'll be feeding off this. I can't help it. If you don't want to keep going, I'll understand."

"I don't care." She sealed her mouth over his as she gripped his narrow hips and pressed him tighter against her body, feeling the hard length of him through their thin layers of remaining clothing. Suddenly, fear of the unknown took over and stories she'd heard in the girls locker room at school surfaced in her memory. "Just promise me you'll go easy."

Khiderian chuckled as he tugged the hem of her tank top up with his teeth and licked the underside of her breast. "I may be a vampire but I still have the same equipment as any human man. You'll be fine. Better than fine once I'm through with you," he added as his mouth found a nipple and began to suckle.

"I mean I-aah..." Marilee's back arched as Khiderian suckled her harder and the simple task of breathing regularly became too hard, let alone explaining to him he'd misunderstood her reason for wanting him to be gentle. As his hand slid into the side of her boyshorts and tugged, the enormity of what was about to happen hit and her limbs trembled in response.

Khiderian laughed against her chest, his breath tickling her skin like a thousand little butterfly wings. "Relax, Marilee. The way you're shaking, you'd think..." His entire body grew taut as he slowly lifted himself up enough to look directly into her eyes. "Marilee, have you ever been with a man?"

She shook her head, and her breath stilled as Khiderian's eyes hardened in what looked a lot like anger before he closed them and hung his head. "Shit."

"What's wrong?"

His jaw clenched as he adjusted her tank top and boyshorts to cover her body and pressed a soft kiss against her mouth before backing away. "This is wrong."

Marilee sat up and watched in confused surprise as he crossed over to the bar and grabbed the slice of cheesecake she hadn't eaten. "You need to eat something, then get some rest."

"What?" Marilee looked down at herself, still dressed in her top and boyshorts, then at Khiderian with his pants on and tried to understand what was going on. True, she was no expert but she was pretty sure they'd been about to have sex. To her knowledge, people didn't stop before the big moment to eat. Doubt reared its ugly head as he settled next to her with the plate in one hand, a fork in the other. "What the hell is going on?"

"I'm sorry, Marilee. I didn't know you were a virgin. If I had, I'd have never touched you." He scooped a chunk of cheesecake onto the fork and held it out to her. "You need to eat. It'll help you recuperate from the blood loss."

Marilee looked between him and the fork, and blinked, sure her brain wasn't registering the picture in front of her correctly. She'd just offered the man her body and he'd rather feed her cheesecake? Because she was a virgin? "You're telling me that if I was a slut you'd have no problem banging me, but because I'm not used up yet you don't want to touch me?"

Khiderian inhaled deeply and licked his lips, avoiding her gaze. "Marilee, just... Please eat."

"Fuck eating!" She slapped the plate out of his hand, sent it sailing across the room. "And fuck you!" She kicked him in the gut, almost succeeding in knocking him off the bed before she fled it herself. She'd barely got to her feet before dizziness set in and she crashed to her knees.

"Dammit, Marilee." Khiderian was on his knees before her in the next second. "Please calm down and allow yourself to recuperate from the feed."

"Go to hell!" She shoved at his chest, his perfect chest that she wished she'd never laid eyes on. "What, am I not good enough for you now because I don't know what I'm doing? I guess you like really skanky—"

"Enough!" His command came out as a roar and he took a big calming breath before running a hand through his hair. "In all my time on this earth I have never had a woman choose me as her first lover, and sweetheart, I've been on this earth a long damn time. Do you have any idea how special you are?"

The hot air fueling Marilee's tirade left her body as quickly as if someone had stuck a pin in her. "If I'm so special, then why don't you want me?"

"I want you, Marilee. I want you so bad I fear it'll one day drive me mad, but that doesn't mean I can have you." He scooped her into his arms and she didn't fight as he settled her on the bed, covering her with a sheet before sitting at her side. "Why would you choose me as your first?"

"I..." She closed her mouth and looked away, allowing a tear to fall from her eye. She loved the jerk, she realized as the words had almost flown out of her mouth so easily. But why tell him when he'd just refused her? "I've had countless men try to get what I just offered you, but the thought of any of them touching me always made me want to go for my blade. You want to know why I was willing to give myself to you, figure it out your damn self."

"Don't do that." His fingertip lifted the tear from her cheek. "I don't ever want to hurt you. If this was just sex, I would have did it in a heartbeat, but your first time makes it so much more than that. Your first time should be with someone more deserving and I'm not worthy enough."

She shook her head as she turned her face to look at him. "Shouldn't I be the judge of that?"

"You don't know me, Marilee, not really." He ran a hand down his face and expelled a breath. "I'm about to train you to interrogate a demon and hope I don't turn you into a monster in the process. And if things go badly..."

"You're going to kill me." New tears ran the length of Marilee's face.

"Yes. Some day I may have to kill you." He kissed her forehead and stood. "I'm a greedy bastard, Marilee, but even I have my limits. I won't take such a precious gift from you knowing I might have to destroy you later."

He crossed over to the sofa and lay down, where he stayed for the rest of the day.

CHAPTER FIFTEEN

Khiderian rose from the ground and dusted the dirt from his once pristine robes. He wavered a bit, unused to supporting himself without the weight of his wings. Even when hidden from the view of humans, they were still there, only invisible. Now they were no more. He reached back with a hand, slid it under his clothes and felt the smooth skin where they'd once been... and where they'd never return.

In the lake ahead of him stood the reason he'd given them up. The woman bathed in the soft glow of the moon. Its light highlighted the ample curves of her nude body as she splashed water, the droplets glistening like diamonds. Her hair, thick and dark, hung past her waist, taunting him. He had to know if it felt like the silk it resembled.

He stepped out of the cover provided by the trees and approached the water's edge just as she turned around. "Oh!" She covered her breasts with her hands. "Who are you? What are you doing there?"

"Khiderian," he replied, lowering himself to sit on a rock next to the one she'd placed her robes on. "Watching you," he added to address her second question.

Her mouth gaped open as she searched the forest area to her right. "I am not alone. The people I travel with have gone off hunting. They are good hunters." Her eyes issued a warning.

Khiderian couldn't decide between laughing or snarling. He'd been in the army of angels that had sent Lucifer to the pits of hell. The threat of a lowly human hunter attacking him was absurd, but the thought of the woman not running into his arms willingly took the humor out of the situation. He was an angel, the most beautiful of creatures. Even if he'd fallen and traded in his wings in the process, he was still carved from perfection. "If I were traveling with you, I wouldn't leave a beauty such as you alone. I would make the animals come to me so as not to waste one moment worshiping your body as it should be."

Her mouth formed an O as mischief danced through her eyes. The compliment had clearly been received well. "So you like what you see?"

"Very much." He grinned as she bit her lip. "May I touch you?"

She gasped, eyes round with shock, before giggling. "You're so wicked!"

Anger surged that such a woman, one who now lowered her hands to expose herself to him dare call him wicked. He was an angel and as such deserved... No. He wasn't anymore. He was human now, and he was acting with the same lustful ideas as she so he could not condemn. The entire reason he'd chosen to fall was to touch a woman, make love to her the way he'd seen, to feel what the humans feel. The thought of loving another being with such intensity had drawn him out of heaven. He loved his brothers and sisters there, but he desired a closeness they were not allowed to feel for themselves. He desired the touch of a human. He desired the woman in the water, and once he had her he would marry her in the human fashion and make their union honest.

"Come out of the water."

She covered herself again, suddenly bashful. "Are you afraid of the water?"

He was a little, he had to admit. He'd never been in it and he was already about to experience one of many firsts. He'd rather test one new thing at a time. "Are you afraid of me?"

She chuckled before lowering her arms and walking out of the water, challenge blazing in her eyes. "I am not afraid of anything."

Khiderian sucked in a breath as she lowered herself to her knees in front of him and started to strip him of his robes. His heart raced in his chest and for a moment he feared it would burst. "You are so beautiful. I will take good care of you."

She looked at him strangely before chuckling. "Of course you will, just as I will of you."

Not understanding, he opened his mouth to ask her what she meant, but she took the opportunity to seal her mouth over his and push her tongue inside. Everything happened so quickly, Khiderian was unable to truly savor every second as he'd planned. The woman kissed him eagerly, her fingernails cutting into his back as she lay on the ground and pulled him on top of her. "We don't have much time."

"We have all the time in the world," he argued with her, earning a roll of her eyes as she rolled him onto his back and straddled him, easing down onto his

erection as if she'd practiced the move a thousand times. Then she was moving, rocking back and forth so fast all Khiderian could do was grab her hips and watch her bountiful breasts bounce up and down in the moonlight. His body started to throb with a sense of intense pleasure he could have never imagined and he felt himself ready to burst, but what the woman was doing would never get him where he needed to go to feel that explosion he craved.

She squealed with delight as he flipped her onto her back, never disconnecting their bodies in the process, and rammed in and out of her as fast as he could, the sense of coming nirvana strengthening the faster he moved. She cried out with sharp sounds of pleasure as he thrust quicker, the sounds fueling his desire to reach the point he sensed ahead. Sweat dripped from his brow, his knees ached from their contact with the hard earth, but he pressed on, climbing higher and higher until... he roared as he spilled his seed into the woman and total euphoria claimed his body before he slumped over her in a heap of shaking limbs.

"Delilah!"

The woman shoved him off of her, their bodies barely disconnected before she scrambled for her clothing. "Oh no! I must hurry."

Khiderian propped himself up on an elbow, looked into the woods where the man's voice had come from. "Stay. I welcome your friends."

"Friends?" She frowned at him as she tugged on her clothing.

"Your friends you are traveling with." Khiderian reached for his own clothing, deciding it was best to meet her friends dressed. His stomach grumbled and he recognized it as the hunger for food humans experienced. "We will feast on what they have caught and tell them of our union. We will be married among—"

"Married?" She straightened her clothes and bent down to cusp Khiderian's chin in her hand. "You poor fool. I'm not with friends. I'm with my husband and his miserable family. He'll kill me and you both if he finds out what we've done." She bent down and kissed Khiderian's mouth, which had parted in surprise. "You were wonderful, such a nice change from the brute I married."

Khiderian watched helplessly as she scampered off into the woods in search of the man still calling her name. She was already married. He stumbled as he pulled on his clothes, his mind reeling. He'd just made love to a married woman. He'd committed a sin.

"It didn't take long."

He whirled around to see Kiara step out of the woods, her long white robes swirling around her. She didn't hide her wings from him, knowing he already knew what she was. He was her brother... or had been. "Kiara, what just happened? I found a woman to make my wife and she was already married."

Kiara crossed her arms and shook her head, her long golden locks blowing in the gentle breeze. "Khiderian, you made the choice to fall and become human. You woke with the same temptations they are all born with, and like many, you gave in. However, I must say I am surprised. You didn't even make it one day without giving in to lust."

"I loved the woman," Khiderian argued. "I intended to marry her."

"The woman?" She laughed, the sound unpleasant. "Did you bother to learn her name before you'd sated yourself with her body? Did you ask her who she was or where she came from? Do you now even know what color her eyes are?"

Khiderian looked away as it dawned on him he hadn't done any of those things, nor had he cared to know the color of the woman's eyes. She was female, nude, and she filled him with desire. He'd wanted her like a possession. "When humans love each other they make love. There is nothing wrong in it."

"Love? Khiderian, you lusted for the woman. You did not love her. You did not allow yourself time to love anyone. You fornicated with the first woman you came across."

He sat down on the rock, his legs suddenly weak, and lowered his head into his hands. "I do not understand this world. It looks so different now. Everything feels different."

"Because you are different. You now feel, think, and act as a human." Kiara sighed. "You were such a fine warrior. You'll never understand how it saddens me to have to tell you goodbye forever."

"What?" Khiderian lifted his head to beseech her. "I don't want this anymore! I don't want a world where people lie and sin. I wanted to feel the love of a woman, not to be used by one. I want to go back."

"That's impossible." Kiara's eyes darkened, her nose scrunched as she looked down at him. "You are impure. You can never rejoin us. You know the rules."

"But—"

"No, Khiderian. You chose to be a human, now you must stay a human. I pray for you that you learn to control temptation. You will not have an easy path to heaven now that you have chosen to leave us. Your sins will be counted just as any other human's, but the expectations of you will be much higher."

He rose from the rock. "Kiara, please."

"I am sorry, brother. You have left us and now you must suffer the consequences of that choice. We could throw you into the fires of hell right now, but your decision is being allowed." She reached out and cupped his jaw with her long, elegant fingers. "I only came to say goodbye since you did not before you made this disastrous decision. I wish you well, brother."

She faded out of view and Khiderian reached out in hope of grabbing onto her, onto something of the existence he'd known before making that fateful leap, but his fingers slipped through air. His human fingers. He looked at his hands, noticed that although they looked the same, they lacked the golden sheen he'd once possessed. He felt things in his body, little aches and strains, which reminded him he was not the being he'd once been. He was something far less superior. He'd traded it all in for the chance of mortal love and he'd come up empty.

Turning toward the woods, he growled. The woman had made a fool of him. It did not matter that he'd not asked her the right questions. She was a married woman. She should have told him. He took off at the quickest pace he could muster in his newly human body and entered the woods intending to find the woman's husband and confess his wife's sins. Then she would learn how a proper wife behaved, and maybe if he was lucky, the man would kill him and put him out of his misery.

He stilled. What kind of thought was that? He'd given up everything for this life and now he wanted to end it with less than a day spent? And why did he think that would solve his problems? He'd barely been in human form a day and had already committed a great sin. He would not be welcomed into heaven after such an act was committed. He had to live, if only to escape the fires of hell longer, he had to live.

A feminine laugh sounded from behind him and he turned, expecting the woman he'd just committed adultery with. But it was not Delilah who stared back at him. This woman was shorter with a narrower waist. Her ample cleavage danced as she laughed, her golden eyes sparkling with mischief. There. He at least had bothered to notice this one's eyes. She twirled a strand of inky black hair as she stepped toward him. "It's a beautiful night."

"Yes, it is," he agreed, not really sure what he was agreeing to. He didn't care what she said, just as long as she kept walking toward him. Then again... "Are you married?"

"Married?" She threw her head back and laughed as if he'd asked her the silliest question, then stepped close enough to run her hands up his chest. "No."

Khiderian forgot what he'd entered the wooded area for as he gazed down into her wine-colored eyes. He frowned as he saw the stains on the front of her robe. "There's blood on your clothing."

"No concern need be raised," she said, pressing closer against him. "You seem... different than most men I've come across recently. Stronger."

He let the statement slip past. No one would believe him if he told them he had been an angel, and after the way Kiara had left him behind after he'd pleaded to go back, why claim them as his brethren anymore? They no longer cared for him. He would live his life as a human, just the way humans did. All he needed was shelter, land to work, and a woman to start a family with. "Are you here with Delilah's family?"

"I do not know any Delilah."

He studied the woman, all five feet three inches of her, and again wondered about the blood on her clothing. "Why are you alone out here? It is not safe."

"I was hunting."

Anger surged inside him. "A man should hunt for you while you wait behind to cook what he has brought for you."

She laughed and batted her eyelashes. "I'm not a very good cook."

"You can learn." He felt a lock of her midnight hair and found it as silky as it appeared. His groin reacted and he wondered if he would find even more pleasure with her than he had with Delilah. "Would you like for me to hunt for you?" The thought of killing one of his Father's beautiful creatures upset his stomach, but if he were sentenced to fulfill life as a human, he had to eat like one.

"Oh yes. Actually..." She pressed in to his body and raised her arms to encircle his shoulders. "What I'd really like..." She ran a fingertip down his throat as she rose on tiptoe to whisper just under his ear, "is for you to hunt with me."

Vicious pain ripped through his neck and the last sound he heard before the darkness claimed him was the cruel sound of the woman's shrill laughter as she momentarily let up from draining the blood out of his body.

SIREN'S SNARE

"Again."

Marilee glared at the tall, dark, and sexy vampire who'd haunted her dreams the entire day before, making restful sleep a joke, and resisted the urge to give him the middle finger.

"Again, Marilee."

Growling a little, Marilee returned her focus to the remaining cactus in front of her. It felt ten degrees below hell. She should be inside, soaking up air-conditioned air at the hotel. Instead, she was standing in the middle of the desert in bum-fuck, Nevada, burning down cacti. "Explain to me again how sweating my ass off is supposed to help me interrogate a demon. I mean, am I actually walking into hell to do it because it feels like I'm already there temperature-wise."

"Hawthorn and daggers won't affect a demon. You have to use your gifts. Now, if you're so bothered by the heat you should hurry up and complete this training session so you can be done with it."

"Easy for you to say." She leered at the irritating vampire, dressed in a black T-shirt and pants with his arms folded over his chest, his face set in the same stern look he'd been using on her all night. Not one bead of sweat dared form on him. He was in total control of his body temperature despite the heat created by her fire bursts. "You're not the one doing this."

A cactus she'd already burned blazed with fire then quickly snuffed out. Khiderian simply raised a single eyebrow as she glared at him.

"Yeah, so you can do it, too. I'd like to see you do it in the daylight and see how well you do then."

"Yeah, I bet you would. As little clothing as you have on and considering the fact it's night, a very cool one at that, you shouldn't be so hot."

"I'm human. I can't use mind-over-matter with temperature like you can, especially when the heat is coming from inside me." She bit back a grin, delighted her choice in clothing—ultra-short shorts and a thin button-down flannel shirt with the sleeves cut off and the lower half cut off and tied below her breasts to bare her lower torso—was getting to him. Khiderian didn't want to make love to her, fine. She'd tease his ass to bits though with her outfits so he knew just what he was missing.

"Again, Marilee."

This time she did give him the finger, but he remained stone-faced, unfettered by her juvenile rebellion. She shook the tension out of her arms and faced the cactus, focused on its green covering, and called upon the fire inside her. The cactus went up in flames as if someone had poured gasoline on it and lit a match.

"Pull it back in."

She took a breath, let it out, then inhaled deeply, calling the fire to her as she did. It died out quickly, her body temperature growing as it diminished. By the time the last flame evaporated her hair lay plastered to her scalp. "There." She wiped her brow with her equally wet arm, simply smearing sweat. "I've burned every cactus in this patch of desert. Are we finally done?"

"No. You've done well with calling out and pulling back in your fire. Now you must learn to use it when needed." He closed his eyes and Marilee felt the vibration of his power in the air, which she only felt when he was doing something major. Her stomach dipped just thinking about what he might be up to.

He opened his eyes and a snake rose from the ground, hissing as its forked tongue flicked quickly up and down. It was at least three feet long with a large head, and Marilee's heart nearly gave out when she heard the distinct rattling sound coming from its tail. "Is that thing a rattlesnake?"

"Yes, and its venom is deadly. I'd suggest you fry it before it gets you."

The snake slithered forward and Marilee swore she saw lethal intent in its calculating eyes. "Are you serious? I have to burn something alive?"

"You're not going near a demon until you've proven you can do what must be done if problems arise. This thing is not a gentle doe, Marilee. It's a nasty, cruel predator. Even Lucifer took on its form when he approached Eve in Eden."

The snake slithered closer and Marilee squealed, moving back. The snake recoiled and slowly stretched its upper half forward, hissing tauntingly. "Khiderian."

"You must learn to do what is necessary to defend yourself against demons. I may not be around when you find yourself face to face with one. Likewise, any number of things could go wrong when we interrogate Dunn.

SIREN'S SNARE

As part of your training I can not interfere. You have to kill the snake before it attacks you."

Marilee stole a glance at the vampire she'd come to think of as her guardian angel, and gaped at the hard set of his features as he stood with arms crossed, feet spaced, watching the action unfold with no intention of helping. "So if it starts to bite me you won't do anything?"

"I can't. You're on your own."

As if waiting for its cue to act, the snake raced across the sand aiming straight for her. Marilee screamed and jumped back, but knew she couldn't outrun the thing. She risked a quick glance at Khiderian, her heart breaking as she watched him turn his face away, not even concerned enough to see what happened to her.

As the snake closed in, the anger mounting from Khiderian's indifference helped her quickly gather the sand in front of her, forming a funnel cloud she used to wrap up the snake and carry it back six feet. Her hold over the sand gave out at that point, dropping the snake back onto the ground. It hissed at her, the sound laced with fury, before charging at her again.

"Tossing it around will only piss it off and make it come at you faster," Khiderian said, his tone giving away nothing. He could have been commenting on the weather for all the emotion he showed.

Marilee created another funnel cloud from the dry desert earth and sent her attacker back four feet. It fell from the funnel cloud as the sand scattered and was racing back at her almost before it touched the ground. Khiderian was right, but besides pissing it off, she was also giving it power. Its fury gave it more speed, more determination. She was only making the damn thing stronger. In the middle of nowhere all she could do to evade it was jump on the car, but she had the suspicion Khiderian would keep them there until daylight if she tried to avoid the outcome he was determined to get from this exercise, and she was too hot and tired to wait around all night while a snake circled the car waiting for a bite of her. The sooner she killed the damn thing, the sooner she could get an icy drink of water and lay down.

It only took seconds for the snake to reach her and when it did she called upon fire, and watched with tears burning her eyes as the creature writhed in the flames eating its body alive. When it finally crumpled in a heap of black smoking ash, she looked over to see Khiderian watching her, eyes cold and empty. "There. Is that enough to prove I can do whatever's necessary to survive interrogating a demon?"

"No." He closed his eyes and flexed his power before opening them to reveal three more snakes and a dozen rats. "Do it again."

Marilee gasped as the snakes slithered her way, the vicious intent in their eyes seeming to shout 'We know what you did to our brother.' She swallowed past the ball of guilt lodged in her throat and set the snakes on fire, fear of three-against-one helping her to act quicker this time. Still, their writhing bodies sucker-punched her in the stomach, and she had to fight down bile as the dozen rats slowly started creeping toward her.

She'd had a pet mouse when she was little, a wild one she'd found in the field by the trailer she'd lived in, and brought inside. She kept it in an old glass aquarium that hadn't been used in years and fed it peanuts and bread. She'd loved it. The thought of killing a member of its family, even if rats were big, nasty creatures she'd never consider keeping as pets, sickened her. Why would Khiderian have her kill an animal who'd never done her harm? *You eat beef*, she rationed with herself. *Cows have never done harm to you either, yet you'll stick a fork in them and grub without a second thought.*

Suddenly, the rats picked up speed and raced toward her. She braced herself to burn their furry bodies, but at the last moment couldn't do it, so she conjured wind and propelled them back. They made it back to the six feet they'd started at and, like the first snake, came at her faster, angrier. Stronger.

Tears cascading down her face, Marilee whimpered and waited until they were almost on her to call upon the fire inside her. Sparks flew out of their backs and they erupted into a frenzy of awful sounds resembling screams as the fire spread over their bodies. The sounds of pain grew louder until Marilee thought she'd go mad enduring it, knowing she was the one inflicting such torture on the helpless animals. She called the fire back in, but all but one rat already lay charred on the ground, dead.

The remaining rodent quickly attacked, latching onto her boot and chewing the leather. Marilee screamed and kicked it off only for it to rebound on her. This time it scrambled up her boot and managed to bite her shin, drawing blood, before she dislodged it and, knowing it wouldn't stop attacking her, she finished what she'd started, covering her ears in an attempt to block out the horrific sound of it dying from the fire she'd wrapped it in.

All of the rats dead, she couldn't fight back the threat of nausea any longer. She bent over and heaved, emptying the contents of her stomach before backing up to the car, too angry to be embarrassed that she'd just blown chunks right in front of Khiderian. "Now am I through or is there something else you'd like me to kill? Maybe a bunny or a kitten this time!"

Khiderian looked at her, his jaw clenched tight, before stepping towards her. He took his time, allowing her anger to fester while he closed in. "You've proven your ability to destroy a living creature if necessary."

"I've killed living creatures before. Plenty of them."

"That's different. You've never viewed vampires as worthy of life."

She shook her head. "How can you say that after the way I am with you? You know that isn't true."

He laughed. "Amazing how you're willing to overlook your obvious hatred for the entire vampire race when your hormones get involved."

Marilee studied his eyes, blown away by the lack of emotion in them. They were dead and cold, cruel, as if he'd blocked everything but the need to kill. "You're a real bastard, you know that."

"You would know, wouldn't you?" Those cruel eyes roved over her. "Your father never stuck around to meet you, never bothered to give you his name. Then again as much of a whore as your mother was who could blame him?"

Marilee's mouth dropped open as Khiderian leaned next to her against the car, his mouth twisted into a sneer almost as ugly as the things coming out of it. "Wh-what did you just say?"

"You ever think you'll end up like her, spreading your legs open for anybody who comes sniffing around?" An evil gleam coated his eyes. "Hell, you did for me. I could have fucked you twenty different ways and made you do whatever the hell I asked without any objection. Your mother was like that, wasn't she? Guess the apple doesn't fall far from the tree."

Marilee blinked, sure the man she saw standing before her saying such vile things was a mirage, but he wasn't. Khiderian stood before her alive in the flesh, his face now totally expressionless as if he hadn't said such cruel things to her. "Why are you saying these things?"

He grinned. "Damn, you're slow. You're an annoying, smart-mouthed, ignorant hillbilly I got stuck on a mission with. Frankly, I'm tired of you and now that we're done with training I can finally tell you how I really feel."

Marilee's eyes burned but she refused to let the tears escape. "Oh, and how do you really feel because it seems you weren't so annoyed by me the other night."

"You're referring to last night?"

"Yes." She folded her arms and braced herself for his response.

"I wanted to fuck you, Marilee. Every nice thing I've said or done leading up to now has either been because I need you to fulfill the mission or because I wanted what's between your legs... until I learned you've never learned what to do with it. I don't have time to deal with the emotions of a clingy virgin so now that I no longer want that and the mission is soon going to be finished..." He shrugged. "Suck it up and move on. That's what your mother excelled at."

Marilee stood still, her mouth hanging open as she registered every horrible word he'd uttered. It had to be a trick. He was trying to rile her up, but why? If he cared half as much as she'd thought he would never say such things. So he didn't care. He meant what he said. What she'd thought was between them was all a lie... and he probably had fed off Lisa by having sex with her right there with her in the same house.

Khiderian cocked his head to the side. "Come on, Marilee. You didn't think we had some special connection, did you?" He crooked his fingers into quotation marks. "I'm a vampire. You're a human. You're just food."

Marilee gripped the cross around her neck, needing the comfort she got from it as she glared at the evil vampire in front of her. "You are a vile, disgusting son of a bitch, and the only reason I'm going to fulfill this mission with you is so Jake can kill you when I save him."

"Your weak slayer can't kill me." Khiderian laughed at the idea. "And you'll leave when I say you leave. As annoying as you are, I can't deny you have your purpose. The ability to draw out demons comes in handy sometimes."

Marilee straightened her shoulders and held his gaze, determined not to back down. "I'll leave when I decide to, and you can't control my ability to call demons like you control everything else."

"You think so?" He stepped closer, invading her personal space. "I haven't tried to control you yet because it hasn't suited my purpose, but if I want, Marilee, I can control your every action. Enjoy your freedom now because if you show me this much sass after we save Jake I'll make you my puppet and you won't like what I make you do."

"You're lying," she argued, more to chase away the chill crawling up her spine than to spar with him.

A wicked grin spread across his mouth. "Why do you think I made you create that mind-link with me, the one with the door I claimed you could use to keep me locked out? The portal to hell thing? All a lie. I knew your gullible ass would fall for it, you dumb hick."

Marilee stepped back, blood rushing through her ears as his words sank in. He'd tricked her into giving him access to her mind, a way of getting in and taking over any time he wanted to and she had no idea how to lock him out, or if there even was a way possible. Anger consumed her and her body burned with rage as she called upon fire.

"You can't burn me, Marilee. Only I know how to find Dunn and get Jake's location."

Marilee expelled a breath and let the heat drain out of her body. "You son of a bitch. I will get you eventually. I will—"

"You will do whatever I say, you worthless bitch. You're nothing on your own. Hell, your own mother told you as much, and your grandparents never wanted you. They just pitied y—"

Marilee punched Khiderian in the mouth, putting all of her weight behind the throw, and knocked him back a few steps as his head flung to the side. She'd barely gotten back into stance to throw another when he straightened up, wiping blood on his fingers. He chuckled, ran his tongue over his bottom lip to seal the wound she'd inflicted, and leered at her with an intensity that quickly formed a ball of nausea in her stomach.

All of the sudden her mind was overrun with images of the night in Hicksville when her world had changed forever. She saw herself killing vampires next to Jake Porter, saw as her throat was ripped into by a woman she'd known all her life. She saw Jake drag that woman kicking and screaming into a cell and then she saw something she hadn't witnessed that night. In her head, she saw Jake set the woman on fire and watch her burn. "Stop it," she pleaded, gripping her head with both hands.

"You haven't reached the good part," Khiderian said as more images filtered through. She saw Judd Perkins kill his own son, Nan Gray rip her own children apart in order to feed off their blood.

"Stop!" She screamed as tears rained down her face. "I don't want to see anymore!"

"You still haven't seen anything yet."

An image of Gram slammed into her head. Gram, smiling as she walked toward the front door with a white apron tied around her wide waist, the smell of apples and cinnamon trailing after her. Gram opened the door and frowned as she saw two men she didn't recognize standing on the porch. Then they bared their fangs.

"Oh God, no!" Marilee covered her mouth with her hands and sobbed, knowing what was going to happen next in the visions she blessedly had never seen much more than that much of. "Don't show me that, please, please..."

In her head, Gram tried to slam the door, but the vampires barreled in, one latching onto her while the other headed to Grampa's den where Grampa sat reading a book, never suspecting his home had been invaded. By the time Gram let loose a scream, the second vampire had found him. "Please, Khiderian. If there is any decency left in you, please don't make me see this!"

"You want it to stop?"

"Yes, yes!"

"Do you want me to complete this mission on my own and stay away from you forever?"

Marilee glanced up through her tear-coated eyes and took in Khiderian's beautifully carved face, the dark hair that brushed over his shoulders. She'd loved him, nearly gave herself to him. Never would she have thought she'd say it, but her mouth opened and, "Yes," tumbled out. "Yes. I'll do anything. Just don't let me see my grandparents' murder."

Khiderian didn't blink, didn't show any emotion, as he held out his hand. "Give me your cross."

"My cr—What?" Marilee gripped the cross in her hand, rubbed her fingers over its smoothness. "Why do you need my cross?"

"It's the key to everything. It's useless to you, but with it I can pass the sirens undetected. I can save Jake. I'll save and release him and you don't have to see me ever again. You don't even have to contact Dunn. There are other ways of locating Porter, but only if I have the cross. Give it to me."

Marilee backed away, her hand wrapped protectively around the cross Gram had given her. *Keep this with you always. It will serve as a reminder that you are God's child. He will always watch over you and no evil will ever come to you if you believe in Him.* Gram had instilled her faith in her, even against her mother's protests. Becky hated the mention of God, thought religion was all make-believe nonsense people used to cope when life screwed them. "I drown my troubles in a bottle and I'm a drunk," she'd say, "but these wackos can go around worshiping someone no more real than the Easter bunny and that's normal. Good, even." She'd roll her eyes, laugh, and keep drinking until she passed out. But Gram believed and she made sure Marilee did, too. "You can't have my cross."

Khiderian's eyes narrowed. "I need the cross. Now."

"Well, tough shit 'cause you ain't getting it." Marilee gripped it tighter and backed away. Suddenly the image of a vampire feasting from Grampa's throat flashed through her mind. She cried in despair, helpless as the image played out in her head, but she didn't loosen her grip on the cross. Gram had given it to her. Gram had loved her, had faith in her. "I'll suffer through these images if that's what it takes, but you're not getting the cross. I'll kill you before I hand it over."

"You asked for this, Marilee."

She saw Gram, her dress savagely ripped from her body to expose more pulse points as a crowd of vampires approached and latched on to various parts of her body. She could feel Gram's shame, watched as she tried to cover herself with her hands, but they were quickly pulled away as vampires latched their mouths onto her arms.

Marilee screamed, dropped to her knees in anguish. She could kill Khiderian. She could burn him alive, but then Jake wouldn't be saved. She could give him the cross and be rid of him, stopping the images in the process, but Gram had given it to her as a reminder. She was never alone. Even after Gram was taken from her, she wasn't alone. Somehow she'd pushed that to the back of her mind in her grief but with the smooth gold in the palm of her hand and Gram's words in her mind, she remembered. She wasn't alone. And there was someone stronger than Khiderian.

"Please, God, help me," she pleaded, fisting her hands together beneath her mouth with the cross tucked inside as the images of Gram being murdered rolled through her head. "Please get me through this. Make me strong and help me do what's right. Help me survive this." The images stopped, leaving her mind blessedly free of the horrors that had filled it seconds ago.

"You passed, Marilee. Now your training is done."

She looked up to see Khiderian looming over her, his hand still outstretched, but this time it was to help her up. She ignored it as she got to her feet on her own and stepped away. "What are you talking about now?"

Sympathy and shame flittered through Khiderian's eyes as he put his hands in his pockets and swallowed hard. "I had to do it. A demon will taunt you with your own insecurities, fill your mind with lies, make you trust it before viciously turning on you, do whatever it takes to break you. I had to make sure you were strong enough to go against Dunn because the demon inside him will try its best to weaken you any way it can when it senses you drawing it out." He nodded his head toward the cross in her hands. "It will keep at you until you're willing to do anything to make it stop, even denounce your faith in God. The last *drac chemare* I worked with took a demon into her own body just to shut it up. I had to destroy her. I don't want to destroy you."

Marilee stared at the man before her, shaking her head as fresh tears, heated by raw anger, fell from her eyes. "So now you're telling the truth? All that horrible stuff you just said was an act?" She laughed, the sound brittle and sharp. "I don't think so, Khiderian. You were pretty damn convincing."

"Marilee, I would never willingly hurt you."

"Funny you say that, because you just damn near tried to rip me apart." She wiped the moisture from her cheeks and sniffed as she released the cross, allowing it to dangle from her neck. Her heart ached, part of it desperately wanted to believe Khiderian had just been testing her, but he'd gone too far. "Once this is over we go our separate ways. If you don't allow me to leave I *will* kill you."

"Marilee, I had to—"

"Shut up!" Her voice came out so shrill she surprised herself, but quickly recovered. "Don't tell me you had to. You wanted to test me, fine. You could have got someone else to do it. Surely the Dream Teller has more than you working for her."

SIREN'S SNARE

"There was no one else who could have tested you, Marilee. Only someone with the ability to get in your head could do it, which means only demons... or me. It had to be me."

She laughed. "Are you actually making an excuse?" She stepped forward. "After the disgusting, horrible things you said? You showed me images of my grandparents being murdered!" She turned away and stepped over to the passenger side of the car. "I was right about you from the beginning. You're not remotely human. No half-way decent human being could do something as cruel as what you did. A demon has the excuse of being a demon. You, however, were once a person. The fact you could form a relationship with someone just to rip their heart out is beneath even them. There's no word for a creature as evil as you and I am beyond glad I didn't sleep with you. I hate you more than I've ever hated anyone, even the vampires who killed my grandparents. I'll never forgive you. You aren't worth it."

Reaching the passenger side door, she turned back and stilled as she caught sight of a single tear glistening in the moonlight as it fell from Khiderian's eye to travel the plane of his cheek. He turned his face away for a second and when he turned it back his cheek was dry as if the tear had never been, and Marilee imagined it had all been in her mind. He didn't utter a word as he walked over and opened the car door. Glaring at him, Marilee sat inside and waited for him to take his place in the driver's seat.

Khiderian slid inside, pulled the door closed behind him and sat there with the key in the ignition, his eyes riddled with thoughts. Finally, he turned the key, starting the car. "The images of your grandparents weren't real."

Marilee tightened her hands against the urge to punch him again and focused out the window, not caring what she looked at as long as it wasn't him. "Don't bother, Khiderian. I'll never trust anything you say again. You're insane if you think it's ever going to be a possibility."

She felt him tense, but he said nothing as he drove them back to the road. Silence rode with them, thick and heavy, as Khiderian navigated the car back to the hotel. Marilee's stomach rolled as she realized she'd have to see the bed she'd almost foolishly given herself to him on.

"I need to feed," Khiderian said softly as he parked the car close to their room. "Go on in and make sure you get plenty to eat and you need to rest well. Tomorrow night you'll have to go through this all over again... with a demon this time around."

"I went through it with a demon tonight," she said as she stepped out of the car, slamming the door harder than necessary behind her, and stomped toward the room. She didn't ask how Khiderian was going to feed nor did she offer her own blood. The bastard could screw or drink from anyone he wanted, but he was never touching her again.

CHAPTER SIXTEEN

"Kiss my pearly white ass!" Jake spat out blood and braced himself for another round of pain.

"I'm beginning to think you get off on being tortured." Rufka, the siren who tended to control the others said as she circled him, tapping the knife she'd been cutting him with against her thigh.

They'd taken him out of the cell and tied him to a metal pole in the basement, his arms raised over his head at a painful degree. He'd given up trying to get loose from them. All they had to do was start that damn singing and he couldn't disobey them. He had to somehow hold on until Marilee and the vampire she spoke of came to rescue him... and pray that he hadn't imagined the young woman feeding him her blood while he lay physically dead on the floor of his cell. His body seemed stronger, which gave him hope his memory was real. "I'm beginning to think you like hearing the word no, or else you're just too stupid to realize you're never going to break me you fugly-ass whore."

The five other sirens working with her stepped forward, tools in their hands ready to burn, cut, or prod him, but Rufka raised a hand. "Ladies, no. I think we've been going about this the wrong way." She licked her lips slowly, seductively, and let out a tinkling laugh. "Most men willingly hand over their souls in hope of screwing their dream woman but Jacob here has already met his. He honestly, truly loves his wife and is completely faithful to her."

"So what do we do to break him?" Lura, the rebellious one, asked. "Torture has not worked and he won't tell us where she is so we can torture her. She hasn't reacted to his pain and come r—"

"Silence, Lura!" Rufka glared at the other siren, who returned a glare filled with just as much venom. "He's a slayer. Never forget that." She turned her cold, calculating, violet-tinted eyes back toward him and patted his cheek. "We don't discuss all of our business in front of him, but to answer your question, we give him what he wants but denies himself."

Jake frowned as the siren ran her fingertip down his bare chest, a slimy feeling following its wake. Never would he have expected a woman's touch to be so revolting, but then again this thing in front of him wasn't a woman. "I know you're not my wife, bitch, even with her image draped over you like a bad Halloween costume. Seducing me won't work."

"Who said anything about seducing?" She laughed as she unbuttoned his jeans. "It seems to me that your worst fear is cheating on your wife. Well, now you're going to do it whether you want to or not."

Jake's heart skipped a beat, his mouth went dry as her intent dawned. Then, he realized it would never work and laughed in her face. "There's a reason women don't rape men, dumbass. I'd have to have an erection, which, trust me, will never happen when I can see your real face behind my wife's. I'd rather fuck a transvestite with a questionable rash."

Her face contorted into a mask of rage, but she quickly brought her anger under control, even pulled off a grin as she closed in on him, licking his earlobe—and consequently causing Jake's stomach to protest—before whispering, "It'll be hard for you to see my face when my lips are wrapped around your dick, and no man can resist getting hard in the midst of a blow job." She chuckled as Jake's blood ran cold. "Oral sex is sex. Like it or not, you're about to have sex with me, then Lura, then all of us, one after the other until you spill your secrets and I'm sure a little something else. That'll be okay though, Jacob. We like to swallow."

He closed his eyes and clenched his jaw against the bile threatening to erupt as the amphibious bitch nibbled on his chest, stirring his nausea even more. She was right. Performing oral sex on him would be sex whether he willingly received it or not, and despite his love for Nyla, she had another point. What man could resist getting hard with the sensation of a warm, wet mouth suckling him? He had to do something and he had to do it now or he could never live with himself. Nyla was everything to him. He'd die before he let another woman touch him intimately. Panic rose as she tugged at the zipper of his jeans, and he wracked his brain for a way out of the situation. He had to fight. He had to break free. He felt stronger after drinking Marilee's blood. Maybe…

SIREN'S SNARE

Rufka's cold breath fanned over his abdomen as she lowered her head to take him into her mouth and Jake sent up a silent prayer for help before pouring all his strength into breaking free from his restraints. His ankles broke free of the rope that had tethered his lower body to the pole and his knees rammed into Rufka's midsection hard enough to knock the wind out of her.

Rufka gasped for air and backed away in shock, placing her in the perfect position as his feet came up. He kicked her under the chin hard enough to crack bone as she flung backward into the siren coming up behind her. Jake broke his hands free of their binds and dodged the claws of another siren, punching her hard in the gut as her own swing went wild. The natural desire to shed blood that consumed slayers flared inside him as he grabbed the mini-torch she'd been carrying and used it on the next two sirens who jumped at him, blasting fire great enough to quickly encompass the front of their bodies.

Another siren, Lura, jumped on his back, her claws digging into his bare and already damaged shoulders as the burning women shrieked in pain and fell to the ground, desperately rolling in effort to snuff out the flames eating at their scaly flesh.

"How did you break free?" Lura screeched as she ripped through his chest with her dagger-like nails.

"I'm a slayer," Jake answered between clenched teeth. "Figure it out, bitch." He flipped her over his back, barreling her into the siren Rufka had slammed into as the creature approached him.

Pain ripped through his body and he fell to his knees as electric volts coursed through his limbs, but he pushed the pain out of his mind and whirled on his knees to grab the leg of the siren electrocuting him with a taser. Two sharp movements and her kneecap broke. She lay shrieking on the cold cement floor as he rose and turned in the direction of the door to see a trio of were-animals gliding down the stairs, hunger raging in their eyes. Lycanthropes. He had natural immunity from their bite due to being a slayer, but it only protected him from catching lycanthropy and becoming one of the beasts. It didn't do a damn thing to keep their sharp teeth out of his tender flesh which was already mottled with cuts, bruises, and burns thanks to his recent torture sessions.

"Don't touch him. He's mine."

Jake turned his head to see Rufka slowly stand, a hand clasped around her jaw. The other sirens, with the exception of the two burned ones currently wailing on the floor, righted themselves and each took a position around him. "We'll deal with him."

"Jaffron says you are not—"

"If Jaffron has a problem with my work he can tell me himself," Rufka snapped at the lycanthrope, and stepped forward.

Jake grinned. "I'll never break and you all know it. Just let me go now or you will all be hurt. He raised the mini-torch and positioned his index finger over the trigger, but before he could apply pressure, Rufka opened her mouth and started singing the seductive song of the siren.

The other sirens joined in as they closed in on him and though his mind fought against the pull of their voices, he couldn't stop himself from following their command. With a trembling arm, he handed over the mini-torch, and then they took their retribution, beating him relentlessly with hands, nails, feet, blades, and fire until he lay a whimpering pulp of flesh on the basement floor. As his vision faded out and the blackness drew him down into a coma-like haven from the pain and humiliation his only thought was, "Thank you God for not letting them molest me."

"Jake."

Jake became alert instantly, recognizing the voice calling his name.

"Dream Teller?" He opened his eyes to find himself lying on the hard earthen floor of a cave in the dream realm, a place he'd visited once before, when he'd learned Nyla carried his child, a child who would be hunted all of his life.

He sat up and inspected his body, finding it unmarred. He generally resurrected in great condition, as if the beatings and other assorted forms of torture never happened, but he didn't resurrect in the dream realm. Being in the dream realm indicated he was unconscious, his physical body left back in the physical world with the sirens. He cringed at the thought of what they might be doing to him.

SIREN'S SNARE

"The sirens are dragging your body back into the cell they've been keeping you in," the Dream Teller informed him as she entered the open part of the cave he sat in, a taller, young, beautiful golden-haired woman at her side as they came through the short tunnel close to the mouth of the cave. "You are near death so they will dump you there and come back later after you've passed and resurrected yet again." The old hag-like woman rubbed her temple. "That is all I can see, I am afraid."

"Did you see what they were doing to me before you drew me here?"

"Ganging up on you while ensnaring you with their song," the old witch answered. "I saw very little before you faded into unconsciousness and I was able to call you here."

"Where have you been? I've been there for weeks." Jake rose, glaring at the witch despite knowing she couldn't see the anger in his eyes. As hot as it raged he imagined she could feel it though. "I've been unconscious several times since being trapped there."

"The sirens are working with powerful enemies of ours." The Dream Teller lifted her chin. "If I could have gotten to you before, I would have, if only to let you know help is on the way. You will be rescued, Jacob."

"Yeah, well, you know how to get me here, you gotta know where I'm at. Have you sent in the troops yet?"

"It doesn't work like that." The witch shook her head, gnarled wisps of white hair falling out of her hooded cloak. "All I've been able to see is the cell, but we have warriors in place to find your location and they will be coming in for you soon."

"Marilee and her vampire."

"Yes." The Dream Teller pressed her thin, shriveled lips together. "There is a reason why those two were chosen to rescue you, just as there is a reason you were captured."

Jake balled his hands into fists as memory of his last visit to the cave flooded his mind. "Not this fate shit screwing with me again." He huffed out a breath, barely able to keep from starting a shouting match. Fate had put him and Nyla through the wringer in order to bring them together. It seemed everything in his life was part of destiny's design to fulfill the ancient Blood Revelation prophecy. "I thought I was captured because the dark side wants to locate the three pre-destined immortal warriors."

"They do," the blonde spoke, her voice soft and almost song-like, but in a way far different than the sirens. Being a slayer, Jake could tell what any non-human being was, but he couldn't get any impressions off the stunning woman in the bright white toga-like robe, other than the feeling she held immense power. "They will continue to do so until they are destroyed, but there is a reason why you were captured at this time, and why you will be rescued by Marilee and Khiderian."

"Who the fuck are you?"

The woman's eyes sparked with ire. "Watch your tongue with me, slayer. I demand the utmost respect."

"Not until you tell me who and what the hell you—" Jake's demand fled as he watched large, white-feathered wings form from the woman's back. Her unusually golden skin glowed as light emanated from her body. He shook his head, blinked a few times, but the image he saw before him remained. "Fuck me sideways. You're an angel."

The angel closed her eyes and inhaled, the way his mother used to do every time she got a call from the principal or some girl's angry father about something Jake had done. When the angel opened her eyes, the golden orbs were full of disdain. "You may address me as Kiara, and you may watch your language in my presence."

Jake shrugged, the past few years of his life coming back to him in a flash of images. "Why? Because you demand respect?" He scoffed. "You know what I demand, lady? I demand to know why the hell I'm down here slaying monsters and demons left and right if angels are real. What the hell are you doing while I'm down here fulfilling a prophecy to kick Satan's pimply red ass?"

Excruciating pain filled Jake's body and he crashed to his knees, his hands going to his abdomen where it felt like his intestines were being tied into knots and wrapped around his other organs. The pain released him quickly, leaving him gasping for air. "I repeat, you may address me as Kiara and watch your language in my presence. I will not be disrespected."

Jake looked up at the woman and growled. "Funny. That didn't seem very angelic behavior."

"Don't believe everything you've been told about us," Kiara responded, her expression smug. "As you can clearly see, we don't wear halos."

Yeah, 'cause it wouldn't fit over your horns, Jake thought but knew better than to say as he picked himself up off the ground. "I asked a valid question. This fight is against Satan and his minions. Why aren't the angels fighting it?"

"The angels are fighting it. We've been fighting it since further than your mind could wrap around, but the earth is where humans exist. When the enemy sends his soldiers into your land, you must help protect it." Her features softened. "Angels do walk among you when needed, but we don't always show ourselves."

Jake shook his head as he ran a hand through his hair, trying to sort through the mass confusion in his mind. "Alright, so I was supposed to be captured to fulfill some other little puzzle piece of my grand destiny. Marilee and this Khiderian dude are involved. How, why, and what? Give me the details."

The Dream Teller hung her head as the angel took one step forward and answered. "Marilee is not a normal human being. She is a dangerous weapon that must be neutralized."

"Neutralized?" Jake looked at the Dream Teller and found her still hanging her head. His gut told him the normally hard-assed woman didn't approve of what the angel was saying. He returned his attention to the blonde beauty. "I'm a slayer. If someone's not human, I can tell, especially if they're evil. Marilee fought right at my side in Hicksville when we took out an army of vamps directly involved with the Blood Revelation."

"Did you know I was an angel when I walked into this cave?" Kiara raised an eyebrow when he didn't answer. She had him there. "Some life forms have a natural defense against slayers. As you've learned already, sirens can still snare you with their voice. You may be able to tell an angel is powerful, but you can't really locate us like you do vampires and shapeshifters, and the one being you absolutely cannot pick up on your radar is a *drac chemare*."

Jake frowned at the unfamiliar term. "What's a *drac chemare*?"

"Marilee Mills is a *drac chemare*. Physically, she comes off as a human, which by technicality she is, with psychic abilities and the extremely rare ability to call demons." Kiara's expression hardened. "Her kind cannot be allowed to exist. Khiderian has the ability to kill demons. Not just exorcise them, but kill them permanently. We sent him on this mission with Marilee so he could train her to use her ability in order to locate you."

Jake shook his head. "Wait. Marilee can call demons, as in draw them from hell?"

"Yes."

"And you need her to do this in order to find me, and are essentially having her trained to do this?"

The Dream Teller lifted her head. "When you wiped out the vampire army in Hicksville and left town with Curtis Dunn, I came to you and told you that he must not be hurt. You remember our conversation?"

Jake nodded. "You said he was a vital part to this prophecy being fulfilled and that his new soul was on our side. I put him in a mental institution and used a hoodoo spell to keep him from leaving to ensure he stays out of trouble."

"Yes. We knew that eventually we would need his help. Marilee is going to get your location from the demon, then draw it out of Curtis Dunn's body so Khiderian can destroy it, leaving Curtis free to finally live in peace."

Jake swallowed past the ball of disgust in his throat. "So you're using the girl with full intention of killing her afterward."

"*Drac chemares* are conduits for demons," Kiara explained. "When Marilee was just a little girl she released a pack of them onto a group of children. All but two were killed violently. Had Khiderian not destroyed the demons, all the children would have been killed."

Fire burned in Jake's gut as his slayer instinct took over. "You're serious?"

"Deadly." Kiara looked him in the eye. "She was just a child then. In order to locate you part of Khiderian's job was training her to use her abilities, which in addition to making her better able to interrogate Dunn and find you, she is now also far deadlier than ever before. *Drac Chemares* have the tendency to draw demons into themselves and when they do the demon takes full control, gaining the ability to release other demons from hell."

"Will Marilee draw a demon inside her?"

Kiara sighed. "We can't afford to wait and find out. Khiderian was appointed her guardian since he has the ability to destroy demons. He is the only soldier we have on Earth who could destroy her if she takes a demon inside her, but he has fallen in love with her."

SIREN'S SNARE

"So he'll hesitate." Unease slithered in Jake's gut. He couldn't imagine killing the teenager who'd aided him in Hicksville, especially now that she would be rescuing him from the sirens, but she wasn't a teenager anymore. She was a grown woman, one with an ability that could get millions killed.

"Hesitate?" Kiara shook her head, the saddest grin he'd ever seen tugging at the corner of her full lips. "He'll probably allow her to kill him just so he doesn't have to make the choice. Her destiny is to rescue you. By doing that, she will redeem herself of the horrible act she committed in her childhood. By killing her right after your rescue, you'll be doing her a favor. You'll stop her before she has the opportunity to kill again and you'll save the world from catastrophe."

"Killing her is for the best?"

"Yes." Kiara nodded her head adamantly. "Jacob, if she calls a demon inside herself that demon will call every demon from hell before you can blink an eye."

Kiara and the Dream Teller flickered as Jake felt the tug of the real world calling to him. "I must be resurrecting. I'm being tugged back." Panic slammed into him. "They were going to molest me. I can't survive there much longer!"

"You will not be violated," Kiara said, her tone firm. "You called upon God to save you. You will not be forced to go through anything you can't handle, but Jacob, you will be rescued soon. When the time comes..."

"I know." He pushed his sentimental thoughts aside, ignored the guilt in his heart. "If she's that dangerous, I'll do what I have to do as a slayer. I'll kill her."

He'd barely gotten the declaration out before he woke on the floor of the cell he'd been imprisoned in, alone. Scooting back against the wall, he studied his newly healed body and sighed. There was nothing left for him to do but wait. Wait to be tortured more by his captors, and wait for Marilee to rescue him so that as payment he could kill her.

CHAPTER SEVENTEEN

Khiderian leaned over the railing of the balcony, gripping the cool metal tight as he closed his eyes and tried to push the horrors of the evening out of his mind. Ravekkah was back. She always came back, and no matter how far he ran, how well he tried to hide, she always found him throughout space and time. She owned him, like a pet kept on a tether, allowed to move only so far before being yanked back.

A scream ripped through the night, coming from within the house. It was a female scream, which meant Ravekkah was torturing the lady of the house, or one of the servants. He prayed the child would remain unharmed. She'd never harmed a child in his presence, but he knew she was capable of it. She was capable of unmentionable evil, including turning him into a monster.

A hot tear trickled down his face as more screaming erupted from within the large plantation house. So many centuries had passed since the night she'd drained him of blood and filled him with her own poison. He'd only wanted to be human, to experience love and joy the way those who walked the earth did. If he had known he wouldn't make it a day before being attacked by unmentionable evil, he would have never fallen. He would have remained in heaven, watching over the humans from afar rather than trying to become one of them. He hadn't just traded in his wings that night. He'd traded in his soul.

"Khiderian! Come in here, darling! Don't be a bore!"

He hung his head, gripping the railing as if his life depended on it, because once he let go he would be walking inside to where she was... entertaining their hosts. She loved to entertain, to toy with the humans like a cat toyed with a mouse. She became drunk off their fear before feasting on their blood, and she thoroughly enjoyed sharing her meals with Khiderian... and making him perform.

SIREN'S SNARE

Ravekkah couldn't do the things he could do. She didn't have his psychic abilities which enabled him to burn flesh off bone, coerce people to do his bidding without using any force. He could creep into a human's mind and turn them into living, breathing, walking puppets. He'd done it for her countless times. But he'd never done it to her. She was his sire. She owned him. Controlled him. He was the puppet dangling from her strings.

"Khiderian! I'm growing impatient!"

He looked down at the vehicle parked on the front lawn and sighed. He'd been with Ravekkah since humans wore robes and traveled by sandaled feet. They'd changed so much during the centuries, from their style of dress to the way they traveled. Automobiles had replaced carriages, and he imagined the future would provide something to replace those. The humans were always inventing new things, striving for a better world. Yet they grew uglier inside. The very land he stood on had once held hundreds of slaves, humans oppressed because of the color of their skin, the same color of skin many of his angelic brethren had bore.

"Khiderian!"

He growled low in his throat, tired of feeling helpless under the control of a villainous creature. "Help me, Father. Help me, please. I can't hold on to decency without you." *Ravekkah knew he loved women, loved their sweet smell, their soft skin, the musical sound of their feminine laughter. She taunted him with them, torturing them until he gave in and drank them to death just to put them out of their misery. He knew what he would find if he walked back into the house.*

I have never left you, my child.

Khiderian stilled as the voice he'd given up on ever hearing again registered. "Father?"

No response. He didn't expect one. It had taken more centuries than he could count just to get the message he'd just received. Khiderian choked back a sob as hope flared inside his chest for the first time since his fall. "Please, Father, I know I am no longer worthy of your mercy. I have done such cruel, vile things, but I beg of you for the humans, not for me, please help me to break this monster's hold over me. Please."

"Khiderian!"

He ground his teeth against the pain in his head formed by his sire's shrill voice. Her patience was nearly gone. He looked up to the heavens, closed his eyes, and turned. As he crept through the hallway, the tangy scent of blood assaulted him, and his stomach tightened in response. He hated this game.

Khiderian reached the bedroom where Ravekkah waited and entered, taking in the carnage around him. Two servants lay in a mutilated heap to his right, their blood, what was left of it, stained the cream silk-cushioned chair toppled over beside them. The dark, plush carpet absorbed the rest. The owner of the home lay at Ravekkah's feet, eyes wide open in death, a large cavity in his chest. Ravekkah licked blood from her fingers as she stepped over his dead body. "There you are, darling. It's time to play."

Khiderian locked his jaw as he turned his attention to the large four poster bed where a woman lay. Her wrists were tied to the bed with scarves, her clothing missing. He could see vicious scratches on her body where she'd put up a fight. Now she stared at him through the sheen of tears coating her eyes as her bottom lip quivered. Her heart raced so fast the sound was deafening in Khiderian's ears, whetting his appetite. He really hated this game.

Ravekkah prowled over to the woman and ran a fingernail down her chest. The woman whimpered in response, closing her eyes tight as she turned her head away, oblivious to the fact she was just giving better access to her throat while trying to avoid seeing what Ravekkah did to her with her hand. Her concern should have been with what Ravekkah might do with her fangs. "Delicious, isn't she?"

"You always think kindhearted people who invite you into their home, offering you shelter, are delicious. My tastes are different."

Ravekkah laughed, her amber eyes sparkling with wickedness. "I so enjoy this game, darling, and hard as you try, you will eventually give in to me."

Khiderian looked at the woman, his heart aching at the sight of so many tears cascading down her face. He wondered if she'd truly loved her husband, and imagined the pain she must be in to have seen him murdered in front of her while she lay helpless. He could have dipped inside her psyche and experienced firsthand the emotions going through her, but knew doing so would cripple him.

She squirmed and Khiderian realized she was struggling against her restraints, desperate to cover herself from his view. He turned his eyes away, glaring at the cruel woman who now crept toward the end of the bed, closer to him. "It's time to play, Khiderian. You know the game. Take her and I will let her live."

SIREN'S SNARE

Khiderian growled. "No."

Ravekkah rolled her eyes. "Khiderian, Khiderian, Khiderian, always brooding Khiderian. You make no sense. You say you don't enjoy killing humans, yet every time I give you the opportunity to save one, you choose to kill instead."

"Taking a woman against her will is not saving her." Khiderian glanced at the woman as she gasped, a quick glance, knowing she didn't want him looking at her while she lay exposed. "You were human at one time, Ravekkah, why do you want to inflict such horror on people?"

"Because I became something greater than them!" Her eyes burned with anger. "So much time together and yet you have learned nothing. The humans will never love you, Khiderian. All they know how to do is fear you. You need to learn to revel in it."

"I'm not as cruel as you."

Ravekkah shook her head. "You're a vampire, Khiderian. You feed off humans and you enjoy it, even if you lie to yourself. I will break you and make you fully embrace what you were meant to be, my pet. When you come into your full potential, you'll thank me."

The desire to call forth fire flared to life inside Khiderian's chest and for the first time since he'd been changed into such a vile monster, the bond between sire and fledgling didn't hold him back. "You're wrong, Ravekkah. I was never meant to be a vampire, and when I do become the being I want to be you won't be here to thank."

Her eyes widened as he called forth fire and enveloped her in the flames, pinning her in place with his mind so she couldn't escape. Khiderian used his psychic abilities to unbind the scarves keeping the woman tethered to her bed and cover her with a sheet. She watched in open jawed-horror as Ravekkah twisted in the pillar of fire, her screams dying out as her body succumbed to the fire's wrath.

Khiderian watched Ravekkah's body turn into a twisted pile of burnt flesh and bone and felt a sense of freedom wash over him. He was free to go anywhere he wanted without Ravekkah finding him, making him witness her warped idea of fun.

"What are you?"

He turned toward the woman in the bed. Her long auburn hair hung in ringlets around her tear stained face as she clutched the cover over her breasts.

"I'm not sure anymore," he answered honestly.

She frowned, her gaze swinging between him and the pile on the floor that used to be his sire. *"What are you going to do with me now?"*

He studied her, licked his lips as her heartbeat taunted him. The smell of blood around him called to the hunger inside and his stomach clenched, yearning to be filled, but as he took in the scene he imagined the raw emotions that must have coursed through the woman as she'd witnessed Ravekkah's brutality.

"Nothing," he answered before turning and finding his way out of the house.

"If you feel you aren't ready for this, now's the time to let me know."

Marilee glared at the vampire next to her. She'd awakened to find him staring at her, suffered through a gut-busting meal he'd forced her to eat, and lost track of how many feeble apologies she'd had to cut off during their drive to the hospital where Curtis Dunn was being held. She spoke to him while they used the crystal to locate Dunn, but other than that she felt communication with the bastard wasn't necessary. "I'm a big girl, Khiderian, and I believe I've already proven I can handle a demon."

Marilee stepped out of the car, slamming the door behind her. Despite being desert, Nevada was actually quite cool at night so the light jean jacket she wore to carry the bottles of holy water in shouldn't have felt so hot, but sweat trickled between her shoulder blades anyway.

"You're upset with me and I get that," Khiderian said as he emerged from his side of the car. "But if we go in here we have to do this together or there could be horrific consequences."

"Upset with you?" Marilee fisted her hands on her hips. "If you forgot my birthday I might be upset with you. What you did was on a whole other level."

Khiderian raised his hand, palm out. "Enough. I've tried to apologize, but clearly you and I will not see eye to eye on why I did what I did. The fact remains that whether you want to admit it or not, whether you like it or not, you need me in there. If we are fighting with each other, the demon is going to use it as a way in." He stepped forward. "I want us to both walk out of here alive so we can rescue Jacob."

Marilee shook her head. Yeah, saving Jake was the goal and she needed to remember that at all times. He didn't want them to both walk out alive because he gave a damn about her. He just wanted to complete the mission. Well, fine. So did she. She didn't give a hoot what he did afterward. Reminding herself of that, she nodded. "I can be as professional as you can. I've been trained, correct?"

He frowned, guilt flashing through his sapphire eyes. Served him well. "Yes."

"Then there should be no problem. I'm ready." She turned toward the hospital and started walking forward. "Let's get 'er done."

She couldn't help chuckling at the confused look on Khiderian's face as she quoted Larry the Cable Guy. "Are you sure we're going to be able to get in there carrying weapons?"

"The weapons are covered." Khiderian squinted his eyes. "I don't see any type of metal detectors by the doors. Even if there are, I can disable them."

"Think we'll run into any problems getting into his room? What if they don't allow visitors?"

"It doesn't matter what they do or don't allow. They won't even notice us being here."

He'd be mind-controlling them. A little spark of ire formed in Marilee's chest. If he was so concerned about them being prepared to go against the demon and knew he'd have to use his psychic power to control the entire staff of a mental hospital… She rolled her eyes. The man had treated her like a worthless slut, taunted her with images of her grandparents being slain, and she was actually wondering if he'd had sex the night before to strengthen his psychic abilities. How pathetic did that make her? "How long should this take? I'm ready to save Jake and move on."

Khiderian shot her an annoyed look as they reached the front entrance of the hospital. "Every demon is different. Depending on the strength, it could take anywhere from ten minutes to several days to get the desired information during an interrogation."

"Several days?" Marilee was aware her voice had risen yet no one paid them any attention as they stepped through the entrance. "You're already controlling everyone, aren't you?"

"It's best that no one remember what you look like or that Dunn had any visitors in case things get messy."

Marilee's stomach rolled at the thought of what messy meant in this scenario. "You're going to be able to keep this up for days if needed?"

"I doubt I'll have to. You're much stronger than the last *drac chemare* I worked with, even if you've just discovered some of your powers. You remember what I've taught you?"

"Block and hit. Never let up."

Khiderian's mouth turned up at the corners. "Remember that and we shouldn't have any problems."

No, they wouldn't. After experiencing the man she'd thought she loved abuse her so cruelly, Marilee severely doubted a demon, a creature she already knew was evil, could affect her at all. Even if the demon forced Dunn to run her through with a blade she wouldn't hurt nearly as bad as she had when Khiderian called her those vile names and used her own insecurities against her. There was no greater pain than what he'd already put her through. The demon would not break her. "Where do we go?"

"You tell me."

She felt something shift inside her head and realized it was Khiderian pulling back the little piece of him he'd planted there. With just a fragment left, she heard the call clearly.

Mistress...I'm here... Come to me.

"This way." She located the stairwell and guided Khiderian to where she sensed the demon coming from. "Why didn't I hear him like this in Hicksville?"

"You must remember that this demon is different than most you will encounter. It is inside a body already, but it didn't take a full possession, and it does not have the ability to switch bodies on its own or it most likely would have a long time ago. Curtis and Alfred battle each other constantly. You wouldn't hear Alfred like this if Curtis didn't allow him to call you."

Marilee remembered the battle in Hicksville. "I didn't sense any trace of the demon in Hicksville. Curtis must have good control over it."

"Curtis has gotten stronger, but he will never be strong enough to cast the demon out or survive a regular exorcism such as what a Catholic priest might perform. Having a *drac chemare* pull the demon out of his body is his only chance of a normal life."

"Normal?" Marilee shook her head. "He's in a mental hospital. How normal of a life will he have?"

"Whatever life he leads from the moment of freedom, it'll be better than the one he's had thus far." Khiderian brushed past and opened the door as they reached the top of the stairwell. "I assume this would be our floor since there's nowhere else to go?"

Marilee stepped past him, not interested in speaking to him unless absolutely necessary. The hall they stepped into was pristine white and smelled like every hospital she'd ever entered. Colorful art prints and potted plants served as décor to break up the drab, sterile appearance of the facility, and a trio of nurses in white scrubs huddled together discussing a rather difficult patient, who, judging by what Marilee could overhear, had just thrown a dinner tray at one of the nurses for the third time that week. None of the nurses bothered with a glance as she and Khiderian strode past.

Yessss...

Marilee stilled outside a door marked with a J. Doe nameplate. "John Doe?"

"Jacob and Curtis probably worked some sort of amnesia angle when he was put in here. I doubt they could just release a psychotic amnesiac onto the streets. The state has to take care of him and foot the bill, probably."

"Why Nevada?"

Khiderian shrugged. "None of that matters. What matters is that you trust me in here."

Marilee rolled her eyes. "I trust you to kill me if I mess up. That's about as much of my trust you're going to get." She pushed the door but it wouldn't open. A light flickered red on a black square-shaped box which Marilee realized was some sort of access panel.

Khiderian placed his hand on it and it flickered green then swung open easily. "They don't just let crazy people come and go."

Rolling her eyes, she stepped into the room. Curtis Dunn sat in a wooden chair facing a window with no drapes. An uncomfortable looking cot with a white mattress and no sheets appeared to be the only other furniture in the room. She saw a door that led to what must be the bathroom. What the hell did people do all day in these places? Except maybe grow crazier due to staring at the same blank four walls.

"Who are you?" Curtis Dunn's voice sounded strained. "You've got him agitated."

Marilee looked at Khiderian for guidance and he nodded as he stepped away to stand across the room. "Talk directly to Alfred." To Curtis, he said, "Allow Alfred to take over so Marilee can question him. The Dream Teller promised you something. We're here to deliver."

Curtis turned around, his hopeful eyes shining brighter than his shock of red hair. "Really?"

"Something's off." Khiderian frowned. "Alfred should be taking over immediately with a *drac chemare* willing to speak with him so close. What do you feel?"

Marilee focused on the man in front of her and dipped gently into his mind. It took her a moment to figure out what she was picking up then she realized there were two minds. One was cowering. "Now that I'm here, Alfred is trying to hide, but..." She focused on what she felt. "He's anxious to talk to me at the same time."

"Call him, but be careful."

Marilee looked at Khiderian, received a nod, and took a deep breath before redirecting her gaze on the thin man in front of her. He looked absolutely harmless, but she knew what appeared harmless could contain deadly venom. Khiderian had taught her that when he'd shown her she could be foolish enough to fall in love with a man who had no heart. Closing her eyes, she breathed in deep, cleared her mind of her personal heartache, and summoned the demon. "Alfred. Alfred, I command you. Speak to me."

There was a stirring inside Curtis Dunn's mind, a slight growling, and then the demon's voice fell from between Curtis Dunn's lips. "Why do you bring this man with you? He is not your friend."

Marilee glanced over at Khiderian to see him arching an eyebrow, directing a look at her that said *I told you so*. Grinning despite her soured feeling towards him, she returned her attention to the man sitting in the chair harboring a demon inside himself. "Ignore him. I'm here to talk to you."

"Make him leave."

"No."

"Why?" Dunn glared at Khiderian, his eyes flickering red for a brief moment. "Because he tells you that you need him? Are you really stupid enough to fall for that? Or..." He grinned impishly as he angled his head to meet Marilee's gaze full on. "Are you really as weak as he says?"

Marilee laughed, earning another red flicker. "Is this the worst you can do? You're the weak one. Now..." She took a step forward. One step. While inside the body of a human, a demon could control it and she didn't want the thing lunging at her, especially after they'd instructed Curtis to unleash Alfred. "My time is valuable and I'm not big on games. Tell me where your friends are holding Jake Porter."

"What's in it for me?"

Release me. Release me from this weak body so I can protect you. This vampire does not love you. He looks at you and sees only plain features and a boyish body. I would worship you.

"Enough!" Marilee took a deep breath and shook her head at Khiderian, noticing his concerned frown. Concerned he would fail at his mission to free Jake, she reminded herself before pressing on. "Begging me to release you like a crybaby little girl won't work, Alfred. I'm not doing anything for you until you give me what I need."

"And you need to find Jake? Why? Not strong enough to fight on your own? And why do you fight against us? Are you really that much different than we are?"

Marilee started to deny the accusation, but realized the tactic for what it was. The demon, although it desired to be freed by her, could sense Khiderian would kill it once it was released from Curtis's body. It was trying to rile her up so she would make a mistake, allow it some way to get inside her where it thought it had a chance to kill Khiderian before he could kill it. Little did it know, Khiderian didn't care about her and would kill her before the demon drew its first breath inside her body. "I'll ask you one more time. Where is Jake Porter being held?"

"Up your grandmother's cunt."

Marilee gasped, looked over at Khiderian. "Did he really just say that to me?"

"Yes," Khiderian answered. "I believe he did."

Anger warmed Marilee from the vicinity of her heart. "He should pay for that, don't you think?"

"Yes. I would have to agree."

Marilee nodded, turned her head back toward Dunn and called fire, envisioned it coming to life deep in the man's intestines. Curtis Dunn let out a howling scream, tears springing forth from his eyes as he jumped out of the chair and started writhing on the floor, his cries of pain shrill enough to wake the dead. Marilee's eyes shifted between Khiderian and the door, expecting security to come bursting in.

"No one can hear anything beyond these walls. You are safe to do whatever you feel necessary to make him speak." Khiderian watched the man twist and turn on the white tiled floor as if he were nothing more than an insect. Not even that.

She, however, had a heart and knew that although Alfred Dunn deserved the pain, Curtis was in there too. She called the fire back and visualized Dunn's intestines unharmed, but when the man coughed up blood she knew she'd really damaged him.

"Bitch," he spat out along with more blood.

Release me from this body. Don't hurt me. I only want to serve you. I'll do whatever you want. This vampire has filled your head with so many lies you don't know what to believe. I only want to love you. Curtis is saying these evil things, not me!

"Where is Jake?"

The demon laughed in her mind. *Try to ignore me all you want but it won't work. We're the same, you and I. Both misunderstood, both cursed by our abilities.*

"Where's Jake? If I have to ask again you're going to feel some pain."

Like the pain you feel because of this vampire? I sense your heartbreak. I know he's hurt you. He will continue to hurt you. He's only using you to find Jacob and then he'll drop you. It's what his kind does. You don't know what he truly is.

"Newsflash, Alfred. I'm only using him to find Jake and then I intend to never see him again." Marilee noticed the tightening of Khiderian's jaw but pressed on. She didn't have time to worry about his ego when he cared nothing of hurting her. "Quit fighting and just tell me what I want to know so we can leave you in peace."

And who will leave you in peace? Do you think Jacob Porter cares for you? These people are using you. They destroyed your town. Killed your grandparents. Do you think it was all coincidence they came to your town? Quit thinking with your heart and use your brain. Unlike this vampire, I know you have one.

Marilee stepped back, shaking her head desperately, wishing she could dislodge the fears that had been planted there. What was real? She had wondered why Jake had come to her town. What were the odds the same slayer who came to her town would need her to one day save him?

"Block and hit, Marilee. Block and hit."

She glared at Khiderian, the fear in his eyes increasing her anger. So much for the faith he'd claimed to have in her abilities. "I'm not as weak as you think." Turning back toward Dunn she braced her shoulders, narrowed her eyes and delved inside Curtis Dunn's mind. *Curtis, what does Alfred fear most?*

Her head filled with pain as Curtis struggled to overcome Alfred and answer her, but she kept her focus strong, determined to break the demon and finish her mission.

God. Angels. Light.

Marilee pulled out of Curtis's mind and rubbed her forehead, the pain instantly subsiding as the man before her growled. Curtis had clearly relinquished control back to Alfred. Angels? Well, what was she supposed to do with that little nugget of intel? She supposed she could pray to God in front of him. As far as light went...

"In the name of God I command you to tell me where Jacob Porter is being held." Dunn shrieked, shook his head back and forth violently as he clamped his lips together. Marilee knew she had him. "In the name of God I command you to tell me!"

The demon's screams became so shrill Marilee checked her ears to make sure they weren't bleeding. He was agitated, visually disturbed by the use of the Lord's name, but still he clung to what he knew, refusing to relinquish it. She had to use light against him. Marilee took a deep breath and visualized the door inside her mind that she shared with Khiderian, hating the fact she'd need to ask for his help, but before she could open it an image of her mother slammed into her mind.

Becky straddled a man in her bed, rocking back and forth on top of him so quickly the bed started to inch across the floor. Marilee tried to block out the vision, not wanting to see her mother in so intimate an act but it wouldn't go away. *Her mother made sounds of pleasure, eventually screaming before she fell over, a heap of exhausted limbs, sweat dripping down her bare back.* "You are not a normal kind of guy," *she managed to press out in between pants.*

"Sweetheart, you have no idea," a very familiar voice said before shoving her off and rising. Khiderian stood in her mother's bedroom, naked and proud as he leered down at Becky. With a snap of his fingers his clothes were back on and Becky was sound asleep, her mind wiped clean of what had happened.

"Marilee."

Marilee shook her head as she came out of the vision. Dunn's mouth twisted into a wicked grin, his head hung forward as he stared up at her, eyes flickering red. Khiderian's brow showed deep frown lines as he studied her, his eyes wary. "What's he doing, Marilee? It's affecting you. Block and hit, sweetheart. Don't let him trick you."

Marilee stared back at the vampire, tried to swallow past the lumps of confusion and panic in her throat. Had he slept with her mother? Demons lied. She knew that. But she knew that because he'd told her. What was truth and what was lie? Who was friend and who was enemy?

"Sweetheart—"

"I'm not your fucking sweetheart!" Marilee conjured wind and slammed Khiderian into a wall, his eyes wide with shock as his body connected and he slid down to the floor.

Rising up, he squared his shoulders and stared at her, head lowered like a bull about to charge. "Please, Marilee. Don't make me have to destroy you. I'm begging."

His eyes registered fear. Not of her, she realized, but of what he would have to do if she took the demon inside herself. Did he care or was he just upset he'd have to do it without getting Jake's location from the demon first?

He's a great actor. Remember how he acted like he cared about you yet tossed you away when he thought you'd be too much emotional trouble? The image of her offering her body to Khiderian only to be rebuffed assaulted her, bringing fresh humiliation in its wake. *Truth was, he wanted you because he thought you'd be like your mother. He always thought you were a whore. In fact, that's what he'd found desirable about you. He likes women he can use and toss aside. You know that. He's already told you.*

Marilee swallowed hard and fought back tears, remembering the previous night's training. Khiderian hadn't blinked an eye when he'd said those things to her. He'd certainly appeared to be telling the truth.

You don't even know the worst about them, these so-called friends you're helping... Another image plowed into her and she was forced to watch against her will.

"Coming!" Gram called as she made her way toward the front door, straightening her apron. She glanced at the clock, wondering who it was at this time of night.

Hoping whoever it was wouldn't take up too much of her time while she was baking, she swung open the door and blinked as she saw neighbors she'd known all her life. Yet... they didn't look alright. "Jon, Bob, Ray... You fellers alright? You look sick."

Their eyes roamed up and down her body in a way that made her feel dirty before they smiled, showing teeth far sharper than any person's teeth should ever be. They looked like wolves, and if she recalled correctly, Bob and Jon didn't have many teeth in their mouths. Yet, now... "What in tarnation?"

The men barreled through the door, fangs bared. Two grabbed her while the third headed down the hall to where Lyle sat in his den, reading his paper. She opened her mouth and let loose a scream as the two holding her sank those razor-sharp teeth into her body but the sound of Lyle's own scream told her he'd been attacked too.

The pain seemed unending as they ripped at her flesh, more of their kind entering her home to join in. She could smell the apple pie burning as she faded in and out of consciousness. She struggled to stay alive, desperate she would be saved somehow. Marilee knew things. She'd always had a special gift. Maybe Marilee would sense trouble and send help.

"Your granddaughter won't save you," a man said as he loomed over her. "I've blocked her ability to sense anything. Sorry, old lady, but I need you to die so she can become the huntress she's meant to be."

The man came into view as her vision cleared. He was extremely attractive, a face beautiful enough for an angel, with long black hair and eyes bluer than blue. "Who are you?" *she managed to whisper past her pain.*

"Khiderian," he answered. "I'm the man who's going to use your granddaughter's gifts before killing her."

Marilee cried out as the vision ended, stepping backward on shaking legs. The demon in front of her smiled, knowing he'd shown her something guaranteed to make her rip Khiderian's heart out. "No."

"Yes," Alfred hissed through Curtis Dunn's mouth.

"Dammit, Marilee! Don't let him play you!" Khiderian yelled, hot angry eyes focused on the man sitting before them.

Tears slipped free from Marilee's eyes as she looked between them, trying to determine who the liar was. It should have been so easy to pick, but she couldn't. Her emotions were way too involved to think clearly. If only she'd seen with her own eyes what Gram had gone through that night she could rule one of them out.

The cross sitting over her breastbone suddenly felt heavier. She lifted it and the smell of apples, cinnamon, and fresh bread floated around her. "Gram."

I'll always be with you, Marilee. Remember, you have a destiny to follow, my sweet girl. You know things nobody else knows, and see things others are blind to. You will be called to do great things one day, and your gifts will bless many.

She could see her grandmother clearly in her head, smiling as she told her how special she was, that she had a mission to fulfill. She'd nearly forgotten the nights her grandmother would tuck her into bed after reading from the bible, reminding her to never lose her faith no matter how hard others would try to rip it away from her, and she wondered...Was she the only psychic in the family? Did Gram really know what she was talking about when she mentioned a mission? Had she known what Marilee's future held? If Gram had known of her mission and encouraged it, it couldn't have been bad.

Marilee lifted the cross to her mouth and closed her eyes. If Khiderian and Alfred could call visions out of thin air, maybe she could too. *Show me the truth, Gram. I can handle it now.*

Marilee swayed as dizziness set in, and suddenly she was back in Gram's house. She watched helplessly as vampires drained her of her life's blood. Her stomach rebelled, threatening to erupt, but she refused to shut down the vision. She had to see it through so she suffered through the screams, the blood, the vicious cruelty. As Gram clung to her life, Becky walked in, eyes widening in terror. She screamed and jumped on the back of one of the vampires. Marilee watched in stunned horror as her mother fought the monsters with tooth and nail, desperate to save her parents' lives. As Gram lay lifeless on the floor and Becky faded in and out of consciousness, Demarcus, the vampire who'd sired Nyla and turned the inhabitants of Hicksville into bloodsucking killers, entered the home and loomed over her.

Becky coughed up blood as she glared up at him. "Touch my daughter and I'll come back from the dead to destroy you all."

Demarcus laughed as he lowered his fangs.

Marilee blinked, rubbed the cross between her fingers, and pulled herself out of the vision. She'd seen enough to know the vision the demon had shown her had been a lie. Khiderian hadn't been there.

Studying the man before her, she saw no change in his features. His mouth still curved into a grin, and his eyes still flickered red, a twinkle of victory in them. He thought he had her. "You know, Dunn. You have seriously underestimated me."

Within the few seconds it took for Dunn to blink in surprise, Marilee reached inside her jacket, removed a vial of holy water and popped the lid off. He made to leap at her, but Marilee called upon her power to pin him down. He writhed and kicked, but couldn't move as she straddled him and poured the clear liquid down his throat.

He opened his mouth to spit it out, but she covered it with her hand, forcing him to hold the liquid inside himself as it burned him from the inside. "Curtis said you feared light and foolishly I thought he meant actual light, but then it hit me that you're not a vampire. Sunlight doesn't affect you. But the light of God, which can show itself in love, truth, and faith can destroy you. I'm full of the light, Alfred. I have faith in God and in my grandmother who showed me the truth. We can go round and round all night but you will not beat me."

Blood poured from Curtis's ears as he tried to buck her off of him, tears cascading down his face as the holy water sizzled inside him. "You know what your demon brothers and sisters are doing with Jake and unless you want to go through this torture forever you will tell me where he is being held."

She removed her hand, allowing Alfred to speak. He spit water at her instead. "Bitch! You will get nothing from me until you pull me inside yourself. It's the only way to win this. You think you're so smart. Now that I've had access to your mind, I can taunt you from anywhere. I can fill your mind with such horrors y—"

"So can I." Marilee called forth images of church and sent them directly into the demon's mind. His red-tinted eyes bulged as he opened his mouth wide and let out an ear-splitting scream. "Ready to confess?"

He shook his head violently and sent an image of Khiderian thrusting inside her grandmother into hers. The idea of Gram getting it on with Khiderian was so absurd Marilee laughed out loud and the image dissipated. She counter-attacked with every gospel song she'd ever heard Gram sing, and coated the lyrics with the love she shared with the older woman. Dunn screamed, the sounds panicked, providing the perfect opportunity for her to pour more holy water down his throat.

He gurgled and spit the liquid out, then sent the image of Khiderian laughing at her into her head. Again, Marilee laughed.

"Is that all you have? You're weak."

She closed her eyes, breathed in deep, and recalled the vision she'd received after asking Gram to show her the truth. She sent the truth into Alfred, including all the love that went into her mother's dying declaration to kill Demarcus if he touched her.

Dunn screamed louder, his eyes filled with pain and horror, then the image of Jake being tortured in his cell flooded her mind. The picture changed and Marilee felt like she was on a roller coaster as everything moved so quickly. She appeared to be moving up the stairs, through numerous rooms filled with men and women, and eventually she stood outside in the vision looking at a building. It was an old building, closed and boarded up. A large body of water loomed beyond and behind her a hill rose to hide the building from view. Suddenly, she was moving up the hill at warp speed. Once she reached the top, she looked up and saw a building covered with neon signs promising the prettiest dancers in Pacifica. All nude, all the time. The largest sign, set dead center, read *The Pearly Pink Nipple*. Surely, that would be easy to Google.

"I've got Jake's location," she said as she rose and stepped away from the man twisting in pain on the floor. "I know how to find him. Are you ready?"

She looked over at Khiderian to find him staring at her in wide-eyed wonder. Blinking, he shook his head before nodding. "I'm ready."

Marilee breathed in deep and searched inside herself for the place she tapped into when she heard Alfred talking to her inside her head. A cold sensation crept through her and she heard the distant sound of chanting. She focused on it until it grew loud enough for her to make out the odd-sounding words and join in.

As she chanted the strange words, heat stole over her body and she opened her eyes to see Dunn cowering from her. His eyes flickered in between red and their natural green color as his body began to tremble.

Khiderian stood between her and him, off to the side enough to not break her line of vision as she chanted louder. She could feel Alfred inside Curtis's body, trying desperately to deny her call as he realized her intention, but Marilee was stronger. She raised her hands, and put everything inside her, every last bit of power she had into pulling the demon out of Curtis Dunn's body.

Dunn's mouth opened and a cloud of red, wispy smoke poured out, transitioning into the shape of a large, vicious, snarling dog-like creature as its clawed feet hit the floor. It hunched down, growled, and prepared to attack, but before it could leap Khiderian held his hand out and released a beam of pure white light from his fingers. The room shook as his eyes shone with the same white light and the demon howled in pain before exploding into shards of bright colors.

Marilee felt her own power snap against her and fell to the floor. Khiderian knelt at her side the next instant, cradling her upper body against his chest. "Are you alright?"

She nodded. "How is Curtis?"

Khiderian glanced over at the man lying on the floor. "He took some damage but he'll recover with the aid of human doctors. As soon as we get out of here I'll put the thought to check on him in one of the nurses' heads."

"Good." Marilee took a fortifying breath and pulled away from Khiderian's embrace. It took a minute but she managed to get to her feet and remain upright. "We need to locate a strip club called the Pearly Pink Nipple in Pacifica. Jake's nearby."

"You're sure?"

"Positive."

Khiderian nodded his head and glanced back over at Curtis. "Marilee, what the hell did you do in here?"

She frowned. "I interrogated a demon like you showed me."

Khiderian shook his head. "Whatever you just did, I didn't train you to do. I've never seen anyone interrogate a demon like that. It worked though."

"That's all that matters, I guess." She studied Curtis's prone form. "Are you sure he's going to make it?"

"Yes."

"Then come on." She walked toward the door, stumbling a little. "Let's go rescue Jake and get this shit over with."

CHAPTER EIGHTEEN

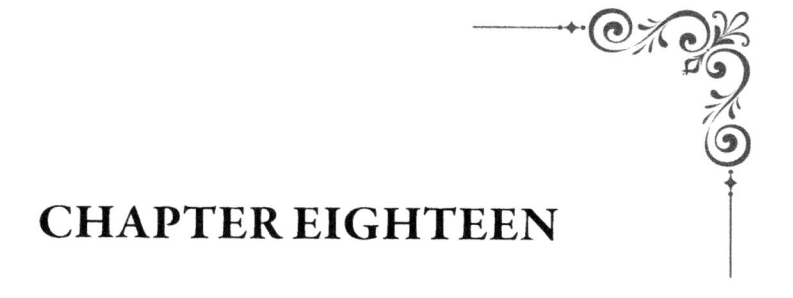

Khiderian kept his hands fisted at his sides in order to keep from reaching out to help Marilee as she weaved through the parking lot. All the while he prayed the wind would stay calm. It wouldn't take much to knock her over after the energy she'd spent inside the hospital.

They made it through the parking lot without incident, but as they trekked through the wooded area next to it where he'd left the car hidden in shadows she stumbled and fell. Khiderian quickly stepped forward and bent down to help her up. The moment his hand connected with her shoulder, she whirled on him, punched him square in the mouth. His head snapped back but before he could recover she was beating her fists against his chest. "Don't touch me! I hate you! I. Hate. You!"

Khiderian scooted back out of the way as Marilee crumpled over, letting loose sounds of agony as her tears flooded the ground. A quick lap of his tongue sealed the cut lip she'd inflicted on him, but nothing could heal the pain in his heart as he watched her suffer, knowing he couldn't do anything to help her because she didn't want him near. She hated him, and despite his intentions being good when he'd said those horrible things to her the night before, he couldn't blame her. What had the demon showed her? He could only imagine the sickness in its vile mind. Helpless to do anything else, he sat in silence and waited until her sobs subsided.

As the last sobs left her body, Marilee straightened up and wiped her eyes. "My mother died with my grandparents that night, and protecting me was the last thing on her mind." She shook her head as silent tears leaked from her pink, puffy eyes. "I always hated her because she was so easy. She embarrassed me so much and I resented her but when she lay there dying her thoughts were of me. I'm a horrible, horrible daughter."

Khiderian's gut clenched as she broke down again, sobs wracking her body. "Marilee, the demon will show you anything to upset you."

"That wasn't what the demon showed me." She heaved in a breath as she choked back another deep sob. "After he put so many visions in my head about that night and I couldn't tell what was real anymore, I asked for help."

"You prayed?" Shock mixed with pride crept through Khiderian's chest, warming him.

"I think so. I had my cross and I smelled my Gram like she was there with me. I asked for the truth and they showed me what really happened. She died with me on her mind. I am such a miserable daughter."

"No you're not. Marilee, you were old enough to leave your mother but you stayed with her. Whatever problems the two of you had, you didn't leave her and she didn't put you out once you were raised." Khiderian sighed and leaned his head back against the tree behind him. "I know what a horrible child is. I left my Father for the stupidest, most selfish of reasons. I've regretted it ever since."

She looked at him, frowning. "You never talk about your past."

"It's not worth knowing. Like I told you before, I'm a greedy bastard."

Marilee sniffed as she raked her fingers through her hair. "You were right. The demon sensed what was going on between us and used it. He showed me an image of you having sex with my mother."

Khiderian's mouth dropped open. He knew demons were evil, master deceivers but he'd never expected an image like that to be projected into Marilee's mind. "Marilee, whatever you think of me, I hope you know I would never—"

"I know." She looked at him and he would have said she grinned, but there was no humor in the slight upturn of her mouth. "I don't know how I can still believe you wouldn't do such a thing but in my heart I just know it. You are a bastard, Khiderian. You do whatever it takes to get what you need to finish your mission, and now that I've completed my first demon interrogation I understand why you did what you did, but..."

"But what?" Khiderian asked, his heart in his throat.

"But I could have never done that to you. I could never purposely hurt you, even if it was for a good reason, and that's why I know you don't care for me in the way I cared for you."

Cared. Past tense. Khiderian closed his eyes and grit his teeth against the anger rising inside him. He'd spent centuries suffering through hell on earth. He'd survived Ravekkah's cruel games, being cast out by his brothers and sisters, only hearing his Father's voice once since falling, and completing missions one after the other that required him to kill so many. But nothing hurt him as bad as hearing Marilee say she'd cared for him in the past tense.

"I loved you, Khiderian, and you used it against me. I can never forgive that."

He nodded his head while swallowing past the urge to scream over the unfairness of the situation. "But despite everything, you know what the demon showed you was a lie?"

"You're a bastard, Khiderian, but you're not that damn low." She pulled herself to a stand and wiped dirt off of her clothes before starting toward the car.

Khiderian rose and followed her. "I'm thankful that you at least know that, and whether you believe me or not, I do care for you and I'm very proud of you for the way you handled the demon. I've never seen a *drac chemare* hurt one with love before."

Marilee shrugged off the compliment. As they reached the car she opened her door and stood, looking at him over the roof. "That would mean a lot more to me if I wasn't just the key to saving Jake. I mean, if you really cared about me you would want to be with me afterward. Do you?"

Khiderian held her gaze as he reached the driver side door, noting the hopefulness in her blue eyes, still beautiful despite the puffiness from her crying spell. It would be so easy to assuage all her fears with a simple promise to be there for her after they saved Jacob, but it would be a lie. Despite what he wanted, he couldn't have her. He wasn't naïve enough to believe they had a future together. He'd already had a vision of her death. Fortunately, there were other prophesies besides the Blood Revelation, and one prophecy he knew of would save Marilee. But in order to fulfill that prophecy, he couldn't share a life with her. He had to let her go. "Even when you can't see me, Marilee, my heart will always be with you."

She rolled her eyes as a tear slipped out. "That's what I thought." Marilee slid into her seat and slammed the door behind her. The sound of it ramming closed so angrily cracked like a gunshot and hurt just as bad.

Khiderian took a deep, calming breath, reminded himself that the pain he was going through was for Marilee's benefit, and took his position behind the wheel. "You know where to go?"

Marilee already had his laptop in her lap, searching the internet. "I have the address." She input the information into MapQuest and pulled up directions. "Head out west on the expressway. Pacifica, California is only four hours from here. We'll reach it before sunup."

"Good," Khiderian managed to say through the pain of a breaking heart. His time with her was almost over and he had no idea what to say to make her believe he loved her. "Why don't you go ahead and get some rest while—" He stopped speaking as he realized she'd already fallen asleep with her head leaning against the window. He tilted the laptop so he could see the directions and drove through the night in silence, stopping at the first hotel he reached in Pacifica.

As he carried a sleeping Marilee to their room, an errant tear fell from his eye as he realized it was the closest he'd ever get to carrying her over a threshold.

"That's it." Marilee curled up her nose at the distasteful club as Khiderian entered the parking lot and stopped the car. "Jake's being held in an abandoned building down the hill."

Khiderian situated the car in a parking space and cut the engine. He closed his eyes and inhaled deeply. Marilee could feel the thrum of power rolling into him. "What are you doing?"

"Feeding."

"Feeding? On what?" Marilee looked toward the strip club and her cheeks flamed. Again, she'd assumed. "So feeding off sex doesn't always include you physically having sex, does it?"

He shook his head as he continued drawing energy from the club into himself. "The club is full of aroused people, and the emotions are abundant. Shame, pity, excitement, sadness, joy, fear... all mixed in with lust. So much energy." He opened his eyes and they shone with golden light for a moment before blinking out. "With the club so close I'll be able to replenish any psychic energy I use during the rescue mission easily. This is good."

"Good." Marilee opened her door. "Let's get this over with." She stepped out of the car and took a deep breath, exhaling slowly to soothe her frazzled nerves. She wanted Jake safe but she wished someone else had been chosen to rescue him. "What if the sirens snare you and turn you against me?"

"Kill me." Khiderian stepped around the car and started toward the edge of the hill overlooking the building where Jake was imprisoned.

"What?" Marilee jogged after him until she reached his side. His eyes held no hint of sarcasm. "Kill you. Just like that?"

"Yes. If it comes down to you or me, kill me. Let them kill me. Whatever you have to do, just get Jacob and get out alive. And hide. Never let anyone know what you are." They reached the edge of the hill and could see the building below, next to the ocean. "The trees surrounding the property should provide adequate coverage for us to sneak onto the grounds," Khiderian murmured as he turned and started down the hill at an angle that would keep them hidden from view.

Marilee struggled to understand the man before her as she followed along. He'd been sullen since she awoke to find him sitting on the sofa across from her, watching her sleep. He'd stared at her while she ate the food he commanded her to eat in order to build up her strength, his features drawn, eyes dull, almost depressed looking. Now he was ordering her to kill him? "Do you want to die or something?"

"No." He didn't look back as they continued their trek down the hillside. "To be honest, I fear it."

Well, now he really wasn't making sense. "But you want me to kill you if the sirens ensnare you?"

"Yes."

"Why?" She glanced around as they reached the bottom of the hill and entered a patch of trees, half-expecting some kind of creature to jump out.

"Because you are more valuable than me."

Of course. Marilee sighed, tried her best to ignore the sharp stab of pain in her heart. She could defeat the sirens and save Jake. It all came down to saving Jake. The mission. The job. She was just part of the way Khiderian could complete his job. She should want to kill him after the way he'd hurt her, but her heart ached at the thought. "We're both getting out of here alive."

He looked back at her but said nothing. As they reached the edge of trees four feet away from the building, Khiderian extended his arm, halting her. His gaze roved over the area, seeming to study the outlay of the property. "There are four were-animals walking this way but it'll take them about five minutes to get to this side of the building. There's a back door right there we'll go through." He nodded toward a door at the back of the building. "It's guarded by a magical ward. Once I use my power to unlock it and throw it open, the alarm will be raised. We have to get in and get Jake, killing everything and everyone in our way. Are you prepared for that?"

Marilee nodded, remembering the last battle. Those things weren't human or animal as far as she was concerned. They were monsters. "Killing the rats got to me. These things? Not so much."

"Good. Make sure you don't get bit."

"Trust me, that's in the forefront of my mind." Marilee shivered at the thought of long, sharp teeth coming down on her. The hawthorn oil she'd covered herself from neck to ankle in protected her from the vampires, but were-creatures would chomp right through it. If only getting bit was the extent of her problems. "Khiderian, what other surprises am I going to run into in here? I need you to spill everything right now."

His brow creased as he turned toward her. "I've told you everything, trained you for this."

"No, Khiderian." She shook her head, trying to keep her temper under control. "I know you and Seta were hiding something from me. When this started you made it out like we were looking for Curtis Dunn to ask him about the serum, but that wasn't the case at all. You knew all along that my job was to draw that demon out of him. I want the truth and I don't want any more surprises."

He looked past her, beyond the tree line. "Three minutes until those weres are here."

"Khiderian. I need to know the truth." Marilee folded her arms and stood with her feet firmly planted. "Now."

Huffing out a breath, Khiderian ran a hand through his hair. "When this is over with and Jake is free I'll tell you what Seta and I kept from you. I swear it. And I swear there will be no surprises in here. We're going in to get Jake out. There's no ulterior motive."

Marilee looked deep into Khiderian's eyes and knew he was telling the truth. "Alright. I guess there's no more stalling then."

"Actually, there's one more thing left in case I don't get the chance afterward." Khiderian grabbed the back of her head, where his hand wouldn't connect with hawthorn oil, and smashed his mouth down on hers. He kissed her long and hard, pouring a passion into the action that curled Marilee's toes before he pulled away and rested his forehead against hers. "I love you. I always have and I always will... and I'll always regret not making love to you."

He pulled away, held up a hand and behind her, the three were-creatures he'd seen from far away went up in flame. "Let's go. Don't stop until Jacob is free and we're all back up that hill. Kill everything you have to kill."

Marilee blinked, still affected by the shock on her senses the unexpected kiss had caused, but she shook it off. It was time for battle. Taking her cue from Khiderian, who held his sword in his hand, she thumbed off the safety of her gun, which now contained silver-tipped hawthorn bullets—She'd miss those silver hoop earrings—and readied her finger over the trigger as they made their way inside the building.

Khiderian was right. Once he unlocked the door and they ran through, their enemies inside were alerted. They pressed down a hall, shooting, and slicing everyone in their path. They'd passed three doors before those doors opened and more of their enemies poured out of them, surrounding her and Khiderian.

While Khiderian fought against the vampires ahead of them, Marilee took on the enemies behind them, enemies who looked human but quickly shifted into tigers, snakes, and ravens. Panic clogged her throat as they came at her, prepared to eat her alive. Khiderian had warned her against draining her energy quickly by using her psychic power, but with all the shape shifters coming at her she knew there was no way she could avoid being bitten while trying to shoot or slice them. Calling upon fire, she sent a large ball of flame hurdling down the hall, charring everything in its path.

She pulled the fire back into herself and turned to help Khiderian fight their way into a large, open room. She emptied her gun quickly and switched to the sword Khiderian had made her strap to her back before they'd left the hotel. Back to back, they sent heads and limbs flying in every direction as they fought their way to the staircase leading down into the bowels of the building. Unfortunately, they found themselves surrounded once they reached it. "Let me into your head, Marilee, so I can protect you from this."

She didn't ask his intentions or fear he might trick her. Khiderian was a soldier before anything else, and she trusted him at her side in a fight. She flung open the door they'd formed along with their mental link and allowed his energy inside her. As soon as they connected, a halo of light formed around them and grew quickly like a sonic boom, pushing back all of their enemies. As their enemies' bodies hit the walls, the boards covering the windows blasted out letting in the moonlight to cast a pale blue glow over the bodies scattered on the floor. "Are you alright?"

Marilee nodded. "I'm fine."

"Let's go. You first down the stairs in case we run into sirens."

Marilee took the lead, her heart in her throat as she imagined a hand reaching up from under the stairs to grab her ankles. She'd definitely watched too many scary movies growing up. They made it down the stairs with no trouble, but two steps into the dark, moldy-smelling basement they were met by three bald men dressed all in black, their mouths twisted into identical wicked grins.

"Pranic vampires," Khiderian announced as one of the men hurled a fireball at them. Khiderian pushed her down, carefully grabbing her by her cloth-covered shoulders to avoid coming into contact with the hawthorn oil on her skin, allowing the fire to sail over them, and gave her a push in the opposite direction. "Find Jacob while I handle these guys. We could use a slayer right about now."

Marilee ducked out of the way of another fireball and ran in the direction she knew led to Jake's cell. Just as he came into view, three women who looked just like Nyla stepped out in front of her. As she skidded to a stop, she felt the hair rise on the back of her neck and knew more were closing in behind her. "You really don't want to screw with me, ladies," she warned as she raised the sword, positioning it to swing.

"Oh, but we do," one of the sirens taunted, "and we really can't wait to play with the vampire you came here with. I think we'll make him kill you before we pay you any real attention though."

SIREN'S SNARE

Marilee's heart hammered in her chest, the organ beating so loud she struggled to hear over it. They intended to turn Khiderian on her which meant she'd have to kill him. She couldn't do it. Even if he called her a slut all over again, she couldn't bring herself to kill him. So she had to make sure the hell-hussies were dead before he finished with the trio of vampires and joined her by the cell. "It'll be hard to do that when you're dead," she advised as she lunged forward, swinging the sword in a smooth arc to slice one of the sirens straight across the throat.

The siren gurgled on her own blood as she fell forward. Marilee jumped back out of the way, as if she wasn't already speckled with the crimson fluid, and stepped right into another siren's waiting arms. As the siren locked her arms behind her back, the other sirens approached, each one holding some sort of tool used for torture in their hand.

Jake rattled the bars of his cell, shouting for her to do something. As the sirens closed in she drew on her energy and directed it into the lock on Jake's cell door. The lock burst, allowing the door to swing open.

Jake stood stunned for a second but recovered quickly enough to charge through before the sirens could use their weapons on her. They spun around as Jake charged them, giving Marilee the break she needed. She stomped on the instep of the siren holding her, and flipped her over her back while the hussy was too surprised to fight the move.

Jake had managed to tackle one of the sirens and break her neck, but his aid was quickly cut short as the sirens began to sing, lulling him into submission. Tears escaped his eyes as he held on to Marilee's gaze, desperately trying to break free of the sirens' hold, but not able to pull it off.

She was growing weaker, could feel it deep in her bones, but Marilee had to do something big. She couldn't fight all of the sirens alone with just a blade, especially if they used their song to turn a powerful slayer against her. She had no idea how many more enemies awaited them on their way out of the building, but she had to destroy the sirens and trust Jake and Khiderian to get her out safely if she was too weak to fend for herself.

Jake stepped toward her, murder in his eyes, and Marilee drew upon every ounce of energy she had, formed fire inside her body, and directed it into the sirens. They immediately caught aflame, their songs ending as they shrieked and writhed from the pain of their flesh burning off their bones.

Jake's eyes widened as he shook his head, snapping out of the trance. He made a small sound of shock in his throat before stepping back from the sirens closest to him. His mouth hung open as he watched them burn, twisting and turning on the floor, mouths open in horrified agony as they morphed into piles of burnt flesh and charred bones. "What the hell?"

Marilee swayed, her knees suddenly weak, and wished she'd slept or ate a little bit better. It took her a moment to get her vision clear enough to see in front of her and remember to keep moving. "Come on." She tossed the sword in her hand to Jake and retrieved her dagger out of her boot. "We have to get out of here. There's bound to be more here waiting to attack."

Jake glanced at her sideways, his eyes narrowed, and turned to lead the way back to the stairs. "I've never seen anything beyond this point. Do you know the way out?"

"Same way we got in, I suppose." Marilee cut in front of him and took the lead. "I left Khiderian back this way to fight off pranic vampires. We need to see if he needs help."

"Khiderian is a prannie too?"

"How do you—" Marilee stopped herself. "That's right. Slayers sense paranormal beings. Do you know what else we're up against here?"

"Shape shifters up ahead. Lycanthropes. Don't let them bite you."

A chill skated along Marilee's spine. "I'm so tired of those things."

She'd no more than finished the statement when one jumped out of the shadows and lunged for her. She sidestepped and lost her balance, falling to the floor. The sound of air whooshing over her head warned her to stay down and she saw a head rolling to her left as two more shape shifters approached, transforming into the biggest wolves she'd ever seen.

Jake made quick work of them with the sword she'd loaned him, allowing her to get back up just in time for a small army of the creatures to spill down the stairs and surround them. "There's a witch among them," Jake warned as he positioned himself so his back touched hers. "Try to take out as many wolves as you can while I get that bitch."

Before Marilee could nod, a wolf leapt at her and she was forced to act. She dodged its massive jaws as they came toward her throat and raised her dagger, embedding it deep into the thing's heart. She barely managed to pull the dagger out before she had to do the same move on another. "Jake! There's too many!"

"Burn them!" he called from somewhere behind her, a grunt mixed in with his order.

She focused on the place inside her where she formed fire, but barely managed a few sparks. "I can't! I'm too weak!"

She ducked as another wolf leapt at her, and sliced its middle as it sailed over her head. Where was Khiderian? She'd left him in this area fighting the pranic vampires. Another lunged and she struck but her dagger got stuck in it. She yanked harder as she saw two wolves jumping toward her out of the corner of her eye. She finally managed to pull the dagger free from the wolf she'd just injured, but knew as she turned that she was going to lose this fight. There were just too many beasts coming at her and without her psychic abilities, all she had was a dagger. It wasn't enough. She was going to get ripped to shreds unless...

Marilee fell to the floor and rolled, narrowly avoiding a chest full of teeth and claws while she searched inside herself for that place she accessed when she called the demons. If she were near a portal they would be talking to her already, but still... Maybe if she intentionally called them, she could do it from anywhere. She focused on remembering the chant as she jumped to her feet and leapt out of the way of a snarling set of jaws. It came to her softly and she started chanting along as the cadence grew inside her.

Yesssss. Yessss. Free us so we can serve you.

One condition, she answered back in her mind while gutting a wolf. *You attack only the lycanthropes.*

Yessssss Would love to.

Marilee finished the chant and fell to her knees as icy cold raced up through her chest, followed by white-hot pain. Then she found herself looking into the eyes of two huge hellhounds created of fire and dark maroon scales. "Destroy the lycanthropes," she commanded and collapsed against the wall as the demons shredded their way through her attackers.

Fear clawed at her insides. She'd just released demons into the world, hoping they did as told, but what if she'd just made the biggest mistake in her life? What if they went after Jake or Khiderian? Khiderian. He had to stop them before they went too far. *Khiderian, I need you. I released demons.*

Hold on. I'm—There was the feeling of a grunt down their mental link—*coming. Don't call them back into you, no matter what they do!*

Marilee sighed in relief that he'd heard her through their link, and searched the room for Jake, praying the demons left him alone. She saw him ducking as the woman she'd seen in the field during the first battle she'd shared with Khiderian flung green light at him. His gaze shifted to the demons, eyes widening before narrowing on her seconds before he dodged another attack from the witch.

Marilee searched inside herself, struggled to find the fire so she could help Jake with the witch, but she couldn't produce the energy needed. Still, she could fight hand to hand. She rose to a stand, ignoring the aches in her body as she crept forward. The demons were devouring the last of the shape shifters and for all she knew, would go for Jake next. She had to protect him.

The dog-looking beasts finished with the lycanthropes and turned, their heads down as they set their sights on Jake.

"Don't!" Marilee warned, capturing their attention. "I pulled you out of hell and I can send you back."

No you can't. You can only take us inside you.

"Don't push me," she warned, stepping back as the beasts stalked toward her, red, sizzling saliva dripping from their jaws. "I'll never take you inside me. You have to play my way or no way."

You'll take us inside you to keep us from killing your loved ones.

Marilee swallowed hard to cover a whimper, trying her best to appear strong in front of the creatures. *Khiderian, where are you?*

Khiderian appeared at her side, eyes glowing white as he stared down the demons. They cowered away but didn't move very far before they went up in pure white flame, bursting into a thousand shards of color, their shrieks deafening.

"Where were you?" Marilee asked.

"Killing things." Khiderian didn't explain further as he blasted the witch Jake was barely able to hold off with pure energy, sending the woman careening backward into the far wall. "Get Marilee out of here while I take care of the witch."

Marilee opened her mouth to protest but Jake latched onto her arm and yanked her forward, forcing her up the stairs as Khiderian stayed behind to battle the witch. "We can't just leave Khiderian," she cried as they reached the upper floor.

"He's a pranic vampire, he'll be alright." Jake slipped in blood but regained his footing without falling, and shoved her forward. "Which way?"

Marilee pointed toward the corridor they'd entered. "Is there anything here except the witch?"

"I don't sense anything else. Did you kill that fucker, Jaffron? Long, red-haired bastard with a big nose and a scar running down the side of his face?"

"I never saw anyone like that," she answered as they exited the house and started up the hill. "Khiderian might have. He stayed behind to fight some vampires, but wasn't where I left him when we reached the stairs. Obviously he found more enemies to take out while I got you. How are you doing?" Her legs ached as they stumbled up the hill but Jake's tight grip on her arm wouldn't allow her to rest.

"Good. I'd just woken renewed from their last torturing session about ten minutes before you two arrived. Another five minutes and I might have been beaten and useless."

"Thank goodness we came when we did."

"Yeah." Jake reached the top of the hill and turned around, releasing his hold as he stepped backward.

Marilee looked over the edge of the hill to the building below, her heart beating ninety miles a minute. "Do you think we should go back and help Khiderian? Can you contact Seta or something?"

"That won't be necessary. I'm grateful to both of you for helping me get out of there."

"No apology needed. You'd do it for anyone." Marilee bit her lip, watching the building below her for sign of Khiderian. Suddenly, the hair along the nape of her neck stood up and she sensed danger at the same moment she heard wind whipping toward her head. She ducked and turned in time to see the sword in Jake's hands swing over her head.

Gasping, she rolled away and quickly rose to her feet. "What the hell? You're trying to kill me?"

"I have to, Marilee." Jake's hazel eyes showed remorse before turning into steel. "There's no other way."

He lunged at her with the sword and Marilee quickly sidestepped, sticking her foot out to trip him. "Are you crazy?" She danced away as he rose to his feet. "I just saved you!"

"Yeah, and I saw how you did that." He swung again, narrowly missing the opportunity to decapitate her as she ducked at the last minute and punched him in the stomach as hard as she could before running behind him.

"Jake, I've helped you before. I only kill vampires and shape shifters. I don't kill people!"

"You killed children," he accused her as he grunted and straightened from the hunched over position her punch had forced him into. "Innocent children."

Her jaw slackened as she realized he knew the truth about her deadly accident. Tears welled in her eyes. "I didn't mean to."

"I'm sure you didn't." He lunged for her again but a dark blur barreled into him, knocking him down.

Khiderian quickly jumped up and blocked Marilee with his body. "What the hell are you doing?"

Jake wiped his bloody lip and carefully got back to his feet. "You're cool with me so far, Khiderian, but I have orders from an angel. She has to die before she draws a demon into her and it calls a thousand more."

"Son of a bitch!" Khiderian roared. "Show yourself, Kiara! I know you're here. I already had the vision of you trying to kill Marilee."

Marilee shrank away, her entire body going numb. Angels? Angels were real, and they'd ordered her death? By Jake's hand?

"Why?" she asked.

"I'm sorry, Marilee," Jake said, shaking his head, "but you have an ability that can't be allowed."

"Kill her, Jacob, and you're killing your sister."

Marilee gasped again, her gaze switching between Khiderian and Jake, whose mouth hung open. Suddenly the Latin used in the spell Seta cast made sense, as did their secrecy.

"Khiderian!"

Marilee jumped as a beautiful blonde woman appeared out of nowhere, big fluffy wings sprouting behind her, white as the immaculate toga-like robe she wore.

"Kiara." Khiderian growled the name. "I expected you to kill Marilee, but to send her own brother to do the job? That's sickening."

The beautiful angel jutted out a proud chin. "Half-brother," she clarified, "and it's not as if they were created together as you and I. You still left your family, severing all ties. Obviously, family isn't of that much importance."

Created together? That meant Khiderian was an angel. The man she had thought of as her guardian angel really was an angel. Marilee shook her head. Her mouth opened, but words wouldn't form.

"Wait a damn minute." Jake stepped forward, the sword falling from his hand. "You're for real? Marilee is my sister?"

"Half-sister," Kiara repeated.

"Think about it, Jacob." Khiderian shoved Marilee, who was still too stunned to utter a sound, behind him to protect her from both the angel and the slayer. "You look nothing like the man you've thought of as your father and there's always been a strain between you two. There's been a strain between you and your mother, as well. Every time she looks at you, she sees the face of the man she cheated on your... Jonah's father, with."

Jake crouched down on his heels, raked both hands through his hair. "Jonah's just my half-brother, too."

"Yes, but that shouldn't change anything between you." Khiderian glared at the angel. "You're not killing Marilee. She's done nothing to deserve a death sentence."

"She's a *drac chemare*," Kiara advised, drawing the title out. "Or did you overlook that while lusting for her and forgetting your duties?"

"I'm aware of what she is, and what she isn't." Khiderian held the angel's gaze for a breathless moment. "She used love against a demon during an interrogation. She prayed in the presence of a demon!"

Kiara's eyebrow rose as she glanced at Marilee, and she shrank away, not knowing if the angel—her mind still tried to wrap around that—would show any sign before attacking.

"I'll admit those are not normal activities for one of her kind," the angel said softly, returning her attention to Khiderian, "but she must die. She has served us well in the Blood Revelation, but she has grown even stronger now that you've trained her to be a better warrior and interrogator of demons. She can call them at will and we can not allow it."

Jake snatched up the sword he'd dropped and leapt to his feet. "You're not killing my sister!"

Kiara raised a hand and the sword flew into it while Jake was picked up and tossed aside, landing behind Marilee. "You may be powerful, slayer, but I am out of your league."

"Jacob, take care of your sister." Khiderian stepped forward to face off with the angel. Marilee cried out and grabbed for him, but he sidestepped her grasp as Jake grabbed her from behind, holding her back.

The angel frowned. "What are you doing?"

"The Blood Revelation isn't the only prophecy," Khiderian said as he stepped right in front of Kiara. "Another prophecy states that when an angel willingly gives his life for a *drac chemare*, she may live in peace of her curse."

Marilee lunged forward as Khiderian's statement registered, but Jake's arms wrapped around her like steel bands. "Don't, Marilee."

"Let me go!" She squirmed but couldn't break free. "Khiderian!"

Kiara's eyes widened, showing her surprise, before she tilted her head. "Do you know of an angel willing to die for her?"

"I can still destroy demons and I'm far more powerful than other pranic vampires. I must have some angel left in me."

"No!" Marilee yelled, reaching out for him, but he ignored her.

Kiara frowned. "You fell of your own choice. How do you know your death will save her?"

"I've got to try." Khiderian's throat bobbed as he swallowed hard. "Either way, if she dies I don't want to live."

"You know angels can't go back," Kiara warned. "You've killed, done horrible things in the name of lust and greed. Khiderian, you will go to hell and burn for eternity. Walk away now, brother, while you can."

Marilee whimpered as Jake held her tighter to him.

"Life without Marilee would be a greater hell," Khiderian said. "Knowing I allowed her to be destroyed would be unimaginable torture. Take my life for hers. Throw me into the burning pit. I promise you, the flames consuming me will be nothing compared to the pain I'll feel if I let you destroy her."

Marilee sobbed, falling back against Jake's chest. "Do something, Jake."

"I can't, sweetheart." He squeezed her tighter as if willing comfort into her body. "I don't know how to, or if it's even possible, to kill an angel. And sounds like he's saving you."

Kiara cocked her head to the side, studying the man before her. "You willingly fell from the heavens because you wanted to feel what humans felt. You said you sought love, but you always gave in to lust. Now you're telling me you will die for this woman you have not had sex with? You truly love her?"

"Yes." Khiderian nodded, a tear spilling from his eye. "It took centuries to learn what love for a human truly felt like, but now I understand." He looked toward Marilee. "I wish I'd shown her better."

"Khiderian!" Marilee sobbed as she tried to escape Jake's hold. "Khiderian, don't! Don't risk hell for me!"

Khiderian turned toward the angel. "Take me. Do it now in exchange for sparing her and setting her free of her curse."

The angel nodded, eyes watery as she raised the sword. "It may not work, Khiderian. This is your last chance, knowing that. Do you still wish to die for her?"

"Yes."

"So it is to be." The angel closed her eyes and prepared to strike, the sword glowing with white light.

"No!" Marilee twisted in Jake's arms, striking him in desperation to get out of his grasp and reach Khiderian, but the slayer's hold would not break. She watched helplessly, screaming as the sword swung through the air, entering Khiderian's chest and coming out through his back, sending bolts of lightning through his body in the process.

As Khiderian fell to the ground, Marilee threw her head back, connecting it to Jake's face, and broke free. She surged forward, her intent to scratch out the angel's eyeballs when she was hit with pain so great it blinded her. Her chest felt like it was ripping open, molten lava pouring out as she fell to the ground and sank into oblivion, Jake's horrified yells ringing in her ears.

CHAPTER NINETEEN

"She's waking up."

The sound of a female voice registered as Marilee fluttered her eyelashes. Her eyes felt grainy, as if she'd slept for days. Where was she? She searched her memory, remembered saving Jake and then...

"Khiderian!" She jerked into a sitting position and discovered herself in a small room that looked as if it had been carved out of the ground and boarded up with planks. She lay on a bed with plain blue sheets, and next to her sat Jake Porter, his wife, Nyla, standing behind him with her hands resting on his shoulders. His wife, which would make Nyla her sister-in-law, or half-sister-in-law.

"How do you feel?" Jake asked, leaning forward. "You've been out for almost two days."

"Two days?" Marilee scratched her head, trying to remember what happened to her. She saw Khiderian dying in her memory and tears fell in response. "What happened to me? Why do I feel so..." She struggled for a word. Something was different about her. She'd never felt this way before, so... "Something's missing in me."

"Khiderian gave his life for you so that you could live as a normal human. Your ability to call demons was ripped out of you as he died."

Marilee heaved in a breath as the enormity of Khiderian's sacrifice hit her. He hadn't even known it would work. "He died for me, and I didn't think he loved me." Tears poured from her eyes as she sobbed, gasping in between for air. "Why did he do that? The angel said he'd go to hell. Oh, God, he's burning in hell right now!"

"Well, actually, about that... Khiderian! She's up!"

Marilee's mouth fell open, her heart stopped beating as she stared at her newly discovered brother while heavy footsteps neared the room. "What?"

SIREN'S SNARE

"Had to force him to leave you long enough to eat something," Jake said with a smile as he turned toward the door.

"Marilee!" Khiderian stood at the door, chest heaving from running to her. He wore a black T-shirt and pants, his usual attire. His hair was just as black and long, his skin just as golden, his eyes just as blue as they sparkled with love ... and life.

"Khiderian!" Marilee jumped from the bed and ran to him, kissing him the way she'd wished she'd kissed him goodbye, pouring every ounce of her love into the exchange.

"Let's leave these two alone for a minute before they start going at it like were-bunnies," Jake said with a chuckle as he guided Nyla toward the door. Stopping next to them as they came up for air, Jake gripped Marilee's shoulder. "I'm sorry I almost killed you. That was a pretty shitty thing to do to my own blood."

Marilee laughed, tears of joy sprinkling her cheeks as she hugged Jake and gave him a big smacking kiss on the cheek. "You didn't know. We'll get everything figured out later."

Jake nodded, grinning as he patted Khiderian's shoulder on the way out behind his wife.

"How do you feel?" Khiderian hooked a piece of Marilee's hair behind her ear.

"How do I feel?" She laughed, then alternated between that and crying. "I don't understand. I saw you die." Remembering the moment the sword sliced through his body, she slugged him in the chest. "What a stupid thing to do, Khiderian. I'm not worth your life!"

"Ouch." Khiderian rubbed the pectoral she'd hit. "Watch it, sweetheart. I'm not a vampire anymore."

"You're not a—" She backed away, slack-jawed. "You're an angel again?"

"No. Once you fall, there is no way of going back." Khiderian took a deep breath. "I did die, but I didn't go to hell. Apparently, my love for you was—and is—so pure and so great it bought me a second chance. I'm human, Marilee. Completely."

"Human? Really?" Marilee ran her hands up and down his chest. "No blood-drinking? No powers?"

He frowned. "Do you mind?"

"Are you kidding?" Marilee wrapped her arms around his neck and delivered another kiss. "This is wonderful. You can grow old with me!"

A white-toothed smile split Khiderian's face. "Well, I guess that answers the question of if you'll marry me."

"Yes!" She jumped up and down as fresh tears fell. "Yes! Yes! Yes! Oh, Khiderian. I feel like I'm dreaming."

He wiped a tear from her eye. "It's all real. You're free of the abilities you've always despised. You have a brother, an adorable nephew, and you have me as long as you want me."

"I'll want you until the day I die, Khiderian, and even longer than that." She sniffed. "Wait. What about the Blood Revelation?"

"We're out of the game as far as fighting. With no birth record or record of education, being a human has its road-bumps for me, but Jake has hooked us both up with jobs. We'll do some detective work with his brother, Jonah, who just started his own private investigation company, and we'll be doing some behind-the-scenes stuff, looking out for signs of demon activity and helping to keep tabs on known enemies from afar, like this Jaffron, the vampire who directed the sirens to capture and torture Jacob. Our days of going into battle against vampires and shape shifters are over, though. Is that alright with you?"

She nodded. "Marrying you, working with you... It all sounds wonderful."

"Good." Khiderian smiled. "Let's go see what your brother and nephew are doing. There's a lot to explain to you about how you became a *drac chemare* and how Jacob became a slayer."

"Wait. Our father. Is he still alive?"

"No." Khiderian frowned, his eyes touched with regret. "He died not long after your birth."

"Oh." Marilee couldn't help feeling a little bit deflated.

Khiderian tipped her chin up with his fingers. "But you have a brother now, and a handsome little nephew. And you will always have me."

"I know." She kissed the man who'd chosen to go to hell for her. "That's more than enough."

Khiderian kissed her back before taking her hand in his and walking her outside the room to meet her family waiting beyond.

Did you love *Siren's Snare*? Then you should read *Vampire's Halo*[1] by Crystal-Rain Love!

A past he can't remember. A temptation he can't resist. A sacrifice that must be made.

Being run out of his church by hunters isn't a new thing for Christian, but the feelings he has for the woman caught up in danger with him are.

Awakened as a vampire centuries ago, with no knowledge of his past and only his strong faith and a deep-rooted desire to be of service to others, the minister doesn't think twice about protecting Jadyn, a woman who unknowingly brings danger to him. However, as he gets closer to her and discovers they share a very special connection, the more he realizes finally learning the truth of his past comes with a high price.

As the mystery of his past comes to light, prophecy is revealed, and Christian must make a choice: Reclaim the divine life he has spent centuries

---

1. https://books2read.com/u/mZK9By
2. https://books2read.com/u/mZK9By

trying to find his way back to, protecting all of mankind, or throw it all away for the only woman he's come to love?

Read more at https://crystalrainlove.com.

About the Author

Crystal-Rain Love is a romance author specializing in paranormal, suspense, and contemporary subgenres. Her author career began by winning a contest to be one of Sapphire Blue Publishing's debut authors in 2008. She snagged a multi-book contract with Imajinn Books that same year, going on to be published by The Wild Rose Press and eventually venturing out into indie publishing. She resides in the South with her three children and when she's not writing she can usually be found creating unique 3D cakes, hiking, reading, or spending way too much time on FaceBook.

Read more at www.crystalrainlove.com.

Printed in Great Britain
by Amazon